Kunim
RAISE ME UP

DELIA J. NZEKWU, PhD

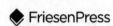

FriesenPress

One Printers Way
Altona, MB R0G 0B0
Canada

www.friesenpress.com

ISBN
978-1-03-918185-4 (Hardcover)
978-1-03-918184-7 (Paperback)
978-1-03-918186-1 (eBook)

1. FICTION, CULTURAL HERITAGE

Distributed to the trade by The Ingram Book Company

Dedication

To you, dearest grandma, Mama Awele, your compassion lives through my stories. I can still hear your beautiful voice and see your lovely smile and gestures as you told me the folktales for my B.A dissertation. May you continue to rest in peace. Thank you.

To you, dearest Isioma and Ike, Henry, Stella, and Vivian, for all your love and support, thank you.

To you, dear Dan Lepine, for the very special friendship and inspiration, and for being just you, thank you.

And to you, Maarten, for motivating my first contemplation of publishing my collection of short stories sixteen years ago and for your technical support, thank you.

Kunim owes its debut to you all.

A Word From Delia

Kunim tells of three different journeys, taken by young adults, to find a sense of belonging, acceptance, and happiness in their families and communities.

The main location of the three short stories is my hometown, Ibusa, in Delta State, South-eastern Nigeria. However, all characters, names of places, and currencies are fictional. The stories are drawn from my experiences growing up in Nigeria and regularly visiting Ibusa in the seventies and early eighties with my parents and siblings during school holidays. The local language used throughout the stories is a variation of the Igbo dialect spoken in some parts of Oshimili South local government area of Delta State, which includes Ibusa.

Kunim serves three main purposes; first, to be an entertaining read; second, to be didactic and contribute to the wealth of literature on diversity and inclusion. In this regard, the intra and inter-cultural stereotyping and discrimination depicted in "Fate" and "Shadows," and allyship in all three stories denote a call for partnership for change. Choosing the title "*Kunim*." which symbolically means "raise me up" in the Igbo language is a deliberate effort to speak to community. Third, *Kunim* celebrates family, quality education, gratitude, and the preservation of local languages.

Contents

Fate

No sooner had she pegged the last pair of sheets to the second of two rubber lines—tied to the large trunk of the orange tree in the backyard—than the heavens opened up. Heavy drops of rain clattered on the zinc roof of the pale-pink bungalow, built with red mud and plastered over with cement. Lamie began to chastise herself for not listening to her own weather forecast, for when she'd woken up this morning and gazed deeply into the skies, her instincts had told her that the uneven layers of dark clouds, heavily clustered together in boulder-like bundles, spelt rain. It was the peak of the rainy season, and without warning, the weather often changed from scorching heat in one moment to grey skies and torrential downpours in the next. Before eleven a.m., she had also observed the appearance and disappearance of the sun behind the clouds multiple times, as though there were a battle raging between the sun and planet earth for supremacy. Lamie remembered that, on days like this, her father sometimes alluded to the interesting idiomatic comparisons the elders often made, describing the earth as "polygamous" or "polyandrous" and swearing that when the sun and clouds—two of the earth's spouses—fight the way they seemed to be doing this morning, rain—another spouse—is always the fair arbiter.

It was Friday and a public holiday, and Lamie's younger sister, Hassa, was having a fun time on the front balcony with her school friends, Yvonne and Harriet, who lived in the neighbourhood and had come to visit, just as they often did on Fridays after school. She was playing Ayo, a local seed game, with Yvonne as Harriet looked on, ensuring no one was cheating and waiting for her turn to challenge the winner of the two.

"Hassa!" Lamie called out to her sister.

Hassa had also noticed the change in weather, and she and her friends had already agreed to quickly finish the round in progress and pack it up as Yvonne and Harriet's homes were three- and five-minute walks away respectively. Looking up, Hassa said, "Sister Lamie's calling me. It's about to rain really, really heavily. Let's pack up. I must go. But hey, remember, Yvonne, that I've eaten two of your houses. We'll continue next Friday." Hassa quickly stood up. Yvonne and Harriet stood up too, bid her goodbye, and ran home as Hassa packed up the game, stowed it away in the living room's cupboard, and met Lamie near the guest room, where her sister had taken up a big metal basin, chipped in many places around its base, and was scurrying back to the drying lines at the back of the house.

Hassa was eleven years old, five years younger than Lamie and the only survivor of a set of twins. Lamie doted on her little sister with passion and motherly forbearance. Their actual mother, Osarimi, had died shortly after giving birth to the twins.

Home alone at around noon, after having walked Lamie to school, two blocks away from their home, she'd had plans to clean the house, de-shell some pumpkin seeds, and grind ingredients for cook dinner. Osarimi was only halfway through the bowl of fresh pumpkin seeds when her water had broken, and she'd quickly gone into labour in the kitchen. Falling to the kitchen floor, screaming in excruciating pain as she tried pushing out the babies herself, the first baby, a boy, came after about fifteen minutes, laying limply between her thighs. The second baby was taking much longer.

In excruciating pain as she held tightly to the kitchen table, near the door, she'd been drenched in sweat and breathing so hard that her chest was heaving ... so badly that it seemed likely to blow up any time. Osarimi had screamed and pushed in agony. Meanwhile, Auntie Oka, their next-door neighbour, had been busily sorting out old clothes to donate to the church, whistling to herself, when she'd thought she heard someone shouting. Opening the door to her room, and stepping outside it to listen more closely, she'd soon realized it was coming from Osarimi's house, and that it was a scream of pain and fear.

"Oh my god!" she'd said. "What's going on?" Knowing that her neighbour was due to give birth any time, Auntie Oka had quickly grabbed a big cotton scarf from the head of her bed and run from her house, tying the scarf around her head in a dishevelled manner. As she'd made her way over, she noticed that her neighbour's car wasn't in its usual parking spot and suspected that the father wasn't home. She'd impatiently knocked three times on the door, and without waiting, turned the handle. The door was unlocked, so she let herself in. As she walked into the living room, she heard the scream again.

"Osarimi?!" she'd called out, making her way through the house. "Osarimi!!" As soon as she'd entered the kitchen, she'd spotted her. "Holy Father! Father Lord! Father Lord!"

* * *

Osarimi was on the kitchen floor, drenched in sweat, a baby lying face down on the floor between her legs as she continued to push. Auntie Oka panicked at the sight and wondered how long her pregnant neighbour had been in labour. With no time to waste, she removed her scarf and laid it on the floor, then cut the first baby loose and laid him on it. She could see that there was another baby coming and began to help Osarimi through the process of pushing it. Osarimi had hardly any strength left but she pushed, and just as the second twin, Hassa, emerged, Osarimi fainted with exhaustion.

Auntie Oka laid Hassa next to her twin, revived Osarimi, and helped her with the afterbirth. She then fetched drinking water and old newspapers from the dining room and fanned Osarimi with them, as she seemed to be sliding in and out of consciousness. When her eyes moved and opened up in a narrow but steady slit, Auntie Oka raised Osarimi's head enough to enable her to drink some water. Once she was certain Osarimi was fully conscious, she quickly rummaged around the kitchen and bedrooms to find towels, rags, and other items she immediately needed, and then put on some water to boil.

Hassa began to cry but her sibling was quiet. Auntie Oka was worried, so she quickly cleaned the gunk off the baby boy, rubbed him gently to stimulate him, and lightly slapped his buttocks to elicit a cry, but not a single whimper emerged. She kept at it, but after many attempts to make him stir, listening to his chest, and checking is inner elbow for a pulse, she had to accept that the baby boy was not going to respond. He was dead. She cleaned him and wrapped him in a towel. With Hassa also clean and now lying quietly on the scarf on the floor, gently kicking her legs and hands, Auntie Oka, cleaned Osarimi with warm water and soap and helped her into clean clothes and sanitary napkins. Helping the new mother to her feet, and letting her lean against her for support, she slowly walked her into the guest room where she laid her down and made her comfortable. Auntie Oka then left her for a moment to get the babies and brought them into the room to be with their mother, sorrowfully telling Osarimi that the boy had not lived and placing him in her arms to cradle for a while, and before laying him on a rubber mat near the bed, on which she had spread a blanket. She then placed Hassa on her mother's chest.

Leaving them in the room to bond, Auntie Oka cleaned the mess in the kitchen, sprinkled some kerosene around to stave off flies, and then rushed home to get some food. She knew Lamie was due back home from school at two-thirty, but was unsure if her father, Butem—a prolific trader—would be back soon or much later in the evening. Lamie was usually walked home by a schoolteacher, commonly called the "sweet woman" by parents and children alike. For a small fee, the sweet woman shepherded school children whose parents were unable to meet them at the close of school.

Auntie Oka knew the sweet woman would soon be at Osarimi's front door, holding Lamie's hand. Just like her own two boys, who attended a different primary school, Auntie Oka knew that Lamie would likely be hungry and need a snack before dinner, which wouldn't be until around six-thirty. So, she grabbed some boiled cassava chips and pieces of coconut from her family's previous day's snack and brought them next door.

When Lamie returned from school, Auntie Oka instructed her to stay with her mother while she went back to her place to make local pepper soup for Osarimi. For the next several hours, Auntie Oka shuttled between her house and her neighbour's, bringing them food and drink and making sure Osarimi remained well until her husband, Butem, finally arrived home at seven-thirty to find his wife so weak that she could barely speak.

Auntie Oka told him how the day had transpired, showed him his lifeless son, and then went back to her home. But at five o'clock the next morning, Butem knocked on her door, explaining that he urgently needed to drive his wife to the hospital. Osarimi had taken a bad turn during the night and was extremely sick and pale. Something was seriously wrong. Osarimi was in pain, and she weakly told her husband that she was bleeding heavily. Butem was certain having twins had taken an unusual toll on his wife and hoped that this was all it was, rather than something far more serious.

Auntie Oka offered to babysit Hassa until Osarimi returned home, and the struggling mother was admitted to the hospital. At eight a.m., a doctor and a midwife began to attend to Osarimi but nothing helped, and she soon went into a coma and never recovered.

After the death of Osarimi, Auntie Oka became like a foster parent to Lamie and Hassa, while Butem continued working, extending his trading to neighbouring towns. Butem was happy to have Hassa live with Auntie Oka, as he felt that he lacked the parental skills required to be a single parent to a new infant while also looking after a five-year-old daughter. So, when he got back home from work each day, Auntie Oka would bring Hassa to him so he could spend time with his newest daughter. As Hassa got older, Auntie Oka happily left her with her father and Lamie much longer, only stopping by to check on how they were all getting along before taking Hassa back home with her at night.

Butem paid for Hassa's upkeep, but Auntie Oka refused to be paid a wage for fostering her, and occasionally, Lamie as well. The day Butem broached the idea of financial compensation for her efforts, Auntie Oka took offence and curtly expressed her anger. Looking at Butem with wide eyes, and angrily shaking her head from side to side, she admonished him. "Brother Butem, I've already told you no twice, and now you insult me by asking for the third time. What don't you understand about *no*? If what happened to Osarimi had happened to me, don't you think your late wife would have done exactly the same for me, and even more than I'm doing now for you and your children? If this is your way of telling me that you want to end my relationship with the girls, then please say so. You're their father, and I have no legitimate right to overrule you, but let this be the very last time you offer to pay me for minding these innocent children. Have you heard me, Brother Butem? I say, no more. No more, please."

Butem bowed his head in embarrassment. All he'd wanted was to show Auntie Oka his appreciation and not take her generosity for granted, but he could see that he had clearly crossed the line despite his good intentions. He owed this benefactor, who was not even related to his family, so much gratitude. He didn't think he could ever offer her anything that could fully compensate her for her kindness. The last thing he'd wanted was to hurt or offend her in any way.

Desperate to apologise and make amends, Butem stretched out his hands and brought them together as though in prayer. "Auntie Oka, from the depth of my heart, I'm terribly sorry for having raised this topic again. I didn't mean to offend you in any way. You've been a saint, and I only wanted to show my appreciation and not take your kindness for granted, but I do understand now how my attempts to do so anger you. Please don't be offended, and I swear to God that I won't ever broach this topic again. Please, forgive me."

"No problem, my brother. I understand."

And with that, the matter was closed.

* * *

By the time Hassa was four years old, she had grown so fond of Auntie Oka that she refused to fully return to live with her father and sister. As Auntie Oka was a next-door neighbour, had become more like family, and their co-parenting arrangement had fallen naturally into place, Butem didn't mind that his younger daughter spent just as much time with her foster mother as she did with him. On weekends, though, from Friday after school until Sunday night, Hassa stayed at her father's. He insisted on this as he also wanted to be sure she attended church with him and Lamie and joined them in the family's weekend visits to friends and distant relatives.

When Hassa was nine years old, Auntie Oka's eldest son, who lived in the "big city," asked his mother to leave the small town of Pembute and come live with him and his family of four in Soglo. He told his mother that it was time she stopped doing the "back-breaking" manual labour of housework and started using sophisticated electric tools and equipment for chores like doing dishes, washing clothes, blending ingredients, cutting grass and weeding, and cleaning the floors. Auntie Oka argued that the life her son was offering, in exchange for the one she currently enjoyed, would make her bored, sick, and age faster than her peers.

One of the many things Auntie Oka loved about her life in Pembute was her subsistence farming. She had resigned from her meagre-paying job as a kindergarten teacher to focus on farming and found the latter much more fulfilling and economically rewarding. After many months of protesting and hesitating to forgo her life in the small town, just to move to a new city to learn a completely new way of life, Auntie Oka decided to finally oblige her son, as daunting as she found the prospect.

She knew that leaving her foster daughters behind would be the hardest thing she had ever done. She had grown to particularly adore Hassa, whom she'd helped to birth just like her own biological children. She was going to dearly miss the girl's wilful yet thoughtful personality. And she loved Lamie nearly as much.

Hassa was an inquisitive child and spoke her mind freely. In so doing, she had a tendency to make people blush in embarrassment or upset them with her direct questions and observations. She always reminded Auntie Oka of exactly how joyful (and sometimes annoying) the purity of a child's heart can be.

One day, just back from school, Hassa had complained to Auntie Oka, whom she called "Mami," that her class mistress had scolded her sternly because she'd bluntly asked a female classmate if she'd eaten beans yet again that morning because she was tired of her "farting" all the time. The classmate had cried and reported Hassa to their class supervisor, who'd summoned Hassa to her office and threatened to send her home.

Auntie Oka sat Hassa down and explained why her class mistress had been right.

"Hassa, you can't just say whatever you want, however you want, anywhere you want, or else you'll hurt people. It's disrespectful and rude. Suppose your classmate is ill? You embarrassed her and hurt her feelings. Imagine yourself in her place. How would you feel?"

"Okay, Mami, then what should I have said and how should I have said it?"

"You should have said nothing. And if the farting was simply making you *too* uncomfortable, you should have asked your teacher to allow you to sit somewhere else for a little while."

"But if no one tells her, she'll keep letting out foul air, Mami, and I sit directly behind her and can't concentrate. Am I to keep asking the class teacher to allow me to sit elsewhere all the time? Then it looks like *I* have a problem."

"Then you should have found the right time and gone to talk to your class mistress in her office about the problem, instead of in the class, right in front of everyone. Your class mistress would then know how to resolve the issue, and your classmate wouldn't even know you'd said a word about it. Do you understand?" Hassa kept her gaze on the floor and nodded meekly.

After a moment, she looked up and quietly asked, "Mami, why can't she just eat bread, or yam, or boiled potatoes in the morning, like we do? Lamie says beans makes one 'fewww and feel sleepy all the time.'"

Auntie Oka threw her head back and looked at Hassa with her eyebrows raised in surprise. "And what does 'fewww' mean?"

Hassa pouted her lips and tucked her tongue in her cheek before answering: "Air from the butt."

Auntie Oka couldn't believe her ears. Clapping her hands in amusement, she said, "My goodness, you kids these days! Your language is truly going excitingly haywire." Hassa stared at her foster mother, awaiting her answer. "Listen," Auntie Oka said, bending her head to look Hassa straight in the eyes, "I don't know about beans and 'fewwwing' and sleeping. What your classmate eats is none of your business. Just don't ever rebuke her about this matter in the class or anywhere else. Do you understand?"

Hassa gazed at the floor and wriggled her toes and then nodded. Auntie Oka wanted to be sure she had made sense, so she repeated: "Have you heard me clearly?"

"Yes, Mami, I have," Hassa said grudgingly. With that, Auntie Oka gently tapped Hassa on the shoulders and told her to run along.

When Auntie Oka broke the news about her plans to leave for Soglo, Hassa cried for days, struggling to picture her daily life without "Mami." She begged her father to allow her to go live with her foster mother, but neither Butem nor Auntie Oka would hear of it. Instead, they promised

Hassa she would vacation at her foster mother's in the future.

When Auntie Oka finally moved to Soglo, Hassa returned to live full-time with her father and Lamie.

Hassa was growing up to be an incredibly wise young lady under the guidance and protection of Lamie, who loved to act 'Mother' when their father was away, particularly on long trade trips to the borders. Lamie knew that her little sister had a sharp tongue and didn't often understand diplomacy or courtesy when she spoke her mind. Although Hassa was still a kid, Lamie feared her younger sister's tendency to be overly outspoken could get her in a fight, and the consequences could be dire. Each time Hassa told Lamie about a quarrel with a friend or an acquaintance in school, it always turned out that the situation had been escalated due to Hassa's language and tone. So, Lamie made it a primary responsibility of hers to guide Hassa on choosing her words carefully and watching her tone.

Hassa also learnt to be domesticated, cheerfully carrying out whatever task Lamie delegated to her. She also learnt how to wash light clothes. "Pay more attention to the collars, necklines, underarms, and hems." Lamie repeatedly shared such instructions in the early days of teaching. Hassa mastered the intricate art of brewing a local rice beer, how to skin and dress chicken, and her favourite of them all, how to polish drinking glasses till they shone like mirrors. Hassa always proudly called Lamie to inspect her polishing, knowing that her sister would be very generous in her praise for a job well done.

* * *

It had now become windy and very grey. At the back of the house, Hassa knew exactly what to do as soon as she saw Lamie with the large metal basin. With the unfinished Ayo game with Yvonne still on her mind, she rushed back into the kitchen to fetch a smaller plastic basin to assist her sister. She began to unpeg the white clothes, which Lamie was intentionally leaving on the lines in order to separate them from the others, and put them in the plastic basin.

Lamie had once told her, "Never mix whites and colours, especially when they're wet or damp, and never put whites in the metal basin when they're not dry, as rust stains are bound to get on them." Hassa had never forgotten. Hassa quickly got all the whites down from the two lines. The rain seemed to be waiting for the two girls to finish as heavy grey clouds moved briskly across the skies, casting a darker shadow over what had earlier been a bright day. The afternoon looked like late evening.

With fewer clothes to unpeg, Hassa finished earlier than her sister and covered her basin—now half-full with white linen, shirts, and singlets—with a large bedsheet and stowed it away by a corner in the guest room. The electricity was out, as was generally the case whenever a heavy downpour was on the horizon. It was the government's way of trying to prevent surges and potential fires from lightning. It had become too dark in the house, so Hassa lit two kerosene lamps, set one on the dining-room table and the other on the floor in the bedroom she shared with Lamie. The wind grew ferocious, banging windows and blowing debris around in the backyard. All around their house, they could hear neighbours scampering around, trying to tidy things up before the rain came down. Chickens clucked, goats bleated, and dogs barked. Hassa rushed to close the window in the living room and pull the shutters of the one in their bedroom mostly closed, though she left a small opening for light to peek through.

Hassa loved the rainy season. She adored the peak of this season even more, as the heavy skies forbid outdoor play in the wet afternoons that became wet nights. Lamie always allowed her to lie down and read when there was nothing else to do but listen and wait out the rain. It was three p.m., still four hours before dinner at seven.

Hassa sat on the edge of her double bed, bored and kicking her legs in and out as she looked around the room and wondered how to spend her time. At the peak of the rainy season, when it was often cold at night, Lamie always brought out two striped military blankets from the metal trunk at the corner of their bedroom and spread one at the foot of each of their beds for cover. Thrilled at finding something to do, Hassa quickly stood up and headed for the trunk box, took out the blankets, spread one blanket at the foot of Lamie's bed, and had just finished spreading the other on hers when Lamie walked in.

"Ah, well done, Hassa. Thank you. I was just thinking of doing that. It's going to be cold tonight."

"Yes, it will be. We also have no idea if we'll get electricity back for a little while, but looking at the rain, we'll need the lamps for the rest of the day."

"Well, as you know, it may be a few days before the lights come back on, and until Papa returns on Sunday, we can't use the generator. Oh, by the way, let me check how much kerosene we have left." Lamie grabbed the umbrella from where it was leaning near their built-in wardrobe and dashed out of the room to the back of the house, where they stored a twenty-five-litre keg of kerosene.

Torrential rains were coming down with a vengeance as Hassa laid on her back with her head at the foot of her bed, gazing at the shuttered window in delighted amazement. She listened intently to the rhythm of the wind and rain as they slammed on the rooftop and against the wooden shutters and began to contemplate what to do with her free time. A few minutes later, Lamie rejoined her sister in the room and announced that the keg of kerosene was still a quarter full and should last for at least a couple of weeks.

"Lamie, what are we going to have for dinner?" Hassa asked as Lamie sat at the makeshift dressing table by the window with its round, tinted mirror.

"I'm not sure. Emm… let me think. Emm… We still have some of the leftover vegetable soup, and we could either have some boiled plantain or a maize meal with it," Lamie replied, staring off into space.

"Can we have yams instead?" Hassa asked, certain her sister would say no.

Lamie immediately began to mentally review what they'd eaten for dinner that week in order to determine what they'd eaten the least frequently. "Hmmm… Yes, maybe we should have boiled yellow yams with the vegetable soup."

"Yes!" Hassa said in surprise. "Yes! That would be so good, sis!" Excited, she sat up.

Hassa loved yellow yams, and Lamie knew it. She liked the fact that they always had a slightly rough crunch to them, even when cooked for much longer than normal. Having yellow yam with vegetable soup would certainly make her evening more special.

"Yes, yes, yeeellooow yams," she sang, her shoulders dancing with the glee of a child, stretching the "yellow" for emphasis. "I promise I'll peel the tuber carefully and slice the yam into the shape and thickness you showed me. I promise I'll cook it with the right amount of salt. I promise… I promise…" Hassa was rambling excitedly, and Lamie couldn't help but smile broadly at her young sister's exuberance.

"Okay, yellow yams it is for today. If you were allowed, Hassa, I know you'd eat yellow yams every day until the stalks grew from your stomach." The two girls began to laugh.

"Thank you, Lamie," Hassa said, clapping her hands and pouting playfully as she rose to fetch a new picture novel from her schoolbag. Then she laid back on the bed, opened a page, and pretended to read while she watched Lamie applying makeup.

Why does she like that red dirt she calls powder, she thought, *and the black shimmery ash she lines her lower eyelids with? They make her look different. Old, sort of.*

Lightning flashed and thunder roared, interrupting her thoughts, as the rain poured down.

"Lamie, are you getting ready to go to the usual townhall meeting in this rain?" Hassa asked, even though she believed she knew the answer.

"No, not today. Remember, it's a public holiday," Lamie answered offhandedly, eyeing her sister. "I'm only going to go buy Papa's back ointment and hair dye. That's all. He gave me some money and asked me to buy them before his return, and remember, it's Friday, and he said he'll be back on Sunday."

"Why don't you wait till after the rain or go tomorrow? You could get blown away by this wind. Just listen to it! And most of the paths will be flooded. Besides, most shops will be closed."

"I know, but I just feel like getting this done now and out of the way because I'll be busy tomorrow."

"Okay but be careful. It seems like we're going to have one of those famous seven-day rains, and from the look of the weather now, it's going to get much worse before it gets better."

Indeed, the wind's wheezy, woozy sounds were loud as the rain pounded the roof and slapped the windows and walls. Suddenly, as though to reconfirm Hassa's fears, the wind banged their room's shutters multiple times. Lamie stood up, noticing that rain was coming in through the small opening in the shutters that Hassa had left. She pulled them fully close and locked the window, inspecting the bolts on both panels to ensure they were properly pushed into the holes that had been drilled into the seals. The wind kept on coming, hitting the window with loud clapping sounds. Lamie stood there and gazed at the tiny spots of light streaking into the room around the hinges.

Hassa sneezed three times, and after each, Lamie turned to her with a smile and said, "Bless you" before returning her attention to the window. Tired of standing and listening to the wind, she finally walked back to the dressing table, sat down in resignation, and carried on with her makeup.

Hassa opened the novel again and buried her face in it, pretending to be reading. From the corner of her eyes, however, she watched her sister's every gesture in front of the mirror. Lamie was taking her time as she waited for the rain to subside.

An hour later, with the lightning and wind having subsided, leaving only heavy showers, Lamie tidied the dressing table and fetched her bag from the wardrobe. Hassa watched Lamie tuck some money into her bra like she always did, which signalled her readiness to leave.

Teachers of higher education had been on strike over better working conditions for four months. Lamie had just finished A Levels and gained admission to the local university to study Public Administration but couldn't register until after the strike, so she'd been keeping herself busy with volunteering. After lunch every Saturday, she went out to community-development meetings at the community centre's townhall. With the support of their father, Butem, who believed she'd make a fine politician or advocate someday, she volunteered as an active member of the Anti-Domestic Violence Committee. When Lamie dressed up for those meetings, Hassa would watch her like a cat spying on a rat. Sometimes, and true to character, she bluntly told Lamie that her lip gloss was too much or that her eyelids were too heavily lined, and that she looked like those unattractive women in magazines. Lamie always listened to her sister's reservations. She would take a second look in the mirror, tone down the makeup, and turn back to Hassa for approval.

"Okay, Madam Wardrobe Director, how do I look now?" she would tease.

"Let's see. Hmmm... That's better, sis," Hassa would proudly reply, pouting her lips and tilting her head as though to warn Lamie that she was all grown up now as well.

These past couple of weeks, however, Lamie had gone out every day after lunch, except on one Sunday when she'd stayed home to do the ironing as they'd had electricity again after three days without a flicker of it. Every day, she'd planned dinner, gotten dressed, put on some makeup, tucked money into her bra, and told Hassa she needed to run an important errand and would be back in a couple of hours. Hassa soon began to find these daily post-lunch errands her sister was undertaking strange, but she never asked her for details. Given the weather today though, she was worried and unhappy and couldn't help but wonder who in their right mind would venture outside if it weren't for an emergency.

As Lamie put things into her bag, Hassa was perplexed that her sister always seemed to take plenty of money with her to these meetings. Their father always gave Lamie more than enough money for household expenses as well as additional pocket money for each of them. Lamie always kept the house sufficiently stocked, though with the cost of living rising, there was nothing extra for luxury.

So, Hassa could not help but wonder if Lamie was spending her pocket money at the meetings. Lamie was never comfortable with being watched so closely, so when she could, she was careful to keep Hassa engaged in other things. But today had been different. The rains had kept them both indoors, and unable find anything else for Hassa to do, Lamie contented herself with simply enjoying her younger sister's company as she prepared to go.

The heavy rains subsided still further, becoming a drizzle, but the skies were still heavily overcast. Satisfied with her overall look, Lamie rose from the stool and sat down close to Hassa on the bed so she could peek into her picture novel.

"What story are you reading?" she asked with genuine interest.

"*Ladi and the Magical Nunu,*"[1] Hassa replied, even though she hadn't read a line since opening the book.

"Umm... Sounds like it an interesting story," Lamie observed as she looked at the glossy picture of a young Fulani boy embracing a jug of fresh milk, straight from the cow. "Listen, when you finish reading this story, why don't you write down what the story's about for me, so I can see how much improvement you've made in your writing skills." She ran her hand affectionately through Hassa's cornrows.

"Okay, Lamie. But you remember I got 75 percent in our class's last essay test, right? And our English teacher said that my spelling and grammar had improved a lot."

"Yes, I remember, and I'm very proud of you," Lamie said, squeezing Hassa's shoulder lightly. 'The more you read and write, the better you become, and you'll see … in the next essay test, you'll score much higher than seventy-five."

"I'm going to try and score 85 percent or higher at the next test, sis. You'll see. I'll be top in my class."

"Of course, Hassa. I'm sure you will." Lamie smiled and gazed at the book for a while. Glad to see Hassa engaged and happy, she rose from the bed and put on her sandals. Then she turned, and in a regret-laden voice at having to leave the young girl all by herself on a day like this, asked, "Is there anything you'd like me to buy for you from Yaya Abu's?"

"Goody-goody, Lamie, please."

"Goody-goody, Hassa? First, you know how Papa feels about Goody-goody, which is why he barred us from eating that candy years ago. Second, I don't even know where to find it as I haven't bought it in years!" Lamie looked at her sister suspiciously then from the corner of her eye. "Now, tell me the truth, have you been eating Goody-goody in school, Hassa?"

"No, no! I swear I haven't. I only buy lollipops. The kiosk that sells Goody-goody is too far away from the playground, and there's always a long queue there for eggrolls, so Yvonne, Harriet, and I never bother going there."

"Okay, I believe you. At least you know the kiosk that sells it. Right?"

Hassa nodded. "That's true, Lamie."

Lamie bent her head down a little and looked at Hassa like she needed reaffirmation. Then wagging a forefinger at her, offered a warning: "Now, this must be a secret between us; if I do succeed in finding Goody-goody, Papa must never know it, or he'll kill me. Do you hear me?"

"I know, Lamie. I'll keep it a secret, I promise. And it's just this one day. Please?"

"Good. Again, as I said, *if* I find Goody-goody, I'll buy one for you, maybe two, but if not, I'll buy those malt and milk biscuits we both like. Is that okay?"

"Yes, I love those biscuits too. Thank you, Lamie."

Lamie felt a strong need to compensate her sister for leaving her home alone in such inclement weather. Although Hassa was old enough to look after herself, Lamie knew that leaving her alone today was inappropriate. So, she made a mental note not to be out for long and to buy some sweet treats on her way back. Then she slung her bag on her shoulder and took one long last look in the mirror.

"I have my keys, so I'll just lock the living-room door on my way out. You can relax and carry on reading," she said, turning to look at Hassa before leaving the room. Then she grabbed the second biggest family umbrella, which was rainbow-coloured, from behind the kitchen door and left the house.

Hassa laid back on the bed, and this time, really began to read. The room grew darker as the clouds gathered again, and Hassa felt very lonely. The winds returned, scaring her sometimes, banging the windows and shaking the doors. She imagined masquerades that danced with scary masks at big festivals walking into the room. She shut her book, pulled her blanket over her head, rolled on her stomach, and buried her head in the pillow. It began to rain heavily again for a while, and then became a light drizzle. As the grey clouds disappeared, the room lit up a little, and Hassa began to feel happier.

She opened the window again, just a little, to let in natural light, and continued reading. When she got to the part of the story where the cows could no longer produce milk, Hassa dog-eared the page, shut the novel, and tucked it under the pillow. It was 4:20 p.m., and Lamie had been gone for nearly ten minutes. An idea suddenly crossed Hassa's mind. She jumped out of bed and fetched her raincoat from the wardrobe. She hurriedly put it on, pulling the hood over her head and knotting the string under her chin. Then she slid into her rubber sandals, patted down her bed to straighten out the sheet, quickly inspected the room to ensure everything was fairly organized, and then stepped out into the very wet and grey afternoon, locking the door behind her. Hassa held fast to her hood's strings, bent her head down, and began to walk.

The paths were thick with mud, and Hassa had to constantly struggle to walk fast as her feet kept sinking deep into the mud. It was quiet outside, and she seemed to be the only one walking the face of the earth while everyone else was indoors. She arrived at the concrete fence leading to a neighbour's farm, and standing on four bricks set against it, she jumped over the fence and carried on walking through the windy rows of ferns and vegetables. She reached a bushy path on which stood some of her favourite paw-paw trees. Yaya Abu's shop was not far away from here. She climbed one of the short trees and looked around but found the shop closed. She sat on one of the tree's branches and waited up there for a while, hoping to see Lamie, knowing that when it rained, petty traders often carried on with what they called back-house selling. No one wanted to lose money if they could help it. Tired of waiting and convinced Lamie wasn't there, Hassa gently climbed down from the tree, holding its slimy branches, then began to walk back home.

This time, she took a different route. The wind played with her rain-coat hood, blowing it off her head occasionally. Hassa struggled to keep it permanently in place, holding it on her head with one hand and clutching the string with the other. Bent almost double against the wind, she walked. When she got to an open field, an idea struck her. "I think I know where sister Lamie might be," she told herself loudly.

It was a long walk, but curiosity drove her on. Scurrying through the wet grass and into the bushes, she reminded herself that she needed to be back home early to cook the yam and heat the vegetable soup. Ahead of her, she recognized Wuka, a friend of her father's, approaching with a severely deformed umbrella. *Oh dear! Where do I say I'm coming from now in this harsh weather?* she thought, trying to quickly come up with a story. She couldn't allow him the opportunity to ask her too many questions if she wanted to avoid complications. Settling on an explanation, she redoubled her strides as she approached Wuka and then began to jog as she got much closer to him.

"Good afternoon, Uncle Wuka!" she waved, pretending to be in a hurry.

"Good afternoon, Hassa. Where are you coming from in this rain?"

"To buy matches," Hassan shouted back, jogging on.

"You must hurry up because the rain will likely start falling hard again soon," Wuka called back, no more eager than she was to stop and exchange pleasantries, considering his unreliable umbrella, which seemed to be conniving with the rain to drench him even more. Feeling saved from that situation by providence, Hassa jogged on. She came to a big field at the outskirts of the market and stopped for a while to decide which way to go. Wuka crossed her mind, and she immediately realised that to play it safe, she should buy some matches in case Wuka stopped by the house unannounced to say hello and referred to this chance meeting. The only problem she had was that she didn't have any money on her.

Wondering what to do, she finally decided to go to a longtime customer of the family, from whom she and Lamie bought Golden Penny Flour. This detour was going to prolong her journey a little, but Hassa believed it was well worth it. She turned away from the direction of the market and walked in the opposite direction to a small house with a kiosk at its corner. The kiosk was built from discarded wood, and at its front, a small opening covered with metal gauze was created from which bric-a-brac items were passed to buyers. Like all other shops shut due to the weather, Hassa didn't expect the kiosk to be open, so she hastily made her way to the back of the house. She had to knock on the door four times before a boy of about seven years old opened it, looked her over from head to toe, and greeted her sharply. "Good afternoon."

"Good afternoon. I want to buy some matches. Can you tell Sisi that Hassa would like to have two boxes of Three-Crowns matches please."

"What is your name?" the boy asked, either unaware that Hassa had already given it, or simply having missed it.

"Hassa. Tell Sisi it's Hassa."

"Okay. Wait." The boy shut the door against Hassa, and she waited. Before she could even collect her thoughts, the door opened again, and Sisi was there, smiling broadly with her hand outstretched with the boxes of matches.

"Good afternoon, Hassa. Why did you wait to completely use up your matches before buying some more? This is not the kind of weather to be outdoors you know."

"How are you, Sisi? You're right. I forgot until I was about to set the pot of yam I'm cooking on the fire. Can I come pay when my father is back on Sunday?"

"Of course. Anytime, Hassa."

"Thank you, Sisi."

"No problem. And watch the paths. Debris has flown everywhere."

"I will," Hassa almost shouted back as she left hurriedly.

With Lamie nowhere in sight, and Sisi not hinting at having seen her, Hassa was now convinced that her sister had lied to her. She pulled her hood down and began to walk to the venue of the townhall meeting Lamie attended. She believed that, for some reason, her sister was actually going there and hadn't been honest when she'd said she was only running an errand for their father. Hassa resolved to uncover the truth. Shoving the boxes of matches into one of the raincoat's deep pockets, she headed back towards the part of the road from which she'd made the detour. Then choosing to walk through the market, she briskly headed in that direction.

As she reached it, she was amazed at how chaotic the market seemed even though it was quiet and completely empty of people. The rain had overturned table slabs and chairs, kicked up and moved debris everywhere, and pulled down several electricity poles. She meandered through piles of rubbish and made her way down a narrow bushy path to a field, on which was being erected some new residential buildings.

Hassa looked around to see if she was being watched or followed, but nobody was in the street. Close to a crossroad, she saw a female figure from afar. She wasn't absolutely certain, but seeing the raincoat and watching the woman walk, her gait was like Lamie's. As she fixed her gaze on the woman, Hassa's instinct told her that this was her sister. She quickened her steps and followed the woman at a safe distance.

As the woman turned suddenly off the road and onto a narrow path, away from the one that led to the townhall venue, Hassa clearly saw that it was indeed Lamie, and her curiosity heightened. She watched as her sister disappeared around a corner up ahead and frowned. Lamie wasn't going to the townhall after all, so where was she going in this weather? As she followed, she soon doubted that she had taken the same path Lamie had, as she found herself pushing through thorny weeds and emerging adjacent to the t-intersection. She realized she had lost Lamie and began to run through the path her sister had turned onto. Then she saw her again. Lamie was walking into a dilapidated building, which stood on higher grounds.

Hassa stopped. She didn't know what to do—whether to walk straight into the building and confront her sister with a lie, which she would need to concoct quickly, if that was her option, or else find a way to spy on her inside the building. She chose the latter and searched for the best way to do that.

Near the building, Hassa walked into what seemed to be abandoned farmland, judging by the rows of dead stalks of corn, sugarcane, and overgrown weeds. It was partly fenced off with weak concrete walls, whose unevenly laid bricks looked like they could collapse at any moment. The stench of animal dung was putrid in the rain. Hassa kept her eyes on the building and maintained a path that kept her across from it, soon finding another broken concrete fence. This one had three blocks of cement stacked one on top of the other, near the corner of the lot, surrounded by trees and shrubs. This fence was in direct view of the building, although it was a bit of a distance away.

Climbing up on the blocks, she discovered a large hole in the fence through which she could look without being seen. The building was about a block away. Its walls were awash in green mould and plants, sticking out of every corner. Its broken, sunken roofs had rotten boards jutting out and dangling down. Then she spotted her sister, just inside a wide glassless window, embracing another lady who quickly disappeared, reappeared, and by her hand gestures, seemed to be showing Lamie some things Hassa couldn't see. Then she disappeared again. Hassa kept watching. The room wasn't well-lit, and she couldn't make out the face of her sister's companion.

From time to time, a male silhouette would also appear, conversing with Lamie in the window, only to disappear again. Hassa kept watching, looking on as the pair reconnected once more, laughed, and then bent down to do whatever it was that had been keeping them busy for a while. Hassa kept waiting for a stronger clue about what could be happening out of view of that window. Lamie and her male companion seemed to be moving about, in and out of Hassa's view. Suddenly, she saw smoke, and the shadows disappeared, one after the other, first the companion, then Lamie. The smoke seemed to be rising from the ground as it snaked up to the ceiling; one moment, it was thick, and the next, it fizzled out.

Hassa grew increasingly confused by it all. She stretched to the fullest on her toes and craned her neck, moving it up, down, left, and right, in her search for answers. She patiently looked on, growing more curious each time Lamie's silhouette reappeared. When she hadn't seen her sister's frame for a long time, she started to panic, pushing her face further into the hole in the fence to try and see better. "What's going on?" she whispered, covering her mouth with both hands. "What are they doing? Where's Lamie? What's happening to my sis?" She relaxed her toes for a few seconds and then stretched herself again to the fullest, but she now saw only a thin veil of smoke and nothing else. Hassa waited, moving on and off her toes to peer into and through the hole, waiting for the shadows to reappear, but her wait was in vain. When she could no longer see smoke, or any silhouette, she started praying that her eyes were not playing tricks on her and that Lamie was safe.

Confused and scared for her sister, and of the repercussions to herself for coming out to spy should she be caught, Hassa stooped low and bit her fingers, not sure what to do next. *Why would Lamie wear makeup to come to this dingy place and appear and disappear like a ghost?* she asked herself. She believed her sister was a good person, but this "errand" in this filthy building didn't make sense to her. Their father had brought them up properly, and this seemed the devil's work.

"This is bad, bad, bad. God will be very angry with Sister Lamie if she's doing bad things here," she repeated to herself, upset and close to tears. Hassa stood on her toes again for one last look and then gave up trying.

Hassa felt a light breeze on her face, and though she had no idea what time it was, she knew she needed to start heading back home. As she pulled her hood back to get some fresh air, she heard rustling noises around her, and her heart started to pound in fear. Someone had spotted her, she was sure. Hassa stooped and stayed as quiet as a mouse, looking from left to right. As she heard still more rustling, she raised her raincoat and skirt to her lap and pretended to be easing herself, in case someone came upon her and asked what she was doing there. She felt like her pretence to need the toilet lasted for eternity as she waited for a voice or a bark, but nothing came. When the rustling sound had stopped, Hassa stood up, patted her skirt down, and in a flash, remembered dinner.

Satisfied that she had been able to confirm where Lamie had been, if nothing else, she pulled the raincoat's hood back up over her head and began to scurry back home. As she made her way through the narrow paths of swamps and marsh, she came upon two goats feasting on rotted maize and vegetables that seemed to have been left there when someone emptied their trash. Hassa assumed that, perhaps, the goats had made the noise she had heard earlier. She moved further to the right side of the path, putting more distance between herself and the goats as she watched them hungrily chewing on the vegetables. Hassa felt her heart ease, and she decided to quicken her steps, skipping from the left to the right, avoiding puddles of mash and debris.

"Aha!!"

Hassa was startled by a sudden voice, sounding feeble and shrieking all at once. When she turned around to see who it was, and if the person had been addressing her, her legs sank into a pit of muddy water that rose up to her calves, and she fell forward, landing on her stomach. "Ouch!" Crying out in pain, she dragged and pulled herself forward, clutching the slippery shrubs in front of her with all her strength to free her legs. As her feet finally came unstuck from the hole, a sharp pain shot through her left ankle. Stopped abruptly by it, Hassa laid flat on her stomach for a moment, folded her hands in front of her, and rested her forehead on them. Then she began to cry. The pain was steadily increasing. Rolling over to her side to sit up and examine her leg, she saw dirty feet just ahead of her, with unkempt nails sticking out from a pair of badly worn sneakers, the soles of which were cracked and missing a few parts on both the front and sides.

In tears, Hassa looked up to see a very old man staring down at her, holding a small basket. He was wearing a wide-brim raffia hat and had a long cane pressed under his left arm. He was chewing something, which pushed his sunken cheeks in and out in an unusual way, and thrusting his lower jaw forward in a way that made it look much longer. Hassa looked the old man over from head to toe and wasn't sure what to make of him. Finally, she let her gaze fall on her left leg. Her ankle was bleeding right through the thick slush of mud that was plastered around it. Between the stinging pain that crawled through her calf, and her anger over Lamie's false errand, she started to cry seriously as she pulled the leg up to her chest to examine the ankle, wiping off the mud with her hands to expose the injury. She had scraped the back of it quite badly.

I have to get home. I have to get home, she thought as she tried to lift herself from the ground. She had almost forgotten about the old man until he stooped down next to her. Setting his cane and small basket down, he moved behind Hassa, grabbed her from under both her arms, and lifted her up to her feet, breathing heavily at Hassa's weight. Hassa winced in pain and stood limply, resting most of her weight on her right leg and leaning against the man's chest. Hassa did not like the strong smell of stale local tobacco and gin that was coming from his breath, so she quickly hopped three steps forward and turned to face her helper. The man sucked his cheeks in, grunted, turned his head to the left, and spat. Then he cleared his throat three times, with deep grunts, and looked at Hassa, waiting for some explanation.

"Thank you, Papa," Hassa said, swiftly looking at the man and then down at her feet, ashamed and sorry like a child caught with her fingers in the cookie jar.

The old man shook his head and rolled his eyes. Giving Hassa a "you-naughty-child look" and grabbing her right hand, he lisped, "Try your best to walk. I'm too old, and my bones are brittle from nearly seventy years of farming, otherwise, I would carry you on my back. You see the clouds over there?" He pointed to the horizon, and Hassa's eyes followed the direction of his finger. "Do you see how grey it's becoming, the clouds racing to blanket the skies? It'll soon start to pour yet again. So, let's go before you catch a cold in addition to an injured ankle."

The old man gave Hassa no chance to respond. Still holding her hand firmly, he leaned down and picked up his small basket and cane with his free hand, then began to walk, almost pulling Hassa along. Hassa tried to pull her hand from the man's grip, but she couldn't. Not sure what to do, she limped next to him. In about five minutes, they arrived at a forked path. Hassa looked around, and to her delight, she recognized the road that led to the main market to her left, but the old man was walking straight ahead. She began to panic as she tried pulling her hand free, this time much more forcefully, but the old man only tightened his grip. She desperately needed to turn back and take the path to the market. Her ankle hurt badly, and she tried to stop walking to attract the man's attention, but when he walked on as though Hassa was nothing more than luggage, she began to slap his arm with her left hand. "Papa, Papa, please, I must stop. The road that takes me home is to the left of the junction we've just passed." The old man ignored her and quickened his steps.

The day grew darker as light-blue skies quickly disappeared, and the clouds closed in. Lightning repeatedly flashed, and a distant roaring of thunder could be heard. Strong winds soon came, followed shortly thereafter by thick raindrops. Hassa tried pulling her raincoat's hood over her head with her free hand, but the wind wouldn't let it stay. "Papa... Papa... Papa..."

She tried three more times to stop the old man before finally giving up as he marched on like a soldier. As the rain got heavier, Hassa gave up and meekly hobbled along. She felt pain from every part of her left leg, ankle, calf, knee. Hassa cried in the rain. This was not her plan. She chastised herself. Why had she come out at all? Why had she bothered to try to find Lamie? She didn't know where the old man was taking her and was scared that she was being kidnapped. Lamie had told her stories of young children being kidnapped and used for rituals, and she was suddenly sure the old man was a ritualist. She should have been home cooking dinner and looking forward to sliding under the sheets in her bed afterwards to carry on reading her novel in this kind of weather.

"Papa, please! I'm sorry... I'm sorry... Please let me go..." She sobbed as the rain got heavier and blurred her vision.

The old man turned right at the next junction, and not far away, Hassa saw a cluster of bungalows. They walked past three huts set sparsely in front of them and onto a compound with high fences on its sides. As they walked up to a wooden door, Hassa looked back and around her. She longed to see another person so she could shout and attract attention. But unsurprisingly, it was desolate. The old man knocked on the door, and in a few seconds, it opened wide. A young lady in her mid-twenties held the door handle and looked at Hassa in shock.

"This young girl fell in a pit near my farm. She has a wound on her leg. Please take her in and clean her up." Hassa was surprised to hear the old man who'd refused to listen to her address the lady at the door in a compassionate voice as he moved past the two girls and went inside the house.

"Come," the lady said. "Follow me." Taking Hassa by the hand and drawing her inside, she shut the door behind them. As they walked through a sparsely furnished living room, she noticed that Hassa was limping. "Oh, sorry, sorry..." She looked at Hassa, who was wincing in pain, and slowly led her out to the backyard where she helped Hassa out of her raincoat and sat her down on a bench in a long L-shaped corridor, which ended in a kitchen. Hassa noticed two orange trees at positions adjacent to the kitchen and remembered the backyard of her own home.

The rain was coming down in torrents. The endless sound of thunder and wind frightened Hassa as she sat there and thought about Lamie. The lady quickly went back into the kitchen, came out again, and then walked into one of the rooms off the corridor. When she came back out of the room, she was holding a calabash, which she then carried into the kitchen. It took a little while longer before the lady reappeared with a bucket in her right hand and the calabash held to her left side. Hassa could clearly see steam from hot water swirling out of the bucket. The lady set the bucket and calabash down by Hassa's feet, then scurried back into the kitchen and grabbed a small wooden stool, which she placed in front of Hassa before seating herself upon it.

"Okay, my name's Angelina, but everyone calls me Angel. I'm an assistant nurse and work at the hospital. The old man that brought you here is my grandfather. Everyone calls him Hope. That's not his real name, but it's stuck in the neighbourhood because it is commonly believed that if you have a problem and can't find a solution, you can count on him to either help you directly or refer you to someone or something, anything, that could be of help. Hope is super connected at all levels. He knows anyone who matters, and I haven't yet seen or heard of a problem brought to him that was too great or complex for him to solve." Angel smiled into Hassa's eyes and asked, "What's your name?"

"Hassa."

"Okay, Hassa, you look very young. What were you doing out around Hope's farm all by yourself on a day like this when the heavens seem very angry and are expressing it with such a ferocious downpour?'

"I went to buy matches when I realised we had used up what we had in the house, and as our usual seller and all kiosks in our quarter were closed,

I decided to find where I could buy some near the market. I think I walked too far from the paths I know and got lost."

"You said 'we.' Who do you live with?"

"My older sister, Lamie, and I live with our father. But he's working out of town for some time."

"I see." Angel paused then, and looking down into the Calabash, asked, "And your mum?"

"She died after I was born."

"Oh, oh no, I'm sorry to hear that." Feeling sorry for the young girl seated in front of her, Angel turned her attention fully to examining Hassa's leg. "Now, let's look at your injury."

Angel spread an old towel on her lap, leaned forward, and gently pulled Hassa's left leg forward. Hassa raised her skirt out of the way, tucking it between her thighs and pulling it back into folds on her lap. Angel placed Hassa's leg gently on the towel and turned it so she could easily see the gash. It was bleeding heavily. Taking a soft hand towel from the calabash, Angel dipped it in the hot water, pressed out the excess between her palms, and gently washed the mud from Hassa's wound.

Hassa shouted in pain and wriggled on the bench as Angel cleaned it, and concerned at the sound, Hope came out to find out what was going on. Seeing him by the dining-room's door, Angel addressed him urgently. "Papa, I will need spirits to clean the wound, so it doesn't get infected. There's plenty of dirt in it. I don't have any here, and because of the rain, the shops aren't open." Hassa looked up to catch the gaze of the old man who'd marched her there in the rain. He had cleaned up, and barefoot, he was now wearing a pair of khaki knee-length shorts, and a pale-blue short-sleeved shirt. On his head was a beret.

"What *do* you have then?" Hope asked, clearing his throat with a now familiar grunt, he stretched his neck forward and peeped into Angel's calabash.

"Emmm... let me see..." Angel rummaged through the calabash. "Just iodine, cotton wool, bandage, plaster (bandage), emm... raw unfiltered honey, coconut oil, and Panadol."

"Hmmm... Okay, let me see what I can find in my room." He turned and disappeared into the house. In a short while, he was back with a small bottle containing a brown liquid.

"Here, try this. I'm sure it does the same work as spirits."

Angel took the bottle from him and opened it. She sniffed its content, and immediately threw her head back with a look of disgust. "Ugh." Angel immediately recognized the brown liquid as a locally made gin, which the villagers often joked could easily kill a lion.

As Angel got to work, cleaning the wound with the gin and applying iodine to it, Hassa screamed and cried, flapping her hands all over the place at unbearable burning sensation. The sting of the gin and iodine felt like a red-hot knife burrowing into her skin, shooting through her leg like a bolt of electricity.

"Sorry... Sorry, my sister... I know this must hurt terribly," Angel repeatedly cooed in sympathy as the blood quickly began to clot. After a few minutes, she gently rubbed some virgin coconut oil over it to soothe the pain before putting a large waterproof bandage over the gash. With the wound dressed, she massaged Hassa's foot gently with the coconut oil, rubbing her heel in circles with her thumbs and lightly pulling on each toe. She repeated the same with the other foot after washing it with hot water.

Hassa was amazed by Angel. She didn't think a stranger could be so caring and kind. Being marched down here against her will to Hope's home from a spying trip that had landed her in a ditch only to be so kindly tended to by Angel was like an event meant for a storybook. She was grateful but couldn't find the right words with which to express it. So, she simply said, "thank you" as many times as she could muster.

"No problem," Angel replied as she set Hassa's right foot gently on the ground, quickly packed up her first-aid kit, and cleared out the temporary nursing station.

Hassa offered to help put things away with Angel's guidance, but Angel would have none of it. "No, no! You sit right where you are and rest that foot. There's no errand for you to run here."

Hassa obeyed and watched Angel as she scurried in and out of various rooms. It was still raining, but the skies were beginning to clear up.

"How did it go? Did my spirits help?" she heard the old man call from the living room with a slight teasing tone to his voice.

"We're done, and yes, it helped. Hassa did not lose her leg, Papa. Thank God, and thank you," Angel called back with a chuckle.

"Okay, I knew it would work. I told you so."

Angel shook her head and smiled at Hassa. "Grandpa swears by that gin."

Hassa looked down shyly at her injured leg and returned Angel's smile with a grin. "That gin is hotter than pepper."

Angel concurred. "Aye, so it is. It can kill a lion."

Hassa sat quietly and watched the rain. She knew Hope would not let her leave before the rains had stopped, even if she wanted to take the chance and find her way home. She was bothered about time. Her mind kept drifting back to Lamie and what she had witnessed not too long ago, frustrated that she'd gone looking for answers with her spy escapade but had instead been left with more questions.

"Here."

Hassa's reverie was broken by Angel offering her a plate with a large cob of corn that had obviously just been scooped from the boil. She was surprised. Beside the corn were three pieces of cooked African pear, onto which Angel had sprinkled some salt. The aroma from the steam that curled up from the cob was enticing, and Hassa was eager to dig her teeth into it. She looked up and accepted the plate. "Thank you, Angel."

"No problem. If you'd like some water, let me know, and I'll fetch some for you."

Angel quickly left Hassa to her snack and marched back to the kitchen. Hassa saw her come out with another plate of steamy corn and pears, head to the living room, and give the plate to her grandfather, who then prayed over it and blessed her as well.

Then Angel returned to sit next to Hassa with her own plate of corn. Together, they munched quietly and listened to the rain until Hassa got worried again. "Angel, do you know what time it is?"

"It's about twenty minutes past six now."

Hassa's eyes widened, and she began to silently panic. She needed to get home and cook the yams before Lamie returned, but the way things were turning out, she was going to have to explain her absence and injury to Lamie, and knowing that was driving her crazy. When they had finished their snacks, Angel took Hassa's plate away. The rain had now subsided significantly, and Hassa was itching to head back home. She was certain Lamie would have returned by now and be worried sick about her.

"My leg feels better. I'd like to leave for home now," Hassa said to Angel who had just finished sweeping the kitchen and was standing in front of her.

"How does the leg feel? Stand up and tell me if you're having any tingling sensation in the wound, anywhere on the leg or even on the other leg." Hassa did as she was told. After about twenty seconds, Angel asked again. "How do you feel?" Hassa told her the truth that she felt fine and could walk better.

"Thank God. Now, tell me, can your sister dress your wound at home?"

"Yes. She did so once when I slashed this finger here"—Hassa raised her left forefinger and pointed to the tip—"while cutting my nail with a razor blade."

"Alright. Let me tell Hope you'd like to go. The rain has stopped, and from the look of the skies, there isn't likely to be more rain tonight." Angel left Hassa and went to speak to her grandfather. When she returned to the courtyard, she fetched Hassa's sandals and raincoat. "Hope says he'll walk you home," she told Hassa, who eagerly got dressed and was thrilled to leave even though she wished she could get to know Angel better, ask her questions about nursing, and maybe share stories from her novels with her. She liked Angel, likening her behaviour to that of a true angel and wishing she could have her as a second sister.

"Are you ready?" Hope's voice interrupted her thoughts. Hassa saw him standing at the door, but he had changed again, this time into a pair of brown trousers, a pair of black rain boots (into which he tucked his trousers from the calf), and his famous wide-brimmed hat. He was also holding a walking stick and a big silver torch.

"Yes, Papa," Hassa replied.

"Now, before we go, can you tell me what you were doing out on my farm in this terrible weather when kids like you should be indoors?"

Angel answered on Hassa's behalf. "They ran out of matches, and she went looking for a kiosk to buy a packet. Because all the shops were closed, she didn't realise she had wandered too far off her path and ended up on your farm, lost. I'll say she's lucky you found her."

"Hmmm… And who do you live with?"

Again, Angel responded as though to save Hassa the energy of speaking. "She says she lives with her elder sister and her father, who's currently away at work at the borders."

"And where was your elder sister when you wandered out in search of matches?"

This time, Angel was silent and looked at Hassa for a response, realising she hadn't thought to ask Hassa where Lamie was and why she, the younger of the two sisters, was the one who'd had to go buy matches on a day like this. Hassa was caught off guard but quickly made up an excuse.

"My sister had gone out to buy some ingredients to make soup for dinner. I only realized we had run out of matches long after she had left when I needed to light some lamps."

Hope cleared his throat and grunted. "Well, thank God, I found you. Okay, come on. Let's go."

"Come," Angel said, smiling and taking Hassa's hand. Together they walked behind Hope, who led the way to the front door. Outside the house, Angel looked into Hassa's eyes. "Walk gently and be careful with that leg. Don't go into puddles. If you get to a large puddle, remind Hope about your injury, and he'll happily find the strength to carry you over. Never mind if he's told you he's old, feeble, and tired. He says that all the time, but he's stronger than an old horse, this Hope. I tell you."

Hassa giggled at Angel's description of her grandfather. Hope carrying her was the last dream she wanted to imagine having. But she nodded. "I won't forget. I promise."

"Good and tell your sister to change your plaster every two days. Do you understand?"

Hassa nodded again. "I will."

She began to walk away with Hope but suddenly stopped and turned back. Walking up to Angel—who stood waiting for her grandfather and the young girl to disappear from sight—she hugged her tightly. "Thank you, Angel."

Angel was surprised by this show of emotion and wrapped her arms around Hassa for a while before gently pulling herself from the embrace.

"You're already like a kid sister to me, Hassa, and I'm really glad I was able to treat your injury, and we didn't have to take you to the clinic for stitches or more. Now, run along and don't keep Hope waiting. You know he walks like a soldier, and you may soon start needing to, literally, run after him."

Hassa nodded and headed back out after the man, who'd already begun walking away, then turned around and waved one last goodbye before falling into step with Hope, sometimes having to scurry to keep up with him. For his age, the old man truly did walk faster than a soldier.

"Where did you say you live?"

"Not very far from the main market. When we get there, or to the road leading to the townhall, I'll be able to find my way home from there."

Hope cleared his throat and grunted. "How does your leg feel?"

"It still hurts a little, but not as much as it did before Angel treated it."

"That's good. Angel is a good nurse and a very compassionate woman. I'm lucky she lives with me. Whenever I have a medical problem, she saves me a lot of time and money, treating me at home. I truly feel blessed by her."

"Yes, she's wonderful. She gave me hot corn and pear. I like Angel. I wish she could be my second sister."

Hope smiled at Hassa's words and nodded, confidently marching on, turning in and out of bush paths, and Hassa followed. She wondered why he couldn't stick to the clearer routes she saw in front of them, as the over-grown weeds and ferns they had to go through annoyed her, especially as Hope wore rubber boots and she only sandals.

"Is this how you walk all the time?" Hassa looked at her companion as she quickened her strides to stay level with him.

"How am I walking?" Hope wouldn't look at the young girl next to him as he stomped on, and so didn't notice that she was breathing hard, strug-gling to keep up with him.

Panting slightly, Hassa replied, "Like a military man. Were you once in the army? They're the only ones I know who walk like you do. You even walk faster than my father, than my sister, than our teacher... I mean, you really walk fast, fast, fast." Then she tugged at his trousers, forcing him to stop as she did.

"Slow down, Papa. Must you walk so fast? Have you forgotten, sir, that I have a wound on my leg? You're wearing rain boots, and I'm wearing rubber sandals. With the way you're walking, I'll need a motorcycle to catch up with you, and I don't have one here!"

Hope raised his brows and looked at Hassa, wide-eyed and in shock. Her abrupt and fearless tone had amazed him. "Goodness me, children these days! What an insult! Where is this world headed?" He shook his head and grunted. *In times past,* he pondered, *no child would speak to an elder with such sarcasm and in such a tone.*

Growing up, he recalled, Hassa's language and tone could easily have earned her family a fine of at least a cock or hen, some kola nuts, and a bottle of gin, as well as an apology, at least in some circumstances. Rolling his eyes, he shook his head again, shrugged in surrender, and stood with his arms akimbo. Hassa's body language was defiant as she pouted and squinted at him. As he looked at her, he realized that he truly hadn't been considerate of the young girl and chided himself for being selfish and shirking his responsibility to put her first. He was old enough to be her grandfather and felt ashamed for having set a poor example.

Silently thanking her for admonishing him, Hope moved closer and drew Hassa to him, wrapping her shoulders with his arms. "I'm sorry, my child. This is how I've always walked, but I haven't behaved like an elder should. I should have remembered that you're a child and can't walk as fast as I do. But even more important, you're nursing an injury too. Come." He took Hassa's hand, and they both walked on in silence with him tailoring his pace to hers.

Hassa fixed her eyes on the ground and concentrated on watching her steps, one foot at a time, as they walked through little puddles and muddy slush that had washed down from the untarred roads. She didn't even notice at first when they arrived in a heavily flooded area, with a very big pool of stagnant water covered by floating leaves and debris. It was in their way, so Hope stopped and looked around. Just as Hassa was going to ask if they needed to go back, he pushed his hat firmly down on his head, tucked his walking stick and torch under his left arm, and lifted her up like a large cassava being pulled from the ground, resting her on his right shoulder and gently carrying her through the pool of water. The pool was deep, covering Hope's boots to just under his knees. In three minutes, he was out of the water and put Hassa down, then stomped several times to free the debris plastered on his boots and adjusted his hat again.

"Thank you, Papa Hope. I could have drowned were I to cross that water alone. Angel told me you're very strong, and it's true. You're as strong as a wrestler!" Hassa was looking at him in amazement as he pushed at the crown of his hat.

Hope sniffed and turned to her. "Was that what Angel told you now? Did she also tell you I snore like a lion?" Hope eyed the young girl by his side, took her hand, and began to walk again.

Hassa was genuinely surprised by this new revelation, which she found interesting. "You snore so loud? Really? No, Angel didn't tell me that. Maybe she forgot. But she said you're very wise and kind and that the neighbours all rely on you for advice and help when they no longer know what to do. And it's true too. That's why you found that stuff she used on my injury. Oh! That liquid burned like fresh, hot pepper! What was it?"

Hope quietly observed once again Hassa's tendency to be inquisitive and direct.

"What liquid?" he asked, disinterested.

"The one you went into the room to fetch when Angel told you she no longer had mentholated spirits? When Angel smelt it, she made a disgusted face." Hope ignored the question. He wasn't about to divulge one of his favourite "tools of guilty pleasures," as he called it, as doing so would only inevitably illicit still more questions from Hassa, and perhaps, a lecture and rebuke. He quickened his steps a little as an indication that the conversation was over.

Hassa got the message and fell silent. In no time, she saw the market a few yards ahead. "There!" she pointed excitedly. "That's the market. The road to where I live is to the right of that kiosk with the corrugated roof. Do you see it?"

"Yes, I do. And how far is it to your house from there?"

"Emm… Not very far. Let me say ... emm … just about five minutes from there."

"Okay. Let's go." Hope wasn't going to let Hassa walk home from the market all alone. He had promised himself to walk her to the door of her house, and that was exactly what he was going to do.

When they arrived at the kiosk Hassa had pointed out, she'd expected

Hope to bid her farewell and leave. But instead, he turned right onto the road she had described. "Thank you, sir. I'll be fine from here on. I know my way from here, even in the dead of night," she said, trying to dismiss the old man walking beside her.

"No problem, but I'll see you to your doorstep for my own peace of mind." Hope looked at her and gave her a tired smile.

Close to their house, Hassa noticed that it was still eerily quiet. No one was outside, not even the chickens that occasionally crossed the paths. Her heart began to race as she wondered what Lamie would think when she saw Hope. Until this moment, she hadn't quite thought about what her story would be to avoid annoying her sister who'd expected her to stay home. If they didn't have another box of matches left in the house, going out to buy matches, playing, and getting lost would have been a credible excuse, even though Lamie would have been very unimpressed by it. But there was still a box of ten packets left, so Hassa couldn't use that explanation.

What, what, what will I tell Lamie? she thought, her heart pounding and her countenance growing sad. Then it struck her. *I'll simply tell Lamie the truth! I was very scared staying home all by myself and decided to go find her at the townhall!*

At the front of their house, Hassa looked up at Hope with a victorious smile. "Here we are!" Hope stood outside the fence and looked on as she walked up onto the front step and opened the front door. Looking back at him, she said, "Thank you very much, sir, for bringing me home. Please greet Angel for me."

Satisfied that she was truly home, Hope pulled up his trousers, adjusted his hat, and acknowledged her gratitude. "No problem. We thank God. You stay home and take care of your leg. Do you hear me?"

"Yes, I will. Thank you." Hassa waved then and moved inside, locking the door behind her.

She removed her raincoat and sandals just inside the door, not wanting to drip water or mud anywhere, then gathered them up and carried them to the back of the house. It all seemed still unusually quiet, Hassa observed. She looked at the clock on the living room wall. It was 6.45 p.m. She'd expected Lamie to have rushed to the front door as she'd opened it, but thought that she might just be busy in the room or kitchen and hadn't heard the door.

Placing her sandals near the tap, reminding herself to wash them later, she hung the raincoat on the line and looked everywhere, but there was still no sign of her sister. She went to the bathroom and called, then opened the door, but Lamie wasn't there. She went back to their bedroom and noticed that Lamie's handbag and sandals were still not there. Convinced now that her sister had yet to return home, Hassa quickly tidied herself and dashed into the kitchen to cook some yams for dinner. She turned on the switch on the wall, and to her surprise, electricity was back (although the current was low). Relief and fear made her nervous as she peeled the yams. She didn't need to explain her absence and that felt good, but she also hadn't expected her sister to be out for this long. Lamie had told her that she was only going to be out for a couple of hours, so even if she'd left the dingy building a little later than Hassa had imagined, she should still have been back home by now.

Hassa's head felt dizzy as a million questions rushed through her mind. She sat on a small stool in the kitchen and watched the yam cook for a while. Then she brought out the vegetable soup from the fridge and warmed it in a small pot. When the yam was done, Hassa sat in the back of the yard and thought about her relationship with Lamie, and how full of love it was. They were honest and talked straight with each other. She didn't like the spying she'd engaged in today and was going to confess it to her sister and just ask her some questions. She expected Lamie to be honest about what she'd gone to do in the building, and if not, well ... she was going to tell her that God would be very angry with whatever she was doing and then plead with her to go to confession.

She loved her sister dearly; she was kind and generous, and they shared a very close bond. She couldn't bear to see her hurt. Yet Hassa was afraid her sister would despise her for spying on her and began to wonder if it was worth breaking her trust by confessing. She rose and went to check the time. It was 7.25 p.m., and the day had grown darker than usual because of the rain. She remembered her sandals then, quickly washed off the mud that had caked on the soles, and then dried them with a rag. Next, she removed the raincoat from the line and returned it and the sandals to their bedroom before returning to the backyard and sitting very still, just gazing at the starless sky.

It was calm now, with no wind or rain. Hassa felt lonely as she sat there, letting her imagination travel to distant planets and the possibility of life beyond as her eyes searched the skies for stars while she waited and waited for her sister. Eventually, she brought her thoughts back to earth and began to seriously ponder what had kept Lamie from returning for so long. Suppose she had fallen in a ditch like she had herself when Hope found her. Suppose she had been kidnapped by ritualists?

Hassa shut her eyes tight then and prayed: "Please, God, please... Let Lamie come home. Let her not be kidnapped by evil people. Please, God."

The song her father had taught her when she was about five years old came to mind then, and she sang softly, keeping her eyes shut.

"Jesus loves me, this I know,
For the bible tells me so.
Little ones to him belong.
They are weak, but he is strong.
Yes, Jesus loves me...
Yes, Jesus loves me...
Yes, Jesus loves me...
For the bible tells me so."

Hassa opened her eyes and sang it two more times. One Sunday evening, as they'd sung church hymns after dinner, which they did every now and then when he was in the mood, Butem had told his daughters that they would always be protected by the invisible hands of God. He'd taught them this song then, and after the three of them had bellowed it out about half a dozen times, accompanied by claps at the end of each line, he stretched the last word, "so," and led the girls in a long final clap to signal the end of the song.

"Whenever you feel happy or sad, sing this song and pray, and know in your heart that Jesus is hearing you," Butem had assured his daughters.

As the evening wore on, Hassa's mind was tortured with the worst possible scenarios. Her greatest fear was that she would have to sleep alone in their house. A day like this had never happened before, and she was beside herself with worry. She decided that if Lamie had not returned by 7:40 p.m., she would have dinner, lock up, and go to either Yvonne's or Harriet's house to stay the night. But when she went to check the clock again, it was already 7:45.

She would give anything to have Lamie back and have dinner with her as they did every day. Finding that despair had replaced hunger, Hassa went to their bedroom and laid down on the bed, wondering if she was being punished for spying on her sister. Tears rolled down her face as she cried and muttered to herself.

"Where are you, Lamie? Where are you? Please don't leave me, please. I'm sorry for what I did." For the first time in her life, her mind went to the photos of her mother and her wedding, which their father had shown her, and she wondered what life would have been like had her mother not died. Aside from the day he'd showed her and Lamie the photos, their father had never spoken about her. Auntie Oka had told her a little though. Hassa remembered the one thing her foster mother had always emphasized as she smiled and pulled at her cheeks playfully for being too forward and asking too many questions: *"Hassa, you've taken your mother's quick wits and sharp tongue. Be careful."*

As she laid there crying, she felt a chill, and suspecting her mother's presence, she curled up like she was being given a loving, motherly pat on the shoulder. "Mama, please bring Lamie back. Please." Hassa shut her eyes then and finally drifted off to sleep while she prayed.

"Hassa, Hassa, Hassa!!!"

She opened her eyes to a shadow bending over her and gently shaking her arm. She pushed herself further back in the bed, and soon recognised Lamie, sitting on its edge and smiling at her. Hassa jumped to her knees and into Lamie's arms in a long, bear hug. "Oh, Lamie, Lamie, it's you," she said into her sister's neck. "I was so afraid that something had happened to you."

Lamie ran her hands up and down her sister's back. "It's okay. I'm fine, and I'm sorry I came back so late. I was delayed, that's all."

Hassa remained in the tight embrace, as though to be certain she wasn't dreaming, as Lamie rubbed her back lightly as though she were a baby.

After a while, Hassa pulled back and settled into the lotus position, throwing the blanket over her lap.

"When did you come in? I must have dozed off. I didn't hear you. What happened to you? Where did you go? It's been almost five hours since you left!"

Lamie wasn't ready to answer Hassa's questions just yet. "Have you had dinner?" she quickly asked and stood up, taking her younger sister's hand.

"No, I haven't. I lost my appetite while waiting for you, but I'm hungry now and could eat a whole cow. I cooked the yams you asked me to, but it may be cold now, even though I used the wrought-iron pot. I also warmed the vegetable soup."

Lamie laughed. "Okay then. Thank you. Let's go. By the way, I see we have electricity. That's a bit of a surprise considering today's storm and rain. I wasn't expecting it back for another two or three days."

Hassa was thrilled to see her sister back home. That was all that mattered to her at the moment. She rose from the bed and followed Lamie, feeling like she hadn't eaten in many days. She suddenly covered her mouth with her right hand, silently suppressing the "oh no" that almost escaped, and slowed her steps. Like a light bulb had suddenly lit up, she remembered that she had not done the assignment Lamie had requested of her. Her heart began to beat fast. What would she say? She quickly decided she'd tell Lamie she had fallen asleep after she'd left on her errand, woke up to do the cooking, and then dozed off again while waiting for her. She would promise to do it tomorrow after breakfast.

Lamie didn't feel the need to have them go through the ritual of setting the dining table. It was late now and eating in the kitchen felt more convenient and faster. So, she brought out the small stocky, wooden stools that they sat on whenever they had a meal in the kitchen, and the wooden bench on which the plates of food would be placed. She set the bench between the chairs, so she and Hassa could face each other. As Lamie dished out some food onto plates, Hassa brought out plastic cups and set them on the right-hand side of where the plates would be set.

"Should I get water from the fridge, or do you want it from the clay pot?" she asked Lamie, who had just finished dishing and was covering the pots. "Emm… Do we still have plenty of water in the clay pot? Papa will be back on Sunday. Let's drink the water from the fridge."

Hassa fetched a large bottle of water from the fridge, filled their cups, and set the bottle down on the floor. Lamie never missed refilling the big clay pot with clean drinking water, which she fetched from their back neighbour's tap, which delivered it from a private borehole. Their neighbour's borehole water was much cleaner than theirs, which sometimes looked cloudy. Butem had been told by a plumber that he hadn't dug the borehole deep enough. The plumber had even promised to get his team of experts to help Butem sort out the problem whenever he was ready. Lamie and Hassan agreed that water from the clay pot tasted better and was as pure and sweet as the smell of rain on parched earth. Their father had told them that the clay pot was like a natural filter. Dirt and minerals settled, clung, and died at the bottom of the pot or in its rough internal edges. The villagers described the clay pot as a "poor man's fridge," for water stored in it and placed indoors was just as cold as refrigerated water. Butem preferred to drink from the clay pot and would only serve visitors water from the fridge.

The two sisters sat down, facing each other. "Lead us in prayer, Hassa, will you?" They shut their eyes.

"Bless this food, oh Lord, which we're about to receive from thy bounty through Christ our Lord," Hassa prayed. The two girls made the sign of the cross and then settled down to dinner in silence. Hassa's young mind was as hungry for answers from her sister as it was for the yellow yams in front of her. Several times, she wanted to speak, to ask Lamie about her errand today, but found herself tongue-tied. Sometimes, she stopped eating, lifted her cup to her lips, pretending to be drinking while stealing gazes at her sister. Lamie soon noticed that Hassa seemed to have something on her mind and tried to make her speak up.

"Is everything okay?"

"Yes, Lamie," she lied, looking into the plate of food.

"You must have been so frightened being on your own, considering the bad weather."

"I was. The room was so dark at some points, I imagined masquerades walking in."

Lamie smiled through a pang of guilt. "Well, you know that would never happen. But don't be mad at me. I didn't plan to be late. You know I never stay out late. Papa forbids me to. Today, I just got delayed."

"I know, but where did—"

"Well, I'm here now," Lamie said, interrupting Hassa's question. "I'll not leave you in such a condition again. I promise." She reached out and touched her younger sister reassuring on the shoulder, then lifted her chin so she could look into her eyes for belief and trust. Hassa looked at her sister and nodded, and they both smiled.

Hassa loved her sister very much. So, for the rest of dinner, she worked hard at consciously pretending that she had been nowhere unusual. Each time Lamie wasn't looking though, she stole a glance at her and looked away with a little frown. She wished she didn't know that Lamie had secret and began chastising herself for her inquisitiveness and unsolicited detective work. She'd believed her sister was lying, and now she too felt the need to lie. It churned in her stomach and was ripping her heart apart, but she didn't want to spoil a beautiful moment made possible by Lamie's return. Next time, she decided, she was definitely going to ask Lamie for some explanation, lest this secret kill her, even though she knew she'd be in big trouble with her sister.

As Hassa stood up to clear the plates at the end of the meal, Lamie thought to tease her. "Hey, is someone forgetting something important?"

Hassa looked at her sister wide-eyed and confused. "What, Lamie?"

"Okay, since you're no longer interested, let's forget it." Eyeing her sister, Lamie giggled, stood up, and joined Hassa in tidying their dinner area. Just as she was stowing away the chairs, Hassa suddenly screamed playfully.

"Ah, I get it!"

"You do?"

"Yes, Lamie. Goody-goody!" Hassa was excited as she searched Lamie's face for confirmation.

"What's that?" she responded, trying to look confused. "What's Goody-goody?" They both began to laugh. "Okay, you're right. I found some Goody-goody, but I'm not going to tell you where I bought them from. That's my secret. However, you and I are going to enjoy that sweet together once we've tidied up the kitchen and switched off the lights. Oh, and you know what? I also bought those spicy plantain chips we and Papa like."

"Yeah! Goody-goody, chips, chips!" Hassa danced now, unable to contain her joy. "Thank you, sis! Thank you for walking in all that mash and debris outside to find the sweet. Oh, what a mess outside!" Quickly realising she was on the verge of giving herself away, she raised her hands joyfully in the air and flung them down, circling Lamie's waist in another bear hug.

"Yes, it was absolutely a mess out there today. You should see it, Hassa! I feel sorry for the sellers." Lamie rolled her eyes and shook her head. "The wind knocked down some of their stalls. They're going to have to rebuild. Poor, poor traders. Ah!"

Hassa moved back a little. "Oh, I must tell you, Lamie, I totally forgot to do the assignment you asked me to. I slept and slept like a log after you left."

Lamie walked past Hassa, smiling and nodding like she'd caught her being very naughty. "Aha! *I* kept my promise, but someone didn't keep *theirs*. Let's have a rethink about sweets tonight then, shall we?"

Hassa clasped her hands in prayer and pleaded. "Oh no, please, please, sis. Okay, I'll start the assignment tonight and finish it tomorrow after breakfast. Please?"

Lamie wanted to make up for her lateness, so she embraced her sister. "Come, it's okay. One Goody-goody for each of us tonight. Okay?"

"Yeah!" Hassa threw her hands up for joy, clapped, and then scurried to the sink to do the dishes while Lamie stored the leftovers, stowed the furniture away, and began to sweep the floor.

"My God, Hassa! What's that on your leg?! What happened to your leg?!" Lamie had spotted the bandage as she'd made to sweep the floor around Hassa's feet and was about to ask her to step aside for a moment. Hassa had completely forgotten about her injured ankle but now felt a bit of a sting coming from the wound. Her sister's discovery had taken her unaware though, and she was lost for an explanation. Dropping her broom and standing with her hands on her hips, Lamie looked back and forth between her sister's injury and her face, waiting for an answer.

Hassa twiddled her fingers, sucked in her cheeks, and stared at the floor. Lamie pulled her sister forward and gently turned her around, then bent down so she could look at the injury more closely. "That's not a small cut. And this plaster... We don't have this kind of plaster at home," she noted, as she stood up. She turned to face her little sister again. "Hassa?" Lamie was visibly angry, her voice was firmer and louder, demanding an explanation.

Hassa slowly raised pleading eyes to meet her sister's. "I fell," she answered in a soft, barely audible voice.

"You fell? Where? How? When? And you didn't tell me?" Lamie eyes were wide in surprise, wondering what her younger sister had been up to outdoors in the rain, where she must have been to have fallen and cut herself that badly. She just couldn't imagine what she could have been doing, and where in the backyard or on the balcony or anywhere in the house, to have fallen and hurt herself seriously enough to need the sort of dressing she'd just seen. Had she decided to go be with one of her friends, Harriet or Yvonne, and fallen on the way?

"And where did you get that big plaster from?" Lamie asked, believing that the bandage would provide some clue. Confused and shocked at the same time, her questions rushed out more quickly than Hassa could answer, and not knowing how to start, the young girl took the easier way out.

"I will tell you ... after I finish washing the plates."

Exasperated, Lamie hissed. "Jesus, Hassa! So, if I hadn't seen this wound now, you would have kept silent and carried on trying to hide it from me? And if it got worse, then what? Papa would be mad and scold me for not keeping an eye on you! For not caring for my sister enough!"

"I'm sorry, sis! I didn't mean to hide it from you, I swear. I meant to tell you later." Hassa's voice broke as she begged Lamie to understand.

Lamie was silent, still in disbelief. After a while, she breathed out heavily and dropped her shoulders. "Alright, let's finish with our tidying, but then I want to know what happened."

A heavy silence descended on the two sisters as they tidied the kitchen. Lamie's heart was racing with guilt and anger, and Hassa's with how to explain her injury. When Hassa finished her share of the chores, she returned to their bedroom and sat meekly at the foot of her bed, waiting for her sister.

Lamie checked to ensure that everything was in place. She switched off the kitchen light and checked the windows and living-room door, then did the same for their father's bedroom and the guest room. With all lights switched off, she finally walked into their bedroom, pulled out her dressing stool, and sat down.

"Lie down on your stomach and let me look at that leg," she ordered Hassa, who did as she was told. Lamie pulled the stool close enough to enable her to examine the injury. Although, in her mind, she played with the idea of pulling the bandage back to see the size of the cut and redress it, she knew that doing so could make things worse, so she decided to rely on her sister's words and reactions. Feeling around the area, she noticed Hassa inhale sharply and winced.

"Does it hurt badly?"

"Yes, when you touch it like that," Hassa quickly answered.

"How big is the cut?" she asked, and Hassa raised her forefinger and held it just under the joint in the middle. "Did it bleed a lot?"

"Yes."

"Okay." Lamie pushed her stool back so she could rest her back against the dressing table, folded her hands on her lap, and demanded an explanation. "I'm waiting, Hassa. What happened while I was away?"

Hassa slowly rolled to her side and sat up. It was time to tell her story, and as she usually did when caught being naughty or breaking a rule, she needed to ensure clemency before she could begin. "Please, Lamie, promise you won't be mad at me. I did something bad."

Lamie was accustomed to her younger sister's way of neutralizing her anger by taking the winds out of her sails before confessing any wrong-doing. Tonight, though, she was also angry at herself for leaving the young girl alone in such bad weather and for so long, so Hassa's plea pushed the guilt deeper into the depths of her heart, and she succumbed to compassion.

"I promise I won't be mad. Just tell me the truth about what happened."

Hassa began her narration, and Lamie was gobsmacked by its revelations. She'd really believed that her younger sister had wandered off to play with her friends, but nothing could have prepared her for what she was hearing, and she couldn't hide her shock.

"What? You followed me to know where I was going?" She leaned forward on the stool and stared at her sister.

Hassa stopped speaking and nodded, waiting for further rebuke from her older sister, and when none came, she continued her story, only to be interrupted again.

"What? You went as far as the community centre?"

Hassa paused again for a short while and then carried on with her narrative.

"Jesus, Hassa! You really followed me right until I walked into the building?" This time, Lamie stood up abruptly, with her arms akimbo, rocking her body back and forth and looking at her sister in utter disbelief. Suddenly, seeing tears rolling down Hassa's face, she remembered her promise not to be mad and threw her hands up in exasperation. Then she shook her head, sat back down on the stool, and crossed her legs. Hassa stayed silent and cried, sniffing and wiping her eyes with her hands.

It had turned into a quiet night, and the two sisters could hear the intermittent whistles of birds and the bleats of crickets. Gusts of wind softly pressed against their bedroom window, and the light in the bedroom periodically dimmed. Lamie got up and went outside, returning a short time later with a lit kerosene lamp, turned it to its lowest glow, and setting it down with a box of matches in a corner, far from the window.

They both knew that the electricity would go back out soon, and Hassa was grateful her sister had been proactive. The last thing she wanted was to be in total darkness, even for a second. Imagining the repercussions for her detective escapade was more than enough darkness on her mind. The soft glow from the lamp and the dim light from the bulb on the ceiling lifted Hassa's spirit. The room was brighter now, feeling like welcome sunshine to the young girl.

Lamie was struggling with her emotions. She was angry, and yet she wanted to be compassionate. Going out to fetch the lamp had removed some of the heat from her anger. She quickly sat back down on the stool, rested her back against the dressing table, and demanded to hear the rest of Hassa's story. "Okay, go on, Madam Private Investigator. I'm listening," she teased, indirectly scolding her sister in a voice filled with disappointment.

Hassa decided not to tell how she'd stood against the broken fence and spied into the dilapidated building, feeling that this part of her story could cost her Lamie's forgiveness.

"When I saw you walking towards the building, I turned around and decided to come home. It was on my way back that I fell into a hole. I didn't see it because the path was flooded with muddy water." Hassa then began telling Lamie about her encounters with Hope and Angel, her voice growing almost joyful, especially as she described Angel and her kindness, her boiled corn and pear snack, and her insistence on washing up the plates.

Lamie couldn't help but smile at her sister's description of Hope and how he'd lifted her onto his shoulder to cross the pond. "He carried me like a cockroach, sister! That man, Hope ... he's very old but very, very strong, I tell you, as strong as Zuma Rock."

When she reached the end of her story, Hassa looked down at her feet as she waited for her sister's reaction.

Lamie leaned forward on the stool, rested her elbows on her lap, and clasped her hands together on her knees as she looked sternly at Hassa.

"Tell me," Lamie said in a scolding voice, no longer trying to hide her anger. "Suppose you'd been kidnapped, fallen into a bigger, deeper gutter or gully, or gotten bitten by a snake?" Lamie's voice rose further the more she spoke, echoing into the night now. "Suppose Hope and Angel were wicked people and had abused and killed you? What would I do, coming back to find you not at home and not at Yvonne's or Harriet's home either, enh? What would I tell Papa? How would anyone know where you went or where to even start looking, enh? Sometimes, you're very stubborn, Hassa! I've been telling you that always!"

When she finally sat back against the dressing table and folded her arms on her chest, she looked at her sister with frustration and concern clear on her face. "So, tell me, what did you benefit from trying to spy on me aside from a big cut on your leg?"

Hassa wriggled her hands, kept her gaze on the floor, and remained quiet. The silence in the room was broken then as a gust of wind shook the window. In the distance, they could hear the nervous barking of a dog. Then the electricity went out and both girls faced each other and saw only shadows. Lamie got up and increased the glow of the lamp, brightening the room nicely again, then moved to sit next to Hassa on the bed.

Turned towards her, she addressed her in a firm but gentle tone. "Do you understand the seriousness of what you did, Hassa?"

She nodded. "Yes, Lamie, and I'm very sorry. I won't repeat it, I promise. I was just afraid of being on my own. The weather made me afraid of the day."

Lamie put her hand around her sister's shoulder and drew her close. "I understand. If you had gone to Harriet's or Yvonne's house, I wouldn't have minded. I'm your big sister. But I have the responsibility to look after you, and I would have been blamed for negligence had anything bad happened to you. Papa would not have forgiven me; he would *never* have forgiven me. You do understand what I'm saying, don't you?" Hassa nodded.

Lamie pulled back. "Look at me," she ordered. Hassa turned to face her sister, and Lamie bent her head so it almost touched hers, staring right into the young girl's eyes and seeking reassurance. "Now, I will take your word that you'll never play this kind of game anymore. Not ever! Are we clear?"

"Yes, I promise, sis. I'll never repeat it."

"Okay. I'll look at your injury again in the morning and maybe change the dressing."

"Angel is an assistant nurse. She said you should change the dressing every other day."

"Okay. But I'll check it every day anyway, and if you begin to feel more pain there, you must let me know."

"Alright, I will."

Lamie got up and sat back on the dressing stool, facing Hassa with a little smile playing on her lips, which confused Hassa until she spoke up again. "Now, I did promise us Goody-goody tonight, didn't I?"

"Yes, yes!" Hassa clapped in delight.

"Well ... it's almost ten thirty and too late for a sweet, don't you think?"

Hassa's lips pushed outward in a pout even as she frowned. Lamie still felt the need to compensate her sister for her long absence though, and even more now after hearing how Hassa had spent the rest of her day in her absence.

"Hmmm... Alright, how about we share just one tonight, and then we can have some more tomorrow after lunch?"

"Yeah! Thank you, Lamie. You're the best sister ever!" Hassa clapped, leaped out of the bed, walked to her sister, and flung her arms around her waist.

Lamie laughed and was happy the tension between them had thawed. "Okay, okay. It's only halfy-halfy tonight then," she reminded her sister.

Lamie dug into her bag and brought out a Goody-goody. She tore the wrap open with her teeth and found the mid-point of the candy, then pinched the soft caramel deeply on a straight line in the middle from end to end. Twisting it nonstop until the candy separated in two in a long gummy stretch, Lamie cut it with her thumbs and forefingers and gave Hassa one half. Hassa thanked her sister and excitedly returned to sit on the bed to enjoy her candy and watch Lamie busy herself around the wardrobe, the dressing table, and her bed, enjoying her own Goody-goody in small bite-sized chunks.

Hassa finished her sweet, licked her sticky fingers, then went to the bathroom to wash her hands. She changed into her nightdress then and slid under her blanket, pulling it up to her chest and covering her shoulder as she turned on her side to continue watching her sister, who was now seated on her own bed, holding a small notepad and a pencil, and reading off what Hassa believed was a list.

When she was finally ready for bed, Lamie cleaned up in the bathroom and fetched the lamp. Blowing it out, she set it down near the head of her bed, with the box of matches, so she could easily reach them when she woke up in the morning.

Hassa still had a lot on her mind, mostly why Lamie still hadn't told her why she'd gone to that rundown building or what she'd been doing there. After confessing to spying on her older sister, she'd expected her to clear the air and explain herself, thus quenching her curiosity. Since that hadn't been forthcoming, she decided to try and draw a response from Lamie.

"Em ... so ..." Hassa yawned and paused before continuing. "That building I saw you going to is really terrible. Why were you going there, sis?"

"I can't tell you now. That's a chat for another day." Lamie looked over at Hassa, and even though it was dark in the bedroom, she could not help but imagine the unsatisfied look that was surely on the young girl's face. Finally, she relented somewhat. "Well, if it will make you feel better, Madam Detective, I didn't go there to kill anyone, to steal, to fight, or to commit any crime."

Hassa yawned again, plumped her pillow, adjusted herself under the blanket and remained quiet. A few minutes after, Lamie's racing thoughts were interrupted by Hassa's voice yet again.

"Lamie?"

"Yes?"

"Have you ever seen Mama's ghost, or felt like she was around you?"

"Emmm… no. Why do you ask?"

"When I was sleeping, just before you returned and woke me up, I think Mama came to me in this room. I felt her around my bed … emm … like she was touching my shoulder and telling me everything would be fine. I was crying and very afraid you might never come back."

"Are you telling the truth, Hassa?"

"Yes, in God's name."

"Hmmm… Well, maybe her spirit really was here to comfort you, but I've never recalled seeing or feeling her. Or, perhaps, I just didn't recognize her presence."

"My twin brother that died at birth... Do you know if Papa gave him a name?"

"No. He doesn't seem to have lived for even a minute, according to Auntie Oka. Why do you ask?"

"Nothing. I'm just curious. That's all."

"Okay. Let's sleep. It's late, and I'm sure that, just like me, you must be very tired."

"Yes. Goodnight, sis."

"Goodnight." Hassa turned to face the wall and drifted off.

Saturday morning was cool and bright. The sun rose very early, as it usually did near the peak of the rainy season after a torrential rainfall like the one of the previous day. It was almost seven when Lamie opened her eyes to the repeated sound of a cock's crow and the blinding glare of the sun streaking into their bedroom from the window, which she had risen to open at about two a.m. and left a little ajar to let in some fresh air. She stretched, yawned, squinted, and frowned. As though the sun was an unwelcomed guest, she turned on her side and pulled the blanket over her head, wishing she could just lie in bed the whole morning. Her mind was fully awake and already active though, itemizing and prioritising what she and Hassa needed to do that day.

Saying her early morning prayer, she then pushed the blanket away, flinging part of it to the floor as she grumbled and stood up. Quickly making her bed, she moved over to her sister, who had heard Lamie's noise as she walked around the room and turned her back to her, covering her head with her pillow.

"Hassa?" Lamie softly called as she gently shook her sister on the shoulder. "Hassa?"

"Huh?" Hassa grumbled from under the pillow.

"Wake up." Not waiting for another answer, Lamie left her sister and went to take a shower, confident that the young girl was awake.

Lamie had just finished sweeping the front of the house and was returning the brush and dustpan to the kitchen when Hassa met her by the dining room.

"Alright, Hassa. I've swept everywhere, including Papa's room, so wipe the furniture and join me to get breakfast ready."

"Okay. I sorted yesterday's laundry while you were sweeping and put the ones still a bit damp out on the line to dry. I don't know when we'll be able to iron though as there's still no electricity."

"Hmm... yes, let's see... em..." Thinking hard, Lamie pinched her lips together with her left thumb and forefinger. "Well, if electricity isn't back by tomorrow morning, is there anything else we can do other than take the laundry to the washerman on Monday for ironing?"

"No, nothing. You're right, Lamie."

A thought flashed through Lamie's mind then, and she walked briskly to the tap in the backyard. She turned the faucet and water burped out in splashes at first and then a trickle. Lamie knew that they would run out of water from the tank in no time, and although she was relieved their father would turn on the generator and pump some water into the tank on his return the next day, she found waiting till the next day tiring. She hissed loudly and turned the faucet off before angrily storming off, muttering to herself, "I don't understand this rubbish. We have a tap that's no better than exterior décor when water in the tank is too low. If Papa didn't have a private borehole and a generator, it would be this difficult all the time, fetching from the neighbours' or walking five minutes to the public taps at the square all the time."

After breakfast, Hassa did her assignment and assisted Lamie in making okra soup and stew for the week in anticipation of their father's return. As they left the soups to rest on the burner, the sisters frolicked in the back-yard, first taking turns to throw stones from afar to gauge the middle of a round circle Lamie drew on the ground, and later, challenging each other to see how far either of them could skip rope nonstop a hundred times with one of the thick twisted ropes Butem's roofer friend had left behind a couple of years earlier when he'd come to replace the rusted zinc sheets above the guestroom.

"My God! Lamie, what's that in your hair?" Hassa stood up abruptly from the ground where she'd been sitting with her sister as they rested after skipping.

Lamie jumped up, scared, brushing her hair all over with her hands so that whatever it had been would fall or fly off. "What's there?"

Looking closer and then backing away, Hassa's eyes widened, and she pointed. "Ha! Looks like you have lice! I see tiny things like their eggs on your hairline."

"What?! Lice?! They're so, so dead!" Lamie ran off to their bedroom to fetch a large and small mirror so she could get a better view of her hairline in the daylight. Hassa started to giggle as her sister dashed off.

She soon rushed back. "Now, where are they?" Lamie stood next to Hassa with one mirror held at the back of her head while she looked into the one in front of her. "Where are they, Hassa? I can't see any eggs!" Lamie looked from her right ear to the left one, as Hassa moved further away from her sister, waving her hand forward to indicate that she wanted to keep her sister as far away from her as possible.

"I don't want to get close, Lamie! They'll jump onto my hair, and the agony of camphor or shaving my head again is the last thing I want."

Lamie eyed her sister, hissed, and carried on looking into the mirrors.

When they were much younger, the girls always got infected with lice at school. Auntie Oka had tried several remedies prescribed by her friends to get rid of them. First, every day for one week, she'd sprayed the girls' hairs with insecticide just before bedtime and tightly wrapped their heads in a scarf. That didn't work. Then she tried a mixture of camphor and kerosene, and on the very first day she applied it to their scalps, Lamie and Hassa had screamed and cried from the unbearable burning sensation. From his bedroom, Butem had heard the girls crying out and rushed out to the backyard.

He'd found the sisters jumping up and down, running from one wall to the other and flapping their hands in pain as Auntie Oka tried to calm them down, telling them that the burning sting would end after a while. Butem couldn't bear to see his daughters in such pain, and unnerved by the commotion, he'd intervened. "Auntie, please let's wash that concoction off their hair right now," he'd ordered Auntie Oka. Without waiting for any response, he'd run into his bedroom and fetched shampoo and a bucket. Auntie Oka had taken Hassa to the tap, bent her head under the faucet, and lathered her hair with the shampoo while Butem filled a bucket with water and washed Lamie's. Not knowing what else to do about the lice infection, Auntie Oka had suggested the last remedy she'd been told about.

"We'll have to cut their hair right back to the skin, and then they must keep washing their scalp with a bit of Dettol mixed in their bath water. It's the only way to get rid of the lice, not having anywhere to hide and breed."

Butem hadn't been happy to have his girls modelling shiny bald heads, but it seemed better than camphor and kerosene and more sensible as a permanent solution. So, he agreed. Lamie and Hassa knew they had no choice, so they grudgingly went with Auntie Oka to the barber.

In addition to the haircut, Auntie Oka had removed all the beddings from the girls' beds and washed them and their bath towels in disinfecting hot water. She'd also taken out their mattresses and placed them on mats on the floor in the backyard to get plenty of sun, brushing each side down with boiled water every couple of hours.

The sisters had been teased in school about their new look, and Hassa had gotten into a bloody fight with a classmate, who'd called her "wally" or "mirror." She scratched her classmate's face so badly with her fingernails that the others had gotten scared and stopped teasing. The class teacher had scolded Hassa and her mate for fighting, and when she'd learnt from the others that Hassa was being teased for her shaved head, the teacher had sternly warned the class about such behaviour, told the brawling classmate that if she teased Hassan again, she'd be suspended, and had taken the matter no further. Auntie Oka's last resort had worked, the sisters' hair had grown back, and they'd never gotten lice again.

Lamie was shivering as she focused on the mirrors, afraid the lice nightmare was back, but as she stared in the mirror, nervously looking to catch the tinniest glimmer of what could be a louse egg, she wondered if perhaps the mirrors were useless.

"Now, truthfully, Hassa, I don't see *any* lice eggs on my hair." Lamie was becoming really agitated and teary.

"Oh God, Lamie, they're there. Can't you see them even with two mirrors? Should I go bring you Papa's standing mirror to add to the hand ones?" Seeing the worry etched on Lamie's face, Hassa walked to the dining-room door, and facing her sister, declared victory. "Yeah, Lamie! I was just joking! That's my payback for losing the skipping and the stone-throwing games to you. Next time, try not to beat me. I'm younger."

Lamie blew out a loud gust of air, relieved but exasperated with her sister. Throwing her hands up in the air, she shook her head, hissed, and began walking to their bedroom. Hassa, ran off to the front deck, laughing out loud and thoroughly amused and excited by her prank.

After dinner in the evening, and with nothing else to do, Hassa sat on the veranda singing hymns with her sister and enjoying the evening. She teased Lamie, telling her she sang like an "over-fed toad" when Lamie couldn't hit some very low notes and warning her that the writers of the hymns would be so disappointed that Lamie was "murdering" their verses. Sometimes, Lamie laughed and chose another hymn more amenable to her voice, and other times, she ignored Hassa and carried on bellowing the song, shifting tones as it suited her.

The night was cool and still, and the sky absent of stars, as the girls got ready for bed at nine-thirty. Lamie reminded Hassa that they needed to wake up at six a.m. to be in church for the eight a.m. mass. As they made small chatter in their bedroom, Lamie suddenly stopped and said she thought she'd heard the sound of a car pulling up. Hassa listened but didn't hear anything. Then they heard the sound of feet shuffling on the veranda. Lamie grabbed the lamp she had lit, and Hassa followed her into the kitchen. Grabbing a pestle from behind the kitchen door, Lamie gave Hassa the lamp to hold, and raising the pestle above her head, she tiptoed through the living room to the front door with Hassa at her side. The door creaked open then, and Lamie raised the pestle, intending to hit the intruder, but when the door opened further, both girls stopped, with Lamie dropping the pestle and Hassa the lamp.

"Papa!" The two girls shouted and simultaneously flung their arms around their father, who was holding a suitcase. Butem almost fell back from the force of the embrace, and quickly put the suitcase down and wrapped his daughters in a tight hug.

"Oh, Papa, we thought it was a burglar!" Lamie said quickly, excitement and relief pouring from every word.

"Yes, Papa, Lamie was ready to break the thief's head with that pestle," Hassa pointed to the weapon on the floor, "and I-I would have shouted so loud, the neighbours would have gathered here in no time!"

Butem laughed, pulled back a little, and looked at his daughters in pleasant surprise. "Jesus! You girls are real warriors! Where have I been all these years to have missed this training you have?" Butem kept laughing and gave the girls one more tight squeeze. "I'm sorry I surprised you this way. I missed you both, and since I'd finished my trade, I didn't feel the need to wait till tomorrow. I'm so happy to be home." He then pulled out of their embrace. "Okay, my children, let's get in. I've had a very long journey, and I see you both were ready for bed. Besides, we need to go to church in the morning." Butem picked up his suitcase, locked the door, and went into the living room with the girls. "Oh, and please," he added, "let's attend the ten a.m. mass so I can rest for a little longer."

He flicked the switch near the door on and off. "I see we don't have electricity."

"No, Papa, it went out last night and hasn't been back since then," Lamie replied.

"Okay, I'll turn on the gen in a little while."

"Please, Papa," Lamie said, "can you pump some water into the tank when the gen comes on? We've run out of water."

"No problem. Now, both of you, please go to bed, and I'll see you in the morning."

"Goodnight, Papa," the sisters chorused.

Back in their rooms, the girls carried on chatting, more animated now as they each expressed how shocked and delighted they had been to find that their father was the "burglar" they'd expected to find lurking behind the door. They'd both been looking forward to his return the next day, but having him back tonight felt like Christmas had arrived much earlier.

The next day, Butem and his daughters drove to church. Neighbours who knew he usually returned home on Sunday, and preferred to attend the Sunday evening mass when he could, showed delight at seeing him with the girls in church that morning. After church, when he stopped to exchange pleasantries and told them he was home for another month, or perhaps a little more, before travelling back to the border, he was inundated with invitations and requests. Some promised to stop by the house for a beer or two. Butem knew the ones who'd invited themselves over for a drink whether he liked it or not, and was not surprised. He simply said, "Of course."

Another acquaintance told him offhandedly about his son's upcoming traditional marriage. "You must come. I've already saved you the fabric we've chosen as the uniform. I'll bring it to you during the week!" With that, the man walked away without waiting for Butem to accept or decline the invitation. Another offered to take him for fresh fish pepper soup and palm wine "one of these days," and another told him he had a new stock of beautiful organza and damask fabrics he'd bring over to the house so he could buy some for his daughters, if not for himself.

Hassa and Lamie stood next to their father as the greetings went on, and Lamie began to grow impatient. Each time a new person approached, and she thought to herself, *Right, this must be the last and then we'll go*, another acquaintance would appear from nowhere, and soon two or three more, all taking turns to shake her father's hand, ask after his trade, when he'd gotten back, when he was leaving again, what new things he had, and so on and so forth. Not sure when it would end, she quietly dipped her hand into her father's trouser pocket and took out the car keys. Together with Hassa, they sat in the car and waited for him. By the time the pleasantries were finally over and Butem got in his car to drive home, he wondered if had really been to mass at all, as the solemnity of collective prayer and meditation seemed to have worn thin and church had felt like being in a market on a very busy day.

Determined to bring back some piety to their day, Butem introduced hymns and belted them out at the top of his lungs, almost drowning out his daughters' voices. The girls clapped to the songs in rhythm, and their father tapped the steering wheel, sometimes honking the horn accidentally in the process. Back home, the day turned out to be busy in Butem's household. Neighbours came and went, some for a quick hello or to gossip, not bothering to sit, while others made themselves at home while Lamie and Hassa served snacks and drinks.

At about seven, after a dinner of rice and fish stew, Lamie told her father that she needed to bring him somewhere to show him something quickly. Butem tried to get his daughter to reveal what it was and asked if it couldn't wait till the next day, but Lamie wouldn't disclose anything and pleaded its importance. "Please, Papa, we won't waste time. I promise you," she begged with her hands clasped.

"Okay. Do you want us to walk or drive?"

"Let's drive, please, Papa. That will be faster, and we'll be back before it gets too late."

Butem obliged and went into his room to put on his sandals and fetch his car keys. Lamie told Hassa to change into her sandals and join them.

"Where are we going, sis?" Hassa asked almost half a dozen times.

"Somewhere. Just come along, and oh … wear your covered rubber shoes," Lamie added hastily.

Lamie and Hassa joined their father, who was already revving the car and waiting for them. Lamie directed her father as they drove, and in a short while, the dilapidated building came in view. A few yards from the building, within the premises of the large field where Hassa had leaned against a fence to spy on her sister, Lamie showed her father where he could park his car and urged him and Hassa to come with her. Hassa didn't know what to think as she took her father's hand and together walked slightly behind Lamie, leading the way, advising them to be cautious as they walked through debris and little puddles of water. Hassa was shocked when they came to the entrance of the building, and it dawned on her that Lamie was really taking her and their father into the same structure she'd believed her sister had entered for some clandestine activity just two days earlier.

As they got closer to the building, Butem expressed disgust at the sight of it. "Goodness gracious! Why can't the chief just pull down this eyesore. It's been standing empty for over twenty years! I mean, just look at the state of it!"

"You know about this building, Papa?" Lamie asked.

"Yes, who doesn't? It's been the subject of a lawsuit forever. Since the owner died, his children have been fighting over its ownership and what to do with it. Three judges have passed during the process of litigation. It looks like the case has stalled." Butem shook his head. "What a shame, fighting over such a material thing. Just look at it! Tell me, who has won now? The poor dead man must be rolling in his grave over such wastage."

Hassa listened attentively, taking in her father's words. She moved to stay in the middle between Lamie and their father as they arrived at the entrance. As they began to enter the building in a single file, carefully watching their steps to avoid slipping, Butem noticed the bandage on his younger daughter's leg.

"Hassa! What happened to your leg? When did you get that injury? Did you fall in school? Is the cut deep?" he asked, like he could already guess the answers. Lamie and Hassa stopped briefly. Lamie's eyes met Hassa's and then she flashed their father a look and turned to face front while Hassa in turn gave her father a quick look, turned away, and replied only to the second and last questions.

"It was on Friday, and no, Papa, it's not really deep. It doesn't hurt anymore."

Relieved it wasn't anything to worry about, and sure that Lamie was efficiently nursing the cut, Butem gave his daughter what sounded like both a warning and advice. "Be careful, Hassa. You must walk very, very carefully when it rains, and at this time too, when the ground hardly dries out from one rainfall before another comes pouring down."

Hassa simply nodded, and the trio walked on. The building had no door and was much worse inside than Hassa had imagined. The front hall, which looked like what was meant to be a living room or an office space, was like a skip and smelled bad. There were small heaps of refuse everywhere, empty beer cans, soft-drink cans, food remnants, takeaway packs, and cellophane bags from which burst rotten meals, empty corn cobs, and rags. It looked like someone had tried sweeping the rubbish into controllable, packable heaps and had just done a poor job of it.

The two large windows on either side of the room were bare, just large open squares with decaying wooden seals around the frames. The ceiling was concrete, and in one quick look, Butem could see mould, water stains, and chipping everywhere. Part of the plaster was peeling off in different places and hung loosely from the ceiling like dead leaves about to fall from feeble branches. He and his younger daughter pinched their noses closed as they carefully tried to make out flatter piles of trash to step on. A rat ran over Hassa's feet, and she jumped and shouted, "Papa!" grabbing his arm. Lamie turned and grimaced apologetically at her family.

She seemed a little less bothered than they were and confident of where she was going as she meandered through the piles of rubbish and down the hall to two flights of broken stairs on the right. Before she could start climbing, Butem stopped her, confused and almost angry that his daughter had brought them into this building that looked like something out of the ruins of ancient Greece.

"Wait, wait, wait, Lamie," he said, still pinching his nostrils together. "Where exactly are we going in this dump? Where?"

"Papa, you will see. You and Hassa should just follow me."

"No, no, my daughter. We can't follow you like a flock of rudderless sheep. I'm your father. I'm supposed to protect you and your younger sister, but you're now asking me to shirk my responsibility by blindly following you into a hellhole. No way! Tell me now where you're taking us or let's get out of here right now! Do you hear me? I say out we go or else speak up!"

"Papa, please, there's something I want to show you. If there was danger here, do you really think that I'd be crazy enough to bring you and Hassa here? And at this time of day? Have I ever taken you to a place like this before?" Lamie stood with her hands on her waist and stared at her father wide-eyed. "I'm sixteen, Papa! I'm grown up!"

Lamie was visibly upset, and her voice rose in anger as she continued. "You trust me to look after Hassa and the house when you go to the border for business. Have you ever returned to find a problem at home or heard a bad report from anywhere, from anyone, about your daughters? Look at this place again, Papa. You think I love this and enjoy coming here? Rather than just being patient, you can't even give me the benefit of the doubt?! You're just shouting at me! I'm angry now, Papa! I'm really angry! If you want to go home, fine! Please just go. But I'm not leaving. I have work to do upstairs, and I'm begging you to come with me, but as I said, if you want to go ... then go. I'll find my way back home." Lamie folded her arms across her chest and looked away from her family.

"And just who do you think you're talking to in that tone?!" Butem yelled, lashing out. "How dare you speak to me like that! I'm asking you—"

"Papa!" Hassa loudly interjected before her father could finish, throwing him an impatient look that bid him to stop.

Hassa had never heard or seen her sister this angry before. As she had privileged knowledge of Lamie's previous visit to the building, she wanted to understand it, but she trusted that her sister must have some reasonable explanation for bringing them here, so her empathy was with her. The filth and stench of the environment was getting to her though, and while she was dying to uncover Lamie's secret mission here, she also wanted it revealed quickly so that they could all go home.

She looked from her father to Lamie repeatedly, waiting for one of them to break the ice of mutual displeasure that had suddenly enveloped the hall where they stood. Just like his younger daughter, Butem was stunned both by Lamie's tone and the content of her rebuke. For the first time, he wondered if he was failing as a father and deeply missed his wife. Was he being too focused on his business and missing out on the emotional growth of his daughters? He wondered if there was more to raising girls that he should know but didn't.

This outburst was not one he would have ever expected from Lamie.

Everyone knew Hassa as the one with the touch-and-go fiery side and tendency to be curt in speaking her mind, just like her mother. Butem's immediate family and extended relatives, however, had always drawn strong comparisons between his grandmother and Lamie, with many of them unequivocal in their belief that Lamie had Butem's calm, yet stubborn demeanour, even though she had also inherited her mother's physical features, just like Hassa. Taken aback by Lamie's stinging reprimand, Butem was seeing her "stubbornness" in an entirely new light, a reflection of himself that had lain dormant until poked. *Our people always say that "the coconut never falls far from the tree." How right they are*, he silently told himself. He sighed and addressed his daughter in a conciliatory tone.

"Alright, Lamie, don't be angry. I know you're a very sensible young woman. This building overwhelms me, and I'm afraid of not being able to protect you and your younger sister should we be attacked or encounter evil. That's all. Let's go." With that, he waved them along.

Butem's heart pounded in trepidation as they began their climb upstairs. He desperately wanted to believe that Lamie had inherited the art of emotional control when it matters most, but he was afraid that this had to be learned, and that his regular absence from his daughters was stealing from him both the privilege and responsibility of guiding them on that path. His friends and neighbours' anecdotes told of current challenges with the intergenerational gaps they were experiencing with their children. They often told him that their problem wasn't with the number of years in between generations but with the distinct nature of the culture shifts and constantly changing modes of expression aided by technology. One of his business friends at the border had once mocked him about his own many futile efforts, explaining to Butem how he was learning to adapt to being constantly teased by his three teenage children for not being "up-to-date," awarding him the "snail" medal in his household for always trying to catch up with them like "a dog with its tail between its legs."

Butem preferred to describe himself as a "modern father" and was proud of the warm, open, and civil relationship he had with his daughters. Right now, however, he wondered if he was "slow" just like his friend. Had Lamie just displayed strength of character nurtured by wise conviction or an insolent rebellious spirit? Butem hoped that the former was the case and prayed that whatever she wanted to show them wouldn't contradict those hopes. His daughters were growing up fast, and he was beginning to realise that he didn't know them as well as he should.

The first flight of stairs, which had no banister or handrail, was five uneven steps—some rectangular with chipped off edges and others looking like huge chunks had been broken off, making them extremely dangerous to navigate. The second flight was another set of five steps, though a little less precarious than the first, with more of them appearing whole, though crooked and just as fragile looking. Both flights of steps were held in place by a wall with crisscrossing cracks all the way down to its base, and a high ceiling overhead.

At the landing of the second flight of stairs, Lamie walked through another door-like entrance into a room a little smaller than the hall downstairs, the window to the right blocked with makeshift cardboard panels. Hassa was immediately struck by the open window to her left as she walked into the room. It was partially covered with tinted plastic. She wondered if that was the window through which she'd seen Lamie on Friday. By the window was what looked like a makeshift kitchen. On a rectangular concrete block stood a one-burner gas cooker, and next to that on two similar blocks, set close to each other, were two small pots in which were neatly stacked a few plastic plates, bowls, and spoons. Beside these was a cardboard box containing various foodstuffs. At the end of the wall, near the window, stood two plastic buckets, one filled the water and the other half-full. Butem was confused by it all but soon had his questions answered when Lamie made a gesture with her hand, pointing to the right corner of the room, not directly in view. Her father and sister looked and were stunned by what they saw.

"Papa, this is Marvelous. Call her Marvel," Lamie said, stepping back a little to stand with them.

"Jesus!" Butem exclaimed and then fell tongue-tied. His eyes widened in amazement and looked first at Lamie, then at the young, heavily pregnant woman who was lying on a raffia mat with a large brown towel covering her legs up to her hips, and then back at Lamie.

Marvel had heard the loud voices downstairs and recognized Lamie's among them. She'd wondered who was with her kind benefactor and arguing with her, and reminded herself that Lamie knew her story and had promised she'd keep it to herself rather than not endanger her with unwanted exposure. She wanted to go check what was happening, but she felt very tired, so she simply laid back, trusting Lamie, as she heard footsteps coming up the stairs.

Butem figured that the pregnant woman was no more than twenty-five years old. Hassa scowled, looked at the woman, and took a few steps back, uncertain as to what to expect from the woman on the mat, who could very well be mentally ill or violent. Positioning herself like a cat ready to pounce if attacked, she looked around at the makeshift kitchen, scanned the room with her eyes, and then shifted her gaze back and forth between the woman and her elder sister. Next to Marvelous's head was a zipped, woven, plastic bag.

Seeing three pairs of feet near her mat, Marvel got scared. As she tried to quickly sit up, Lamie read her mind and stepped forward to help and reassure her. "Easy, easy, easy... No problem. It's just my father and sister," she said softly as she held Marvel's back and shoulders to help her sit with ease and stretch her legs out.

"It's okay, Papa, Hassa... Marvel's not dangerous or mentally ill," Lamie said, imagining their fears.

"Good evening, sir," Marvel greeted Butem, looking at him briefly, bowing her head, and then looking away. Butem noticed that the young woman's feet were swollen from water retention, given how heavily pregnant she was, and shook his head in disbelief at the entire scene.

Lamie sat in a kneeling position next to Marvel and took her hand in hers. "Papa, Marvel has been living here for three weeks now. Her immediate family and relatives threw her out. Her story's a complex one, but not mine to tell. In terms of how I came to know this place and find her here ... I first saw her standing under the cherry tree by the townhall two weeks ago. She greeted me and Abel, our committee head, when we walked past her on my way home, and I thought she was just waiting for someone. Then two days later, when I took my shoe to the repairer near the market, I saw her standing near the usual rice and stew queue. I immediately recognized her and was surprised to see her there.

"This time, she just stood and watched the queue go by, so I sat in the repairer's shop to observe what she wanted to do. When the seller had served the last man in the queue, she packed some food for Marvel in a bowl and gave it to her with some coins. Initially, it surprised me to realize that she might be another crazy destitute walking around begging, but when I recalled our cursory meeting at the townhall, something didn't add up. So, I got up and followed her as she left the seller, keeping a good distance between us so she wouldn't suspect that she was being followed. Well, I saw her walk into this decrepit building, and I knew something was really wrong.

"Papa, imagine seeing someone so heavily pregnant come in here with food!" Lamie craned her neck and looked at her father. Butem listened attentively, with his hands folded across his chest, nodding every now and then as she continued.

"So, not long after Marvel walked in here, Papa, I came in to see for myself what was going on."

Butem raised his brows, shocked and a little displeased by his daughter's risky behaviour even though, from all indications, it seemed like it had been for a good cause. How could Lamie have come here all by herself not knowing who this woman was, what she did here, and who else she may have had as company?

"Well," Lamie said, her voice getting his attention again, "I was shocked to find that Marvel was squatting here with almost nothing, sleeping on the floor. When she saw me, she begged me not to take her away. I reminded her of our meeting at the townhall, and she remembered me. When she realized that I meant no harm, and after I promised to tell no one she was here, she reluctantly told me her story. Like I said, Papa, you'll hear her story later, assuming it's okay with her. In any case, to make her stay here a little less difficult, given her condition, I had to buy her those cooking things you see over there so she need not go out to get handouts anymore." Lamie pointed to the makeshift kitchen.

"Imagine it raining all day or even for days non-stop in this rainy season, like it did two days ago, making it so she couldn't get out to buy food, or if she felt too unwell to be up and about. I also got her some provisions in that bag behind her." Lamie pointed to the zipped, woven-plastic bag. "This mat here, the pillow, and this towel."

Lamie ran her hands over the large towel on which she was partly seated. "I brought her some other items as well. Initially, I was coming here on my own to help Marvel. But I confided in Lovely, and he and I have been meeting here every day to help cook, fetch water, run errands for Marvel, and help her in any way we can. I don't know what else to do. She forbade me from telling anyone else about her or getting her help from the church."

"Aww! Lamie!" Hassa had been as silent as a mouse, moving her gaze from Marvel to her elder sister as she called out in lament. She couldn't help but recall spying on her sister. It felt surreal how she seemed to have replicated Lamie's action, following and spying on Marvel. They'd both even been driven by inquisitiveness, though she'd been severely scolded for her own spying trip. Looking at Marvel, however, instead of being upset by the apparent hypocrisy, Hassa felt nothing but love for Lamie and wanted to express both her awe and delight at her sister's act of kindness. This was the strangest scenario she could have imagined discovering here.

She could definitely see why Lamie had been so angry at their father downstairs. Her sister's secret visit here also became much clearer, and guilt descended upon her like dark clouds portending an impending storm. She had wrongly suspected her sister of doing something untoward, convinced that whatever Lamie was doing was somehow devious and warranted retribution in one form or another. Now that she realized how Lamie had truly been spending her afternoons after lunch, she had a strong urge to run to her sister, hug her tightly, and tell her how sorry she was to have judged her so erroneously. She knew Lovely, a casual friend of her sister's, and was happy that he'd been the male silhouette she had seen from the fence. The smoke she had also seen coming from this room also made more sense now, being obviously from the makeshift kitchen. And the other female silhouette, Marvel, and the movements up and down now all made sense to her. What Lamie had been spending her money on, in particular, filled Hassa with admiration, and in her mind, she traced an imaginary halo over her sister's head.

Butem's emotions were mixed, swinging from amazement at this find, love and pride for his daughter, and humbled by her act of altruism. He was so proud of his daughter that he was finding himself almost mesmerized by her. He bowed his head for a while to let it all sink in. Then, giving out a very loud sigh, he addressed Lamie.

"Alright, my dear. To say that I'm stunned and at a loss for words would be an understatement. As a parent, my immediate fatherly instinct is to rebuke you, first for the risk you took by doing all of this without consideration for your own safety. But ... I'm unable to do that now. I sincerely apologise that you felt that I didn't trust you. All I can say for now, therefore, is that I'm deeply proud of you. Thank you. There's obviously much still to hear from Marvel, and it's getting late, so, first things first..."

Butem sighed loudly and stooped so Marvel could look directly at him as he addressed her. "Marvel, from what my daughter has just told me, I know you're afraid, you don't trust anyone, and you think you're safe here. But you're not. I'm not going to leave you here in this dump all by yourself. I wouldn't even if you *weren't* with child. So ... you're coming home with us and—"

"No, no!" Marvel had been too ashamed to look Lamie's family members in the face as Lamie spoke, but she could not stay silent anymore, and looked up at Butem. "No, I can't. Please, I can't. They say I'm cursed, and I'll bring you trouble if they know I'm in your house. Please, let me stay here. Once I've had this baby, I'll be strong enough to move out of here and start the process of rebuilding my life."

Butem and Lamie pleaded with her, trying to convince her to go with them, but Marvel was adamant. Time passed as they continued to cajole and assure Marvel that she wouldn't be thrown out again come what may.

"I don't think you really understand, sir," she said. "Listening to you, my heart wants to believe that it's your kind nature that runs so deep in Lamie. But I'm afraid that ... that you'll soon judge me like everyone else back home and start finding ways to exclude or avoid me. What would I do then? Come back here? Look for a new place to squat? Haven't I been traumatized enough? Please forgive me, sir, but I can't... I can't leave here." Marvel began to cry and tried to explain again but was fiercely interrupted.

"No, no, no!" Hassa said quickly, adding her voice to the fray. "You *can't* stay here anymore, Marvel!" She rushed forward, stooping to join her father's and sister's appeal. "You've been lucky so far. God has been merciful on you. Don't push His kindness and your luck by saying you'll stay here when you can come home with us! Suppose something happens and my sister and her friend can't come here to help you anymore? You cannot have your baby here, among the garbage with rats everywhere. I would be very angry at my parents if I learnt I was born in a dingy hole like this when they'd been offered a better choice. Not fair to the unborn child. If you don't want to risk it for yourself, please, please, Marvel, risk it for your baby."

Marvel was stung by the young girl's words and abrupt tone, and threw Hassa an unhappy look that didn't even put a dent in the young girl's defiant stare. *Such a sharp tongue and stubborn nature,* Marvel silently decided and looked away, crying now.

Butem could feel his younger daughter's disenchantment and placed a hand on her knee, squeezing gently to quieten her lest she anger Marvel and make her even more determined not to leave. The room was quiet. Butem and his daughters all looked at Marvel, expressing their sympathy and urging her to stop crying as they waited for her final answer.

As she sat quietly, considering their offer and reassurances, Marvel thought about her mother, Destiny, and the phenomenon of "fate" in her encounter with Lamie, and the inherent goodness of human beings weighed against all the pains that had been inflicted on her by others. Destiny had been routinely abused by Marvel's father, verbally and physically, and then on a bus trip to the city, all the passengers, including Destiny, had been robbed by armed robbers on the highway, twenty miles from the city limits, and all her money and merchandise had been stolen.

Marvel had been told afterwards that a dealer in gemstones and jewellery, named Promise, had been on that bus, taking a few unfinished samples of raw gems to his fabricator partner in the city for evaluation and production. Aware of the perilous nature of road trips, where bandits occasionally emerged from the bushes and attacked travellers, Promise had smartly taped the sample gems into his underwear like he always did, and the robbers hadn't looked there. After the robbers had left them stranded on the road with nothing but the clothes on their backs, Promise had gotten Destiny and five other passengers onto another bus to the city.

On arrival in the city, two of the passengers who were able to make alternative arrangements for their upkeep had alighted from the bus. Promise had then asked the bus driver to take him to his bank, where he took out some money and gave the remaining three passengers, including Destiny—who had nowhere to turn—taxi fare and additional money to buy clothing, food, and lodging for the night if they needed it.

On the bus, before arriving in the city, Promise had socialised with the passengers. In the process, he'd learnt that Marvel's mother did beadwork and fabric weaving. Excited by the prospect of trading with her, he'd told her about his jewellery business and invited her to the meeting with his partner. Destiny had declined the meeting invite but told Promise that she was open to seeing his finished samples whenever he was ready to retail them. She was hesitant to get into bijouterie, being that it was a completely new area of business for her. She was also unable to entirely trust Promise at first, in spite of his generosity, but more importantly, Destiny was terrified of telling Marvel's temperamental and extremely conservative father about Promise's no-strings-attached business proposal, knowing that he would fly into fits of jealous rage and beat her like he often did. Promise had gradually earned her trust, staying in touch with Destiny and visiting her weaving shop only to order customized designs whenever he was in the city and within her vicinity. Without putting pressure or any other demands on her, Promise helped Destiny to start her jewellery trade, referring her to his other retailer in town to enable her to gauge her prices, and regularly supplied her stock from his enterprise. Marvel's mother kept the jewellery side of her trade a permanent secret from her husband even as her business grew and thrived. She never opened a bank account, afraid that her husband might one day discover it, even though Marvel had urged her many times to do so, preferring rather to bury her income in the floor of her store.

Marvel's recollection of her home growing up was one of fear and commotion more than love and good cheer. When she was fifteen, angry, frustrated, and helpless, she'd once asked her mother why she stayed in an abusive marriage when she was economically independent. Destiny had looked at her daughter pitifully, and crying, had said, "Marvel, I know this home is not emulative, and it isn't the kind I'd wish for you and your brother. And I don't know why I'm staying. It's more complicated than I can explain. I still love your father and want to believe that he'll change, as my relatives and the priests continue to tell me. Maybe I'm staying for you and Believe. Maybe I'm afraid of the stigma attached to being divorced in our society, especially on women. Maybe I'm afraid of the prospect of suddenly being alone. Maybe… Marvel, the truth is, I really don't know."

When her mother had fallen gravely ill and passed, her father had remarried two months after her funeral. His new wife believed that Marvel and her brother were going to be a liability and strain on the marriage. So, Marvel's father and his new wife soon left town and never again contacted her or Believe, her elder brother. Marvel and Believe had agreed to close their mother's shop after her death and split the earnings.

As Marvel sat and remembered what had brought her to this destitute situation, she remembered her mother's smile as she'd explained to her how she'd gotten into the jewellery business, and the undeniable truth that there was a silver lining behind every dark cloud. She'd then tried to explain to young Marvel that many things in life, like her "fateful meeting" with Promise, are beyond human comprehension, that life sometimes connives to make us meet the right person at the right time, and that we call it fate.

"*Since it's a waste of time trying to make sense of the inexplicable,*" Destiny had instructed her daughter, "*all we must do is accept and multiply the good from such situations.*"

Marvel had always found those quiet and deep conversations with her mother the most solemn of her life, and as she went through a tumultuous situation with her in-laws, she'd taken refuge in her mother's philosophical words, which she'd found most uplifting. And right now, as she pondered the huge decision she had to make, she could hear her mother's voice, repeating one of her favourite sayings: "*When you think God is far away, look within and around you.*"

In the company of Lamie and her family, Marvel couldn't agree more with her late mother. She squeezed Lamie's hand in a gesture of faith and gratitude. In this young girl, she saw "God," and after a long silence, she finally agreed. "Okay, sir, I will come with you."

She was nervous, of course, but Lamie had never given her any reason to distrust her. In fact, she had become a good friend, and hearing her family's assurances, she realised that she simply had to believe that, wherever they were taking her, it couldn't be worse than where she'd spent the last three weeks.

Lamie clapped softly and excitedly stood up. "Okay, Hassa, let's help Marvel pack up," she ordered, her voice urgent. As the girls took things down and organized them in movable stacks, Butem helped Marvel up, so that he could roll up the mat on which she was resting. He pulled down the cardboard that covered the window near where Marvel slept, and threw out the water that had been stored in the buckets in the kitchenette, as his daughters gathered the cooking utensils and cutleries. Lamie left Hassa to complete the sorting and headed out of the room. Hassa stopped what she was doing and scurried after her.

"Where are you going, Lamie?"

"To fetch Marvel's bath stuff. There's something like a bathroom in this other room here, where she bathes, though she goes downstairs to the bushes when she needs a toilet."

Hassa stood by the open doorway of the small, dark cubicle in question as Lamie went inside, returning a moment later with a loose sponge, bath soap, toothbrush, toothpaste, and face towel. She put the items in the smaller bucket, and then put that bucket into the larger one. With everything organized, Butem led the way outside, with his daughters following, one on either side of Marvel and making sure she navigated the steps carefully.

It was about eight-thirty when Butem pulled up in front of his house that night, revved the engine and parked. The night was slightly breezy and would have been pitch-black but for the scattered glow of light coming from some of his neighbour's homes, lit either by their noisy generators or kerosene lamps. Butem took a torch from his car's pigeonhole and helped Marvel out of the car and into the house, settling her into a chair in the living room as the girls brought her things in from the car.

Before long, Butem had the generator on and the girls moving Marvel's items into the guest room. Lamie quickly opened its window, made up the bed with fresh sheets, and dusted down the table and chair near the room's wardrobe. Hassa then heated some water on the kitchen's cooker for

Marvel's bath. When the water had boiled, she mixed some of it with cold water in a large bucket and carried it into the shared bathroom for Marvel.

When she was done bathing, the sisters settled Marvel nicely into the guestroom, ensuring she had everything to make her comfortable, and then went to the kitchen to make her some dinner. Thirty-five minutes later, they returned to fetch Marvel for dinner and found her seated on the bed in the guestroom, crying with her head bowed.

"What's wrong?" both girls asked in unison, seating themselves on either side of Marvel and watching her heaving sobs.

Lamie placed her hand on Marvel's shoulder and rubbed gently. "What's the matter, Marvel?"

"All of this. This kindness from you and your family... I just don't know what I've done to deserve your kindness. I don't know why I was lucky enough to be found by you. I don't know how to thank you. It's too good to be true, and I'm wondering... I'm afraid I might be dreaming."

Lamie and Hassa didn't know what to do or say to her, so they simply took turns assuring their guest that they and their father were very happy she had agreed to leave the squatter dump and to have her join them as family.

After dinner, once Marvel had retired for the night, Butem sat with his daughters in the living room to discuss stocking up a little more on food and toiletries and buying a couple of maternity gowns and sandals for Marvel. He told Lamie how proud he truly was of her and thanked her again for both her boldness and kindness. Then he led them in a short collective prayer before they all went to bed.

After Hassa had left for school the next day, Lamie checked in on Marvel and was happy to find her making the bed and in good spirits. "Good morning, Marvel. Did you sleep well?" Lamie asked with a big smile on her face and quickly jumped in to help her straighten the sheets.

"Oh, you ask me that? Who wouldn't in this kind of comfort?" Marvel said, returning Lamie's smile.

"Well, it's modest, but at least it's clean. You sure you weren't bitten by mosquitoes?" Lamie teased and walked to the window to open the shutters.

"Mosqui what? I didn't hear any annoying buzzes, and to be honest, even if they'd feasted on me, I wouldn't have noticed as I slept like a log."

"That's good then. We always shut this window after four p.m., and Hassa sprayed the room lightly with insecticide last night while you were having dinner. Did you notice?"

"Yes, I smelt it, but please, bother not. You took me out of garbage, remember?"

"Hmm… Listen, Papa and I want to go to the market. Is there anything you'd like?"

"Yes, please. Wait…" Marvel moved over to the chair, upon which she'd spread out a blouse and the wrapper she tied over it. Lamie watched as she began to undo the knot at one end of the wrapper. Once it was undone, Lamie saw that there was a wad of cash repeatedly folded into a small square. Marvel unfolded the notes, took one out, and offered it to Lamie. "Here, please buy me some knitting tools. Different colour balls of wool, different sizes of knitting needles—I'll give you the sizes—some ribbons, and a needle and thread set."

"No, no, no," Lamie said, gently pushing Marvel's hand away. "I can't take your money. Please keep it. Papa will buy the tools you need."

Marvel tried hard to insist, but when it became clear that Lamie would not budge, she gave up and thanked her profusely.

"By the way," Lamie said, smiling and clasping her hands in excitement, "I didn't know you knit, Marvel. Maybe you can teach me! Hassa might be interested too."

"Yes, I do. I learnt it from my mother. Remember I told you she wove fabrics?"

"Ah, yes, you did. I'd forgotten. I'm eager to see you at work."

"No problem. I'll be happy to teach you, Lamie. Knitting will help me take my mind off things. My emotions have been on a roller coaster this past month. My thoughts were sometimes suicidal. If not for you…" Marvel squeezed the young girl's hand and looked into her eyes. "Thank you, Lamie. Thank you for saving me."

Tears welled up in Lamie's eyes as she got up, gave Marvel a bear hug, and left the room.

Back from the market, Lamie busied herself with unpacking and putting the shopping away. When she gave Marvel a big bag containing clothes, a pair of sandals, a sanitary set, a small box with a few baby items, as well as the knitting tools she had requested, Marvel opened her mouth in shock. She wasn't expecting the gifts that had accompanied her knitting kit, and Butem's thoughtfulness and extensive generosity brought tears to her eyes. She thanked Lamie more times than Lamie could count and then clapped for joy like a child.

Marvel was clearly happy, dancing and shaking her bum, making her big baby pouch wobble, and making Lamie hysterical with laughter as she began to clap out a dancing rhythm in support. As soon as her dance was done, Marvel immediately walked to the living room where she found Butem seated and reading a newspaper, knelt down a little distance from him, and began to express her gratitude for the items he had bought her.

Butem flung the newspaper down and jumped off the couch, embarrassed and displeased to see her kneeling. "Please, you must not. Never do that, Marvel," he said gently as he helped her up. "I'm not God, you know. You've thanked me ... and that's more than enough."

Marvel genuflected, returned to her room, and immediately began to unpack the kits, eager to start knitting.

About an hour later, Butem knocked on the guestroom's door and was quickly invited in. He exchanged pleasantries with Marvel, whom he'd found busily knitting. She immediately stopped and told him about learning the knitting skill from her mother and how it calmed her nerves. Butem was surprised and delighted to see the difference the change in Marvel's living environment had made to her spirits. He pulled out a chair at her table, sat on its edge, bent forward slightly, and with his hands locked together, began telling Marvel why he was there.

"First, please trust me, Marvel. I'll do you no harm. My daughters and I already see you as family, and we hope you'll accept us as such. I just want to ask you some questions to enable me to understand your situation better." Marvel nodded, and so Butem continued in a quiet voice. "Thank you, Marvel. Now, please tell me... What is your family name and where do you come from?"

"My maiden name is Memukha, and I married into the Castari family from the town of Nembelele."

"Castari? That's a unique name." Butem frowned slightly, hoping for some clarification from Marvel.

"Yes, it is. My husband, Tanta, told me that his grandparents had been forced to change their family name to Castari when the government had been looking for a notorious rebel kingpin, with the same surname as theirs, and placed a bounty on his head. Even though they were not related, bearing the same name as the kingpin had brought their family a great deal of harassment, with his great grandfather even being accused of hiding the fugitive, thrown in jail, and tortured for many weeks."

Butem grimaced sympathetically and nodded. "I understand. And I know changing surname was common in those days, especially during the war... How old are you, Marvel?"

"I'm twenty-five, sir."

"Please call me Butem, or brother ... whichever you're more comfortable with."

"Okay, Brother Butem."

He smiled. "Thank you. Now, Lamie insists that it is you who must tell me your story, and I do want to know how and why you ended up squatting in that building. I know it must be hard for you to talk about, but as I'm old enough to be your father, I would like you to talk to me like one." Marvel nodded.

"So," he continued, "do you still have family, and if so, where are they?"

"I have only one brother. He's older, and his name is Believe. My mother has passed, and my father remarried soon after her death, left town with his new wife, and never contacted me or my elder brother again. I married four years ago, and five weeks ago, my husband fell ill and died."

"Oh dear," Butem said, looking at her sadly. "I'm very sorry to hear that." Silence fell between them for a short while, before he sighed and asked his next questions.

"How far along are you in your pregnancy? And is this your first?"

"I'm eight months this week, and I have a two-year-old son. My husband's relatives threw me out, and with nowhere to go, I asked my brother to foster my son for the time being."

Butem raised his brows in shock and confusion, shifting in his chair a bit as he tried to digest this. "My God... So, that means your relatives threw you out on the street at seven months pregnant? Why? What happened?"

Marvel was quiet as she turned and squinted out the window as her troubles came flowing back to her. After a long, painful moment, she slowly turned back towards Butem, though she couldn't meet his eyes. Gazing down, she answered as well as she could.

"Three months ago, my husband, Tanta, who worked for the city's development corporation, fell very ill. His relatives didn't want him taken to hospital but treated him at home with prayer and local herbs. His family was split into two contesting camps that could not agree on how he should be treated, or what exactly was the cause of his illness, though both camps believed his ailment was caused by some invisible negative power. Some directly said that it was witchcraft and accused me of being the witch.

"Because Tanta was extremely religious, those relatives who shared his religious zeal came to the house for three days, praying and chanting continuously over him as he laid on his sickbed, getting worse. Whenever I insisted that my husband be taken to hospital, they engaged me in a war of words. On the third day of him lying sick in that bed, a cousin of his who visited us occasionally brought an herbalist, without consulting me, to brew him some fever concoction.

"The herbalist's group and the religious group soon clashed and things came to a head. On that fateful day, I was angry, mad at them all, and forbid any of them to touch Tanta anymore. A fight ensued. Neighbours gathered. More accusations were thrown at me by my husband's relatives, saying that I had bewitched their brother, turning him into a zombie who would take my side on any argument. I was assaulted, my blouse torn and almost ripped from my body, so I locked myself in our bedroom with my son and my husband, refusing to come out until they had all dispersed.

"Close to midnight, I came out of the room, strapped my son on my back, and went to the house of a man who ran a private taxi service. The taxi brought me back home, and we took Tanta to the hospital, where he was diagnosed with typhoid fever. When his relatives came back the next day and learnt that I had taken Tanta to the hospital, and he had been admitted, they almost brought the roof of our house down, raining abuses on me. After a week in the hospital, my husband got better, returned home to continue his recuperation, and was soon well enough to return to work.

"Three of his relatives, two of them his older siblings, came to the house one evening a couple of days later, at about six or so, and accused me of disrespecting them in a serious argument, and started a fight with my husband for marrying someone they called an 'atheist' and 'voodooist.' Of course, he defended my innocence and my actions. He reminded his relatives that he had chosen me even though they had severely pressured him to marry someone else, and that I wasn't beggarly or living under some bridge when he'd met me and that I'd never needed him to look after me. Tanta reminded them that he was the one who'd pleaded with me to become a stay-at-home parent till our second child turned seven years old, in order to give the children the attention of a full-time parent, while he gladly worked and catered for us.

"When my husband told them to get out of our house, as he would no longer tolerate them describing me so disparagingly, his brother punched him in the face, gave him a black eye, and almost broke his nose. A huge fight ensued. I screamed, and even with my pregnancy, I tried to come between the brawling brothers. If neighbours hadn't quickly intervened, one of us would certainly have been killed on that day."

Butem was leaning forward, resting his elbows on the table and listening intently to every word.

"About eight p.m.," she continued, "after the fight, two police officers came to our house. They said that an assault report had been laid against my husband and asked Tanta to follow them to the police station. I insisted on accompanying him, and at the police station, seated at the front desk, we met the brother who had fought him, and one of his sisters. The police officers were taken by the fact that Tanta was an executive for a public company but shared the details of the report that had been filed against him. It was full of inaccuracies and blatant lies.

"Tanta told his own version of what had happened, and I corroborated his version, filling in the gaps my husband had forgotten. Seeing his black eye and bloodied nose, and hearing that I'd also received some punches as I came between them, the police officer asked if I'd been injured, and I showed him the scratches on my neck and arm."

Marvel paused briefly to show her still healing bruises, faded to a pale yellow now, to Butem before continuing. "The officer in charge listened, considered our statements and what he had seen, and decided that he would not take the matter any further, but advised him and his siblings to settle things within the family. They also warned his relatives to stay away from our house or else be arrested and locked up. Unfortunately, the rumour was already being spread that I was a witch, and the whispers and finger pointing in town were not discreet."

She looked up into Butem's eyes, her eyebrows furrowed. "Being accused of witchcraft is a very serious matter in Pembute, Brother Butem. I'm sure you know that too. One is often guilty until proven innocent."

Butem nodded his head but stayed quiet, not wanting her to feel interrupted or rushed. Marvel wiped a tear from her eyes before continuing. "Six weeks after that big fight, Tanta fainted at work and could hardly breathe. His office took him to hospital, and again, he had to be admitted. Seeing his second hospital admission as proof that I indeed practiced witchcraft, more people began to believe the worst about me. Even those who didn't know me, or had never even seen me, began to swear that I acted strange, belonged to no religious group, and would not attend the clan women's meetings.

"Unfortunately, this time, Tanta wasn't getting better as the doctors had expected and more extensive tests had to be done. Luckily, at the time, there were medical experts visiting the hospital to supervise and further train the doctors and nurses, and they were the ones to do the tests." Her voice grew quiet. "They found that Tanta had never had typhoid but sepsis.... And the wrong initial diagnosis and treatment had complicated things and damaged his organs. His relatives who visited him in hospital were shocked by the state he was in and then came to our house. When I explained the tests results to them, and told them that the prognosis wasn't good, they threatened fire and brimstone should Tanta pass. They said that such blood disease did not run in their family and only something supernatural could have caused it."

Marvel stopped speaking then. Butem could see deep sorrow etched on her face as she scowled and shut her eyes, struggling to hold back tears. He shook his head, furious on her behalf but forcing himself to remain silent and supportive, and sat back in his chair, folding his arms across his chest.

"Well," she continued once she was ready, "Tanta didn't make it. He never made it back home. He died on his fourth day in hospital." Marvel's voice broke then, and she began to cry.

Butem leaned forward. "I am so sorry, Marvel," he whispered and allowed her the time to cry out as much of her pain as she could.

After a while, she sniffed and cleared her throat. "Trying to bury my husband was a nightmare. His religious relatives only wanted a religious funeral, and the others insisted on giving him a traditional one, and so they clashed again. I was caught in the middle, though my opinion didn't matter to either side. I really didn't care what kind of funeral he had. I just wanted him to have a decent one. But even trying to get this most basic right for my husband seemed like moving the proverbial camel through the eye of a needle."

She sighed and shook her head. "The relatives finally dispersed after agreeing to do both a church and traditional funeral, and I'd hoped I would be left in peace to mourn him. But two days after this meeting, one of Tanta's female relatives, who had visited us only three or four times before, came to our house, accompanied by two middle-aged men I hadn't seen before but who described themselves as 'emissaries from the clan head's office.' They sat me down and read me a long list of mourning 'dos and don'ts,' which they said were 'customary and approved by the clan chief.'"

She chuckled humourlessly then. "I was expected to swear over a shrine that I was not a witch. I was to shave off my hair, wear only black clothing, not leave my bedroom for eight months and only have a bath once a month during that period. During those eight months, I was to sit only on the floor, roll on the ground to look dirty and sorrowful, be escorted out at midnight every day to wail at the top of my lungs that I'd lost my husband, speak only when I'm spoken to... I was told what I could eat and what I could not, and most importantly, I was not to see or be with my son for those entire eight months.

"All these things were written out plainly, and I knew immediately that the list was fake. I was astonished at how low they were willing to go in order to punish me, hoping that I'd be too naïve and helpless to fight back."

Butem clapped in anger. "Heavens! How backward and devilish!! Reinventing and trying to impose harmful and inhumane customs, centuries old and already outlawed!?" He was visibly upset as he stood up and started pacing around his chair. After about a minute, he sighed, shook his head, and sat back down.

"Yes, Brother Butem. I'm aware that, after many decades of women fighting the indiscrimination and abuse of mourning traditions in Pembute, most of what was on the list had been outlawed. So, I told them outright that they should be ashamed of themselves for what they were trying to do to me, parading a list of ancient so-called 'customary laws' now banned. 'You think I'm a fool because I'm a woman? Let's go! Take me to the clan chief who approved this nonsense list!' I shouted at them."

Butem's eyes met Marvel's, a little surprised by her boldness. Her body language had suddenly changed, and she now looked ready for any challenge, and he admired that. She held his gaze and continued.

"I had barely finished speaking when a female relative tried to forcefully grab my son off my lap, telling me that if I wouldn't obey custom as ordained by the chief, I wouldn't see my son anymore. I screamed and held my son tight as we both pulled him in opposite directions, with him crying. I fought the idiot sister and bit her hand so hard that she ran out then, cursing me. I told them that I'd rather die than have them take my son from me."

"They truly tried to snatch your son away from you!?" Butem asked in disbelief.

"Yes, Brother Butem." Marvel gave him a look that acknowledged how hard this was to imagine and nodded. "By this time, neighbours had gathered, and there was a commotion. My son was crying, and I was explaining to the crowd what had just happened and begging for help. The cousin's two middle-aged companions swore they would make me pay. Then they stormed out, warning that they'd be back to burn our house down. Seeing how vicious Tanta's relatives had become, I decided not to take any chances. I strapped my son on my back, got on a motorcycle, knowing it would be faster than going for a taxi, and travelled to Believe's house in Oni, a one-and-a-half-hour ride away."

"Yes, I know Oni. I sell some things in that town from time to time," Butem interjected. Marvel sniffed and continued.

"Believe was aware of the problems I'd had early in my marriage with some of Tanta's relatives but not what had transpired during his sickness, or that he had died. I arrived at Believe's house late that evening, and after telling him everything, I pleaded with him and his wife to keep my son with them for the time being as he wasn't safe with me. Believe and I were never very close, but he was very upset by what I was going through and wanted to go to the police. But his wife didn't try to conceal her fear and discomfort with me being in the house that evening, given all the witch-craft accusations. With it now looking like I was also breaking a custom-ary law and defying the clan chief, she begged Believe not to get involved, terrified the situation could get even nastier. However, she did promise to look after my son in the interim while I sorted things with my in-laws. Because it was late in the evening, and my pregnancy far gone, Believe refused to allow me to return to my house that night. So, I stayed there, and the next morning, I took a motorbike back home."

"Oh, my god! In your condition!? How unfair!" Butem exclaimed, looking up at the ceiling for a moment before returning his attention to Marvel and looking her in the eye, his admiration growing. She struck him as a fighter, and he even thought he could see a bit of his own daughters in her.

"What else could I do, Brother Butem? Meanwhile, my husband was in the morgue, and I had no clue how or when I could lay him to rest." Marvel paused again, staring off into space for a moment before continuing. "I got back home later that morning and thought I had arrived somewhere else. I couldn't get inside. Heaps of gravel almost as high as the roof had been piled in front of my house, blocking everything. A neighbour got a ladder and climbed over one of the piles, hoping to open the door with my key and help me bring out some personal items, but my key would no longer open the door. My neighbour told me that the lock there looked new and there were splinters of wood on the ground around the door. The lock had been changed.

"I didn't know the clan chief that Tanta's relatives said had signed the list, as there were several of them, so I walked to the one who closest to report the incident. His name was Kekere, and he looked me over from head to toe suspiciously. He was shocked by what I told him, saying that he was unhappy that the village's laws and well-known customs were being abused, and that he hadn't been involved in any list. Given the accusations of witchcraft against me, he promised to look into the matter and sent me away—"

"What a disgraceful state of affairs!" Butem said, interrupting her in his frustration, stomping his foot hard on the ground, slapping his thigh, and almost spitting in anger. "In this age, women are *still* being treated like they're second-class citizens? Like they're some piece of furniture to be used and discarded at will? How wicked! A heavily pregnant woman just widowed should be commiserated with and cared for emotionally not abused in such a cruel way! The devil truly takes human form at times," he hissed.

Marvel breathed out loudly and carried on. "Yes, he does. In any case, I walked about twenty minutes to another chief's house, one whom the neighbour that brought the ladder had referred me to, but his children told me he had gone to a meeting. I asked if I could wait for him to return as it was an urgent matter, but the children wouldn't let me. They said it was no use as the chief was only going to be back very late that evening. I walked back home and sat outside at the bottom of a pile of gravel, not knowing what to do. The neighbour with the ladder offered to accommodate me for the night, but I was tired and in pain, and I just couldn't take it anymore, Brother Butem."

She met his eyes and held them. "I just couldn't take the trauma anymore. Happy that my son was out of immediate danger, I walked to the market, got on a motorbike, and asked to be brought to Pembute. I was let off at the primary school near the huge concrete signage at the main road, and wandered around there till the pupils had all gone home for the day before sleeping in one of the classrooms for the night. The next day, I searched for a place to squat temporarily till I'd had this baby and found the building where Lamie then found me."

Butem was at a loss for words. Covering his face with hands, he began muttering things Marvel couldn't make out. When he brought his hands down, Marvel saw tears in his eyes. He leaned forward on his seat and tried to comfort her in the best way he could.

"Marvel, this is your home. What's important now is that you stay well and deliver your baby safely. I lost my wife eleven years ago, following the birth of Hassa and her twin brother, who was stillborn. That loss is still fresh in my heart, because when she went into labour, she was all alone until a very kind neighbour, who eventually became my children's foster mother, found her long after she had delivered my twin son, who had already died."

He paused a moment to gather his thoughts, and then sighed. "I can't bear to see you alone and would hate to see you go through anymore complications. This is a modest house as you can see, but we really don't lack for anything essential. So, if you need anything, please tell Lamie or speak with me directly."

Butem coughed then and lowered his voice. "I also want to plead with you to consider bringing your son here once you've had this baby and are strong enough to make the trip to your brother's house. I'll be glad to take you there when you're ready. I trust your brother will look after your son like his own, but he is better off with you. With his mother. I also know you begged Lamie and Lovely to keep your story and whereabouts secret. But one way or another, we *will* have to solve this problem. So—"

"No," Marvel said, quickly interrupting him. "No, please Brother Butem, I beg you. Cases of witchcraft are complex, and my son may soon be in danger too. I'm so grateful to you for my life, but please, promise that you'll not expose me."

Butem was quiet for a while and then nodded. "Okay then. If that's what you want, Marvel. No problem. Now, let me ask you a silly question... Do you believe in witchcraft?"

Marvel shrugged, threw her hands over her head, brought them down forward, and then clicked her forefingers. "God forbid! What is witchcraft? Of course, I hear it exists, but it was never once mentioned in my family while I was growing up. As abusive as my father was towards my mother, one thing he never accused her of was being a witch."

Butem chuckled. "Well, your in-laws really have a problem, and they're the ones witch-hunting you. Stupid people. Do you go to church?"

"Well, Brother Butem, I was born Protestant and used to go to church but not anymore. I'm sorry. Please don't think I'm criticizing your faith. Your family is exemplary, the perfect example of godly behaviour, but I don't believe one only finds God in a church, or in any religious building. I believe God is in every living thing. But most of all ... God is in our hearts."

"You're right, Marvel, and I respect your views and your choice. I just wanted you to know that my daughters and I try to go to church on Sundays, and if you ever feel like joining us, just to leave the house for a short while, you'll always be welcome. Let's leave things as they are for now. I feel deeply pained by what you've been through, Marvel. Thank you for sharing your story with me."

Butem had already made up his mind to find a way to solve Marvel's problem with her relatives, even though he really didn't know where to start, and he didn't intend to tell her. He got up then, pushed the chair back in its place, and turned to reassure her, placing his hand on her shoulder. "Don't worry, Marvel. Everything will be fine."

Marvel stood up, thanked him again, and made a small genuflection.

Butem walked out of the room with a heavy heart, quickly putting distance between them so he could finally voice his frustration without upsetting her. When he reached the far side of the house, he almost shouted, "How can human beings be so wicked to others? I don't understand it! She's a witch?! What nonsensical rubbish! How would they know such a thing even if she were, and who made them her judges?" he hissed loudly.

"We label, label, and tag people like merchandise in a store! They want her to conform to their label only to lend credence to their long-standing desire to ostracize and steal from her!" Butem gave out a long hiss, unable to stop expressing his dismay. "What is the *matter* with these people? What busybodies! How is she interfering in their lives or hurting them *in any way*? Jesus! What they've put her through! And all for what?"

He didn't realise how loud his voice had become, but Lamie heard him talking to himself and hurried into the living room to find out what was going on. She found him standing with his hands behind his back, shaking his head.

"Papa, is everything okay? I heard you talking."

Butem unfolded his arms and turned to face her. "No, my dear daughter, I'm not okay. I've just finished chatting with Marvel. Her story has infuriated me."

"Yes, I know, Papa. I felt that way when she told me too. Crazy and scary, isn't it? That in this day and age, women are still being subjected to such brazen abuse and indignities under the guise of custom? I wanted to see how the Anti-domestic Abuse Committee I serve in could help Marvel, but sadly, because she's adamant about keeping her affairs secret, warning me that she'd disappear forever should I expose her ... I relented, Papa."

Butem closed the gap between them, put his hands on her shoulders, then bent and stared deeply into his daughter's eyes. "Listen, should you or your sister ever choose to get married, whether I'm alive or dead, no in-law, rich or poor, aristocrat or common, not in this life and not in the next ... will ever ... *EVER* ... contemplate doing to you what's been done to Marvel."

Lamie's face was sober as she looked into her father's eyes and nodded. "That won't happen, Papa. I promise you."

"I know Marvel has some few small opportunities for justice in Pembute, which she's not pursuing because of her condition, fear for her son, and fear of the repercussions from being labelled a witch, but—and I need you to keep this to yourself—I'm going to help her take advantage of whatever recourse is available to her, and if one way isn't successful, we'll find another, and another, until we are successful. Otherwise, what her in-laws have just done to her will be replicated by others." Butem hugged his daughter reassuringly then, before leaving her and going to his room.

Things carried on much as usual in Butem's household. The neighbours did not know that Marvel was living there. She helped around the house as much as she could and carried on with her knitting, creating colourful bonnets for the girls, which they gladly wore to church to show off, and then began knitting a sweater for Butem. Hassa took easily to Marvel, and like Lamie, began to take knitting lessons from her. Lamie knitted booties for Marvel's unborn child, and Hassa, a bonnet with a pink and blue bow on its side. When the night was well-lit by the moon, the ladies sat outside, and Marvel told them folktales. Hassa gave Marvel novels to read and Lamie shared recipes she'd gotten from Auntie Oka.

One Wednesday, during Marvel's fourth week at Butem's home, Hassa went to work on a practical assignment with Yvonne and Harriet after school hours, and Lamie went to a townhall meeting. Butem was polishing his shoes in his room when he thought he heard someone call his name.

He stopped what he was doing, listened, and then heard the call again.

"Brother Butem!"

It was Marvel. He scurried to her room and found her on the ground, partially seated and partially lying down, holding her back and groaning.

"Marvel!" Butem called out, rushing to her side and kneeling down beside her.

"My water broke, and I think it's not going to be long now before the baby is born."

Butem nodded, then ran to his room, threw out the items in the large overnight bag on his bed, and ran back to Marvel. He opened the wardrobe in her room, and with her guidance, quickly stuffed the empty bag with clothes and any necessary sanitary items he thought she might need. Then he retrieved the small box of baby items Lamie had chosen, grabbed it, tucked it under his arm, and picked the bag back up with his other hand. Then he ran to his car, put the bag on the front passenger seat, and turned the ignition on.

That done, he ran back into the house, quickly changed his clothes, put on a pair of leather slippers, and hurried back to Marvel. Helping her to her feet, he then led her to the car, with her leaning against him for support, and settled her into the back seat. On his way back to lock the front door, he remembered that he needed to leave a message for his daughters, so he ran back to the car, grabbed a notepad from his pigeonhole, roughly tore out a sheet, and scribbled a quick note: "Hospital with Marvel." Dashing into the living room, he placed it on the centre coffee table and rested a drinking glass on it. Then he rushed back outside and drove her as fast as he could to the town's hospital.

When Hassa returned home, she immediately saw the note, grinned in excitement, and sat down eagerly to await Lamie. As soon as she saw her sister approaching, she ran outside and grabbed her hand. "Sis! Papa has taken Marvel to the hospital!"

"True?"

"Yes, yes! He left us a note on the coffee table! Hurry, we must go to the hospital!"

In no time, the sisters were on their way to the hospital on a motorcycle. When they arrived, they spotted their father seated in the reception area with his legs crossed.

"Papa," Lamie called as they rushed to him, "is Marvel alright?"

"I think so. The nurse informed me a little while ago that she's been taken to the delivery room. So far, everything's fine."

As the other iron seats in the reception were already occupied, Lamie and Hassa stood by their father and waited for further updates on Marvel and the baby. Over the next few hours, Butem and his daughters paced up and down the reception area, went out to the balcony, made small talk, returned to the reception area, and enquired with the receptionist if there was any news, always getting the same response: "No, not yet."

As it started getting late, Butem urged his daughters to go home while he stayed behind for news, suggesting they could go buy anything else Marvel might need, but the girls refused. Close to eight o'clock that night, he insisted his daughters go home, and they grudgingly obeyed. Back home, Lamie and Hassa sat in the living room after dinner, waiting for their father, but it wasn't until half past ten that they saw the front lights of a car approaching the house and they rushed out. Butem parked and stepped out of the car with his shoulders slouched, looking exhausted.

"Papa, has Marvel given birth yet? Is she okay, Papa?" The sisters tugged at his hand and shirt as he walked into the living room, eager for answers.

"Yes," he said with a broad smile. "Marvel has a baby girl, and she's doing fine."

"Yay!!!" the girls shouted, clapping their hands and beginning to sing and dance.

"Papa, did you see the baby?" Hassa asked. "When can we see them?"

"Yes, Papa, when?" Lamie echoed.

"Tomorrow, girls. Hassa, we can all go in the afternoon after you're back from school. And, yes, I saw the baby lying on Marvel's chest. She's beautiful, just as you both were when you were born. Now, I'm really tired and need some food and sleep."

"Okay, Hassa," Lamie said, "let's go. Set the table, and I'll heat up Papa's dinner." The sisters left their father, and jumping for joy and chitchatting, they went out to the backyard.

The next day, Lamie and Hassa packed a hamper full of food, nuts, and drinks and set out with their father to visit Marvel. The hospital was busier than the day before, and they waited in reception for fifteen minutes before a nurse came to them and led them down a long corridor to the delivery room, which was divided into three cubicles, each cordoned off with a tall rolling screen for privacy. Their escort pointed to Marvel's cubicle and left.

Butem and his daughters approached and saw a nurse, holding a file, chatting with Marvel with her back turned to them. Marvel saw Butem first, and she smiled and beckoned him forward with her hand. The nurse turned around, and Hassa screamed and ran towards her. "Angel!"

Lamie immediately remembered that name from Hassa's spying story but had never expected to find her here. She placed the basket of food near a chair by Marvel's bed and stepped back to stand with her father.

"Hassa!" Angel called back and embraced the young girl, who had firmly wrapped her hands around her waist and rested her head on her chest. "What a surprise to see you," she said, laughing. Hassa held her tight and didn't want to let go as Lamie and their father looked on, waiting to be introduced to the nurse they didn't know, but who Hassa seemed to know well.

Meanwhile, Marvel sat up. "Brother Butem, Lamie, it's so nice to see you. What's all that you have in the basket?"

Butem and Lamie moved to the far side of the still embracing Hassa and Angel, and saw Marvel's baby girl sleeping in a small pram, covered halfway by a lacy white net. They bowed to look at her more closely and cooed about how beautiful she looked. After his daughters had left the previous night to return home, Butem had gone to a baby shop not far from the hospital and bought the pram, as well as more baby items one of the nurses attending to Marvel had recommended.

Hassa finally released the nurse, greeted Marvel, and excitedly joined her father and Lamie around the baby's pram, her heart melting at how tiny and beautiful she was. After about a minute, she realised she had failed to introduce her family to her nurse friend and stepped away from the baby, moving to stand next to the still smiling woman.

"Papa, this is my friend, Angel," Hassa said, then looked at the nurse. "Angel, this is my papa, Butem." The pair exchanged a quick hello, then

Hassa introduced Lamie, who smiled and thanked Angel for everything, careful not to spill details of Hassa's outing or injury in front of her father, but knowing that Angel would understand.

Angel soon concluded her medical check with Marvel, told her she'd be back in the evening, and then moved on to another cubicle, in which another new mother was lying against her pillows, nursing her own infant. Butem wondered about the nurse, Angel, and how his youngest daughter apparently knew her so well, but said nothing. He simply sat on the only chair in Marvel's cubicle while the girls stood at the foot of the bed and visited.

"Hassa, I see you know Nurse Angel," Marvel observed with a subtle question in her tone.

"Yes," Hassa said, "she's a friend and very kind. You're lucky to have her look after you."

Lamie quickly changed the subject before their father could ask about Angel. "Oh, Marvel, have you thought about a name for the baby yet?"

"No, not really. I have a couple on names in mind, but I'd also like ideas from you all here. So, please think of some for me."

"Sure! I can even give you a dozen pretty female names right now if you want," Hassa answered.

"Of course, you can, Hassa." Butem laughed, and Marvel joined him.

Lamie winked at the new mom. "We're not talking about cartoons or fairytale names, Hassa, like from your story books. No Cinderella, Snow White, or Rapunzel." Butem covered his mouth to stop himself from bursting out laughing again.

"Lamie! What are you talking about? I have beautiful names in mind." Hassa playfully poked her sister in the ribs. Then she turned to Marvel, who was chuckling now. "Marvel, please ignore my sister. Now ... emm... What about Noble, Gift ... Faith, Divine ... emm..."

"Oh, I love Divine, Hassa!" Marvel looked delighted and clasped her hands. "Yes! So beautiful and befitting."

Butem agreed, and even Lamie concurred. "Well done, Hassa!" Lamie hugged her sister, who smiled smugly.

Marvel turned to her baby and joyfully pronounced, "Well, welcome to the world, Divine." She sat up a bit higher, propping her lower back on the pillows. "I already have a local name in mind," she informed her guests then. "My grandmother's middle name: *Emebizie* ... or *Mebiz* for short. Its literal translation is *'Don't spoil your neighbour,'* but it more deeply connotes *'Don't hurt your neighbour.'*"

"Eh, eh!" Butem raised his hands in acknowledgement. "What a lovely name!" Lamie and Hassa nodded their approval.

"And there's one more name I'm giving Divine." Marvel stopped and gave her guests a mischievous look that seemed to be daring them to guess. They had no idea though, and simply shook their heads and waited to hear it.

With a joyful smile on her face, Marvel finally blurted it out: "It's Lamie!"

"Oh my god!" Butem yelled happily. "What an honour! How thoughtful and kind of you, Marvel!" Smiling, he turned to look at his older daughter, who had shyly covered her face with her hands.

"Yes!" Hassa said excitedly, applauding. "Divine Mebiz Lamie! We can even hyphenate the three names into one!" She hugged her sister then, who was still covering her face in disbelief. When Lamie finally lowered her hands, she saw Hassa singing the words "mummy Lamie, mummy Lamie" and dancing happily.

Lamie pinched her sister's ear playfully, and then hugged Marvel and thanked her for the honour.

"I'm the one to say thank you, Lamie," Marvel said quickly, shaking her head, "to all of you really, not just you," Marvel said, then blinking away happy tears, she changed the subject. "Okay, can we share some of those fruits and nuts in the hamper now please?"

Butem tried protesting that the basket's contents were for Marvel alone, but when she refused and made as if to stand up and distribute the contents herself, the sisters told her to lie back down and quickly brought out some fruits and nuts.

Butem and his daughters spent over an hour with Marvel, eating and telling jokes. Hassa had a lot to share about school and amusing times with her friends, Yvonne and Harriet. Lamie shared humorous incidents from the townhall meetings. Although Butem was quiet most of the time, just laughing and enjoying his family, he did tell the girls a few interesting stories from his time at the border.

Before Butem and his daughters left the hospital, the doctor stopped by briefly to check on Marvel and told Butem that he'd like to keep her for a couple of more days, to examine the baby further, but that he would discharge both mother and child on Saturday morning.

As soon as the family got into the car, unable to wait any longer, Butem asked, "So, how come I'm the only one who doesn't know Nurse Angel?"

Hassa shifted uncomfortably on her seat in the back, and Lamie quickly spoke up. "Oh, Papa, you can't know all our friends now, can you?"

"I suppose you're right," Butem agreed, turned the key in the ignition, and silently told himself that as long as his daughters were making responsible friends, like that nurse, he had nothing to worry about. He knew Hassa's friends, Yvonne and Harriet, and could relate to their decent upbringing, so whenever Hassa was in the company of her two girlfriends, or either of them, he was happy and at peace. He had also heard about Lamie's friend Lovely a few times, though he hadn't visited the house. If Lamie found Lovely worth confiding in about Marvel, Butem was certain he must have a fine character.

When Angel got home after her nightshift, she told her grandfather that she'd had a very special day and asked him to guess what could have made it special for her. Hope had scratched his head and grunted as he thought of possibilities.

"You successfully delivered quadruplets?"

Angel laughed out loud. "No, Grandpa."

"You got a raise?"

"No, Pa"

"A young handsome man came to propose marriage to you?" Hope smiled with this question and winked at Angel.

"Pa!" She laughed. "No!"

"Okay, well I've exhausted my guess cards. Tell your old man before he dies of curiosity. What was it that made your day special?"

"Do you remember Hassa, Pa? The—"

"Of course, I remember her!" he exclaimed, interrupting her. "Who could forget her? That was the young, sharp-tongued girl who fell near my farm and cut her leg, right? And I brought her home for you to treat?"

"Ah yes, indeed, Pa. That's her. She came to the hospital today with her father and older sister to visit a new mother, one Mrs Marvel Castari, whose baby I was assigned to look after during my shift. I was with Mrs Castari, heard my name being called, and when I turned around to see who it was, I saw Hassa and her family. Can you believe it?"

"Hmmm… Quite a surprise that must have been. But wait a minute…" Hope sat forward, close to the edge of his chair. "Did you say the new mother's name is Castari?"

"Yes, Pa."

"Did she tell you where she's from?"

She thought for a moment, and then nodded. "Yes. When she told me that her marital name was Castari, I commented on its uniqueness and asked her where her husband was from. I think she called the place Num … emm … Numbulele? Something like that."

"Nembelele," Hope said.

"Yes! I think that's it."

"Goodness me!" Hope exclaimed. "What a small world!" He abruptly stood up, grunted again, and then added, "That's my aunt's family. My father's sister! So, the two of you are distant cousins!"

Angel looked at her grandfather wide-eyed. "No way, Pa! Are you serious?"

Hope sat back down and tried to explain, telling Angel that, while his father was living in the Congo, his elder sister—who was living in Nembelele at that time—had informed him that her husband had urgently decided to change his family name from Umanuhi to Castari for the safety of their family. Umanuhi had been the name borne by an unrelated, state-wanted fugitive accused of leading the rebellion of his city during the war, and my aunt and her family were not only constantly harassed but her husband had been locked up for nearly a month because the authorities were convinced he was related to the man and either was hiding him or knew where he was.

Hope told Angel that there was no other family in Nembelele to bear the name Castari. "If I'm not mistaken, my aunt had six children, three boys and three girls." With yet another grunt, he shook his head. "So, does Marvel live with Hassa's family?"

"Yes," she said almost without thinking, a bit distracted by her grand-father's fascinating revelation. "From all indications, I think she does, or perhaps she's just visiting them for some time. I'm not sure."

"Curious. I wonder... You know, when I think of the stubborn young Hassa, I wonder if she might be related to us as well." Hope and Angel both began to laugh at the prospect of being distant relatives of Hassa's.

"Hmm..." Angel said, smiling mischievously at her grandfather from the corner of her eyes. "You know, now that you've said it, I'm really wondering..."

Hope caught Angel's look, which screamed of naughtiness. "What? What's that look on your face?"

She laughed. "Pa, while you are certainly almost as stubborn as Hassa, do you think you can smell DNA? Surely the well of human obstinacy is deeper than the Atlantic Ocean."

Hope hissed dramatically and looked away, setting them both into new fits of laughter.

Hope finally got to his feet. "Ah well, you can think and say what you like, my child, but I smell what I smell." Smiling, though his mind was reeling with questions, he left Angel and retired to his room.

Butem and his daughters visited Marvel every day, bringing her food and fresh fruit, and on Saturday morning at eleven, they fetched the young mother and her baby from the hospital. When they got home and got out of the car, carrying bags and a pram, a few neighbours saw Marvel and the baby and stopped to say hello. They asked Butem if this was a relative who was visiting, and each time, he nodded and said that, yes, Marvel was a distant relative of his who would be visiting for some months.

Marvel and baby Divine soon settled in, being constantly doted on by Butem and his daughters. As neighbours often heard the sound of a baby crying coming from Butem's house, some visited, hoping to have their curiosity answered. It wasn't long before news spread about Butem's distant relative who was visiting with her newborn baby. Friends and neighbours began visiting Marvel, some of them bringing her gifts of local foods, toys, sanitary products, and baby clothes.

On Sunday evening, one week after Marvel's return from the hospital with Divine, Butem heard a knock on the door and got up from the living room to open it and found Hope and Angel standing there, with the nurse holding a small bag in her hand. He recognized Angel immediately and was pleasantly surprised that his daughters' friendship with the nurse was so close that she even knew where they lived. Her companion, however, was an older man and an absolute stranger to him.

"Good evening, sir. I'm Angel, the nurse from the hospital. You remember me, don't you?"

"Of course, yes, yes, yes. I know you."

"This is my grandfather, Hope," Angel said, pointing to the old man standing next to her. "Pa, this is Hassa's father."

"Good evening, sir," Butem said. "Please, please ... come in!"

Angel and Hope walked into the living room, and Butem ushered them to two comfortable seats. Believing that they had come to visit his daughters, he called out, "Lamie! Hassa!"

The two girls scurried into the living room and stopped in their tracks when they saw their visitors. Lamie remembered Angel but didn't know the old man seated next to her. Hassa, however, knew them both, and the first thought that came to her mind would have made Hope smile had he heard it: *Oh, it's that stubborn but nice old man!*

Pleased to see Angel again, she quickly walked up to her and Hope, greeting them both. Then Angel introduced Hope to Lamie and turned back to her young friend. "Hassa, you already know Hope, so you don't need an introduction."

Butem looked on, uncertain of what to make of Hassa's acquaintance with Angel's grandfather. Conscious of his role as host though, he pushed that amazement to the back of his mind and told his daughters to go and get soft drinks for their visitors.

Hope and Angel quickly, though politely, declined the offer. "No, my son," Hope said. "Thank you, but we don't intend to stay long. I was just hoping to speak with you briefly."

Lamie and Hassa jumped at this statement, using it as an excuse to excuse themselves, knowing that they needed to discuss how they wanted to handle the possible exposure of their secret. Hassa felt like she had been caught, and Lamie felt like the co-author of a poorly scripted play. So, they hurried into their bedroom and started discussing their options. Although they both agreed that they hadn't actually lied to their father, they also admitted that they were actively keeping a secret from him. There seemed no easy way out anymore, and not wanting to lie their way into a corner, they decided to tell their father the entire truth about what had happened the day before his most recent return from the border.

Once the girls were out of sight, Hope smiled at Butem. "We bring greetings and a small gift to your relative, Marvel, and her new baby, and also to share some surprising news with you all."

Butem leaned forward in his seat. "Oh really?"

Hope nodded. "Yes. It seems that Marvel's husband is my auntie's grandchild."

"No way!" Butem exclaimed. His mouth dropped open in shock as he moved to the very edge of his chair. "How can that be?"

Hope explained the genesis of Marvel's marital name, and Butem—recalling Marvel's story—immediately believed him. Unfortunately, with that belief came panic over what the old man's visit might portend for Marvel, who was ferocious about her desire for privacy.

Hope continued. "I've also heard the rumour that you are related to her as well, and wondered what that connection was. Tell me, is it also on her husband's side or on her mother's? Depending on which side, you and I could also be blood relatives."

Knowing that a truthful answer would inevitably mean explaining how his family had met Marvel, Butem decided to gather his thoughts for a moment and quickly stood up.

"Please don't be offended," he said to his guests then. "Let me just use the bathroom quickly and also let Marvel know that you're both here to see her." On his way out of the room, he looked back briefly. "Are you sure you still don't want something to drink?"

"Yes, sir," Angel said, smiling at him. "We're sure. Thank you."

Butem walked into Marvel's room and saw her breastfeeding Divine. In a whisper, so as not to disturb the baby, he told her about the visitors waiting in the living room with a gift for her. Struggling to find the right words, Butem then went on to tell her about Hope's relationship with her late husband, Tanta, and asked her two questions: first, did she want to come meet them; and second, what unified response should they give Hope and Angel?

Marvel's first reaction was shock that Nurse Angel could be even remotely related to Tanta and that Angel knew where Butem lived. She said nothing for a while, and then suddenly looked at Butem and smiled with a look of unexpected peace and calm, which soothed him as well.

"Thank you, Brother Butem," Marvel began. "This is a big surprise for me, and I know how you feel. I know you're afraid that this might be a revelation I don't want, but please don't worry. I'm ready. All I've wanted since I left my husband in the morgue, lost my home, and ran to Pembute to be safe was to have this baby. Now God multiplied that one wish of mine a million-fold when he brought Lamie and her family into my life. Being part of your family is more than I could ever have wished for. I've felt loved here ... more loved than I ever imagined possible or thought I deserved, and holding onto that love and faith, I feel ready to move on. It is time for me to challenge the abuses I've faced, to regain my dignity, and to do my late husband the simple honour of a decent burial, which is the very least he deserves from his wife. So ... Brother Butem, if you don't mind, please tell our visitors that I'll come out to meet them soon. Thank you."

Of all the responses Butem had expected from Marvel, this one had never crossed his mind. He hurried back to the living room, apologized again for his absence, and delivered Marvel's message to their guests.

About five minutes later, Marvel emerged carrying her daughter. After exchanging pleasantries with her guests, Angel handed her the gift they'd brought and requested to hold Divine. Marvel tenderly passed her into Angel's arms and then sat comfortably on the sofa near Butem. Hope told Marvel that he'd come to visit her, and for clarity—believing that Butem already knew about Hassa's visit to his own home—briefly and offhandedly talked about his memory of having escorted Hassa home several weeks earlier. Hope then went on to mention the names of some of Tanta's paternal and maternal relatives, and various memories he had of them, as well as several places in Nembelele. Marvel was left with no doubt that he was indeed related to her late husband.

After reaching a confirmation of his relationship to Tanta, Hope asked

Marvel the question she knew was coming.

"How is your husband, Marvel, and what does he do for a living?"

From this question, many others followed, and for over an hour, Hope and Angel were welcomed into Marvel's world as she told them her story, holding nothing back.

Butem admired her bravery, but Hope was utterly stunned.

"What? You had to leave your husband in the morgue?! They threw you out of your marital home at seven months pregnant?" He crossed his arms over his head and opened his mouth in silent dismay, unable to handle the knowledge of where Marvel had been squatting, knowing the decrepit building all too well.

Finally, he wailed and jumped up out of his chair. "Jesus! This can't be true!" he repeated as he paced back and forth around the room with his arms folded across his chest.

He could remember throwing garbage from his own farm into that old building ... and to imagine that his relative had been forced to live there even for one day made his heart bleed. Finally, he stopped and addressed everyone, his tone betraying his deep regret:

"Do you all *see* why our people always say: '*Never throw a stone in the marketplace because you never know who you'll hit?*'"

Butem nodded and went on to express his own bitter anger over all that Marvel had been through. Soon, a cacophony of voices in the living room were lamenting and swearing at those who'd abused Marvel so cruelly, promising to find justice for her. Eventually, Hope became so angry that Butem could swear he saw the old man's eyes turn red, and remembering the local saying, 'Old men don't cry in public,' he knew it was time to calm things down.

"Sir, please sit and calm down," Butem pleaded with Hope, afraid the old man might collapse under the weight of his rage. "I promise. We will find a solution."

Angel joined Butem in begging her grandfather to sit and take it easy. Marvel was crying now, and the drama woke Divine, who'd been napping in Angel's arms. The nurse stood up when the baby began to cry and rocked her back and forth against her chest until she quieted again. Then she handed her back to Marvel.

After all was said and done, the men agreed to take up Marvel's matter together, with Hope promising to use his long-standing connections in the local circles of authority and make some visits. Before much longer, it was time for him and his daughter to return home, but before he left, he looked reassuringly at the new mother.

"My dear Marvel, if you don't know who I am around these parts, or what I am capable of, just give people my name, or ask my granddaughter Angel here. She'll be the first to tell you that I'm who people come to for help when they run out of ideas. So, I need you to read my lips and trust me when I say this: These apparent relatives of mine *and* your husband's ... they have no more intelligence or power than babies. They're jokers. They'll have to *prove* witchcraft and explain exactly what crime you've committed, which won't be possible, of course. But even if you had committed some crime, who made them your judge and jury? They think they can deny you ownership of what's rightfully yours?"

He shook his head dismissively and then continued. "They will have to think again. They want to use cruel and out-of-date customs against you? Well, I'll give them customs. If they have buried your husband without your consent, and touched your house in any way, mark my words, they'll be in jail for much longer than they've already lived." He hissed, sniffed, and then blurted out a single word, like the bark of an angry dog: "Nonentities!"

With a grunting cough, he took a deep breath and let it out slowly before stepping closer to Marvel. "You're obviously very happy here, and that pleases me. But never forget that, from now on, your family also includes me and my granddaughter, Angel. Please visit us with Divine, and if you'd like, you can come stay for as long as you want. I'm sure Butem wouldn't mind."

"Of course not," Butem answered.

Turning to Butem, Hope told him that they were now family and that his home was Butem's and his daughters' as well. He thanked him profusely for taking Marvel in and looking after a stranger and her baby as though she were his biological child. Then he invited Butem to meet him at his home the next day around five p.m., so that they could both strategize on Marvel's situation and start making important visits later in the week.

Butem gladly accepted Hope's invitation and promised to be at his place on time. Hope nodded, and then asked Butem to call Lamie and Hassa back in so they could say goodbye. He did, and when the sisters returned, Hope said a prayer for them and expressed his gratitude to Lamie in particular for exceeding all expectations and doing what most adults and teenagers her age would never have even contemplated.

Finally, he turned to the first of them he'd met. "You're headstrong, Hassa," he said with a smile. "I knew that already, of course, but knowing your family now, I also believe you're a nice and well-brought up girl. Thank you. Now, you and your sister are welcome at my home anytime. You know where it is. Please bring your father there tomorrow."

Hassa smiled, bowed, and wriggled her toes, happy with the old man's sentiment, but growing increasingly nervous about the snippets of information he kept sharing with her father.

Hope patted his sides, looked around, and then rubbed his hands together. "Well, all that's left now is for Angel and me to bid you all goodbye and wish you a peaceful night."

Butem stood up and asked if it was alright for them to say a collective prayer, which everyone thought was a good idea Hope asked Butem to lead it. At the end of the prayer, and the chanting that followed, Butem's family walked Hope and Angel to the front of the house and bade them farewell.

Not long after Hope and Angel's departure, Lamie and Hassa knocked on their father's bedroom door and requested to speak with him. Their timing was excellent, as he'd been about to go to his daughters' room to demand an explanation for the secrets he was now convinced they were keeping from him when he'd heard a knock on his door. When he opened it, his daughters were standing there like kittens beaten by rain and in need of shelter.

Following them out to the living room, Butem sat on the single sofa with his arms folded while Lamie and Hassa sat on the three-seater sofa and gazed at the floor, occasionally stealing glances at their father. They looked like scared accomplices caught red-handed in a crime. There was pin-drop silence while Butem patiently waited, stone-faced.

After a while, with her head still bowed, Lamie looked at their father and began. "Papa, we have something to tell you."

"I'm listening," Butem answered sharply, moving his gaze from Lamie to Hassa and back again.

Hassa wriggled her fingers and began their confession: "It started on a rainy Friday some months ago, after I'd helped Lamie to take the laundry off the lines…"

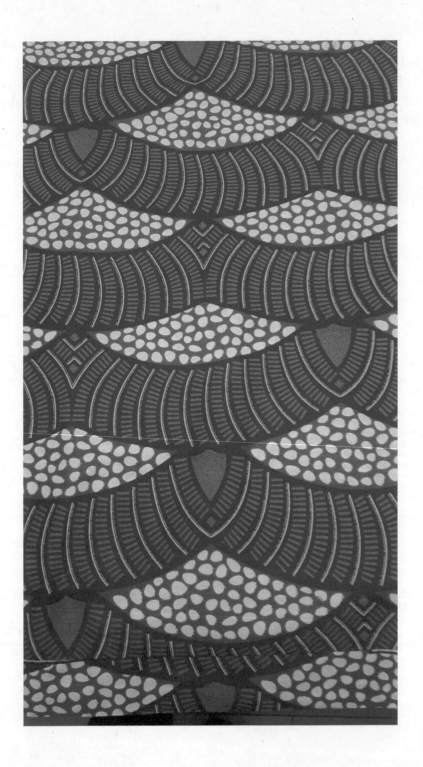

Shadows

It was 6:40 p.m. He fastened his seat belt, yawned widely, and pulled the ivory Lexus Jeep out of the basement parking. *In fifteen minutes, I'll be home. Oh! Do I ever need a shower and a good meal,* he thought, as he drove home.

He spotted his house from two hundred metres away. It was always delightful to see the Victorian-styled gate of his beautiful three-bedroom duplex set on high planes. The huge grounds were lush and green and fenced by well-manicured trees. Michael, or Mike, as his family and friends called him, was passionate about his garden and had deliberately chosen an array of sweet-scenting flowers for all seasons. At the corner of the garden, on elevated grounds facing east, sat his Italian-style gazebo, which he had furnished cozily with an aesthetic chandelier hanging daintily from its ceiling. It was a pleasurable habit of his to sit in the gazebo after dinner and read the tabloids while breathing in the rich and varied fragrances of the flowers. But most of all, he loved to watch the sun set from the gazebo, especially in early fall when—mixed with thick, dusty fog—sunset always looked like a gradual dissolve of yellow and orange watercolours. The huge ball of orange in the horizon cast a breathtaking golden and orange glow over the landscape, mixed with long strips of black and grey skies, was magical and always had a calming effect on his senses.

Mike pulled into the huge twin garage. Holding his jacket flung over a shoulder with one hand and his briefcase clutched in the other, he walked up the wide steps that led to the patio, and with his hands full, he used the corner of his briefcase to ring the bell.

"Hi, darling," said Samantha, his girlfriend of more than a year, as she opened the door for him. They exchanged quick kisses on the cheek.

"Let me take that," she said, reaching for his jacket. "How was your day?"

They both walked up the stairs to his palatial master bedroom. "Oh, well ... it was okay," he replied groggily, signalling that he had a story to tell.

As Mike kicked off his shoes and began to undress in readiness for the bathroom, Samantha stood for a while, waiting for a look at his very fit and well-muscled body. The sight of his six-pack always got her heart racing with a desire to touch each mound of muscle, enticingly arranged in neat rows. Mike paid little attention to her as he unbuttoned his shirt and quickly pulled his hands out of its sleeves. He knew the ritual of being watched undress. When he was down to his briefs, he would look at his girlfriend, give her a sweet smile, and she'd smile back like a child who'd been caught spying, and then leave the room. When Mike finally turned to walk into the bathroom, Samantha headed back downstairs to heat up dinner and prepare the salad.

Samantha was of mixed race. Her dad was Afro-American from New York and her mother part Welsh, from the Isle of Anglesey in northern Wales, and part Thai from southern Thailand. Samantha grew up with both her parents in New York and was the client services manager for a high-end clothing firm in Chicago. She'd met Mike over a year earlier when he came in with a friend to buy a business suit for what he'd called "an exclusively high-profile business meeting and dinner."

From her office that day, Samantha had heard loud, hearty laughter that was quite infectious, as well as ebullient voices that seemed to be arguing, chatting, and laughing together all at once. As the animated conversation dragged on, she decided to get to know the clients. Leaving her office, she'd found two gentlemen in the small public lounge that had mirrors in all four corners. With a sweet smile on her face, she stretched out her hand first to Mike, who was standing in front of a long mirror wearing an Armani jacket from the shop's rack.

"Hi, I'm Samantha," she'd said, giving him her sweetest smile. She immediately noticed how very tall Mike was, as well as his well-toned body. Noticing that he was not wearing shoes, only a pair of grey silk socks, she smiled more broadly.

* * *

Mike smiled and took her hand. "Hi, I'm Mike, and with your authorization, I'm here to steal your lovely jacket, a pair of Italian leather shoes, and a leather belt," he said teasingly.

Mike was the chief executive officer of a new engineering company in Chicago and had a wicked sense of humour that always put people at ease and made them laugh.

Samantha laughed, craning her neck to the left and trying to mirror his humour. "Of course, with all pleasure, please steal as much merchandise as you can. However, please remember to hand the price tags at the till and forget your wallet there too."

The three laughed for a few seconds, and then Samantha turned to Clive, Mike's friend, who was now standing shoulder to shoulder with him and smiling broadly. She shook his hand and introduced herself even as Clive moved to face her directly.

"My friend is an alien, and I've just been teaching him that, here on earth, we pay for the things we buy. Please forgive him. He's a bit of a mumu,"[2] said Clive, feigning a plea for understanding on Mike's behalf.

The newly acquainted threesome burst out laughing. Samantha stepped back, looked around her at the pile of items on the sofa Mike was trying on, one after the other, and then gently throwing her hands up in the air, she gave out a long breath and sighed, satisfied that these clients looked very pleased indeed with their shopping.

"Okay, apology accepted. I believe, though, that your friend is going to choose to stay on earth with us humans as our products remain unmatched in style and price." She smiled, looked from Clive to Mike, and then quickly added, "Well, if you need any assistance, please don't hesitate to ask any of the gentlemen on the shop floor." Samantha bowed her head slightly in acknowledgement then and left the two friends alone.

What an interesting pair, she told herself as she walked back to her office. She liked Mike. She found his rugged looks attractive. At nearly six-foot-two, and with such a well-toned body, she figured that he could be a model for some glossy magazine. He had a fine sense of humour too, and judging by the jacket he was trying on, there was no doubt that he had good taste in quality clothes.

Mike and Clive exchanged naughty winks when Samantha was out of sight.

"Wow! Pretty woman, yeah?" Mike said to his friend.

"Pretty. Sociable too," Clive agreed.

Three days after that first meeting, Mike called the store to speak with Samantha. She accepted his invitation to coffee, and a friendship began that quickly blossomed into an exclusive relationship. Samantha came on very strong, and Mike liked her drive to move the relationship forward as quickly as possible. Exactly one year into the relationship, Samantha broached the idea of moving in with Mike. It was the second time she'd told him that she wanted them to live together as a couple. The first time had been only about six months after they'd started dating. Given Samantha's penchant for following trends and all kinds of advice from her friends, Mike felt that she was asking to move in with him for the wrong reasons. So, he'd stood his ground, rejecting Samantha's suggestion, though she persisted.

"I love you and want to be with you more," she would say. "Colette's boyfriend of three months just moved in with her, and Colette tells me that it's the best decision both of them ever made."

Colette was Samantha's friend and work colleague, and Mike knew the influence they both had on each other. They often shopped together and went to the same salon and gym. "Besides, we could get to know each other better that way," Samantha had argued, that afternoon as they picnicked.

"I love you too, Samantha," Mike explained softly, hoping for understanding, "but living together before marriage is not culturally acceptable in my country, and even though I've lived in the US now for over fifteen years, I'm still pretty conservative when it comes to the idea. Could we please keep it at the occasional long weekend sleepovers for now?"

Disappointed, but willing to respect Mike's culture and conservative nature, Samantha had dropped the idea and promised not to raise the subject anymore. Rocking the love boat she was on with Mike over the issue of moving in wasn't worth it. Not when their relationship was so "beautiful and loving." She understood Mike and knew that he was a proud man, and that his pride was founded on those traditional values he held so dear, and which (he'd once told her) had also been the very foundation of his success. She loved him and would wait to move in with him once they were married. The more Colette flaunted her live-in arrangement with her boyfriend though, the more Samantha was influenced to doubt whether or not Mike truly loved her.

Mike was caring and very generous to Samantha. As her boyfriend, he treated her like what he called (in his native parlance) a "wife." He was proud of her looks and spoiled her with lovely gifts of clothes and cosmetics, always telling her, "My baby, your well-being and beauty are my pride."

Samantha only doubted him occasionally, unsure she pleased him completely. A few times in the past, she'd had a nagging feeling that she (or some other aspect of Mike's life) was lacking somehow, somewhere. But as she couldn't put her finger on what it was, she chided herself for expecting perfection or a cinema fairy tale.

* * *

As she set the table for two, Mike walked down the stairs barefoot, wearing a very light white caftan cut in traditional Chinese style. The combined smell of his shower gel and a dash of cologne was deeply sensual as it filled the atmosphere. He always oozed masculinity and class, which Samantha found irresistible.

"Hi, baby. What can I help you with?" he asked, walking up to Samantha and holding her lightly around the waist.

"Everything's done, really, but you could help with the drinks," she replied, as she began to dish out the meal.

"Hmm… That smells good. What's for dinner?" Mike asked, peering over her shoulder and into the pot.

"I made some sautéed apple casserole with chicken breasts, some penne pasta and herbs, and French salad. And, oh! I found your favourite Haagen-Dazs vanilla and cherry ice-cream on my way here and bought some."

"That's sweet, babe, thanks," Mike answered as he opened the fridge to fetch some water and fruit juice.

Over dinner, Mike told Samantha about his day at work and the meetings they'd with two very demanding and annoying clients. In turn, she shared what her day in the stores had been like and the new line of men's shoes they were expecting. For the most of dinner, however, Samantha eagerly shared her recipe ideas for their next dinner, and her increasing desire to get Botox and register at another fitness club. Mike listened attentively and renewed the promise he had made to her a couple of months earlier:

"Okay, baby, remember, the Botox and the club are on my account."

Samantha blinked at him slowly, and then nodded with a broad smile. "You're always so sweet and kind, thank you."

After dinner, they cuddled up on the big sofa and watched a documentary on the History Channel while sharing a small container of ice-cream. At ten-thirty, Samantha announced her desire to leave before it got too late, and Mike walked her to her car, which she had parked at the side of the garage. They hugged warmly and exchanged goodnight kisses.

"Be careful and call me when you get home," Mike said softly as he opened the driver door for Samantha to get in.

"Sure will," she said as she shut the door.

Mike waved and watched her drive down the road until her tail-lights disappeared.

Back in his lounge, Mike sat cross-legged in deep contemplation and unknowingly began to frown. He missed home. He missed what he called "real home food." Samantha was a very lovely lady and a good cook, but sautéed apple casserole, baked macaroni, lasagnas, and penne were beginning to feel like no food at all. *Kind of boring,* he thought, sucking his teeth. *What I would have given to have pepper soup tonight,* he thought nostalgically. *Or okro, or bitter-leaf soup with eba, fufu, or pounded yam!* He craved cow leg, tripe, kpomo (cow skin) cooked till it almost melted in the mouth, and other local delicacies. He longed for yam pottage made with palm oil, dry fish, and vegetables. He wanted mashed ripe plantain mixed with local spices and palm oil, wrapped in paw-paw leaves, and cooked in boiling water.

He loved Samantha, he told himself again and again. He liked her vivacious nature. She was an extrovert and a bit of a socialite, and it matched his fairly high-flying business lifestyle. But he wasn't sure if she completely made him feel at "home." He paused then, his eyes fixed on nothing in particular, squinting, pouting, and blinking repeatedly as his thoughts ran on and on.

Sometimes, Samantha's sophistication felt like an extension of his office, his business, which he longed to leave completely behind when he was not at work. His eyes lit up suddenly, and he abruptly sat up, slapped his right thigh with his right hand, and almost screamed, "That's it! That is it!!"

For some time now, he'd been trying with no success to unravel the mysterious void in his relationship with Samantha, and it had just come to him. Mike got up from the sofa and hopped upstairs to put on a pair of slippers. He then fetched another packet of juice from the fridge and walked out into his garden. Taking in one long breath, he exhaled loudly, feeling relief that he had finally nailed down the disturbing emotion. Now, he just needed to think clearly about what he should do.

Settling himself in the gazebo, the softly lit garden did wonders for his senses. A few minutes later, he took his phone from his caftan's breast pocket and called Clive, with whom he had been friends for about fifteen years. Clive was the one genuine friend he could unashamedly open his heart to, having become more like a sibling than a friend. Clive loved sarcasm, and their mutually wicked sense of humour enriched their relationship.

Mike knew that he could almost always count on his wise counsel, and had often hinted about the difficulties he had visualizing his relationship with Samantha beyond what they currently had, and that he didn't know why because he did love her. Now armed with what he was certain was the reason, he wanted to share his worries with Clive. As soon as Clive picked up his friend's call, they fell into their normal banter, updating each other on what they had done that day.

"Hey, listen, Clive, you know I've been telling you about my fear that something I couldn't figure out is missing in my relationship with Samantha?"

"Yes, and I've always cautioned you that there's no perfect woman out there."

"I know, I know… but, this isn't about perfection, brother. Samantha's everything any man could want, and as you know, I love her. It's just that … emm…" Mike went silent, and his friend patiently waited for him to find how best to express himself. After about ten seconds, Mike breathed out audibly and continued.

"It's just that … what I think's missing hit me just about fifteen minutes ago. I think I can confidently say that I now know what it is." Mike then went on to share his inner thoughts with his friend.

Having listened to Mike's concerns with no interruptions except for the occasional "yes" or "uh-huh," Clive knew his friend well enough to know when he was excited about something. As he listened to Mike, he could feel his deep sense of relief. Mike sounded like a bird that had been set free from a cage, and even though he had always admired his relationship with Samantha, with what he called "a good dose of envy," he truly wanted Mike to be happy—to follow his heart wherever it was about to lead him. Clive had often told his friend he would always be there to support him unless his decisions or actions became patently self-destructive. So, he began by being as straightforward as he could.

"What can I say, Mike? You and I have been on this journey, searching for love, for a while now. We've debated love at first sight, parental matchmaking, online dating, office dating, church meetings, and even newspaper adverts." He chuckled.

Mike smiled. "Yes, I know, man, and none of it is perfect, but—"

"Yes," Clive said, interrupting him. "And remember, we agreed that, for men like you and me, it's not so much about how you meet that special someone or the sparks that fly from the first meeting so much as its about first knowing exactly what you're looking for, and then looking beyond the sparks to build friendship and love with a firm foundation. I thought you had gone through this process with Samantha—"

"Well, yes, yes, I know, and while I've been trying to convince myself that I have that with Samantha, it's not as easy as A, B, C. I wish it were. I don't know, man. Maybe our foundation wasn't as strong as I thought it was. Maybe our key values are not in synch as much as I thought they were, and would want them to be... Maybe our compromises are annoying me, and who knows? Perhaps, they're annoying her too, and we're both just kicking the love-can down the road and rolling along with it, still afraid to speak our minds even being together for a year. Maybe it's just me, and my preference for something a little more conservative. More traditional." Mike paused to catch his breath and Clive remained silent.

After a moment, with a sober voice, Mike continued. "It's not Samantha's

fault. Maybe it's me who's grown up, evolved, and come to a better understanding of myself and the kind of woman I truly want to come home to
... always."

Clive could feel his friend's agitation and didn't think Mike should be
blaming himself for the complexities that falling in love could sometimes
bring. "Listen, man, don't get hard on yourself about this. But let me ask
you ... the lovemaking with Samantha is good?"

"Oh, we don't have any issues in that department, I assure you. As a
matter of fact, she gives me a run for my money there."

The two friends began to laugh, and then Clive decided to move the
conversation to much lighter ground. "You see, the trouble with you,
brother, is that you have too much of the good things in life," he teased.
"You have a fantastic job, a pretty woman who loves you, a beautiful house
and luxuries, and now ... life's most precious gift of all: confusion galore."

Their laughter rang out into the night. Mike realised that he'd needed
the laughter and was once again glad that Clive was ever ready with lots
of sarcasm.

When Mike's laughter died down enough to speak, he said, "And that's
coming from my own best friend? Should I start to do the frog dance or cry?"

"Try both if you can. But now, seriously ... seriously, I understand perfectly
how you feel. You're the one in the relationship, and you know your heart and
mind. You're the one that will have to live with whichever woman you choose.
So, all that's really important is that you're happy. You can't put a price on that."
He sighed. "Having said that, my dear brother, I also can't help but advise you
to be careful here, man. I don't want to see you hurt. You and I have always
agreed that love is not a shadow. It's a spiritual gift, and we find it and feel it
deep inside once we've cleared the debris from our minds. I hope the choice
you eventually make is one that truly brings you peace."

His friend's down-to-earth words acted almost as a sedative to Mike,
which he found a little unnerving and made him feel a bit light-headed.
His thoughts went to Samantha and the very warm feelings they shared. As
hard as he tried though, he was struggling to see or feel "forever" with her.
He also felt a pang of guilt for not discussing his hesitancy with Samantha
before now. He knew that he owed her that much respect, but he was
afraid—afraid to hurt her feelings, to dash her hopes, to be misunderstood,

and to be judged as arrogant or simply lacking in character.

He'd always prided himself on his good upbringing and now shivered at the thought of Samantha possibly accusing him of being deceptive. As wrong as she might be, how could he defend himself? How could he explain how confusing everything was? That he truly loved her, but that their love was not enough, not because of who she was but because of who she had helped to unravel inside him?

A few seconds of silence fell between the two friends again, and then Mike, without realising he was expressing his thoughts aloud, whispered, "Samantha will never forgive me. Not ever!"

"Yes, brother, I understand that." Clive cleared his throat and rushed to comfort his friend. "I can imagine how you feel with all these emotions buzzing in your head, but you've done nothing wrong. However, my advice is that you sleep on your thoughts for a couple of days and see how you feel then. If you're still certain that Samantha isn't the woman for you at that point, then you'll have to speak to her as soon as you can. Will she be angry at you? Yes, and you must brace yourself for that, but hopefully, someday she'll look back and be grateful that you respected her enough to tell her and didn't choose to cheat when you found yourself at this crossroad."

Mike's spirits lifted, and he sighed, speaking closely into the phone. "Thank you."

"No charge. You still have a healthy credit with me as long as you do the right thing."

Mike chuckled. "I promise, Mr. Reverend Brother. I will. Do you want me to write you an undertaking on my future love life?"

They both burst out laughing. Then to break the ice further, Clive added, "Well, a few years ago, you talked about feeling lonely, didn't you? If it'll help, I'll get a camel to take you to Atacama Desert, so you'll know what true loneliness feels like."

Mike joined in his friend's renewed laughter. "What business do you have being an architect, bushman, when you should be in the seminary? I feel like I've just been to confession."

"Well, sexy men like me don't want to be in the seminary, do we? We'll cause too many catastrophes and be thrown out without our portmanteau on day one."

"Well then, thank you very much for one less potential sacrilege," Mike retorted.

They laughed so loud and for such a long time that Mike teared up, clutching his abdomen with his free hand briefly before removing it to wipe tears from his eyes. He then changed the subject, asking Clive about the proposal he was drafting for a client. From there, the chitchat moved on to other less important activities that they were both planning for the rest of the week.

At the end of this very long call with his friend, Mike felt much better.

For almost a week, Mike avoided Samantha to enable him to gain clarity on his thoughts. The day after his telephone conversation with Clive, he'd called Samantha and told her that some urgent task had come up that he needed to throw himself completely into in order to get it done, and that he didn't want her to erroneously think that she had done something wrong and was being ignored. He proposed that they meet for a snack and walk in the park the coming Saturday.

Samantha thought it a bit odd that Mike was opting for only a park meeting, when they wouldn't have seen each other for a week by that point, rather than one of their typical, cozy dinners at either of their places, after which they'd cuddle up together and either watch a movie together or listen to music while they each read and made small talk. She cautioned herself about reading too much into Mike's meeting preference. She'd meet her sweetheart on Saturday and things would get back to normal between them. She smiled, shut her eyes, and whispered, "Oh lord, I'll miss him so much by that point! I can't wait."

Samantha opened her eyes, gave her figure one quick look, from her chest to her toes and rushed into her room. She stood in front of the full-length mirror next to her armoire and twirled to admire her bum from all angles, then faced the mirror and pushed her lips forward into a long fish pout, turning from side to side to admire her cheekbones. She ran her hands through her long, wavy extensions and pushed the tips up repeatedly to give the waves some bounce. Then she looked at her fingernails and was pleased. The last manicure hadn't chipped yet at all.

Satisfied that she didn't need a salon visit, Samantha went into a frenzy search for what to wear and began to rummage through her wardrobe like she occasionally did on the shop floor when she needed to quickly find a specific garment for a client. After about an hour of trying on this suit and that dress, Samantha's room looked like the site of a catastrophic hurricane. There were piles of clothes and accessories on the bed and the floor. Exhausted, and as yet undecided on what she would wear next Saturday, she dropped down spreadeagled on the heap of clothes on the bed.

It was Friday. Mike was aware that he was going to have a difficult conversation with Samantha the next day and had been practicing for several days, trying to find the best way to approach the topic and the right words to say. Each day, he paced up and down in his bedroom, the living room, the balcony, and his office. Suddenly, the English language seemed inadequate to express his feelings. Every expression he summoned up to pacify Samantha sounded cliché, and he desperately wanted new words or phrases with which to show—more than anything—how sorry he was.

He also needed to rehearse a behavioural response to the lashing out he expected from Samantha, and as the perfect words eluded him, he remembered one of his mother's favourite quotes in their local language, which translated roughly to *"Sorry never brings war."*

He decided that, for as long as he had the opportunity, he would continue telling Samantha how sorry he was, more times than could be counted, and wouldn't blame her if she refused to forgive him.

Tired, Mike walked up to his large fridge, pulled out a bottle of still water, and poured himself a glass. Gazing at the floor, he slowly walked over to the corner sofa in the living room and sat down. He took a big gulp of water and allowed his mind to drift in many directions till it finally landed on his village. One after the other then, images of his relatives appeared in his mind's eye.

He wished he didn't have to think about this now, but he couldn't help himself. He recalled several telephone conversations with his mother in which she'd nagged him about coming home to pick a wife. "You're thirty-two, Mike, and it's high time you settled down. You're a home boy, and you need a young well-brought up local girl who'll look after you, respect you, and bear you lovely children. I still don't support this relationship you have with this American girlfriend you say you love. Listen, I've been told that American women have very sharp tongues, and they don't cook-o. They prefer pizza, bread, bread, bread. You'll be sentenced to eating take-away bread for the rest of your life-o!!! Please come get a wife from home, my son!"

During a few such calls, Mike had been able to sense that his mother was almost in tears. She had always made the same stereotypical argument that White, American, or even non-local women had upset nature's perfect balance by abandoning their nurturing nature and taking equality of the sexes to the extreme. She said she was certain that the high rate of divorce around the world was attributable to a world where the old distinct lines between man and woman were quickly being eroded. It scared her that independent women have become very competitive and increasingly impatient, no longer willing to put in the effort a successful marriage requires like her generation had done. She accused "modern men" of watching too much pornography, and rather than learning to make love to their wives, they now preferred to do so with "strange women" on the computer.

* * *

"Ha! Mama! This is the twenty-first century. Things have changed," Mike said, both admonishing and trying to enlighten his mum.

"But is it not true, my son? By the way, tell me that you're not doing that on the computer."

"Mama! Haba!" Mike almost screamed into the phone. He was shocked his mother even knew about internet pornography, but even more so that she probably feared he could be influenced by it too.

"Well, it's what I've heard! We discuss these things during our church meetings, you know, so that we can understand what's going on with you modern children these days. So, again, I'm asking you … are you looking at naked women on the computer and doing all those…? You know what I'm saying."

"No, Mama, I don't know what you're saying, and no, I don't look at naked women on the computer." Mike was careful to stress every word of this, indicating that he wanted this part of their conversation to end.

"Okay, my son. I just don't want the computer to spoil your good upbringing. Whatever those naked women in the computer have, you can find it here at home. Look at the long, loving relationship your father and I had before he died. I didn't know your father intimately until we got married and I started living with him. Those computers just manipulate your brain and—"

"Enough, Mama! Stop! I've heard enough. Really." Knowing how persistent his mother could be, Mike quickly changed the topic before she could return to it and made sure her thoughts remained fully diverted to other issues for the duration of the call.

* * *

As Mike sat there on the sofa reminiscing, he started to smile. He often told Clive that, when it came to marriage, Mama's mind was like a big barrel of water that never emptied irrespective of the number of times water was drawn from it. The fact that he would repeat her "sermon" again and again, using the exact same words she used every time—though she added new spice to the idioms and references periodically—that it left him wondering if she had the sermon drafted on her palms. Yet, he couldn't help but agree that there were sometimes traces of truth in his conservative mother's thinking, even if it sounded very old-fashioned, sexist sometimes, and unfairly prejudiced against an entire race and continent. He believed that Samantha did not exemplify his mum's prejudices, and he couldn't find his current discontent with their relationship in his mum's biases.

"Maybe I'm the problem," he said to himself. "Maybe I'm delusional."

Mike bought a variety of snacks and drinks on his way to the park on Saturday and arrived ten minutes early at the spot he had told Samantha to meet him and sat on a bench. When Samantha arrived and saw him, she flew into his arms right away. They hugged and kissed passionately and then sat down, asking each other many times how things had been since they'd last met. Mike couldn't help but notice how beautifully made up she looked.

Before she'd run into his arms, he'd been pleasantly surprised and delighted by the new catwalk stride she seemed to have cultivated since their last meeting, throwing one leg sexily in front of the other while subtly swaying her hips from side to side. She radiated such good health and joy that he almost began to second guess himself. He wondered if he was about to do the right thing and if this was the right time to have the conversation. Then he remembered Clive's advice and brought his mind back to the decision he'd made to do the correct and respectful thing.

As they munched on their snacks, caught up with each other, and giggled, Samantha could sense that Mike had a lot on his mind, though he was trying not to show it. When he finally said to her, "Samantha, there's something I'd like to discuss with you," an uneasy quiet punctuated their animated chat, but she was eager to hear what it was and to offer her support in any way she could.

Samantha initially held his gaze, but then looked away from Mike and down at the grass in front of her as she listened to the man that she loved so much and couldn't wait to marry.

"Samantha, you know that I love you, and you've raised the issue of moving in with me a few times in the past."

Samantha's face lit up, believing Mike had given her request to move in with him more thought and had finally realised it was a good idea and a way to show their love for each other. She thought about her friend, Colette, and couldn't wait to tell her the good news.

"Yes, yes, I know that, Mike, and I love you too. Living together will help make our relationship stronger. Remember? I've always told you that we'll get to know—"

"No, no, no," he said, touching her hand gently as he interrupted her. "This is not about us moving in together." Samantha scowled, clearly displeased, but he tried to continue. "I mean..." Mike's voice trailed off briefly as he hesitated, his head swaying from side to side in the discomfort of disappointing her. "I mean … I've wondered recently if I'm being fair to you. I know how much you want us to move things forward and—"

"Well, yes, and you? Don't you?" Samantha asked, slanting her head to the side and looking into his eyes, tensely awaiting his response.

Mike squinted, looked at the ground, and replied in almost a whisper. "That's the issue, and it's with me. Not you, Samantha. You're beautiful, nice, and do your best always, but deep down in me, I'm just not as convinced about us as you are, and as much as I love you, I don't know if it's enough to move our relationship forward."

Samantha's heart sank and began to beat faster as Mike's words hit home. And his next statements only made things worse.

"But because I do love you, Samantha, I must be honest with you... I don't think it's fair of me to waste your time by continuing to give you hope and feed your belief and expectation that our relationship truly has a future. It hurts me deeply, and my heart's been in turmoil for the past few weeks, but you simply deserve better."

Feeling like he had just been freed from a load that had been weighing him down both physically and psychologically, Mike sighed but wouldn't lift his head to look at her. He kept his gaze on the ground, taking in the enormity of what he had just done, ending his relationship with the woman he'd believed he was in love with for some time now.

As Mike's words sank in, Samantha's head began to spin. "What did I do wrong, Mike? Why am I not enough for you?" she asked with tears in her eyes and a broken voice.

Mike raised his head finally and looked at her. "Please, Samantha, it's truly not you. You've not done anything wrong. It's me. It's... There's something about my feelings I only came to understand recently. I feel pained to be telling you this, but it would be irresponsible and cruel of me to string you along and inevitably hurt both of us terribly."

Samantha grew numb as her heart raced. She found herself shaking with disbelief and despair. Mike noticed and reached out to take her hand, but she quickly snatched it away and shifted her sitting position to put more space between them. They sat in silence for a while, but Mike was desperate for Samantha to say something, anything, her silence slowly killing him. He softly called her name twice, but she wouldn't answer or even look at him.

Samantha's mind had taken flight like a jet plane and was rocking back and forth in a thick cloud of self-censure. *What's going on?* she thought. *What's happening to me? How did it all come to this? I've been in a relationship for over a year and now I learn it's been nothing but shadow chasing? What will my family and friends think of me? What will Colette think? I believed Mike and I had a perfect relationship—well... No, not perfect, because we did have disagreements every now and then. But I thought we at least had a good enough foundation that it could withstand the pressures that arise from our conflicting perspectives on life. My friends and acquaintances envied me because they all wanted to have what Mike and I had. What a joke they will gladly make me out to be. I dress well. I'm very trendy. I make sure I look glamourous all the time so Mike kept his focus on me... My god, what more could he want? What?*

Samantha was too livid with anger to cry. She felt like screaming and thrashing things to release all her painful emotions and soon realized that she had unconsciously folded her hands into fists between her thighs and was pressing her fingers so deeply into her palms that they hurt. Mike waited patiently for a while and then moved closer to her and tried again to take her hand.

Samantha could no longer contain her anger, and her hand flew out like lightning, striking Mike hard across the face, and then stood up abruptly. "How dare you, Mike!" she spat out, breathing heavily. "How dare you want to touch me!"

Mike could see the anguished rise and fall of her chest as he rubbed the right side of his face where he'd been struck. His right eye hurt, but he sat still and looked at her. Samantha barked out her next words so loudly that he felt a ringing in his ears:

"Why didn't you tell me this five or six months ago? Why? You wasted my time, leading me into thinking we have a future. All the dreams we shared? All the plans we made? It's taken you *this* long to realise you're not sure? Do you even understand what a laughingstock you've turned me into? What a wimp you are! What a waste of space!! Lose my number and any memory of me!" With that, she turned around and stomped away to her car.

Mike just sat there and watched Samantha until she was out of sight, not sure how he was feeling. Soon though, relief began to take over. He knew he had done the right thing, as difficult as it had been, and as ugly as it had turned out. He'd expected Samantha's outburst, and in a way, was happy that she had reacted just as she had, for if she had quietly sat there and then walked away without a word, his guilt would have known no bounds.

Mike sat there alone with his thoughts for about twenty more minutes. Then he lazily got up, packed up the leftovers and their snack trash into a cellophane bag, and looked around to ensure the space was tidy. Patting his right eye, which was now stinging badly, he walked to the parking lot. Once he was back in his car, he looked at the rear-view mirror and noticed that his right eye was bloodshot. He sighed and shook his head, and as he drove home, he made a mental note of one last thing he needed to do in regards to his relationship with Samantha: He had to go through every room carefully and find anything that belonged to her. He would box them up neatly and courier it to her office.

On the fifth of December, about five months after his park conversation with Samantha, Mike's flight touched down in his hometown. Like Samantha, Mike had indulged in self-flagellation for a couple of months following his breakup with her, assessing his inevitable assimilation of the dictates of the fast-paced corporate world he lived in where glitz and glamour spelled success. He beat himself up for assuming that he could embellish his core values at will rather than attract a woman who shared them, and with whom those values could be nurtured and preserved. He fiercely admonished himself for being the greatest architect of his silent agitation.

Sometimes, his relationship with Samantha had felt like a competition for "what's trending," which he believed was the norm between highflying couples in the corporate world. She was subjected to the same pressure from her world as he was from his, and both worlds clashed in a veiled contest to keep the façade going to meet the expectations of others.

We just didn't communicate enough, he thought. *We were overly active, talking business, fashion, and social media most of the time and neglecting speaking more about the personal things we both wanted in the relationship, big and small. It might not have changed who we both are, but it would have given us the opportunity to decide much earlier whether or not to keep the relationship going.*

When Clive had learned how things had gone with Samantha in the park, he'd been very upset and felt his friend's pain. *It's just as well Mike wanted to break from this relationship though,* he thought. *Something not right always has a way of exploding eventually.*

Mike had to admit that the breakup had been really tough on his mental health, but he did manage to gradually put his relationship with Samantha behind him, and now, with a calm mind, he was keeping his options open.

He had no regrets about Samantha. She had taught him a lot about himself, the most valuable of them all being his newfound understanding of what should really matter to him in his search for a life partner. He sincerely wished Samantha well and hoped she would eventually meet the right man for her.

Mike collected his luggage, flagged down a cab, and drove all the way home with a smile on his face. He loved visiting home in December, where Christmas was always special. The colourful festivals, the coming home of the diaspora with different stories of their adopted countries to tell, and the communal spirit of giving and sharing had never been matched in his experiences in the US. The villagers knew that the diaspora often came home in search of spouses, and festive periods like Christmas and Easter were enlivened with matchmaking.

Mike's mother—or Mama Mike as she was fondly called in the village—was ecstatically awaiting her son's arrival. She had made all the necessary preparations and was happily following the trend of trying to find her son a bride. She really liked Faridah, the niece of an old neighbour, Athen, who was a church colleague of hers. Athen had a reputation in the village for his philanthropic nature. Gossip about him was often mainly about how disciplined and reserved he was, and how much he doted on Faridah and wouldn't let her be courted by any suitor.

Mama Mike liked her quiet and shy demeanour, and it was clear that Faridah was well-suited for domestic life. The young lady was also beautiful, and Mike's mother was certain she and Mike would make lots of beautiful babies—Mama Mike wanted no less than five babies from Mike. At the end of each visit she paid to Athen's house, every other market day for a church meeting, she got increasingly convinced that Faridah was the best kind of woman for her dear son, Mike. Mama Mike secretly hoped that one day soon, Faridah would become her daughter-in-law.

Faridah was twenty-one years old and in her final year at a local polytechnic, where she was studying agricultural science. She was undoubtedly beautiful in an unusual way, with large eyes and a long face on which sat a small, pinched nose. Her cheekbones were set prominently high, accentuating her chin. She was tall at five feet, nine inches, but she carried herself with poise. Faridah had a rustic yet serene aura about her that was captivating, and although often quiet and seemingly shy, she was also outspoken and unpretentious. In fact, she could also be blunt and spontaneous, often to the surprise of her friends in school and her village acquaintances.

Mike's mother found these qualities admirable. Faridah also had a reputation for cleanliness, and the uncle with whom she had lived for twelve years never stopped crediting her for how spotlessly clean their house and its surrounds always were. Many villagers who knew she was an agriscience student relied on her expert advice when they had issues with their crops or soil. They would come to her with samples of their ailing crop, or she'd accompany them to their farms and scoop samples of the soil to test in school. Her teachers regularly indulged her in the labs, because every successful solution Faridah was able to provide to the farmers improved the reputation of the polytechnic, which led to an increase in the number of enrolments.

During Mama Mike's last visit to Athen's for their end-of-year church meeting, she'd invited Faridah and her uncle to the "small welcome party" she was planning for Mike for the Saturday following his arrival back home. She had told Mike one evening, as they both sat on the balcony and sipped fresh palm wine, about the sorts of assistance the church was providing to schools and clinics. She'd then intentionally steered the conversation to the polytechnic and the fundraising the church had held for its renovation.

From there, she smartly moved her narrative to some "very intelligent" students graduating from the school and referenced Faridah as an example. She told Mike that she liked Faridah and how helpful the young lady was to farmers, helping them solve problems with their crops.

As Mama Mike wasn't good at hiding her feelings, her description of Faridah, her uncle, and the polytechnic astonished Mike, who began to wonder if his mother wanted him to donate to the polytechnic. But his mother did not mention any desire for a cash or equipment donation, and believing she was trying not to sound pushy, as his visit was only a few days old, he decided to be proactive.

"Mama, I'll make some contribution to the polytechnic's renovation before I leave."

"That will be wonderful! How kind of you, Mike! Thank you, and may God reward you abundantly," she replied.

Mama Mike was smart enough to avoid pushing her secret agenda too hard, and instead, allowed the subject to be put to bed for the rest of that evening.

The next day, Mama Mike created another opportunity to bring Faridah into her conversation with her son. Given how tough dry stockfish could be, she would normally parboil it whole in a large cauldron with lots of water to soften it before cutting it up to add to her soups. With Mike around, however, she decided not to parboil the fish whole, but rather have Mike cut it up first. *He's a man,* she thought. *He has the strength and energy to do it.* Mama placed the large fish and a cutlass on a large chopping board made from a Iroko tree trunk and called her son.

"Mike? Mike?"

"Yes, Mama, I'm coming." Mike quickly walked to the kitchen and met his mother getting ready to do some cooking.

"Mike, my son, please help me chop up this stockfish into five or six parts. I always struggle trying to do it myself."

"No problem. And you shouldn't be cutting stockfish yourself, Mama. Why don't you have them chopped up in the market when you buy them?"

"Well, the seller normally comes here to deliver stockfish to me whole, and so I have to cut it up myself when I'm ready to use it."

Mike didn't argue. He picked up the cutlass and started cutting up the fish.

In no time, his mother found a way to broach the topic uppermost on her mind and began by revisiting the questions she had already asked Mike the day he'd arrived.

"So, Mike, so how is the US and your work?"

"Fine, Mama. We can't complain."

"And your friend, Clive? He is doing well?"

"Yes, he is. Like I told you, he always asks after you. When I donate to the school, as I told you I would, I'll be donating on his behalf too. I know he'd like to do that."

"Oh, my son, how thoughtful! Thank you, thank you! Our church committee members will be so grateful. Thank you. And … how is your girlfriend. Em… Em… Oh dear, what's her name again? I've forgotten."

Mike wished his mother hadn't brought up Samantha again, but as she was obviously being conversational and repeating a chat they'd already had, he indulged her and answered her questions.

"Her name is Samantha, and she's doing well, Mama." Mike tried to distract his mother and change the subject, picking up a tiny piece of the fish from the many scattered about the table and began to chew. "Mama, this stockfish is really fresh. I can taste it. Is the seller a fisherman himself or does he buy from the fishermen and then dry it himself to sell?"

"Oh, he's a fisherman and dries them himself. That's why I get them for a good price. I think he's said his eldest son helps him in the business too. This one you're cutting up now is among the three I bought from him a day before you arrived."

"Hmm... That's great, Mama. Where should I put the pieces I've cut?"

Mike's mother quickly fetched a large bowl from her shelf and wiped it down with a napkin.

"Here. Use this bowl." She placed the bowl on the table a little away from Mike, and then picked up the cut pieces and examined them. She was pleased with how uniform Mike had kept them. "You're really good at this, Mike. Thank you." As Mama walked towards the window where she'd laid out cocoyams, she couldn't help but wonder why Mike wasn't giving her more details about his relationship with Samantha.

Why does he only keep saying that she's fine? Surely, he knows I'm not just asking to know if she's fine but to learn about where they are in their relationship. Has he met her family yet? Why didn't he bring her along during this visit to meet us? If he's really serious about her, doesn't he think it's about time I got to meet her in person even if I'm not excited about the relationship?

Mike looked up, happy to watch his mother busily examining the cocoyams she'd lined up on a newspaper near the window, but hurried to put the fish away so that he could go, hoping to avoid more discussion of Samantha.

"Mike, my son?" His mother asked then, sounded like she had something important on her mind.

"Eh, nne?"[3] Mike asked, using his term of endearment for her.

"Please don't think I'm being nosy, but ... you know how much I love you and want to see you happy. Your late father would expect no less of me."

"I know, nne, I know, and by the way, I'd love to visit Papa's graveside one of these days when you're free. Let me know if there's anything you'd like me to do, either before or while we're there."

"Okay, that will be good. We'll make a plan. But as I wanted to say, some women have been asking me about you, and because you're eligible, they keep pestering me about their daughters' availability. I wish they wouldn't though, because of all the young women in this village, the one I truly like is Faridah. Now, I'm not saying you should meet Faridah or even give my fondness for her a single thought, but you know ... I know her uncle fairly well, and if there's a respectable family that I'd like to bring into ours, it's Faridah's. That's all I'm saying. Well ... that's just the thinking of an old woman, and you need not pay it any heed."

Mike said nothing. He washed his hands and wiped them with a small towel he found hanging on the cooker's handle. Walking over to his mother then, he wrapped his arms around her as she looked up at him.

"Nne, I came home to take a break from work and all the stress of the big city. I missed you and have come to spend some time with you. I miss the village too and the traditional festivities. Coming to spend Christmas here is a precious getaway for me. I didn't bring Samantha along because I didn't think it necessary at this time, and besides, she is very busy. I know you're eager to know how things are between Samantha and me. I promise you that I'll let you know when or if ever we move ahead in the relationship. Is that okay?" Mike peered down into his mother's eyes, awaiting her response.

His mother looked at him for a long time, as though fishing for some additional clues in his eyes. Then she looked away and shrugged. "Well, whatever you say is alright by me."

Despite her words, she knew her son too well. She remembered how fiercely he'd always defended Samantha and expressed his belief in their relationship during their phone calls. So, hearing him say "if ever" about their relationship deepening let her know everything she'd hoped to hear, and her heart leaped for joy.

Mike had easily picked up on his mother's hints about Faridah but was careful to show no interest, not wanting to give his mother the satisfaction of knowing that he was starting to pay some attention to the name, which never seemed too far from her lips: Faridah. He reminded himself that he hadn't come home to find a wife. He'd needed a break from Chicago, from friends, colleagues, and all the gossip about his failed relationship with Samantha. He needed a break from the things that reminded him of Samantha and their times together. He desperately wanted to forget the black eye she'd given him, which he'd nursed for a week.

The festivities in the village would be a good distraction and far more soothing. He wanted to enjoy living like the villagers and doing simple, ordinary things like walking to the stream, eating yam and stew with his fingers, and bathing outside to the sound of crickets and birds when the night was pitch black, with the only light needed being the one that streaked into the backyard from the kitchen window. He didn't want to entertain his mother's Faridah business, even if she *had* mentioned the name so many times this past few days that his curiosity had been piqued.

Most young villagers, especially distant relatives and casual acquaintances, called Mike "Uncle Chi-chi" in recognition of his residence in Chicago. Faridah didn't know Mike but had heard the nickname and restrained herself from the desire to know him by listening to gossip peddled by neighbours about Mama Mike's son.

The day after he'd arrived, Mike had called on his early childhood friends, Kpele and Udoh, with whom he'd played football on the dusty field on the church grounds whenever he and his parents had visited the village during the summer holidays. Kpele and Udoh both lived in the Netherlands now and were also visiting the village for the Christmas and New Year celebrations, so the three friends agreed to meet at Mike's house a few days later for a drink and perhaps a late-evening visit to a pepper-soup joint to enjoy goat-head pepper soup. Goat-head pepper soup was one of Mike's favourite local delicacies. It had been decades since he'd last had it, and he couldn't wait to join his friends on this proposed walk to one of the famous eateries in the village.

On Friday afternoon, the day before Mike's welcome party, Kpele and Udoh visited him to catch up on one another's lives as they'd agreed. Mike was having a beer with his old friends on the balcony when he sighted a young lady and a middle-aged man in the distance, walking towards them. She was carrying a large basin on her head, from which Mike could see portions of various fruits: pineapple, pawpaw, sugarcane, and corn. Mike looked at the pair with disinterest and soon looked away, carrying on with the ebullient chatter with his friends.

As they got closer to where the friends were seated though, Mike noticed the woman's beautiful dark-brown skin. He noticed how straight and unperturbed the young lady's walk was, even with the basin of heavy fruits on her head. *Goodness!* he thought. *That must be very heavy on her head.*

The pair reached the house and stopped in front of the three friends. The older man greeted them and asked no one in particular if Mama Mike was in the house, while the woman stood behind him, looking down. She almost seemed to be hiding, which Mike found curious. Bringing his attention back to the matter at hand, Mike told the man that his mother was busy at the back of the house and then stood up to escort them to her.

"Please let me help you with that," Mike said, turning to face the woman and raising his hand to lift the basin from her head, but she refused his assistance.

"No, thank you. I can carry it to Mama," she replied, quickly stepping away.

"It's okay," the man said, smiling at Mike. "She can cope." He waved his hand casually to dismiss any assumption that she might need help. "Please don't bother and carry on with your friends. We're no strangers here and can find our way." He thanked Mike again and then follow the woman, who was now standing by the side gate, waiting for her uncle to join her. He did, and then they went through the gate together and continued straight to the back of the house where Mama Mike was indeed seated on a bench, busily picking stones out of a large bowl of beans.

Mama Mike jumped out of the bench when she saw Athen and Faridah, quickly placing the bowl of beans down and rushing to help lift the basin of fruits off of Faridah's head.

"Ah, Uncle Athen, Faridah! What a surprise to see both of you," she said as she and Faridah each took an end of the basin on her head and gingerly put it down on the ground near the bowl of beans.

"Well, we know your son is visiting, and you have this welcome party planned for tomorrow, so Faridah and I thought we'd bring you this little gift."

Mama Mike was deeply touched, placing both hands on her heart and then raising them to cover her mouth, looking at the basin, which was almost overflowing with fruits. "Oh, my god, you call this *little*? Thank you! Thank you! How kind of both of you! Now, what should I offer you?" With that, Mama Mike started to scurry into the kitchen to fetch some drinks and snacks but Athen stopped her.

"No, no, no, Mama Mike. Come, come, please don't bother. We don't intend to stay any longer. We just wanted to drop the fruits off and head back immediately. I'm expecting some people from the church later this evening. I also came to let you know that, should you need Faridah's help with preparations for tomorrow, I'll be happy to free her to come assist you."

"Thank you, Uncle Athen, but everything's fine. I've contracted the cooking out to Best Cooking as it's more convenient. You know Best Cooking, don't you?"

"I think so. Isn't that the company owned by the wife of the former catechist?"

"Yes, that's the same one. They'll do everything and simply deliver the food to me tomorrow afternoon."

"And the beans you were picking when Faridah and I walked in here?" Athen nodded towards the bowl of beans near the foot of the bench.

"Oh, that's for later in the week." Mama Mike glanced at the bowl and looked away quickly.

"Well, okay, Faridah and I must take our leave now. Don't forget, we're not very far from you should you need help."

"I promise not to forget. Thank you." She looked at Faridah and placed her right hand on the young lady's left shoulder, offered her a big smile, and said, "Thank you, my dear."

Faridah genuflected slightly. "Thank you, Ma."

They all turned around then, and Mama Mike walked her guests back to the gate.

* * *

On Saturday, from under the canopy where Mike sat, he saw the same tall lady in the distance, walking with majestic strides beside the same middle-aged man. As they got closer, he was disappointed when they chose to enter the house through the small side gate that led to the backyard, rather than by the front door, which would have given him a better look.

As the house began to fill up with guests, Mike's mother busied herself introducing her son to everyone. Faridah's uncle, who had stepped out of the house and was mingling with neighbours, was formally introduced to Mike at last.

"This is my son, Mike, who lives in Chicago and is visiting till after the new year," Mama Mike said proudly.

"Ah, yes!" Athen said, smiling broadly. "I remember. You're the young man I met outside yesterday, sitting with some other fellows! How are you?"

"Yes sir, you remember right. That's me. I'm well, thanks, and thank you for coming."

Athen turned to address Mike's mother. "I must say, Mama Mike, you have a wonderful son. He immediately got up yesterday and offered to help Faridah with the basin of fruit before we came to the backyard to meet you."

"Is that true? So, Mike, you've already met Uncle Athen and Faridah! I didn't know that, and you didn't say anything!" Mama Mike looked at her son, a look of pleasant surprise on her face.

"Well, Mama, it wasn't like you think. I thought they were simply new guests here and just wanted to show them the way to you behind the house. We didn't get to introduce ourselves in any way."

"Yes, he's right," Athen said. "We just exchanged greetings. I asked him if you were home, he said you were, and I told him we could find our way and that was it."

"Oh, okay, no problem. By the way, Mike, have you met Faridah today?"

Mike rolled his eyes at her, with a look that clearly said, *"Not again."*

"Faridah?" he asked with exaggerated surprise, since he'd already pieced together her identity by this time. "The young lady who was here with Uncle Athen yesterday? That was Faridah?" He shook his head. "No, I have not seen her today at all."

"Oh, okay," Mama said, and glanced around. "She must be here somewhere though."

Sensing Mike's unease, Athen quickly changed the subject, remarking about how regal Mike's height made him and the strong resemblance he had to his mother. Mama Mike joked with pride about that being why Mike was "Mama's child and the one and only after her heart."

They all laughed at the joke, and then Mama Mike led Athen to see some other guests while Mike rejoined his group of friends, sitting under a canopy chatting boisterously.

After about an hour, and with the party in full swing, it suddenly occurred to Mike that he still had not been introduced to Faridah by his determined mother, which he thought a little strange. Big garden eggs and spicy groundnut paste were being served by Mike's nieces, who had been enlisted by his mum to help serve the guests. On seeing the tray with the local fruits, Mike remembered that no traditional party ever seemed to have truly begun without this indigenous starter. It reminded him of all he'd missed about home.

There was plenty to eat and drink, and the local band had gotten many up on their feet dancing. Mike pulled one of his cousins to the dancefloor, and as he twirled around, he spotted Faridah serving a group of elderly guests some palm wine. He watched as she first handed them mini calabashes about the size of traditional English dessert bowls, and then knelt down beside a keg of palm wine. She then carefully poured some of the fresh wine that had been tapped from the tree that morning into the big, funnelled plastic cup in her hand, before filling each mini calabash, one after the other.

Mike danced, more with his eyes than his feet, as he spun and swayed, keeping watch on what looked like a ritual from Greek times taking place not too far away. As Faridah rose to her feet to leave the elders, having filled the last calabash, the chief elder held her back.

"Ah, no, my child," he said. "You must stay and pray with us."

Faridah knelt down again beside the keg of palm wine and bowed her head. The chief began the prayer, pouring libation on the ground three times and asking the ancestors to drink with them and bless them. *"Ise!"* the group answered to end the prayer. Then the chief broke the three yellow kola nuts, which had been served in a china saucer, into many pieces with his fingers, and then placed the saucer at the centre of the table.

He began another prayer, which ended once more with a chorus of "Ise!" Then he threw a tiny piece of kola nut on the ground for the ancestors and took a piece for himself. He then passed the china plate to Faridah, who rose to her feet and passed the plate to each elder for them to take a piece. When her job was done, she genuflected before the elders.

The chief placed his hand on her shoulder. "God bless you. Thank you, my child."

Faridah nodded respectfully then and returned to the backyard.

Mike wished he had his camera with him. *What a beautiful sight to behold,* he thought. This had not been his first time seeing the traditional breaking of kola nut and pouring of libation, but he'd found the scene with Faridah fascinating. He fixed his eyes on her dainty steps and the swinging of her hips as she disappeared to the back of the house.

For the next hour, Mike danced non-stop. Many young women desperately wanted their turn with him, and not wanting to offend anyone, he obliged as many as he could, but he was sweating like a lamb on the grill. Drenched in sweat and tired, he sat down for a short while to cool off, and then excused himself to go freshen up, change his shirt, and return.

He decided that rather than a full bath, since he was going to return to the party, he would simply pour some cold water over his head, wash his face and hands, and use a soapy towel to wipe under his arms. Then he'd change into a clean t-shirt before rejoining the party.

He opted to use the tap beside his mother's chicken cage in the backyard, as that one flowed faster and would save time. Being the one for whom the party was being held, he knew it would be impolite to be absent from the guests for too long.

He walked into the kitchen to fetch a big, plastic bowl, and as he walked out and down the steps to go back outside, he stopped in his tracks. Faridah was seated on a wooden stool with a rooster on her lap, attentively examining the cock's crown and beak. With the loud music still going on, she had not heard Mike in the kitchen or his footsteps as he'd descended the stairs, so he was able to observe her without her awareness.

My goodness! What is it with this girl? he asked himself rhetorically as he tried to harmonise the earlier picture of her serving the elders kola nuts and palm wine with this rural picture of her with the bird on her lap. Without warning, he was suddenly standing beside her. Startled, she jumped up and put the bird down gently on the ground, dusting fluffs of thin hair and feathers from her dress, not noticing that Mike had stretched out his hand in greeting.

"Hi, I'm Mike, Mama's son who's visiting."

Faridah looked up at him, wide eyed and still uncomfortable, but she did faintly remember the face from yesterday. "Good afternoon, I'm Faridah. Are you Uncle Chi-chi?"

"Well, yes. But please call me Mike. Why are you not with the party outside?" he asked, genuinely concerned.

"Em... Uncle Chi—"

"It's just Mike, please," he said, interrupting her with a smile.

"Em, there are too many people out there, Mike. So, I decided to stay with the birds for now, and then later, when some of the guests have gone home, I'll come sit out there with the others."

"But you're all alone here and missing the fun. You must come watch the band, the dancers, and the clown. You must," he urged. "Please."

Faridah smiled shyly, pouted her lips, nodded a few times, and then sat back down on the bench. "Okay, I'll come later."

"No, not later. I'd like you to join us now. Please."

"Okay, Uncle chi—" She stopped and corrected herself. "Em... Mike. I will."

Faridah left him standing there, but Mike's instinct told him that she wasn't headed for the party. Convinced that he had disturbed the young lady's peace, and feeling a little guilty about it, Mike changed his mind and decided to wash up in his room. Something about her made him self-conscious. At close range, he had noticed her large eyes and prominent cheekbones. Her eyes were like mirrors and seemed to be piercing deep into his heart when she spoke. He felt stripped nude by those eyes.

Mike silently cautioned himself about getting carried away. *You're here to get away and relax, Mike. You're still hurting. So ... focus.* As he changed into a clean t-shirt, he still couldn't keep his mind off Faridah. "And what game is Mama playing by not introducing her?" he asked aloud then, shaking his head and smiling at what he perceived to be his mother's craftiness. "Ah! Mama! This woman and mischief!" Finished cleaning up, and whistling lightly, he walked outside to rejoin the party.

Mike was exhausted, but he couldn't take his mind off Faridah. True to his fears, she had not joined the party or gone to sit in the parlour as she'd said she would. He looked around the party arena every now and then, hoping to catch a shadow of her somewhere, but she was nowhere to be found. Tempted to know if she had returned to the backyard spot where he had met her a little while earlier, he walked into the house and headed for the backyard, but she was gone. Mike checked every cranny of the area, unknowingly muttering to himself, "Where's Faridah gone?"

"They've gone home."

Mike turned around abruptly to see his niece, Nissy, standing not far away from him.

"They've gone?" he repeated in disbelief.

"Yes, she and Uncle Athen have gone home."

Mike felt disappointed. He wasn't sure why he should really care, although he'd hoped that, had he met her out there again, he would have taken the chance and asked her to dance. Instinct again told him that she would have declined, but he was willing to try. Faridah seemed to be the only young lady among all others at the party this evening who didn't show any interest in him. Mike didn't like that she wasn't sociable, but he respected it.

Alone with his mum once the last guest had gone and the clean-up had been done, she asked, "You met Faridah, didn't you?" She had seen him speaking with her in the backyard and hastily stolen away, wanting things to happen naturally.

Mike wasn't surprised by his mother's question. He'd expected it and was forthright in his response, hoping that his mother would shed some light on why Faridah was so reclusive and why they'd left much earlier than he had expected. "Yes, I did. It was a shame she didn't want to join the party. I wasn't successful in pleading with her to take part." Mike shrugged, feigning disinterest.

"Well, Faridah is a very shy girl, as you may have observed, and her uncle is very protective of her."

Feeling the need to change the subject to something less sensitive, he asked, "Mama, can you tell me how the clan head is chosen? I'm really curious."

Mama Mike began to narrate the history of how the chiefs of the clan were chosen, and Mike listened attentively, happy that their conversation had now been fully diverted to other matters. The digression didn't last for too long though. At the end of her history lesson, she decided to pick her son's brain and see if any tidbit on Faridah would drop out.

"Tell me, Mike," she said, her voice both teasing and excited, "I could see that almost every young lady wanted to dance with you tonight. What did you think?"

Mike smiled and talked about how lovely all the ladies were, how special they made him feel, and how exhausting it had all become, dancing nonstop for so long. His mother kept smiling as he rambled on about much and nothing in particular. She knew her son very well and could swear, by the look on his face and the tone of his voice, that none of the young ladies he'd danced with really interested him. Something else was preoccupying his mind. Whatever it was, she hoped Faridah featured positively in it. She wanted that very much.

Much later that night, Mike called Clive and told his friend about the party and his encounter with Faridah.

"Can you imagine, man? She was just sitting there like an apparition with a rooster! Never seen anything like that in my life!"

Clive laughed with his friend, and as usual, teased him. "You needed a selfie with her and that rooster, my friend. How did you miss that golden opportunity?"

"I honestly don't know how that happened, brother, but I can tell you this: even my camera would have frozen in fear. No kidding." The two friends laughed for a long time. Then Mike continued. "But... But, seriously brother, it's an image that's imprinted itself on my mind. And you know what? It scares me to say this ... but that image is like a painting of the most beautiful sunrise I've ever seen."

For days after the party, and much to his consternation, Mike thought about Faridah. He wanted to meet her again. He wasn't happy with the way their meeting had turned out during the party. He wanted a one-on-one visit with her—to get to know her and see if the emotion making his heart skip beats at the vision of her serving kola nuts, and sitting with the rooster, was worth pursuing—unlikely as it was beginning to seem. He knew that he couldn't just show up on her uncle's doorstep. That would be rude and give the wrong impression of him, and yet he didn't want his mother involved. There had to be another way to arrange a meeting.

Ah ha! Nissy! he thought joyfully. He could get information about Faridah from his niece, and if possible, use her as the intermediary in planning a casual date with Faridah.

It didn't take long before Mike's plans began to take shape. Nissy was acquainted with Faridah through church events, even though they weren't very close, and occasionally met at the local stream or when her aunt, Mama Mike, would send her on an errand to do one thing or another at Athen's house.

Two days after the welcome party, Nissy came to Mike's home to return the bowl in which Mama Mike had packed her some leftovers from the party. Mike stopped Nissy for a chat at the front of the house on her way back home. He told her about his mother's conversation with him about the local schools and clinics, and his plan to make a donation to Faridah's polytechnic. He said he was intrigued by all his mother had told him about Faridah's competence in agricultural science and needed to know more about her interventions with the farmers, offering them solutions to their crop problems, so that he could perhaps support her and other similar efforts by way of book or tool donations. Nissy was dumbfounded by Mike's generous gesture.

"Wow, Uncle chi-chi, of all the young men in this village who live overseas, you're the first one I know who is offering to donate to the polytechnic and even assist Faridah's efforts. You're very kind. Faridah will be so happy. I've heard her talk about how much better she could be of service to the farmers if only she had advanced crop-testing equipment in the lab."

"Great then, Nissy. I'd like a meeting with Faridah, but do me a favour, please keep this conversation between us to yourself. I don't want anyone to know that I plan to meet with Faridah, not even Mama. I need what I'm planning to do to be a surprise for Faridah, and if Mama knows, she may get too excited and tell her unintentionally. Is that okay?"

Nissy smiled shyly and pouted her lips. "Of course, Uncle Chi-chi. I won't say anything. But wow! I can imagine the look on Faridah's face when she hears what you have to tell her! She'll scream for joy. And... Ah! Uncle Athen will be *so* happy and proud too. Uncle Athen is going to really like you."

"Well, I don't know about that." Mike chuckled and tucked his hands into his trouser pockets. Looking around to make sure his mother was not within earshot, he smiled, focusing his attention back on his niece.

Nissy happily volunteered as much information as she could about Faridah's routine. From her, Mike learnt Faridah's main weekly activities: church every Sunday morning from nine to eleven; choir practice every Friday evening from seven to nine; a trip to the Three-Shoulder stream every Saturday morning before sunrise, where she did her laundry; and then tending to her neighbours' poultry for about an hour on Saturday evenings, usually, from five to six.

Mike was surprised by how busy Faridah's schedule was for a student in college. He knew that the list Nissy had just given to him was in addition to her usual household chores at Uncle Athen's. Mike's heart was filled with admiration for Faridah's dedication to her studies while doing all the other chores Nissy mentioned. He expressed his gratitude to his niece, promised her he'd come fetch her for goat head or fresh-fish pepper soup at his favourite joint in a few days. Nissy clapped with excitement and half ran, half hopped back home.

The popular local stream was called "Three Shoulder" because it converged at a point the villagers called the "Isi", meaning "head" and then clearly branched out in three different directions. The stream bustled more on Friday evenings when most users came to do their washing, believing that all else being equal—especially with no heavy downpour—their laundry would be dry and ready for ironing by Sunday evening. Faridah preferred to go to the stream very early on Saturdays when it was quiet, with most villagers headed for the market. Recalling the image of her with the rooster, and his mother's description of her as "shy," Mike could understand why Faridah would not want to be at the stream when it was busy.

He didn't think he'd like to be there on a Friday evening either.

Church and choir practice seemed too public for a very private conversation with Faridah, and he didn't want to look like a philanderer. In addition, he cringed to imagine his mother getting an earful from the church busybodies about her son's meeting with Faridah on church premises. The neighbour's poultry would be too intrusive in a meeting with her though. And how will he explain his presence there, uninvited, to the neighbour? So, Mike settled for the Three-Shoulder stream. He decided that it was the best place to meet Faridah and chat with little or no interruptions.

On Christmas day, Kpele and Udoh came to fetch Mike at about two, and the three friends joined the crowd headed to the streets to watch masquerades and traditional dances. Mike joined his friends as they danced and clapped with each dance group. He loved the back and forth chase the masquerades gave spectators. He laughed heartily at the ludicrous outfits of the stupidly made-up clowns wearing long, black, fake beards with their stomachs and bums stuffed with cushions and pushed back and forth in a hilarious dance step to the laughter of kids and adults alike. Mike took lots of photos.

The three friends danced their way to the carnival at the Civic Centre, located in a large field. Festivities at the Civic Centre were partly sponsored by the local government and the village king. The city's professional dance band blared high-life music. The city's official dance troop was also entertaining on a different part of the field. The church had a grotto of the nativity set up in a corner of the field, beside a tall tree, and Father Christmas (Santa) sat by the grotto receiving children, giving small gifts, and posing for photos.

There was also a church bazaar, and Mike and his friends bought snacks as a way of contributing to the church. There were all sorts of games and lucky draws and kiosks selling everything from food to artefacts. Mike encountered some of the young women he had danced with at his welcome party. They all exchanged pleasantries, and when Mike showed no interest in carrying on with their acquaintance, they left to mingle with the crowd and entertain themselves.

Around five-thirty, the three friends were at Udoh's house. Udoh's mother and siblings had prepared lots of foods, many of them delicacies Mike had not eaten since he was a child. In Udoh's living room were about six kids between the ages of five and twelve, standing in two rows and singing Christmas carols to the delight of Udoh's parents and an uncle and auntie of his who had also come to visit Udoh's family. The kids reminded Mike of trick or treating on Halloween in the US, and when he saw Udoh's family giving the kids some money at the end of their performance, he did the same. As the living room couldn't hold everyone, Udoh's Mother spread two raffia mats in a corner at the front of the house and sat the kids there. She gave them food and drink and each of them were provided with small gifts of local delicacies wrapped in transparent cellophane to take home.

Mike had a good time. Close to seven o'clock, Kpele requested that they pay his family a visit too as they were expecting them, and his mother and relatives had also done a lot of cooking. Mike knew this was normal in the village at Christmas. People continually exchanged visits until they were tired. Mike's stomach was full. He was exhausted and felt sticky with dust and sweat, but to make Kpele happy, he and Udoh told him they'd just stop by to say a quick hello to his family and then call it a day.

At Kpele's house, it was bustling as well. Traditional music was blaring from a tape player. Friends and relatives of the family were drinking and bantering loudly. Mike politely turned down the offer of food and drink. It was windy, and they sat outside with Kpele and reminisced about the afternoon. When Mike and Udoh were ready to leave, Kpele's mother brought two big bags and handed one to each of them. She had packaged bowls of food and drinks for them to take away as they had declined to eat with the others. Mike hadn't expected takeaways, but he thanked her profusely. Then he and Udoh said their goodbyes and left.

As soon as Mama Mike saw her son with a big bag, she knew what to expect and started to laugh.

"Why are you laughing, Mama?" Mike asked.

"Well, if you go into the kitchen, you'll find about five trays of different kinds of foods from the neighbours. I don't think there'll be enough space in the freezer for them all." She took the bag from Mike.

"So how do you plan to preserve them?"

"Whatever can't go in the freezer, I'll warm up in pots and leave on the cooker and table. Then tomorrow, I'll send some food to the orphanage and to the labourers who normally cluster around the motor park. By the way, Mike, would you like something to eat?"

"Oh gosh! No, Mama. The thought of food churns my stomach. I'm too full. Now, unless you need me to help you with washing up or anything else, I'm going to sit out on the balcony and then walk around till I feel lighter. Then I'll take a bath and go to bed. It's been a lovely but tiring day, Mama. Watching the masquerades and dancers was a real treat though ... even though my feet are sore."

"No, no, my son. You go relax, please. I can manage. And soak your feet in a bucket of hot water before you go to bed."

Mike paced up and down on the porch for a little while. Then he sat on the edge of one of its steps and did some exercises for about thirty-five minutes.

It was Friday, a week after his party, when Mike decided to surprise Faridah and meet her at the Three-Shoulder stream the next morning. So, in the evening, he turned towards his mum and said, "Mama, if you have things to wash, please give them to me, and I'll do them at the Three-Shoulder stream very early tomorrow morning. I haven't been to that stream in such a long time, and I'm itching to be there again ... to bathe and swim in it. You remember how much I used to love going there when I was a kid and we visited during the summer holidays?"

"Of course, of course, how could I forget? You're lucky the Three-Shoulder stream is still pristine. The other ones are no longer what they used to be. Some are completely gone. You should see them now; they're just eyesores. Their once beautiful and peaceful environments have been developed now, and the inhabitants of the houses around them have turned them into garbage dumps.

"Oh no! That's terrible. I remember how my nephews and I used to chase squirrels and catch butterflies, which we brought home from the stream near the clan chief's home. Oh, and those sweet cherries we always plucked from the trees! So juicy and sweet. And you know what, Mama? For days after each visit to that stream, I could still smell the trees, and hear the sound of the river, the sounds of all kinds of birds, and insects ... even in my sleep. It was always so soothing to go there."

"Ah, all that is history now. The felled the fruit trees, dredged and reclaimed the land on that stream, and they're now building a big mall there. Some teachers in the polytechnic protested and took their case to the king. But he ruled that disputes on the alternative lands proposed for the mall had made that stream the most viable option."

"What a shame, Mama. I was really looking forward to visiting all the streams because each of them had a unique environment and shape."

"Yes, my dear son, so it goes... Anyway, you said you'd be able to do some laundry for me tomorrow at the Three Shoulder? I do have a few items. Let me go sort and bundle them together." Mike's mother walked briskly into her bedroom and returned a little while later to the living room, where Mike was standing and waiting for her. She handed him a few clothes tied into a large shawl and knotted into a ball.

"Will you still be able to find your way?" she asked as Mike tucked the ball of clothes under his arm.

"I think I will. Once I leave the main road and get onto the rough, narrow one leading to Utu village, it's straight down the bush path from there. Isn't it?"

"Ah, you haven't forgotten then. Yes, that's the path to take, and as you know, you'll start to smell and hear the stream as you get closer."

Faridah had arrived at the stream at quarter to six on Saturday morning to avoid the crowds, just like she did every Saturday, since at this time of day, traffic was almost non-existent. Because of its vastness and the cleanliness of the water, which flowed through sets of rocks overlooking the mangroves at three different angles, the villagers had the liberty to wash and bathe in private at any of its tributaries. A few often chose to remain at the main source of the stream where the torrent was heavier and the water so clear that it sparkled like a freshly wiped mirror.

For Faridah, the Saturday trip to the stream was both therapy and a ritual. She would catch butterflies, admire their nicely coloured wings, and set them free. She'd chase after big grasshoppers and squirrels and dig for unique seashells in the shallow but very clear water. Most of all, she loved to bathe completely nude in the stream, swimming in the deep end close to its head for as long as possible. As soon as she'd arrived this morning, she'd done her laundry, set it aside in a big plastic basin, undressed, and then began to lather her body from head to toe. Scrubbing herself with a bath sponge made from the inner chaff of coconut shells, she then walked into the stream to wash off the lather. She sang and danced, wriggling like an Indian belly-dancer as she dipped in and then emerged from the water.

From a distance, Mike could smell the stream. He arrived at its source at six a.m. and decided to do his laundry there, where the water was cleanest, before heading further down to the body of the stream. At 6:20, Mike neatly folded his clean laundry into his sling bag. He was getting excited now at the possibility of surprising Faridah and not knowing exactly when she'd arrive gave him butterflies in his stomach. He took a few steps down the path, strewn with leaves, nuts, and stems, and then heard something. As he marched further down the shady, sloppy path, he saw a naked back in the waters and quickly ducked down, hiding in the bush and watching from between sugarcane, trying to make sense of what was going on down there.

Of course, when the figure screamed gleefully as it splashed in and out of water, then emerged and began to chase something he could not see, he recognized it as a woman. "My-o-my! What the heck's going on there?" he whispered to himself. The woman chased whatever it was to a tree and then around and around it. Mike remembered running after squirrels and butterflies at this very stream when he was a child. Smiling, he refocused on the woman in the stream. She seemed to be saying something to the squirrel, or whatever it was, and laughing like a child playing with a puppy.

Confused, he watched on while very quietly moving forward in his hiding place. Then he recognized her. *Goodness! It's Faridah.* Dumbstruck, his mouth dropped open and he covered it with his hand, awed at the scene playing out ahead of him.

Finally, after a long playful chase, she caught whatever it was she'd been chasing, and holding it in her palms, took it with her back into the stream. She then began to sing, dance, and swim, diving into the water and coming back up many times over. He watched her dive down once again, and then waited for her to reemerge. And he kept waiting, uncomfortable in the bushes, being bitten and crawled over, and listening for any sign of her emergence somewhere down stream. It was dead quiet though, with only the whistling calls of birds and insects and the mesmerizing echo of the waters.

The area around the stream was beginning to feel eerie. *Where is she?* he thought, impatiently stamping his foot to get rid of an insect. After waiting for what seemed like eternity, he began to panic, fearing that she might be drowning.

Unable to hold himself back any longer, Mike dashed out of the bush and began to run down the slope towards the head of the stream, calling for her.

"Faridah?" Silence. "Faridah?!..."

He began screaming her name at the top of his voice as he ran to the left shoulder of the stream, as close as he could get to the place he was sure she had dove beneath the surface. With no time to waste, he stripped down to his swimming trunks, dove into the water, and swam the breadth of the left shoulder, still calling her name. Then he headed to the middle of the stream and to the right shoulder, furiously swimming fast and far, calling her name. He dove in and out and turned again to the left shoulder.

"Please God, don't let her drown!" he begged again and again as he called her name at the top of his lungs. *"Faridah!!"* Mike was truly alarmed now and visibly shook with fright. Close to the cluster of rocks on the right shoulder, he thought he heard her voice ... or maybe multiple voices?

He turned around sharply, shouting, "Is someone down there?" Silence. He called out again, as loudly as he could manage. *"Faridah!?"* He listened to his voice reverberate through the waters and echo so far that it seemed likely even his mother would hear him. He felt uncomfortably alone with only the chirps of birds and the soft ripples of the water against the banks for company. He dove in again and swam back towards where he'd dropped his sling bag of laundry, certain Faridah had drowned, and struggling to contain his tears.

It had been more than twenty minutes now since he'd seen her disappear into the water, and he felt utterly helpless. He rushed out of the water, pulled his trousers back on, and grabbing his sling bag, he began to run up the hilly path to the village. He needed to report Faridah missing and get the villagers to organize a search party of divers. It was still very early in the morning and he hoped she'd be found before the stream got busy.

Mike sprinted faster and farther than he had done in his life, and panting for air, he reached home and found his mother sweeping the front of the house. It was almost seven-thirty now.

"Mama, Mama, we ... need ... help. Faridah ... has ... drowned ... in the Three-Shoulder stream," he gasped out between breaths and sat on one of the steps leading to the porch. Unable to understand him, Mike's mother worked to calm him down and asked him to explain what had happened. Wasting no time, he quickly narrated what had happened at the stream as clearly as he could without offering to many details.

"Oh my God, oh my God!" his mother cried. Panicking, she flung her broom to the ground and ordered him to stay home while she went to see Faridah's uncle so they could assemble a search party. She ran into her room, grabbed a scarf, and tied up her dishevelled hair. Sliding into a flat pair of rubber slippers then, and knotting her wrapper tightly around her waist, she began to run to her former neighbour's house, clutching her chest and praying and calling on God to save Faridah.

"God, please, have mercy... God, please have mercy... Holy Father, please have mercy..."

She arrived at Athen's house and banged on the door, startling Faridah's uncle, who rushed to the door and opened it, shocked to see Mama Mike standing there so early in the morning with her arms around her head now and acting like someone whose house had just gone up in flames.

"Mama Mike, what happened? Please come in! Come in and sit down!" he said, ushering her inside. She was nervous right down to her bone marrow. How was she to deliver such bad news at the dawn of a new day? Unsure, but knowing there was no time to waste, she shook her head and just got right to the point.

"Neighbour, my son, Mike, just ran home from the Three-Shoulder stream and while—"

"Good morning, Mama," a lively voice said, interrupted her. She turned her head and almost fainted when she saw Faridah standing in the doorway, having come to discover the source of all the commotion.

Mama looked at Faridah with wide eyes as Athen looked on, confused by her reaction.

"Em... Em... Good morning, Faridah, my dear. Em..." Mama Mike seemed to lose her tongue then.

Faridah's uncle quickly intervened. "Please, Faridah, make Mama Mike some tea. She's clearly distraught." Faridah quickly left the room to do as she was told.

Athen quickly turned back to Mama. "What is the problem? Is Mike okay? I've never seen you like this."

Mike's mum wracked her brain for a different story she could tell to get out of this embarrassing situation. "Em ... neighbour, I had a very bad dream early this morning, a terrible, terrible nightmare. I haven't dreamt in years, and to dream that our dear chief had been struck dead by lightning in the market square was a nightmare that left me crying."

"God forbid! May we not see evil," Athen interjected, swearing and clicking his right thumb and middle finger.

Mike's mother continued. "Have you seen Chief? Is he alright? His leg, his hands... Is everything okay with him?" she asked, trying to make her lie sound more credible.

"Oh, Mama Mike, I was with the chief last night, and..." He left his voice drift off as Faridah walked in with a big mug of tea on a tray.

She handed it to Mike's mum, who looked up, smiled at her with quivering lips, and said, "Thank you, my daughter."

"Thank you, Mama," Faridah replied sweetly and then turned to Athen. "Uncle, if you need me, I'm in the backyard hanging up the washing I did this morning at the stream." She genuflected lightly to her uncle, said goodbye to Mike's mother, then turned around and left the living room.

Once she was gone, Faridah's uncle tried reassuring his guest that she had nothing to worry about. "I'm sure Chief is alive, hale, and hearty. Please don't worry. As they say, bad dreams often mean the exact opposite: good fortunes. But to put your mind at rest because I can clearly see that you believe your nightmare, I'll go past Chief's house on my way to the farm to say hello, and if he's not alright, I'll definitely come tell you. I promise you."

"Okay, I'd appreciate that. I can't rest until I know that my nightmare isn't true."

"You have nothing to worry about, Mama Mike, I assure you."

With that, Mike's mum gulped her tea, thanked her neighbour profusely, and left.

As she walked home, confused and feeling embarrassed by her uncharacteristic visit to Athen's house so early in the morning, and all for nothing as it turned out, she kept wondering if Mike had not been imagining things. *What is going on with my dear son? Is Samantha getting to him? Is Faridah getting to him? Or are there other women haunting him? Looks like his heart and mind are conniving to play dirty tricks on him. How else could he have seen a drowning that never took place? How?* She hissed and breathed out heavily as her thoughts raced back and forth.

For the love of God, I don't understand what happened to Mike this morning. I don't understand it at all. I've never known him to act so strange. Mama Mike was so wrapped up in her thoughts that she hardly realized that she'd reached her home until her son rushed out to meet her.

"Mama!"

She hissed and looked away, a little upset. "Faridah is home," she told her son, throwing him an embarrassed look. "What a fool I made of myself this morning." She walked past Mike and threw herself down on a chair in the living room.

"Hunh? No kidding? She can't be! I mean ... she's home? How?" Mike asked in complete disbelief. Standing and looking down on her with his hands on his hips, he couldn't help but argue. "Mama, she can't be! Not possible! I saw her go into the water! I swam the length and breadth of that stream. I called her name at the top of my voice more times than you've called my name in thirty-two years! Where could she have been? Why didn't she answer my calls? Why? Why, Mama? Tell me."

His mum raised her hand to hush him. "Well, Mike, I don't know what to say. You know the Three-Shoulder stream is vast. Maybe she was at the end of one of the stream's shoulders and you just didn't see her and she didn't hear you. Maybe she was at the deep end and didn't hear you. You must remember that we locals swim better than fish. But she *was*, undoubtedly, at the stream this morning because while I was at their house, she

141

mentioned her trip there this morning to do laundry." She sighed. "So, what am I supposed to think now?"

He shrugged and then shook his head. "Well, okay, good. At least she confirmed she was indeed at the stream, so you know I'm not lying or crazy when I say she was there."

"My son, what's important is that she's alive and safe, and no one else knows what you told me. Please, let's put this incident behind us now," she pleaded, tired from it all, wanting to get on with her morning chores, and happy that the girl she wanted as a wife for her son was alive and well after all. "What would you like for breakfast?" Mike felt the need to again dispel any concern his mother might have about the state of his mind.

"Mum, listen, I'm not crazy. I know what I saw this morning. I know you don't want to believe me because it sounds like fiction, or else you think I may be mistaken, and I don't blame you. But I know what I saw. Why would I want to endanger my own life by diving into that stream to save—"

He cut himself off, seeing the exhausted look on his mother's face and her clear desire to drop the subject. Trying to convince her was clearly a waste of time, so he gave up and threw his hands up into the air.

"Never mind," he said, and walked past her, very upset and just as dumbfounded as his mother clearly was even though she was trying hard not to show it.

Mike had no appetite for food and told his mother so. Then he went to the backyard and spread his laundry to dry on the line before locking himself in his room for a couple of hours. Recalling the stream incident in his mind, he was just as certain as he'd always been about what he'd seen and hated that he was being made to feel like he was hallucinating. "That incident was not an illusion," he said to himself. "Faridah has some explaining to do."

Tired of being cooped up with his thoughts, he showered and decided to go for a walk to clear his head. Suddenly, he felt like he was lost in the village as well as his thoughts about Faridah and how she was beginning to torture his emotions. He walked with his head bowed and did not hear the footsteps coming up behind him.

"What were you doing at the stream so early this morning?"

He almost jumped out of his skin at the sound of her voice, turning around abruptly and looking her in the eyes. "Faridah! Why did you do that?" he asked, angrily. "I want to know right now. Why?"

"Do what?" she asked, surprised.

"What do you mean 'do what?' You know very well what I'm talking about. Why did you play that prank on me at the stream this morning? Please don't pretend you don't know what I'm talking about or try to make a fool of me. Do you realize that you scared the hell out of me? Do you know how much my mother panicked and fell into despair, rushing to your house early this morning to tell your uncle so that a search party could go out to find you in the waters? I thought you'd drowned, and for the life of me, I still don't understand how or why you disappeared for twenty minutes!"

Mama Mike's strange visit to their house this morning all made sense to her now: the frantic banging on their door, and Mama's stammering look of disbelief when she'd stepped into the living room to say good morning. Faridah looked straight and deeply into Mike's eyes and gave him a smile of regret.

"I didn't play any pranks on you, Mike," she said softly. "Yes, I went to the stream, but I go there very early every Saturday morning. I didn't even know you were there. I wasn't expecting you." Her large eyes were pleading for understanding.

"Okay, so where were you then for twenty minutes?"

"I was there at the stream," she answered, still holding his gaze.

"Where? Deep underwater? I don't get it."

"I was there," she said again. "I was there."

Mike was more confused. Exasperated, he rolled his eyes and then shut them, running his hands over his head briefly before bringing them down and resting them on his hips. "Did you not hear me calling you?"

"Yes, I did," she answered, her large eyes still fixed on his.

"I don't understand, Faridah. Where were you hiding and why didn't you answer?"

She looked away and off into space then. "Because even though I don't really know you, I trust you." She looked at him sympathetically and then stepped closer. "You're a good human being, Uncle Chi... Mike. I like you, and I trust you."

Frustrated, Mike threw his hands up in the air again. "This doesn't make sense." He looked at her for a long moment, warm feelings of deep affection rushing over him despite her lack of clarity. "I just feel so stupid now ... diving in to try and save you while you were right there, or not there, or whatever, laughing at me ... enjoying my act of stupidity."

"Mike please. I wasn't laughing at you. I just wished I'd been able to stop you from diving in."

Mike gave up and decided to simply walk on. He was beginning to get a headache and was angry at his own folly. Faridah followed, walking along beside him. Mike stayed quiet, trying to come to terms with the fact that he was apparently starting to fall for a girl he didn't know, and worse, one that had made him look ridiculous to both himself and his mother.

Rubbing his eyes roughly, he then stole a quick glance to the side and found himself looking into her beautiful eyes once more. His heart melted. Suddenly, he felt like wrapping his arms around her. He felt like protecting her—from what, exactly, he didn't know. Faridah just seemed sweetly vulnerable in a strange way. He could feel it deep in his soul. He knew that further prodding wouldn't get Faridah to tell him anything before she was ready. She clearly was not one to be pushed into action. She'd already made that clear when he'd found her with the rooster in their backyard and tried to get her to join the party.

Mike stopped and turned to face her directly. "Listen, let's just forget it for now. I'm happy you didn't drown. I'm happy to see you. You have no idea how scared I was this morning."

Faridah smiled and nodded, and then they both carried on walking. Although Mike had many other questions to ask about the incident, he didn't ask them. The riddle might be driving him crazy, but it was better to let it rest for now. So, he changed the subject.

"Where are you off to, Faridah?"

"Just to see a school friend."

They continued walking in silence for a while, though Mike looked at her in disbelief every now and then. He liked her walking beside him. She was beautiful and elegant. *The sort of woman any man would be proud to have by his side,* he caught himself thinking. But there was something else too—something magnetic about her that he just couldn't put his finger on.

Thinking about what he'd done at the stream that morning, he began to relax and even smile. *"I'm losing my mind, aren't I?"*

"Mike?" Her soft voice jolted him from his reverie.

"Yes, Faridah?"

She stopped and blocked his path. "Are you alright?" She peered into his eyes. "Why did you just say that you're losing your mind?"

He looked at her and then quickly away. The genuine concern in her lovely voice seemed very romantic to him. "Yes, yes. I'm fine," he said, sending her a quick look and a smile. "Something just crossed my mind, that's all."

"You seem lost in your thoughts. I don't think you're here with me at all."

"I am. Forgive me. I was just thinking about my home in Chicago."

To prove that he was indeed there with her, despite the lie he'd just told, as their walk continued, he asked her about herself, the polytechnic, and her uncle, and shared his own interest in her support of the farmers but avoided mentioning his intention to donate to the college.

He noticed that she was evasive when he asked her about her hopes to settle down to marriage and a family, but he put that down to her uncle perhaps not approving just yet, or to an existing boyfriend, or to some pending engagement. Faridah also asked Mike a lot of questions, and he found himself sharing details of his life in Chicago with this young woman who was still a stranger to him, which surprised him. He had no clue why he trusted her, but for some strange reason, he did. He told her about his business, Clive, and even Samantha.

"You do wear your heart on your sleeve, don't you?" Faridah said, breaking his train of thought.

"Yes, I do, but I'm not sure it's always a good thing. As you may have observed, it can lead to me doing things like diving in to save you this morning, even though I could have lost my life in the process."

"Please don't be offended about this morning," Faridah said, regret heavy in her voice.

Mike looked at her and smiled. If only she knew how difficult it was to stay angry at her. "Are you in a hurry? I mean, were you in a hurry to meet your school friend?"

"Well, not really. Why do you ask?"

"I want to keep talking with you. I want us to sit and talk. That was why I came to the stream this morning. I just wanted an opportunity to chat with you."

"Are you still angry with me about this morning, hoping to scold me?"

"No, no, I'm not angry, and I think I've already scolded you enough. I just want us to talk."

Mike looked around and saw some big trees lining the front of a house up ahead in the distance. They could easily provide a huge area of shade where he reckoned they could sit and talk for a little while.

"Come. Let's go over there," he said, pointing and then taking her hand. Together, they walked briskly over to the lovely shaded area. Faridah watched him closely as he looked around and then ran to fetch a block of cement, setting it down under one of the trees and tapping on it. "Sit down. I'll be right back." Faridah did as she was asked. Then he ran back to grab another block from the nearby pile, and brought it back, placing it down beside her, angled enough to enable him to look into her eyes.

Mike sat down and sighed gently then, looking at her. "Faridah?"

"Nnnnn?" She cocked her head to the side and looked at him.

"I realize that I don't know you, and I don't know what happened this morning, but it doesn't matter."

Not wanting to conceal his feelings, but afraid of her response, he chose his words carefully as he explained that he was beginning to like her a lot and how devastated he would have been had she drowned this morning. He spoke again about Samantha and what had been lacking in their relationship, his guilt over having hurt her, his desire to find a life partner, and perhaps, even one from the village.

Faridah listened intently with her eyes fixed on his face. It was slightly breezy, and the flutter of the leaves overhead as she sat with him in the shade was so beautiful that the whole scene felt surreal. She was reading him like a book. She liked that he was a gentleman, his candidness, and even the difficulty he sometimes showed in expressing how he felt. Faridah liked him, but she also felt sorry for him and wasn't sure he'd understand that. So, she told him a little more about herself, why she'd chosen agricultural science, how she'd come to be living with her uncle, and her desire to get into public service in the future, preferably with the Ministry of Agriculture.

Mike noticed that there was no mention of a boyfriend, fiancé, or husband, and it delighted him immensely. He wasn't sure how he would have handled the knowledge of a man already in Faridah's life.

"You sound very grounded, Faridah, and I love that. So, I would like us to explore this friendship further." He took her hands and squeezed them gently. "Would you like to do that too?"

Faridah was scared, but tightened her grip on his hands. "Mike, what is it you want to explore?"

"Friendship, of course, but also the possibility of getting close, real close ... the possibility of a relationship."

"That's going to be difficult for me. I've never had a boyfriend. I can't. I'm not—"

"I understand," he said quickly, interrupting her, "and I promise not to rush you." He thought he finally understood. He was dealing with a virgin eager to maintain that status, but he was more than willing to respect both her wishes and time. He gently rubbed her hands. "Faridah, please don't get me wrong. You're an exceptionally beautiful girl. You're elegant, well-mannered, and from a good family. I like you very much. I liked you from the moment I saw you in the backyard with that rooster, and to be honest with you, I still don't know why exactly. All I know is that you unsettle me, but it's got nothing to do with getting you in bed with me. You're different in a way I can't explain. So, please don't ask me to explain my feelings for you because at this point in time, I really can't. I don't even know what they are. Do I make any sense at all?"

"No, Mike. But it's okay because I know I don't make sense to you either."

Mike chuckled and raised her hands up in his own and pressed them against his chest. Faridah smiled, seeming to be moved almost passionately by this, but there was a hint of regret as well.

"I don't want to hurt you, Mike, so ... I need you to promise me that, whatever happens, you won't hate me for the rest of your life."

"Hate you? Not a chance in hell." He kissed her hands then and felt fluttering in his stomach like he'd never felt with any other woman. "So, we start as friends?" he asked, his eagerness for confirmation clear in his expression.

She nodded. "Yes. We start as friends."

Relieved, Mike's heart pounded with excitement. He shut his eyes and kissed the back of her hands over and over before looking into her eyes once more. "I have an idea. Why don't we do something private and fun this weekend and start getting to know each other gradually?"

Faridah accepted his invitation to meet again at the Three-Shoulder stream next Saturday, which would be his last one before returning to the US on Sunday. He proposed that they do some laundry and swim together. "Maybe you can teach me the sort of deep-diving disappearing act you did this morning." He winked at her. "I'd really love to try that."

"You're sure?" Farida looked at him like he was a lunatic.

"Of course. As long as we're together, we'll be fine, and knowing what an expert diver you are now, I'm sure I'll be in good hands."

Faridah laughed. "Oh, Mike, Mike..." She sighed, clutching his hands tight and looking into his eyes.

Before she could say anything against the idea, Mike quickly spoke up. "Okay, let's get going. Your friend will be waiting for you."

Mike stood up then, and pulled her up to her feet. Faridah dusted down the back of her dress, and together, they continued their walk. When they got to the T-junction leading to the road, Mike moved to embrace her but restrained himself at the last moment.

Faridah noticed and looked down shyly. They said their goodbyes, and then Mike stood and watched her walk on. After a minute or so, Faridah turned around and saw Mike still standing there, watching her. She waved, he waved back, and then she continued on her way.

That night, Mike realized that he hadn't spoken with Clive since his call on the night of the party. He didn't feel the need to give him any update until after his next meeting with Faridah, but his heart got the better of him as his thoughts turned to Faridah. He picked up his phone and called his friend. Mike told Clive that he was afraid he was falling in love with a stranger, who up to that moment had been like a mirage, a shadow. He described what had happened at the stream and the drama that followed with his mother, his subsequent meeting with Faridah later that afternoon, and how after their conversation he'd been left even more bewildered.

"I don't know if her elusiveness and seeming weirdness are what I find so annoyingly attractive," he told Clive. "I just know that she's different in a way that pleases my senses, you know? Like a puzzle I need to solve that something inside me wants to possess ... to unravel. You know?"

Mike struggled to understand his feelings and to express them in a way that Clive would understand. Clive listened without interrupting his friend, and when Mike paused for a long time, awaiting his friend's opinion, he did not disappoint, advising him candidly.

"I don't want you being hurt, buddy. I hear intensity in your voice, and I don't know why, but something isn't sitting well with me about your story so far. I know you've always liked the thought of a girl from home, but please take your time. I think you have to take the coming opportunity of a second meeting with her at the stream to lay it all out on the table again. She must lay her cards on the table. No tricks, no loose-woman tendencies. You're not compelling her to do anything, but you need to know if you can truly start to build a relationship, and if not, I'm sorry ... but you'll need to move on."

Mike agreed with his friend, but he also couldn't blame Faridah for anything. After all, he was a stranger to her. What right did he have to expect her to open up her heart when they were barely acquaintances? Mike confessed to Clive that his straight-to-the-point advice felt like a whack on the head. It made him wonder if he was engaging in "puppy love," being foolish, immature, and acting like a thirteen-year-old schoolboy who's just gained the freedom to meet a girl for the first time.

"Hey, buddy, tell me... Do I sound like a thirty-two-year-old simpleton?"

Clive laughed for some time. He could feel his friend's dilemma. "No. I just bought you a present for your fifteenth birthday." They both laughed, then Clive offered some calming words. "But hey, listen: Follow your heart."

For the next few days, Mike rehearsed all he'd say to Faridah at their next meeting on Saturday.

Faridah was excited to meet Mike. She felt elated that this "Uncle Chichi," whom all the young ladies in the village were falling over themselves to get to know, had chosen her for a potential relationship. She had always preferred to be reclusive, but Mike was pulling her out to chat and play, and more important, he treated her like an equal. But she wasn't quite sure how to handle all of that just yet. Today would be special though; she could feel it. Faridah put together her laundry and packed a bowl of assorted fruits, a bottle of groundnuts, and water.

She arrived at the stream just before six, did her washing, and began to bathe nude in the stream. She was at the far end of it, on its left shoulder, when she saw Mike walking down the slope. She swam up close to him and beckoned him to join her. His mind flashed back to the morning he'd watched her disappear into the waters.

"Where's your laundry?" he asked after they had exchanged pleasantries.

"Done. Look over there." She pointed to a large plastic bag that was half full of wet and neatly folded clothes. "Finished the washing not long ago. Come on. Join me." She beckoned him with her hand.

"No, you go on and swim. I'll sit by this bank and watch you for a while," he told her. *Besides,* he thought, *you're completely nude.* He didn't feel comfortable being close to her in that state. He remembered what he'd assumed were her fears during their last conversation and wanted to show her that he'd meant it when he said that his intention was not to take advantage of her, and that he wouldn't rush her. He was going to respect her nudity until she was ready to be in a serious relationship, assuming they got that far.

"Just warn me when you're coming out of the water, and I'll look away."

Faridah laughed. "Okay, I'll let you know. By the way, I brought some fruits, groundnuts, and water. They're in my bag next to the plastic bag. Please take whatever you want." Before Mike could respond, she slid into the water and disappeared.

Mike sat on the turf by the bank, last night's conversation with Clive reverberating in his head as he watched Faridah swim. She wriggled in the water like a mermaid, and it mesmerized him. She dove under the water and came up several times and waved at him.

"Why are you looking at me, rather than swimming with me?"

"You're absolutely gorgeous, that's why," Mike called back, waving.

"Are you afraid, Mike? Come join me. I have something to show you." Mike promised himself that he wasn't going to swim with her while she was nude. *She'll have to ether wear something or be content with me just watching.* Aside from respecting her, he couldn't take the chance of a villager seeing them both in that state. The news would spread like wildfire in the village, and the gossip and derision would be too much for his mother, Faridah, or her family to handle once he was gone.

"Just let me watch you for a little while. I'll join you later," he shouted back. Then in a split second, she disappeared under the waters, and in the twinkle of an eye, appeared again at the extreme right shoulder of the stream. Mike watched in utter bewilderment. It felt like magic. It was the fastest he'd ever even heard of a human being able to swim. She repeated the feat, disappearing and appearing at the left shoulder of the stream in a flash. Mike was stunned. *My goodness! How does she do that?*

After about fifteen minutes in the water, Faridah swam up to him by the bank where he sat, and without warning, emerged from of the water. Mike looked away.

"Faridah, we agreed you'd warn me. Please put some clothes on. Please."

She ignored him and sat down next to him, pulling her knees up together to her chest. "It's okay," she said gently. "There's nothing to see. I'm covered. And I know you have a lot of questions you want to ask me."

"Yes," said Mike, still with his head turned away from her. "But I need you to put something on first."

"I don't want to. I mean… I don't feel like it… I mean… This is how I am."

Mike's instinct told him that he was wasting his time but pressed her nonetheless. "Faridah, you need to wear something, or at least tie a wrapper up to your chest. Please. If someone walks in on us, you know the villagers would enjoy making up a fictional and exaggerated story about our encounter, and your uncle, my mother, and you, in particular, would have a real hard time living with it and trying to correct the wrong impression."

"I won't. I don't want to. Now, can we talk, please? I'm getting hot sitting out here."

Confused, Mike instinctively turned to face her. "You're getting hot while it's so breezy and cool under this tree? Strange. What would happen to you then were the sun out at this moment? Would you melt before my eyes before I'd found the time to go fetch a lorry-load of ice blocks?" He smiled, searching her eyes for some answer.

Faridah was silent. She stared at him, squinting like she was indeed being hit by rays of sunlight. Mike knew when a topic was a lost cause, so he looked straight ahead at the waters and laid bare his feelings, holding nothing back.

"So, Faridah, I don't know where this might lead me, lead us, but I owe it to myself to be honest, tell you how I feel, and be open to being either accepted or rejected by you."

Faridah was quiet, just staring at him with squinted eyes, so he continued. "Now, I want you to be as completely honest with me as I have been with you. Tell me about yourself, about your boyfriend if you have one, about what you want out of life, and also why you're sitting nude with no shame whatsoever beside a man you barely know." His tone was quiet but firm, as he refused to let himself look directly at her.

Faridah finally drew her glance away from him and stared at the stream. The breeze had picked up strength and was sending the slightly fishy smell of the water mixed with that of the vegetation all around them. It was cool, calm, and peaceful. The water had a subtle music to its flow as it softly splashed against its banks, echoing all around and mixing with the whistling sound of birds and insects. Mike patiently waited for an answer. He felt like he was on a different planet, one with two inhabitants only: himself and the stubborn but very beautiful woman seated next to him.

"I don't know what 'nude' means, but clothes are abnormal to me," Faridah said. Mike shot her a look of shock. She continued. "I accepted your invitation because I want to be honest with you. And I've been trying to find the best way to explain it. Wait here," she ordered, and before he could open his mouth to ask what she meant by that, she ran forward, stretched herself out with both hands over her head, and with her head bent, dove into the water. He sat there and watched the stream, looking out for her.

She was gone for a long time, and even with the last incident fresh in his mind, Mike soon began to feel uncomfortable with the length of time she had been gone, and called out, "Faridah?" It was dead quiet all around him except for the bleating of crickets and countless other insects. "Faridah!" he called again, looking at the waters from left to right.

He was about to call out a third time when she emerged, holding something wrapped in a cloth. Walking up the bank, dripping water everywhere, she returned to the spot where she'd sat earlier and took her position again beside him, with both knees pulled up to cover her breasts like it was the most natural thing in the world to do.

Mike was confused and looked away. "Faridah, why can't you please put on some clothes or wrap the towel around you?"

When she ignored him, he decided on a different approach. Reaching into his bag, he pulled out a bath sheet, opened it, and wrapped it around her. She said nothing. She just casually threw the towel off her shoulder like it irritated her skin.

Mike picked up the towel and wrapped it around her again, this time with a jovial warning: "If you won't stayed covered up, I won't listen to anything you have to say. I'll just leave."

Frowning, Faridah looked at him as though he were making no sense at all, but she left the towel wrapped around her shoulders, wriggling in discomfort from time to time.

Mike turned to look into her eyes. He'd noticed her discomfort under the towel, but he ignored it and smiled. *"Now,* we can talk."

Faridah brought her face close to his, so close that he could feel the warmth of her breath on his face. "Mike, look into my eyes. What do you see?"

Mike slowly ran his eyes from her forehead to her lips and left his gaze there, swearing softly under his breath. *God, I want to kiss her so badly!* He was feeling almost desperate to pull her close and have them dissolve into each other. It felt like torture.

As Faridah clearly wasn't moving until he did as he was told, Mike ran his eyes from her lips, over the tip of her nose, and to her eyes, but he couldn't seem to make himself stare into them. He took one quick look and then kept his gaze fixated on her brows, too afraid that what she'd see in his own eyes would betray him.

Without warning then, Faridah sat back, adjusted herself, and quickly shot out her hands, opened them, and then turned back to him with the loveliest diamond tiara Mike had seen in his life glistening in her hands, right before his eyes.

"Faridah! What is... Oh no! You're not a pirate, are you?" He gazed into her eyes now. "Is that the secret? You steal jewels and come hide them deep down underwater?"

Faridah didn't answer, remaining silent with her eyes fixed on the tiara.

"Where did you get this from?" Mike asked, hoping she had not stolen them and completely at a loss for what to think. Faridah remained silent. Contemplative.

"How long have you been doing this, Faridah?" Mike waited for an answer, an explanation, anything really. But when she finally spoke, it wasn't to answer his questions.

"Hold it," Faridah suddenly ordered, holding out the tiara towards him. Mike was apprehensive, hesitant, and if he was being honest, a little irritated as well. She had not answered any of his questions.

"Hold it," she said again, thrusting her hands close to his face now.

Mike took the jewel slowly and carefully, and almost dropped it when he felt some sort of current rush through his hands. "My God, Faridah, what is this? Where did you get this from?"

Mike touched the peak of the crown then and felt more current pass through his fingers and all the way up to his elbow. "And why does it feel electric? Is it some sort of gadget?" Faridah was silent, just staring at the man seated next to her for a long moment before finally sighing, nodding slightly, and explaining in a soft whisper.

"I'm a 'rebirth,' Mike. What the villagers call 'reincarnated.' I've been reborn as a water being, an Ogbanje."

Mike frowned, still clutching the tiara as he looked at her. "The villagers say you are an Ogbanje? Some sort of mermaid?"

"They do not 'say' it. My nature says it."

Mike had never believed in what he called "the famous ogbanje fable," which he had always heard as a kid when he'd visited his hometown. But now, seated close to a young woman who claimed to be one ... he felt like he had gone completely crazy. Delusional. He withdrew from her a bit so that he could look at her with clearer eyes. Of all explanations he'd expected from her, this was by far the weirdest.

"Unfortunately," Faridah continued, interrupting his thoughts, "though I was born to earthly parents, I still have a life in the water world, and there, I belong to the royal family and was betrothed as an infant. Saturday is the only day I'm able to come spend quality time with my family, and that is why I come as early as I do, before the sun rises when I can, so that we're not disturbed by the other villagers. I can sing and dance with my family when I'm here because it's always like a reunion. I can communicate with the fishes, the insects, and reptiles that dwell here, in and around the stream. We're all family."

Mike shut his eyes and shook his head. This was really beginning to feel like a dream. He pinched himself to be sure he was awake, unsure whether he should be in awe or utterly despondent.

Faridah continued. "When you came upon me last Saturday, you may have seen me playing around that tree." She pointed to the tree Mike had watched her chasing something around. "In any case, my family here says that there are a series of appeasements I must make if I want to cut ties with them and be set free to have a normal earthly life. Until I met you, I wasn't sure if I'd ever want to be free from my world here. I love this family..."

She paused for a while and then continued with sadness in her tone. "You also live in the USA, and I'm afraid I might free myself from the world here, which truly makes me happy and content, only to find that I've just been chasing after shadows on earth once you're gone."

Faridah smiled softly and looked past Mike, scanning the breadth of the stream behind him. Suddenly, she started wriggling again. Mike was confused and unsure about what was going on, but as he watched her beautiful body sway from the side, he began to feel fear. He looked at the tiara again, and then held it back out to her. She sensed his fear and slowly took it from him.

"This is my crown, Mike. It's okay to touch it and feel it. Don't be afraid. The vibration you feel is the waters hydro-electric current. In the water, it doesn't give off any vibration or shock," she said. "All human beings have the energy that attracts or dispels currents, animate or inanimate. That's why you can feel either a negative or positive vibe from anyone you meet, even when they've not said a word to you."

Mike was numb with disbelief. Faridah's words sounded like something from a sci-fi movie, and he wished she would suddenly tell him that she was just joking.

"You're an Ogbanje? A rebirth?" he asked again as though in search of reconfirmation. "Truly?"

155

As a child, he had heard about the elaborate ceremonies associated with casting out mermaids and cleansing families of reincarnations. He'd once even gone to watch such a ceremony at the market square. The villagers had described it as "the release of a teenager from her water world." But he'd never believed in all that "rubbish," and never in his wildest dreams had he thought he'd meet and get to know one this closely. Suddenly, the tiara fascinated him. He gently took it from Faridah once again and ran his fingers around its rim, which was beautifully studded with a rainbow of precious gems. Everything he'd observed about Faridah began to make sense, particularly the incident at the stream the previous week, her deep-diving skills, and her ability to be lost in the water forever. But it was also explained her aversion to clothes while at the stream, as well as her wriggles and dances. Everything made sense to him now, except of course, that she was human.

Still looking at the tiara, he noticed that she was wriggling again under the towel. "Why are you uncomfortable under the towel when you wear clothes all the time?"

"It's because I'm here. I'm one with the water here, just like a fish."

Mike looked away. His heart broke with guilt and pain. He could see that she felt trapped under the towel, but he just couldn't let her take it off because having her sit next to him nude would be more problematic for both of them, and that was a chance he wasn't going to take.

"I'm sorry about the towel, Faridah. I really hope you understand why I need you covered while you're seated next to me."

"I do, Mike, and I don't blame you."

"Tell me," he said then, "does your uncle or anyone in the village know you're an Ogbanje?"

"Only my uncle and the oracle priest of our village know. I fell seriously ill two years ago and was close to death. The oracle priest was consulted when no medicine seemed to make me feel better. The priest told my uncle to bring me to the Three-Shoulder stream to meet my family. As soon as we got here, and some incantations were said, the priest carried me to the edge of the river over there, as I was too sick to walk or even talk."

Faridah pointed to the point of the stream where the three shoulders converged. "Once there, he laid me down in the shallow waters, and to my uncle's surprise, I immediately swam away. I didn't resurface till late at night the following day, at which time, I walked home naked."

This was too much for Mike to process. He handed her back the tiara, and with it back in her hand, he saw her smiling at something in the water. He searched its surface ahead for what it could be but saw nothing.

Then Faridah looked back at him pensively as silence fell between them. Mike looked down and stayed silent as she kept her gaze on him, and it was as though she could read his thoughts.

After a long moment, she spoke in the calmest voice Mike had heard in his life. "You're judging me, Mike, aren't you? Everyone avoids people like me. No man wants to be in a relationship with Ogbanjes like me. Anything negative that befalls my family is blamed on me. Be honest, Mike, I'm not your kind of woman, am I?"

Mike was embarrassed at being caught out. His head was giddy with this sudden self-awareness, as he had indeed been silently asking himself many questions: *Who is she? What is she? How would society view me? What would Clive and my other friends in the US think? People would say that I've completely lost the plot.*

This was unchartered territory, and he didn't know how to deal with it. He remained silent for a while longer and then took Faridah's hands in his and squeezed them gently as he slowly looked up and into her eyes. "Who am I to judge you, Faridah?" he asked softly.

Even seated right next to her, all Mike could see was a beautiful young woman who wanted nothing more than just to be happy. Just like him. *We're both victims of societal expectation, norms, and beliefs, dear Faridah,* he silently told himself.

Faridah smiled briefly and then looked sad. Mike's words had comforted her, but she couldn't trust them. Why would he'd be any different? She suspected that he was in denial about the difficulty of being in a relationship with a woman deemed possessed and treated like an outcast ... at least until she agreed to take part in an elaborate ceremony, or several, that would require her to dig the earth to find the "evil seeds" or charms that were understood to be responsible for her odd behaviour.

Faridah began to wriggle more frequently, and Mike gently squeezed her hands and then let go of them. Holding the tiara, she wriggled out of the towel then, flung it to the ground, and in a flash, dove back into the stream and disappeared. Mike just sat there transfixed. At this point, he couldn't say he yet believed in rebirth or reincarnation. But "belief" was subjective.

One thing he was sure of, however, was that of all the challenges he'd faced in his lifetime, nothing compared to this one with Faridah.

"Mike?" Faridah's call brought him out of his trance. He looked up and saw her waving from the deep end of the stream. "Do you hate me?" she called. He shook his head and waved back, not sure why she'd asked that. *Hate? How can I hate what I don't even understand?* he silently asked himself. She swam up close to him.

"You wanted the truth, Mike."

"Yes. But this is so unreal. I don't know what to do with this truth. I'm wondering if I should have sought it in the first place."

Faridah giggled like a child and disappeared into the waters and then came back up, but this time, half her body remained in the water, her hands slowly moving back and forth under it at her sides, creating soft waves.

"What do you seek now, Mike? Earth or water?" she asked, looking at him with a sympathetic expression.

"I'm still shocked, Faridah. Can you please come sit here? Let's talk. I really need to know what I should do. What *we* can do."

"You're sure you want to do anything about this?"

Mike rubbed and shook his head in utter confusion. "Yes. No, I don't know, Yes, maybe. I need to really understand all this."

"Mike," Faridah called out in that romantic voice of hers that completely melted his heart, "don't you see now that I am not what you need?" With these words, she somersaulted back into the waters and was gone.

"Faridah!" He stood up then, calling her name over and over, but his voice only echoed back to him.

Mike sat there all alone for more than an hour. Faridah didn't come back up. He gradually felt himself calm as it dawned on him that she was not lost, and she hadn't drowned. He felt it strange to admit, even to himself, that Faridah had gone where she felt happiest, but it was also very sad that that place was not at his side.

Tired and sad, he got up and took a long final look at the water. It felt

158

like a huge part of him was under there with her, and he wished the rest of him could be as well. With a sigh, Mike shook his head then, packing his bag and solemnly beginning his walk back to the village. He hadn't managed to do the laundry he had brought with him, so he decided he'd just do it at the back of their house. He was due to fly back to the USA at midnight the next day and had some packing to do as well.

Back home, he tried to act normal, quickly telling his mother that he'd changed his mind about washing the clothes down at the stream to save time because he'd remembered that he needed to go out to buy some local spices to take with him to the US.

Mama Mike took one look at her son and knew all wasn't well. He looked exhausted and down. "Mike, you're not looking yourself. What's the matter? Have you seen Faridah? Have you told her you'll be flying out tomorrow or do you want me to send Nissy to tell her?"

"No, no, Mama. It's okay. I'm well, and Faridah knows that I leave tomorrow. I've already told her."

Mike's mother was delighted. "Oh, you have met properly then?"

"Yes, yes, I have. I actually met her at the stream this morning."

"Oh, that's good." Mama clapped, her eyes lighting up with curious longing for a bit of gossip from her son. "And? Well? Tell me what you think about her?"

"She's a lovely young woman, Mama. And you're right; she's very shy too." Mike wouldn't say more, but his mother was dying to know if he'd felt some chemistry with Faridah.

"And? How did she feel?"

"Nne, please, can we talk about it later?" Mike faked a smile, squeezed his mother's shoulders lightly, and quickly walked past her before she could ask another question.

Mike's mother knew that whatever was bothering her son had to do with Faridah. Although she was thrilled at the news that they'd met this morning and spent time together, she didn't like the air about Mike. *Faridah is a nice and well-brought up child; she'd never hurt Mike.* Mama was sure of this, and so it had to be something else. Mike's mother hoped that Samantha was not making her son miserable. She knew that it would be abominable to ask Faridah anything about Mike. If Mike grew to love her, and they both agreed to have a future together, Mama knew that the respectful thing would be for her to go speak with Athen. It would then be Athen's place to talk to his niece and find out how she felt about Mike. Mama Mike decided to let things be for now. She'd soon find out more though, she promised herself.

Mike immediately washed the clothes in their backyard while Faridah played on his mind. He took a bath, and then went to the market to shop for artefacts and some local spices. He needed to avoid raising his mother's suspicion any further by sulking. So, he promised himself to cheer up, make his mother happy the last night of his vacation, give her the donation for Faridah's polytechnic and another for the village clinic, and steer their conversations to any topic other than Faridah.

Later in the evening, Mike called Clive. He wanted to reconfirm his flight details, so his friend could pick him up from the airport Monday night. Mike was not in the mood to discuss Faridah. He wanted to wait until he arrived in the US, but Clive was inquisitive.

"Hey, bro! So ... how did it go with Faridah this morning?"

Mike was quiet for a while. Then he smiled and chuckled into the phone. "Wacky, crazy, fiction, life on Mars. I'm hydroplaning..." Mike sighed loudly. "You wouldn't believe the education Faridah gave me today. I grew up today, my dear friend. You have no idea!" Mike paused and then decided he didn't want to relive this morning's trip to the stream. "Do me a favour, bro."

Clive sniffed. "Yes?" He could feel Mike's resistance.

"Can we talk about Faridah when I return? At the moment, I just need to be sure I haven't gone dodo in the head, as they say." He chuckled.

"Sure. If you need anything done here before you arrive, just let me know."

"Well, not before. But certainly once I arrive. Tell me, do you think you can be my psychiatrist for maybe a week?"

The two friends laughed. Clive caught the drift, and even though something was bothering him about Mike's tone, he tried to keep the humour going.

"Let's talk about my fees when you get here because something tells me that you'll be my most expensive patient yet."

"I sure will, and be warned, you'll be stuck with this patient for a long time."

Still laughing, they said their goodbyes and hung up. Mike was exceedingly grateful for Clive's friendship. He was looking forward to telling his friend about his experience with Faridah. Clive was the most potent psychedelic drug he needed in his life right now.

Mama could hear Mike's laughter ringing out from his room. She liked it when her son sounded happy. It had been a humid day, so at about seven-thirty, she sat with him on the balcony to enjoy the cool evening breeze and their last night together before he flew back to the US the next day.

Nne brought a tray with two ceramic plates with four large pieces of garden eggs on each, as well as some groundnut paste scooped onto the side. "Ni. Take." She handed a plate to Mike, set hers down, and went back to the kitchen to bring some glasses and drinking water in a plastic jug.

Mother and son munched on their snacks and chatted amicably. Mike heard more village gossip and local politics and made his mother promise to package some garden eggs and groundnut paste for him to take back with him to the US next time he visited. The evening slowly cooled off into night, and soon Nne was sleepy and began to yawn. Mike cleared the dishes, washed them, put them away, and then tidied the backyard. By the time he was finished, his mother was already in her room, so he simply called out a goodnight to her, locked the front door and windows, and returned to his room.

The next morning, Mike's final packing was interrupted by his mother's impatient call: "Mike! Mike! Mike!"

He immediately stopped packing, hurried into the living room, and was shocked to see Faridah standing there. A mischievous smile was playing on Mama's eyes and lips as she looked back and forth between her son and Faridah. Mike turned his head and looked directly at his mother, his expression quickly making it clear that he would like some privacy. So, she hastily disappeared into her room.

As soon as his mother was out of sight and hearing, he looked around as though to ensure Faridah had not brought along a water being or some other strange aquatic gift. He then quickly took her by the elbow and led her to a corner at the opposite end of the house from his mother's room.

"Good morning," Faridah said as soon as they reached their destination, breaking the silence between them.

"Good morning, Faridah! What a pleasant surprise to see you! To what do I owe the honour of this visit?"

"Nothing. I just came to give this to you," she said, dipping her hand into her dress pocket and retrieving something wrapped in banana leaves. Then taking his palms, she pressed the object into them, and then closed his hands over it, making it clear that he was not to open it now. Instinctively, Mike wanted to hold her close and lay her head on his chest, but something held him back. Instead, he simply stood there and gazed into her large eyes for a while.

"Thank you, Faridah," he said finally, distracted somewhat by the rapid beating of his heart. "But what is it?"

"It's something very special. You'll understand in time." Faridah looked down at the floor then, but Mike lifted her chin gently so she could look at him as he addressed her.

"You already gave me the best gift ever: your trust. You trusted me enough to reveal yourself to me, and that means the world."

Faridah smiled very sweetly, her large eyes glistening like polished crystal. "Do you, in the smallest way, understand me, Mike? Do you think you ever can? Or will?"

"I don't know," he said honestly, his voice gentle as he ran his right hand lightly over her left cheekbone, tracing the contours as he looked deeply into her eyes. "But standing here with you in this moment, it's not important. That's my bridge to cross, Faridah, not yours."

"Okay... Well, I wish you a safe journey, and lots of love and happiness. You deserve it." She rested her hand gently on his arm as he caressed her face, running his thumb softly along the bridge of her nose, her eyebrows, and then back to her cheek. Then he moved closer, embraced her, and pressed a kiss to her forehead.

Mike took a reluctant step back from her then and was surprised to see that her eyes had filled with tears. Pulling her close once more in a warm embrace, with her head finally resting on his chest, he closed his eyes and breathed deep. Her hair smelled of lavender, heated shea butter, the local black soap, and the stream. He wished he could just stay there forever, taking it all in.

"I wish you lots of love and happiness too, Faridah," he whispered.

She slowly pulled back from his embrace, turned around, and walked away from him, heading out to the backyard. Mike walked behind her and watched as she continued out of the gate—and out of his life—as his eyes filled with tears.

Back in his room, he unwrapped the banana leaves to reveal a large, glittering golden key with an antique head. Turning it over, he saw that something had been inscribed there in a lovely cursive script: *My Heart*.

Mike smiled and pressed the key to his heart. "Oh, Faridah, Faridah, Faridah..." he whispered, shutting his eyes. "I *must* leave today, but ... how can I leave your shadow behind?"

He sat on the bed for a while, running his fingers all over the key, wanting and even expecting to feel the same sort of vibration he'd felt from her aquatic crown at the stream, but he felt nothing. Examining it closely, he noticed that each time he turned it in his hand, the golden colour seemed to alter slightly, shimmering with shades of green, purple, and blue.

"I wonder where she got this key..." he muttered quietly to himself. "It doesn't look like it would unlock a door or chest... Maybe my mind is just playing tricks on me, and I'm seeing colours that are not truly there."

Shaking his head, he made himself wrap the key back up in its banana leaf and tucked it between his clothes at the bottom of his suitcase.

At midnight, Mike boarded his flight back to Chicago.

Clive had picked his friend up on time, and throughout the drive from the airport to Mike's place, the two friends had bantered about everything that had happened in Chicago in the more than three weeks since he'd left to vacation in his hometown.

Clive thought something was strange about his friend, as every now and then, he caught Mike lost in his thoughts, even though he seemed overly chatty, asking many questions as though he wanted to mask his inner turmoil by ensuring that the conversation remained fixed on Chicago.

Clive decided not to ask any questions about Faridah, as much as he was dying to know more. He knew his friend was in an emotionally delicate place and would confide in him when he was ready.

Back home, Mike was unpacking his suitcase when his phone rang. As soon as he picked it up, Samantha's lively voice came on the line.

"Hey, Mike, are you okay? I've been calling you and have left you messages on your home and mobile phones, but you never called back."

Mike had seen Samantha's messages but refused to listen to them, especially as he'd imagined them to be berating or accusatory. "I'm sorry, Samantha. I've only just returned from the village and—"

"Ah!" Samantha interrupted him excitedly. "No wonder then! How was your mum? And the village? Did you enjoy yourself?"

Samantha was the last person he wanted to speak with at this moment, so he decided to end the call quickly. "I'm sorry, Samantha. I must unpack and dash to the grocery store to get some food."

"Oh, you must be tired. Why don't you give me a list, and I'll pop by the stores and pick up what you need? And I tell you what: You can just relax. I'll be happy to make us a late dinner and just spend a quiet evening together. I know we ended things badly ... but I've had time to think things through, and I really do miss you, and I have so much to tell you, and—"

"No, no, Samantha. It's okay. I'll do my own shopping. Besides, I don't think it's a good idea having you shop and cook for me. Please, let's not complicate things."

"Complicate things? What do you mean complicate things?"

Mike was irritated. And as his mind darted to Faridah, he briefly shut his eyes, opened them, and then shook his head as if to clear away a hazy thought. Just as he was about to politely end the conversation, Samantha's next question jolted him.

"Is there someone else?"

Mike was silent, uncertain how to respond. An image of Faridah popped into his mind then, and he let out a long, slow breath. The beautiful water being in his village had changed his perception of love in an inexplicable way, and he felt vulnerable and emotionally fragile ... like his heart could break into a million pieces just trying to imagine life without her.

There was no basis for comparison between Faridah and Samantha, and even though he didn't know where things stood with Faridah, he was now certain, more than ever before, that Samantha was not the one for him. He reminded himself that Samantha deserved the respect of not being led on about the possibility of rekindling their relationship when he knew for certain now that this wouldn't happen.

Determined to end the conversation before it went further, with a tone as gentle but firm as he could muster, he said, "Yes, there's someone else. I'm in love with someone else."

"I see," Samantha hissed into the phone. "Well, good luck then. But I promise you, you'll never find a woman who'll treat you as good as I have." She hung up before Mike could wish her luck as well.

Mike had been feeling like a lost lamb ever since he'd stepped into his house. Samantha's call was like a torch in a dark forest. Admitting he was in love with Faridah was as surprising to him as it was liberating. Suddenly, he felt like Samantha had helped to lift another heavy weight from his shoulders and given him both additional clarity and the confidence to face the unknown with Faridah. He hadn't welcomed Samantha's call, but he was now grateful for it.

Mike tried settling back down to his life in Chicago, but it felt empty. He missed his village, and ever since he'd gotten back, when he thought about it while looking in the long mirror in his bathroom, he was pleasantly surprised by how relaxed and fit he looked. His skin glowed, and he seemed to have lost a bit of weight, which he liked.

In the village, he never drove his mother's old Ford or biked anywhere. There was no need for any of that. Nothing was too far away, and so he walked everywhere he wanted to go. He missed his mother's cooking, and even her annoying desire to poke her nose into his business. Most of all, he missed Faridah. *Oh, what I'd give to be back at the Three-Shoulder stream!*

As he rummaged through his fridge and cupboards for something to eat, it occurred to him that, for more than three weeks, he had not eaten any boxed or tinned food. His mother had always bought fresh vegetables, fish, beef, and poultry. *Maybe that's why my skin is almost glowing.*

A few days after his return, Mike visited Clive, told him all about Faridah, and showed him the key. Clive listened, worried about his friend, but gasped in awe when he saw the key and agreed that it was like no other he had ever seen. He advised Mike to lock it away in the safest place possible as its value could be mind-blowing. Still, he hadn't liked the story about Faridah. Clive didn't know what to make of Ogbanjes, even though he had also heard about them. So, for the first time in their very close friendship, he simply couldn't advise his friend, which really upset him. Whichever path Mike decided to take seemed fraught with challenges. If he couldn't be with Faridah, he wouldn't be happy, but if he decided to be with her, there was no way of knowing if they could fit into each other's lives.

After Mike left his house, Clive laughed at the crazy thought of Mike becoming a water being, and speaking aloud as though to warn anyone who cared to listen, he said, "If he isn't happy with her, I'll deep-dive into whatever ocean Faridah has taken him, yank the silly crown off his head, and drag him out of that water palace myself." He pounded his chest with his hand and then laughed for a very long time.

As the weeks passed, Mike continued to confide in Clive about his ongoing struggle to get Faridah off his mind and relieve his misery. Clive repeatedly assured Mike that, though it would take some time, he would eventually move past Faridah if that was what he truly wanted to do. He suggested that Mike consider getting on online dating sites, or engaging a professional matchmaker, as a distraction to test his feelings for Faridah and see if he could forget her. Mike agreed that it was a good idea and promised to try Clive's suggestion, but deep in his heart, he believed that it was clutching at straws.

In the two months following his return to Chicago, Mike spoke with his mother three times, always avoiding asking after Faridah. He was surprised as well that his mother never volunteered any information about her. The only time she mentioned her name was to express Athen and Faridah's deep-felt gratitude for the donation to the polytechnic and in support of Faridah's assistance to the farmers. Mike was disappointed his mother had ceased to push the Faridah issue, and told himself that if his mother no longer felt the need to match him with Faridah, it must be because it was truly a lost cause, and therefore, he needed to move on.

One Wednesday evening, at ten-thirty, three months after his return from his village, Mike's phone rang just as he was winding down and getting ready to retire to his bedroom. He rushed to answer it, surprised when his mother's voice came on the line.

"Mike, how are you?" Before he could respond, she followed this up with another question that threw Mike off balance. "Why didn't you tell me? Eh? Why?"

"Tell you what, Mama?"

"About Faridah! Why didn't you give me details about the incidents at the stream? Why didn't you tell me that she's Ogbanje?"

Expecting his mother to start stereotyping Faridah, he prepared himself for vituperations and unsolicited advice. "Please don't be offended, Mama," he said firmly. "It was not my place, and still isn't, to tell you anything about who Faridah is, or who she's supposed to be. Aside from Faridah, the only people who know about her origin, for lack of a better word, are her uncle Athen, and the oracle priest."

"Well, I still would have thought you'd have confided in *me*. I'm your mother, after all. Or don't you even trust me to keep secrets secret?"

Mike wasn't going to argue this point. He didn't think his mother would understand his stance anyway. How could he explain that he was working through his own emotions and still afraid that believing Faridah was an Ogbanje made him sound like an unenlightened fool? He decided to ignore his mother's emphasis on him not trusting her and turned the conversation away from it.

"How did you come to know, Mama?"

"Faridah started behaving strangely after you left. Rather than her weekly trip to the stream to wash and bathe, she told her uncle that she needed to go to the stream every day. Then she disappeared for two days, and Athen was beside himself with worry. He knew Faridah was at the stream though, and knew what to do. He went to the chief priest, who consulted the oracle and discovered that, with you gone, Faridah no longer felt like living on the land ... and that was the problem. When Faridah returned on the third day following her disappearance, Athen fetched the priest, and Faridah confirmed exactly what the oracle had proclaimed."

Speechless, Mike listened to his mother, his confusion returning in full force. He didn't know what to feel: joy that Faridah missed him so much she would choose to return to her water family; or fear that he was about to lose her forever, which would kill him.

His mother continued. "So, the priest asked Faridah if she would be happy to be free from her water family, and she said yes, but *only* if she could be with you. Only if you wanted her. You asked me how I found out? Well, Athen paid me a visit. He was shocked to learn from Faridah that the two of you had met at the Three-Shoulder twice and that she had revealed herself to you. Thinking you had already confided in me, he told me everything. Athen has a lot of respect for you for protecting Faridah's dignity and for saying nothing, not even a peep, to your own mother, but now ... he and the chief priest want to know how you feel about Faridah."

This was all too much for Mike to process. His head felt foggy, and he needed a break. His eyes were blinking rapidly to hold back the tears that were threatening to fall, and he knew that he couldn't carry on with this conversation tonight without breaking down completely.

"Mama, I'm not feeling very well now. My heart is throbbing badly. I need to calm my mind so I can process what you've just told me and think things through. Would you please let me call you back tomorrow night, say about eight p.m. your time?"

Mama Mike felt sorry for her son. Although she had been eager to match him with Faridah, with all she now knew about the young lady, she wouldn't press Mike for any life-changing decision. There was much more on the line here than she had imagined for her son. Although the chief priest had informed Athen that Faridah could be freed from her water family with a three-day ritual at the Three-Shoulder, Mama Mike was afraid that simply freeing her from her water family would not mean that she was no longer an Ogbanje by nature.

"Okay, my dear son. Please think it through, and may the Lord help you to make the right decision. Goodnight."

At the end of the call, Mike was more confused than ever. "How does Mama, a Christian, even believe in the Ogbanje?" he asked loudly.

Remembering Faridah's words at the stream, about society excluding people like her, Mike would have expected his mother to advise him to stay away from Faridah, now that she knew, but she hadn't. She'd almost sounded a little encouraging, which had shocked him.

Mike barely slept that night, but when he did, he dreamed of Faridah in his house, cozied up with him in his lounge, in the gazebo, in the kitchen, cooking, in his bathroom, and in his bed. Then he saw her, like a mirage, heading back into the deep waters and taking him with her. The water turned blue, and suddenly, with their bodies entwined, they both shot up from it, laughing.

Mike jolted up from his dream, sweating, frightened, and a nervous wreck. Afraid to go back to sleep, he got out of bed, slipped into his housecoat, and went into the kitchen to make a cup of sweet herbal tea. Once it was ready, he laid down on the sofa in the living room and turned on the TV, just for some light and noise, feeling like a child afraid of ghosts he believed were under his bed. As he mentally sorted through the things of most value in his life, he began to shiver lightly with the realisation that came to him.

"Dear Lord, please help me. I think I've fallen more deeply in love with a water being than I ever would have thought possible."

With this prayer given voice, he soon felt a sense of calm descend on him. Then he drifted off to sleep and slept like a baby till the next morning, when he woke up and called in sick at his office. He wanted to talk to Clive, but each time he picked up his phone to dial his bosom buddy's number, he held back and clicked off. "No," he muttered. "This is a decision I must make myself and own fully."

After a day spent pacing and pondering, Mike called his mother at eight o'clock as he'd promised.

"Mama, how are you?"

"Mike, my son! It feels like forever since we last spoke, even though it was only yesterday. Listen... please hold the line."

The line went silent, and Mike patiently waited for his mother to return. "Hello? Mike?"

Mike froze at the sound of Faridah's soft voice, which brought her image flooding back into his mind and heart. When he finally found his own voice, it was barely more than a whisper. "Faridah?"

"Yes, it's me."

"Faridah, I'm coming to get you. Is that okay? I *need* you. I *want* you." Mike stressed the words "need" and "want" so that Faridah would feel his emotions.

"Okay, Mike. Then I don't want to be in the water anymore."

"I understand, Faridah, and you won't need to be anymore."

The phone went quiet for a moment then before his mother came back on the line. "Hello?"

"Mama, there's nothing more to say. I'll be back in the village next weekend. I've told Faridah I'm coming for her. Please tell Uncle Athen my decision."

"Okay, my son. I'll have your room and your favourite food ready."

"Thank you, Nne. Thank you. Goodnight."

"Goodnight, my son."

Mike called Clive and told him all that had happened since they last spoke, then booked his flight to his village. When the day finally arrived, Clive drove him to the airport, and enroute, he noticed a twinkle in his friend's eyes and the soft smile playing on his lips.

"Brother, I must say that the energy around you is very nice ... even though I'm still afraid for you, not wanting you to be hurt. You seem at peace."

Mike gave his friend a side look, still smiling. "That's exactly how I feel deep in my heart," he replied, nodding several times.

"Are you absolutely sure about this?" Clive couldn't help but ask.

"Yes, as sure as I am that I have lines on my palms," Mike confidently replied, chuckling.

Clive eyed his friend and finally shrugged. He knew that all he could do was wish his best friend well and hope for the best.

As soon as he arrived at his village and set his luggage down at home, Mike told his Mother that dinner could wait. He wanted to see Faridah and needed her to accompany him to Athen's, as he didn't know where she lived, and in any case, it would have been taboo to show up there by himself on a matter such as the one at hand. As Mike freshened up, his mother changed clothes quickly. Mike then gave his mother a fabric bag containing a gift for Athen. He requested that she present it to him on his behalf when they met with Athen.

In no time, they were both ready, and Mama Mike led her son to Athen's house. They knocked at his door at eight p.m., and when it creaked open, Faridah jumped into Mike's arms.

After a quick embrace, Mike bowed and greeted Athen, who had followed Faridah to the door and broken into a broad smile as soon as he saw who his visitors were. Mike didn't want to waste time. So, he politely asked his mother and Athen to excuse him, and taking Faridah's hand, he led her outside to the front of the house.

The moon was full, and the sky was lit with stars. It was slightly windy, and the rustle of leaves on the trees around the house seemed like consent from the gods. Mike dipped his hand into his trouser pocket, took Faridah's right hand, and placed something on her palm. Faridah unwrapped it and soon uncovered a replica of the golden key she'd given Mike, glistening under the moon.

Her eyes went wide in a delight and surprise, and she gasped, then looked at Mike lovingly, running her fingers over the key's surface.

He adored the sparkle of her large eyes on her chocolate skin as she ran her fingers up and down the key. "Look at the back," Mike urged.

Faridah turned the key over. Engraved on both sides of its head were blue waves, and on its stem, there were words, clearly lit by moonlight, which she read aloud in a soft voice, full of peace and love:

"My heart, My Soul."

Eyes That Speak

She pushed back the wooden chair with its broken backrest and yawned loudly, raising both hands and reaching them behind her head for a full stretch backwards. Then she brought her hands down with a loud bang on her notebook, which lay on the table before her, and rubbed her sore eyes, looking lazily at her shadow on the wall. *Hmmm,* she thought. *My head looks bigger!* Using the shadow on the wall as a mirror, she turned her head slightly to the left, examined it for a while, and then turned it to the right. She took an especially long look at her ears, pinching and pulling them lightly up and down. *Hmmm, yes.* She nodded. *My head looks bigger for sure, even my ears...*

Without warning, Osom Semewe let out another yawn, this one silent, with her mouth shut and making a long "nnnnn" sound. She stretched out her legs, wriggled her feet, and gazed into the bush kerosene lamp that now seemed to blink intermittently as the kerosene ran low. She was thinking about nothing in particular ... just taking in her body's fatigue from sitting for two hours in a less than comfortable chair, studying with a bush lamp.

Suddenly, Osom realized how sleepy she really was, and a nervous thought occurred to her that had her quickly pushing the chair further back and getting to her feet. Looking at the old China clock on the wall, with the long crack in its glass, her worst fear was realized. It was ten-thirty! "Ah!" she cried "It's so late! I must go to bed right away or else I'll

173

wake up late." She scowled then, muttering, "And if I'm late for school, that witch of a class mistress will have her favourite bamboo cane ready. Please-o, I don't want her trouble." Kissing her teeth, she began to pack up her textbooks and organize her school bag for the morning.

There was no love lost between Osom and Ms. Claire, the class mistress—at least not from Osom's perspective. Osom had resented the class mistress ever since early in the school term when Ms. Claire had ordered her to move from her favourite back-corner seat in the class to the first row, right in front.

* * *

"Osom Semewe, leave that back seat and come sit right here in front, in Nadia's place, where I can see you." Ms. Claire's voice cut through Osom's attention as soon as the teacher had put her books and accessories down on her large, square teacher's table at the front of the class, which the class prefect had to ensure was always clean after every class session. Osom couldn't believe her ears. She hated the front row. She didn't like being directly under the nose of any teacher. She also disliked the fact that, during inclement weather, especially the harmattan, those in the front row were always the first to be strongly hit by the cold, dry breeze and gusts of dust that often blew through the door whenever it was opened or left ajar.

If that weren't bad enough, she didn't like that her feet would be exposed up there, leaving her severely stitched-up school sandals under clear scrutiny from under the desk. At least she could conceal them when seated in the extreme back corner. What she hated the most though was the fact that those in the front row always had to submit their tests or assignments first. In short, Osom could find nothing good whatsoever about moving to the front.

Osom frowned, looking stunned by the order, and didn't move, not sure she had heard the teacher right. Nadia, the girl with whom she was to switch places, turned around briefly, but when she saw Osom still seated, she shrugged and turned back to look at the teacher.

"Osom Semewe, hurry up," Ms. Claire said impatiently. "We don't have all day, so there's no time for slow coaches. And Nadia, you heard me. Quickly, switch places with Osom. Hurry, hurry."

Osom grudgingly packed up her books and bag to head to the front row. *Why is Ms. Claire addressing me by my full name as though there are too many Osoms in this class and I must be reminded of who I am?* The class teacher crossed her arms on her chest as she stood in the front of the class, waiting for her students to switch places.

My God! I hate the front position. I hate, hate, hate it!! Why is she doing this to me? I hate the front row!!! Osom grumbled and hissed inaudibly as she took her place at Nadia's desk, barely able to concentrate on her lessons for the rest of the day.

* * *

Preceding that order, on that first day of her new school session as a form-five student, during the students' self-introductions to their new class mistress, Ms. Claire had jokingly told Osom, that her large, bright eyes were frightening from the back seat and unsettled her. Many of the students in class had found this funny and giggled, holding their mouths to suppress laughter, but Osom did not find it funny.

In any other circumstance, she would have gleefully accepted this as a compliment. In fact, if she were being told that by one of her many male admirers, she would have flirtatiously responded with a narrowing of her eyes and pouting of her lips, while pushing her chest outwards like she'd seen some girls do on TV dramas and comedies. But that day, she had scowled. Coming from her class mistress, who had a reputation for strictness, Osom was compelled to interpret the reference to her eyes as a blatant indication of dislike.

* * *

As she got ready to call it a night, Osom's memory continued to play back her first encounter with Ms. Claire. Like a videotape, she fast-forwarded and rewound their conversations and hissed loudly like they had only just taken place a few minutes ago, remembering with anger how Ms. Claire had refused to listen to her pleas to remain in the back corner, where she also loved to rest her body on the wall whenever she felt like it.

"Ah, I'll never forget that day," she whispered as she recalled her mood that day as she'd packed her belongings from her favourite position and moved to a new spot in front of the class. On that day, she had thought that Ms. Claire's directive would be for that one lesson only, but when the class mistress requested this change a second time, and told her and Nadia that it would be the norm for all her classes, Osom and Nadia had quickly switched places every day before Ms. Claire's lessons started, and returned to their usual positions afterwards. Nadia didn't like the back position any more than Osom liked the front, and found it very irritating having to switch, often twice a day. Since she wasn't really friends with Osom though, she approached the swaps efficiently. She was always the first to pack up, walk to Osom's place, and stand there, watching her peer take her time in vacating her seat.

At that first introductory class, as Osom had walked gingerly to the front row with her school bag slung over her left shoulder and the heap of stationery from her drawer clutched to her chest with both hands, she'd clicked her tongue against the roof of her mouth and sworn under her breath and cursed the teacher silently: *If your village people sent you to me, may you not find me.* Ms. Claire could plainly see and feel every bit of the resentment Osom felt about the swap of places, but when Osom tried to make her case for preferring the back seat, the teacher had refused to even listen.

Knowing that being opinionated and eager to assert independence often came with adolescence, Ms. Claire had ignored Osom's grumbling and gone ahead and made a few more changes to the seating arrangements. Once she was satisfied that the class was as organized as she wanted it to be, with ebullient friends separated and quiet and shy students brought to the middle rows, she'd proceeded to call the register, after which she started the English lesson.

Osom was fifteen years old, and in about seven months, she'd finish primary five and start her A Levels. The youngest of the four surviving children in her family, Osom's eldest brother and sister had been sent to live with distant, well-off relatives who lived in different states, and served as domestic help in exchange for being looked after and given a good education by their benefactors. Osom's immediate elder brother was keen to be a priest in the future and was studying at a federal-subsidised seminary in the southwest, where according to her father, he was also the ward of a retired caretaker priest.

Since leaving home, her siblings had never visited, and even though Osom remembered them, they were like temporary treasures that had been lost. She had no close relationship with any of them and had not been given the opportunity to grow to care for them enough to make her ask after them. Once in a while, she could hear her parents sharing good news from their relatives about how well their children were doing at their various stations, and plans for a home visit in the near future.

From the ages of seven to nine, Osom had often wondered if she was going to be sent away too at some point. But as she'd remained with her parents past her eleventh birthday, she'd gradually begun to believe that they had decided to keep her with them after all.

This was Osom's sixth night at home alone. Her father, Tingatu and her mother, Ayere, were on a two-week trip to the traditional and white weddings of her mother's maternal cousin in Fonma. It was going to be an elaborate five-day wedding extravaganza full of pomp and pageantry. Ayere's relatives were rich and excited to display their wealth and social status. Not wanting to look like the proverbial church rats among the affluent, the Semewes had gone out of their way to spend more money than they could afford on the set of six different uniform fabrics that had been specially distributed for the weddings. Tingatu, a trucker, had borrowed some money from a friend to buy the three fabrics chosen for men and the three for women. When Munma, one of Ayere's relatives, had visited to inform them about the weddings, the colour scheme, and the dress code agreed on by the bride and groom's families, and later returned with the fabrics that the Semewes and others were expected to purchase, the Semewes had a deeply fake conversation with Munma.

* * *

"So, Uncle, Auntie, all preparations are now in top gear, and these are the fabrics the couple's families will be wearing for the three-day celebrations."

Munma smiled as she excitedly took the fabrics out of her bag and placed the six individually wrapped bales on the chair next to Tingatu.

"Oh, nice, nice, very nice," Tingatu and his wife exclaimed as they admired each bale in turn. "This is not a problem at all. We'll pay for them all now. In fact, Ayere and I have been preparing for a long time, eager to buy. Isn't that so, my dear?" Tingatu turned to his wife for confirmation.

"Oh, yes! We've been expecting you, Munma, and we can't wait to go to our tailor. Tingatu and I have already chosen our styles. You must let us know if there's anything else we're obliged to do."

Tingatu nodded and agreed with his wife. "Yes, Munma, anything at all. Just let us know, and we're ready." He then quickly rose from his chair. "Just give me a few minutes, Munma, and I'll pay for all these fabrics." Tingatu slid his feet into his rubber slippers and hurried out of the living room, returning in a couple of minutes and standing in front of Munma.

"Alright. Again, how much did you say is the total for the six?" he asked, as though he had recently won the lottery.

"Only seven thousand, two hundred Shinpas, Uncle," Munma said and sat forward, excited as she watched Tingatu proudly show off the wad of notes as he counted off the exact amount.

Ayere sat there, shuffling her body, trying to catch Munma's eyes with a smile that would let her know that they could clearly afford such an expense, even as her heart was in turmoil. *Seven thousand, two hundred Shinpas! Oh lord!* Ayere cried silently. *That is like our entire housekeep income for the year! And Tingatu had to borrow to pay for these god-forsaken fabrics... Oh lord.*

Ayere's head was spinning, and she likened the heat in her body to piping-hot steam, dripping fear from her ears amidst her smiles as she looked at the money in her husband's hands. She felt like jumping out of her seat, grabbing her husband's hand, and shouting at him to stop this folly as there were more pressing issues for which they needed money, and that worry of how they were going to repay this debt was killing her. Her husband's trucking business was not very successful and neither was her work in the second-hand-clothes retail trade. They were always just barely scraping by. And then there was Osom's schooling to think about! Ayere felt like an accomplice in a crime that had been perfectly planned to rob their daughter of a decent education.

With the fabrics paid for, Munma offered more information about the wedding than the Semewes really cared about. She told them all about the different entertainments and foods that had been ordered, as well as who was doing what. The Semewes watched resentfully as Munma tucked the money away. They couldn't change their minds now. An unnecessary luxury had just been paid for.

Tingatu was trying as hard as he could to pretend that he hadn't just done one of stupidest things of his life. He barely heard the many tidbits of information Munma was giving away like a child excitedly describing an ice-cream cone, but still carefully continuing the farce, he interjected excitedly.

"Oh, wonderful! Please let us know if there's anything else we can do to support the festivities."

Ayere sucked her cheeks in sarcastically, and then added her voice to her husband's. "Ah yes, Munma. We've been looking forward to this wedding, so we must be told if there's anything more that we can do besides just buying these."

Tingatu felt like choking at the mere mention of the fabrics. Each time he threw a glance at the glittering bales on the chair, he quickly looked away and forced his mind to try and focus on whatever story Munma was telling them. Her voice was beginning to sound like a church bell that just wouldn't stop ringing. He desperately wanted her to leave so he could secretly wallow in trepidation and regret with his wife.

Finally, to their relief, Munma announced that she needed to leave as she had more fabrics to drop off. Ayere sprang up from her chair, signalling her subtle support for their visitor to speed up her departure, though she veiled it by saying, "Oh, but why? You're leaving so soon?" She asked this with a smile, craning her head to one side and raising her brows, wanting Munma to believe that they truly wished that she could stay longer.

Ensuring that Munma didn't misconstrue those words as an invitation, before she could reply, Ayere quickly countered, adding, "But we understand that you have to get going. You must be very busy at this period with all the preparations. Time runs so much faster when you have much to do. Before you know it, it's nighttime."

Tingatu was lost in regret land, so he blanked out then, not hearing the rest of conversation between the two women, though he kept nodding. Munma stood up with her bags, thanked the Semewes again for buying all six fabrics, and then took her leave.

Ayere pushed the door shut, and carefully looked through the window near it, watching until Munma walked completely out of sight, then quickly locked the door and turned the key twice so the woman couldn't spring any surprises on them by returning unannounced. Then Tingatu and his wife collapsed on the sofas like people who had just completed a ten-thousand-mile race.

Ayere was holding the back of her head with both hands like one deeply in mourning as she leaned back. Her husband sat with legs forward and apart, gazing into space with his hands folded under his chin. No one spoke for about five minutes. Then Ayere attempted to break the heavy silence, turning and looking at her husband.

"My father," she said, using the term of endearment she often did with her husband, especially when she wanted a favour, "what's done is done. Let's—"

"Woman," he said, his attention snapping back to her before she could finish. "Look, just leave me alone and remove all these stupid fabrics from my sight." He looked away; a deep frown etched deeply into his forehead.

Ayere wasn't very surprised by her husband's reaction. She knew his tendency to sometimes go overboard and complicate their lives when they desperately needed simplicity. So, she brought her hands down to her lap, sat up, and leaned forward, facing her husband.

"Leave you alone? Ha! The wedding's in three weeks, and we need to start looking for money to sew our uniforms or else we'll both be wrapping each fabric around our heads like bath towels at the wedding. You know I didn't want us to buy these uniforms. I told you we could wash, starch, and wear whatever we have and wriggle our waists like we're wearing diamond and gold, but you insisted and gave me a lecture on honour... Well, now here we are." Ayere opened her hands, shrugged, and sat back with an expression that clearly stated, *"I told you so."*

Tingatu said nothing. With their make-believe show-off now donning on him, he felt like a man drowning in shallow waters claiming to be an expert swimmer and asking if there was a deeper river he could swim in. He needed some space to process the cost of his pride, but Ayere hissed and continued.

"If you could have seen my heart while you counted out that cash, you would have felt like you were being bitten by a mad dog and changed your mind. I sat here smiling at Munma like a goat being roasted whole for a medieval king's feast, even though I felt like fresh bitter leaf." Ayere paused and hissed again, sighing out heavily before continuing to express disgust at their hubris. "If you could see the bottom of my heart—the very bottom... Oh no. I felt like tearing the money out of your hands and Munma's, but now she's gone and the money with her! Gone, gone, gone like the wind!" Ayere gestured wildly towards the door with her hands and shook her legs, deeply pained by what had just transpired in the living room.

Tingatu pulled his legs back, and even though his wife's words stung, decided not to give in to regrets. He'd eyed his wife as she was speaking, but now turned fully to face her. "Well, we're not the only ones with poverty knocking on our door! We can't go to this wedding having deprivation written all over our foreheads, can we? You want your relatives to think that I'm starving you and Osom? You want your relatives to judge me like I'm less of a man for not buying those uniforms, eh? You can sit there and tell me about us wearing old, washed, and starched clothes to a high-profile wedding, but I know from the depth of my heart that it would not make you happy to see your relatives, friends, and everyone else kitted out to kill and purposefully walking up to you to chat just to show off. You think I don't know that you'd want the ground to open up and swallow you from embarrassment? Look me in the eyes, Ayere, and tell me you'd be thrilled." Tingatu stopped speaking for a few seconds, and then with his eyes wide open in a look that dared his wife to contest his assertions, he continued when she remained silent. "Tell me, what excuse would we give your relatives for not buying the uniforms? Go on, tell me. I have pride, my wife. I have pride."

Ayere knew this was not an argument she'd win. When they'd had the conversation about the wedding uniforms three weeks earlier, she had also suggested just buying one for each of them, to save money, but Tingatu wouldn't hear of it. He'd firmly told her that he wanted them, and her, in particular, to look the part just like everyone else, and if they wouldn't buy the uniforms, they might as well not attend the wedding at all.

Ayere was no stranger to her husband's pride. As she sat and looked at him, she recalled the heated argument they'd had before their own traditional marriage. Tingatu's trucking business had been very successful back then, and he'd felt the need to show that to her relatives. So, even though her dowry was only twenty-five shillings at the time they were engaged, Tingatu, had insisted on paying more than ten times that amount, pounding his fist on his chest and argued that his father had spoilt his mother and "shook the town" during their wedding, and he was expected to surpass that.

When Ayere had tried to explain that the dowry was a symbolic gift, a "token of acknowledgement" to her family and not some price of purchase, a very bad and painful argument had ensued between her and her then fiancé and lasted for over an hour. When Tingatu wouldn't listen, Ayere had gotten her elder sister to intervene.

To please her husband, it was finally decided that Tingatu would pay only the twenty-five shillings dowry stipulated by custom, and that anything in addition to that would be accepted by the bride's family as a separate gift and definitely not be considered part of her dowry. Tingatu grudgingly accepted this decision but swore that he was still "going to move mountains and cause an earthquake" at both his traditional and white wedding to Ayere. And, indeed, he had gone all out to make the weddings the talk of the town.

Listening to her husband now, Ayere knew from long experience that when Tingatu felt that his pride was at stake, nothing would make him budge. So, she sighed, dragged herself up to her feet, looked away, and in a nonchalant tone, said, "Well, okay. Let there be no war. I agree with whatever you say."

She yawned then, stretching her torso and arms fully, and then continued. "I'm going to go make plans now for the shoes and purses I'll need to match these expensive fabrics. What I have would be grossly inappropriate to wear with them. I'll also need to go borrow a set of earrings and a necklace from Sister May at the back of our house. I think I've seen her wear some unique pieces."

Tingatu frowned, opening his mouth to speak but then changing his mind. He didn't like the idea of his wife borrowing jewellery to complement her attire, but he was also aware that he had opened the borrowing gates, let in the Trojan Horse, and wasn't equipped to win another battle about the fabrics—an issue his conscience told him he should have been more circumspect about in the first place.

Leaving her husband, who was still looking very displeased, Ayere picked up the six individually wrapped fabrics and took them into their bedroom. As she busied herself in the room, she heard a groan coming from the living room and stopped to listen closely. It was her dear husband. Walking to the living room to check on him, she found him with his head resting on his arms, which he'd crossed on his knees. He seemed to be crying.

Ayere walked up to him and placed her hand on his shoulder, but Tingatu wouldn't move or even acknowledge her presence. She then ran her hand up and down his back and gently said to him, *"Obim* (my heart), it's okay. It's okay. Nothing ever stays the same. This hard time will pass as well."

In the two weeks leading up to the departure of her parents for Fonma, Osom could sense the tension between them. Sometimes she heard them arguing in their bedroom and then noticed that, for three days after, they would hardly speak. As always happened whenever her parents had a bad argument, her father made or served his own meals, and when he was in the living room, her mother stayed elsewhere to avoid him. Osom didn't like to see her parents giving each other the cold shoulder. It disturbed her greatly and made her lose concentration at school. When all wasn't at peace at home, going to school became more than just a place of learning for Osom; it became her escape and refuge from the tension at home.

Ordinarily, in good times, besides asking her how school was as a matter of routine—and that only rarely—her parents had never really sat with her to have a cordial one-on-one conversation, in which they genuinely wanted to know how she was doing academically, as well as about her psychological wellbeing. When they were at war with each other as they had been for the past couple of weeks, she always found herself inevitably caught between them and having to try not to offend either of them by being erroneously seen as leaning towards one side or the other.

As Osom walked back home each day after school, her heart broke because life at home these days was like walking on eggshells. Like many other experiences at school about which she had questions and would have been happy to have her parents—particularly her mother—give her some answers, Osom was compelled to keep her current stresses to herself. She'd never told her parents about her annoying experience with Ms. Claire on her first day in form five. Given the toxic situation at home, she felt it was useless telling either of them. As far as she was concerned, even when she was experiencing harassment or abuse at school, she believed that it was her problem to deal with. Her parents were too busy with their own affairs. With their own war.

Osom was generally an average student, and her parents often made her feel like they were really not expecting more or better from her. Whenever she got an A in a subject, her father would express shock, tell her a quick "well done," and then speedily dismiss her effort in a way that implied that she'd gotten that grade because the questions must have been much easier than they normally were. Osom, therefore, never saw the need to be better than average. Average was celebrated, below average was regarded with indifference, and above average was acknowledged by her parents with humiliating shock.

Osom also began to internalize blame values that diminished her self-esteem as her parents' arguments and fights over the smallest things intensified. One day, she overheard her parents arguing about her school fees and choice of school, and certain that she was one of the reasons for their fights, Osom had wondered if giving her away to some benefactor as house help wouldn't have been better after all. With her emotional wellbeing taking second place at home, she sought refuge in unempowering silence and acquiescence and soon mastered the art of pretending that all was fine, just like her parents had done with Munma.

After school each day, Tingatu and Ayere's routine question to their daughter was simple: "You're back?" To which Osom simply answered "yes." And the few times when they'd said, "Hope all was well in school today," Osom also gave them the answer she knew they were expecting to hear, which was "yes" accompanied by a cheerful expression, which she always wore around them.

In forms one and two, Osom had been picked on and bullied at school by senior students who found her quiet and easy to send off on errands that occasionally saw her late for class after breaks. Whenever she was asked by a teacher why she'd been late on those occasions, and she gave an honest answer, Osom had been blamed for either being slow on the errand or for not telling the senior student that the errand would make her late for class. Giving the complex power dynamics in the school, she wondered how in the world she could ever do the latter without getting into more trouble with the seniors in question, eliciting a cascading effect on the other seniors one way or another. So, she silently suffered instead, often simply replying with "I'm sorry, sir" or "I'm sorry, miss" when asked why she was late, preferring to be caned by the teacher than expose a senior student to criticism.

Because of these stresses, Osom made no close friends and was teased by her peers as a loner. She desperately wished that her parents would one day look closely enough to see the tears hidden behind her smiley face.

Over the years, as their economic situation deteriorated, her parents' marriage had as well, with the tension building day after day. At one point, Tingatu had been forced to sell his old Citroen car to help increase the family's disposable income. His pickup truck was essential for his trucking business though, so he took time to look after it. The cost of maintenance kept rising though, as it aged, traversed difficult terrain, and gathered mileage, and sometimes, it broke down for weeks at a time, and Tingatu had to order replacement parts from abroad through his mechanic. When Ayere was upset by the truck's drain on their resources, she would fiercely scold her husband, saying that the truck was better fed than the humans in the house. Then Tingatu would reply, "Okay! You know what we must do then? Let's starve the truck and see how well the humans in the house will be fed then!"

Inadvertently, Osom's parents had always projected the growing tension between them on their daughter, and so she began to increasingly navigate the world of growing up as a young woman through the eyes and experiences of others. In form three, just before noon one day in the second semester, Osom had been climbing up the stairs to her class with many other students, after the usual fifteen-minute break, when she'd suddenly felt her right hand being pulled. Turning, she'd seen a student she faintly recognized as belonging in another class.

* * *

"Come, come," the student whispered to her. "I have something to tell you."

Osom hated being late for class, but the student was still holding her hand, and so Osom reluctantly turned around and followed her. Together, they went down the steps, pushing past a throng of other noisy students making their way up.

"What is it? What is it?" Osom asked impatiently, unhappy to have her time wasted.

The student waited till they were on the landing and in the corridor, away from the crowd, before saying, "My name is Kenene. You have a stain at the back of your uniform."

"Stain? What stain?" Osom asked irritably as she turned around to look at her back, craning her neck to find the stain.

"You won't see it like that. I think it's your time of the month. Come. Hurry, let's go to the toilet, and I'll show you."

Osom had no clue what Kenene was talking about, so she pressed for clarity as she was being ushered hurriedly along. "Time of the month? What's that and what does it have to do with me? Please, I don't want to be late for class."

Kenene immediately understood Osom's naivety. "Just follow me. I'll show you. But don't go to class because it may get worse, and everyone will laugh at you."

In the general toilets, Kenene pulled Osom's school-uniform skirt from the back to the front so that Osom could see the large parch of pale red on her light grey pinafore. Osom was shocked and afraid. "I swear by my mother and father, I don't know how that stain got there! I only sat by myself on the football field. I didn't realise someone had poured watercolour on the field."

Kenene smiled. "Listen. It's not watercolour, and it's not a problem. You've never heard about periods?"

"Periods? What do you mean? Am I going to be sick and end up in the hospital?" Osom asked, confused, afraid, and now almost in tears.

"Your mother didn't tell you about it?" Kenene was surprised because she'd assumed that all girls had the same privileged knowledge from their mothers that she did.

"No," Osom said, her eyes widening in shock. "You think my mother knows?"

"Okay, look, don't be scared. It's not a disease, and you're not going to be admitted to hospital. All girls have periods. Mine started early this year, but because my mother had told me last year to expect it, when it happened, I told her, and she bought me lots of sanitary towels."

Kenene then proceeded to educate Osom, based on what her own mother had diligently told her a year before she'd ever seen her period. She told Osom that she would bring a sample of a sanitary towel the next day to show her, and without elaborating, she warned Osom to ensure that she didn't get too close to boys. Kenene told Osom that her mother had cautioned her to wait till she was at least nineteen years old, and in the university or polytechnic, before having a boyfriend, and when she was ready to date, she must confide in her so that they could have what she called a "girl-to-girl chitchat."

It all sounded like Greek to Osom, and she was amazed that Kenene's mother was so close to her daughter that she had taught her these things, and disappointed that her own mother was so far away in her life when she needed her the most.

At the end of her short lecture, Kenene said, "You're lucky. When mine came, I was in so much pain, I thought I'd die. I threw up several times, and my pelvic felt like it was on fire."

"Hun? You were sick?" Osom opened her mouth and eyes wide.

"Yes, but the good thing was that I was at home when it happened. My mother gave me pain killers and took care of me. Not every girl sees her period with pain like I did. I don't think you will." Kenene saw Osom's fear and quickly moved to assuage it. "Don't be afraid. Stay here, and I'll go get some toilet paper." Kenene ran off, and in five minutes, was back with a toilet roll and her cardigan. She showed Osom how to use toilet paper as a temporary sanitary towel and told her to tie the cardigan around her waist to cover the stain.

More grateful than she could express, Osom thanked Kenene and quickly asked, "But what do I say if my class teacher asks me to remove the cardigan? You know how strict the school can be about us dressing properly." She feared that she might still be exposed in one way or another.

Kenene waved off her worry with her hand. "If your class teacher sees the cardigan and asks, just tell him or her that it's your period. They'll understand."

Osom's heart was pounding, and she suddenly became shy and overly self-conscious. *Period.* The more she heard that word, the more annoying it sounded given the embarrassment it had just caused her. This so-called "period" was a very strange occurrence, and she had more questions than she believed Kenene could answer. Most of all, she was angry that her mother had not taken the time to talk to her about this period that was obviously normal, inevitable, and according to Kenene, exclusive to girls. Accompanied by Kenene, Osom scurried back to her class then, regularly tugging the cardigan down to ensure that it was still there and covering the patch at the back of her uniform.

In her classroom, Osom found the chemistry lesson already in progress. She was twenty minutes late. The male teacher took one look at her as she stood by the door, waiting to be allowed in, and asked her why she was so late.

"I'm s-s-sorry sir. I went to ... to ... the toilet. It... The ... the thing... It came." Osom stammered, praying that the teacher wouldn't make her give details. To her surprise and relief, he looked at her cardigan and simply waved her to quickly take her seat and settle down. Osom kept her eyes down as she marched to her desk, afraid to make eye contact with anyone while wondering if her classmates knew the secret of the cardigan around her waist.

From that day on, Osom and Kenene were close friends.

* * *

With her parents away in Fonma, Osom focused on her schoolwork and ensured that her assignments were all completed on time. This evening, she looked at the clock again. It was 10:40 p.m., and she realized just how much her reminiscing had slowed her packing things up. As she tidied up the small table that served as a study desk in her room, she shook her head in sorrow as her thoughts inevitably dwelled on Ms. Claire.

In the past months, she had twice been given three strokes of the cane on the palm of her hand for lateness and for what Ms. Claire called "wrinkled dress and scruffy work." When problems at home weighed her down, Osom usually left home a little earlier than normal and turned off the route to school, heading towards a narrow path to a valley where she had once, by chance, discovered a quiet spot by a small field. There in the midst of the birds hovering above her and singing in the fresh air, she'd put her bag down, sit for about fifteen minutes on the trunk of an old, felled tree, and allow her imagination to run wild as she enjoyed the peace and quiet.

She'd then start scribbling poems she'd never finish. Sometimes, she'd chase butterflies or moths, and catch grasshoppers, admiring and playing with them in her hands before letting them go. Content then, Osom would sling her school bag across her shoulder and walk to school, always arriving late on those days. When Ms. Claire would ask the reason for her lateness, Osom would apologise for waking up late and being slow.

On the days when she just didn't feel like going to school, Osom would dress for school as usual, put her wrapper and a bottle of water in her school bag, and buy biscuits and groundnuts on the way to her favourite place by the valley and just sit by herself. She'd snack on her biscuits and nuts and chase butterflies. When she got tired of sitting on the tree trunk, she'd spread her wrapper on the ground and lie down to read or sketch the nature all around her till she got tired and fell asleep.

Osom would spend her entire day there until she was certain school was finished. Then she'd walk home and give her usual single-word reply to her parents' routine question, "You're back?" and pretend that she had indeed been to school.

Back at school the next day, she would confide in Kenene about where she'd been the previous day and spend her break hours copying her friend's notes to catch up.

As Osom did her homework this evening, she promised herself to show meticulousness. She had agreed with Ms. Claire that she needed to be more careful with the ink from her pen and learn to cancel out her errors more neatly to avoid blotches. After the English lesson on the first day that Ms. Claire had described her as "tardy," Osom had quickly looked up this new word in the advanced learners' dictionary. Although she'd had a faint idea what Ms. Claire had meant, she'd needed confirmation. And in any case, Ms. Claire had advised them to always look up the meaning of a new word in order to broaden and enrich their vocabulary.

Having been described several times as "scruffy," Osom had looked up the meaning of that word too and knew it well. Now armed with the dictionary's meaning, Osom was not surprised at being described as tardy, which she often was, or scruffy. She'd never been the neatest student, and with only one pinafore, two blouses, and a pair of school sandals for nearly two years, most of the time she struggled to look her best, even though her mother had adjusted and resized her blouses and pinafore, lengthening and expanding them to fit. Her leather sandals had had their fronts and sides resewn and their soles replaced twice, and her right big toe was beginning to burst the sandal loose yet again. Still, with two more terms before graduation, Osom was happy to manage her own school gear.

It was now 11:48 p.m. The Semewes were on what was generally known as the "pay as you go" electrical billing system, whereby a pre-paid electricity voucher had to be bought. Tingatu always bought a specific amount of pre-paid electricity for his household only at the end of every month and had laid down the law regarding television. It could only be watched from six p.m. to nine p.m., and all lights in the house had to be switched off at nine p.m., and only kerosene lamps used till six the next morning.

Armed with a small notepad and a pen, every morning Tingatu would religiously check and write down their electricity usage as though his life depended on it. On two occasions, when Osom had forgotten to abide by the electricity rule and had the light in her bedroom on for just a little past nine, her father had shouted at the top of his lungs, lecturing her about wastage and how expensive electricity had become. After the second incident, Osom had sworn never to forget to switch her light off at 8:55 p.m., and she'd kept that promise.

Before surviving on a stringent budget became the new norm at the Semewe household in the past couple of years, Osom had enjoyed watching TV for an hour or two on Fridays and Saturdays. Her favourite sitcom, *Big Mouth*, which was loved by her parents as well, was on every Saturday at eight p.m., and loud laughter could be heard emanating from the Semewes' house as they enjoyed the show.

Now though, since the rule on electricity usage had been imposed by her father, Osom no longer watched TV at all, and gradually, she completely forgot that the big, square screen sitting on a stand in their living room was even there. Still, Osom missed those happy times and often wondered if things would ever return to that lost normal. She had noticed that, as her father grew into an increasingly angry man, her mother sought refuge in the silent treatment, often choosing to ignore her husband, and inadvertently, her daughter as well.

Osom felt like the fragile and fraying middle of an invisible rope with both ends being pulled on by her parents, and tonight was no different. She knew that as soon as her father returned from Fonma, he would first dash to the metre to investigate her electricity usage, so she ensured that, whatever calculations he made, he'd find the result within his expectations.

From nine p.m. on, Osom had worked solely by the light of a kerosene lamp. Before putting her assignment notebook in her school bag with the rest of her things, she took one more look at her work, flipping the pages, and found that she was proud of herself for having no blots, smears, or cancellations. She placed the bag on the floor next to the big cupboard where her parents stored bric-a-brac, and then pushed the chair back under the table. She then went through her nightly ritual of ensuring that all doors and windows were securely locked, pushing down the heavy wooden barrier against her bedroom's door, spreading out her sleep cover, and propping up her feather pillows.

Then she knelt down beside her bed and said her prayers out loud, adding at the end of it, "Thank you, lord, for helping me not have a tardy or scruffy assignment to submit tomorrow. Amen!" Making the sign of the cross, she then stood up, took the packet of matches from the table, lifted the lamp, and sitting on the bed, she blew out the flame. She then placed the lamp and matches on the floor, close to the head of the bed, where she could reach them easily upon waking.

Finally, she slid under the bedcover, and looking up at the ceiling in the dark, she imagined what a lovely day she would have in school tomorrow and soon began to snore softly.

Although not full, the moon was bright, its warm fluorescent glow was filtering into Osom's bedroom through the hedges by the window and keeping the room from being pitch black. The night was warm though, and as the dozing Osom began to feel hot, she flung the bedcover off to the side, adjusted her sleeping position, and soon began snoring once again, sometimes loudly and sometimes like a weasel, and then she began to dream.

She found herself suddenly heading to a plantain forest. The sides of the road were lined with tall oak trees whose branches crisscrossed to form a beautiful aisle of green leaves in her path. She walked for what seemed like eternity, and as she did, the night got darker, and her feet became sore and bruised. Her throat also grew parched. *If only I could get a cup of water to drink,* she thought as she walked on.

The sounds of the night—of owls, crickets, the rustling tree branches above her, and the echoes of all of it—made her run and run until she was exhausted and about to fall. But then, far ahead of her, loomed a mammoth cave with a large door. The huge oak trees lining her path were soon left behind. She could see the cave, yet it looked so far away. She desperately needed to reach the door. She needed water, but the farther she ran, the farther the cave seemed.

She tripped and fell flat on her face then, and as she painfully arose and dusted down her skirt, she turned back and saw Ms. Claire running towards her with an axe raised over her head and glistening in the moonlight. Ms. Claire looked like the caricature of Lucifer in the bible picture book her uncle Daniel had given her for her sixth birthday. Osom's knees were bruised and bleeding, but she ran for her life.

Ms. Claire chased after her, and each time Osom turned to look back, Ms. Claire seemed closer to catching up. As she finally neared the cave, Osom began to scream for help, believing someone would come through the cave's door to save her. But her screams only echoed uselessly. There was no one there. Osom arrived at the cave's entrance, forcefully pushing the door open, and dashed into the cave past cold and mouldy walls. She slammed the door closed behind her then, with shaky hands, and locked the bolts.

Tired, sore, thirsty, and hungry, she rested her body against the door, her heartbeat sounding like a pestle on mortar as the minutes passed. Dead silence. Osom glued the side of her face hard against the door, listening, waiting for Ms. Claire.

"Witch of a woman," she panted, cursing her in a hissing tone, "I hope you rot in hell." Exhausted, Osom shut her eyes then, and with her head still resting sideways against the door, she slid slowly down. She needed to sit and catch her breath. As she settled to the cold floor of the cave, she shut her eyes in relief and turned to rest her back against the door.

When she opened her eyes again a few seconds layer, Ms. Claire was right there, her axe raised and shrill laughter bellowing from her wide-opened mouth. Screaming at the top of her lungs ... Osom woke herself up.

Bolting upright in her bed, breathing heavily, she put her left hand on her heaving chest and realized how much she was sweating when it felt damp right through her night clothes. The moon was gone now, and the room was pitch black. Looking around her room, she could identify nothing.

"My goodness! What a nightmare! What a nightmare!" She was feeling almost panicked, the darkness of her room scaring her. The clothes hanging from a line on the side of the bed looked like monsters. She frantically began to feel around the head of the bed with her right hand for the lamp and matches, found them, and quickly lit the lamp, placing it some distance away on the ground, opposite her bed.

As its golden glow filled the room, Osom finally felt safe when she looked around and was certain she was all alone, and that nothing else in the room had changed. She looked at the clock. It was 3:05 a.m. She grunted, rubbed her eyes, and sat back on the bed, propped up against the pillows.

Her mind was jumpy as she tried to recollect the dream. Not much of it came back and only a few parts of what did made sense to her. Where had she been going? A plantain forest? What cave was that? And why was Ms. Claire chasing after her with an axe?

She paused and rubbed her eyes. The most puzzling part of it of all was how on earth Ms. Claire had entered the cave. She began to feel cold even in the heat of her room. "And that laughter," Osom whispered quietly. "My God! That laughter!" She could feel still the ring of Ms. Claire's laughter right down to her bone marrow and wrapped her arms across her chest, raising her knees to her chest and resting her head on them for warmth.

Osom sat there in the dead quiet for a long time, thinking and remembering bits of the dream, and then wondering what to do till five a.m. when she normally woke up to start preparing for school. She looked at the clock again. It was now 3:40 a.m. She stretched out her legs, settling onto her back, then threw the bedcover over her legs and pulled it up to her chin.

Osom laid very still then, gazing up at the ceiling and listening to the quiet tick, tick of the clock. Her parents crossed her mind then, pondering all the fun they must be having in Fonma. She had heard about the weddings and the expected grandeur of it all. Osom told herself not to care that she was missing it and tried to bring her mind back to Ms. Claire, but it was no use.

If she could have made one wish at this moment, she would have wished for a closer bond with her mother. She remembered how, when she was a little girl, she'd sit with her parents on the living-room floor during very hot days, when chairs felt like furnaces, and together, the three of them would eat a meal from the same plates, while her parents indulged in petty gossip about the goings-on in city life. She couldn't understand where the love she'd once witnessed between them had gone, and why love now looked so painful. She felt like a stranger in her home and had for a long time now.

Since meeting Kenene in form three, even though they were in separate classes, Kenene had become both her mother and father, all rolled into one, and the only person in the world she could share things with without restraint. She benefitted from her friend's upbringing because everything Kenene's parents taught her at home, she shared with Osom. As her friend's values increasingly became her own, Osom began to see her parents as being of biological relevance only, which she knew was not normal.

Osom squinted in the dark and muttered, "I wish things were different with Mama. I wish I could tell her that I feel a hole in my heart where she and Papa ought to be, and that she's become like morning dew to me, here for a moment but quickly disappearing as soon as the sun comes out."

Osom's heavy eyes slowly shut as her body relaxed in the faint smell of kerosene mixed with the murkiness of the room. She allowed her thoughts to drift between Kenene and her parents as her earlier fears dissipated and were replaced by a smile.

Osom's eyes opened again as she remembered good times and some funny incidents with her parents. Ayere sometimes struggled with her huge headgear, whenever she had a party to attend. She'd call her husband and ask him to hold this part or that, to push this side or that side down so she could pin this or tuck that. When Tingatu made a mistake or pulled a little too hard, Ayere would grumble and blame him for messing up her style.

"Oooh, you want to kill me? You're pulling it too tight," she'd complain and look at her husband like he had a predesigned diabolical plan to compress her skull. She'd scold him, and in anger and frustration, undo all that had already been painstakingly done. Tingatu would stand akimbo in utter frustration, not sure whether to give in to his exasperation and leave his wife with her headgear problem or be patient and help her. Then they would both breathe out heavily, as though they were climbing Mount Kilimanjaro, and start the head-tying process all over from scratch.

In no time, it would be Tingatu's turn to scold his wife. "Oh dear, you women! Why can't you just wrap this forsaken thing around your head like a turban and rest? Look, my hands are hurting, and I'm fed up."

Eventually, amidst all the grumbles and complaints, the headgear would be done, and Ayere would turn around to face her husband, strike a pose, and ask him how she looked. After a marathon of hard work with the headgear, Tingatu knew better than to say anything other than "Wow, you look absolutely beautiful, my dear wife!" Then Ayere would clap and flutter her eyes flirtatiously at her husband like a new bride.

Osom smiled weakly as her eyes slanted with drowsiness and recalled the chase around the neighbourhood her father had once given a chicken that was to be cooked for a meal before breaking free from the pole to which it had been tied. "Hmmm... Papa, that chicken was dribbling you, left and right, left and right, like the two of you were playing soccer," she mumbled, chuckling as she drifted off to sleep again.

This time, she slept soundly.

Osom suddenly woke up, confused and concerned. Usually, when she woke up during this transitional period from the rainy to the dry season, it was still quite dark even at six-thirty, and judging by daylight streaming through the gaps between her window's wooden blades, she suspected it was already past seven. A quick look to the clock on the wall only heightened her fears, and she sat up, alarmed. It was 8:23 a.m.

"Oh no!" she cried. "Oh dear! I'm late! I'm very late! I'm so late!" She rushed out of bed, grabbed her bath towel and the plastic bowl with her bath accessories from the foot of her bed, slung the towel over her shoulder, and ran out to fetch water from the kitchen's tap using one of the large empty paint buckets in the backyard. The tap in the family bathroom, which she shared with her parents, had been broken for a long time, and this morning, she wished yet again that her father would try harder to fix it.

While her bucket was filling up, Osom contemplated the fastest way to get ready for school and figured that walking to the family bathroom, which was closer to her parents' bedroom and some distance away from the kitchen, would only add time she simply didn't have to spare. So, she decided to bathe in the open space behind her bedroom window, which was hidden from the public by the low fence around their house.

Osom brushed her teeth, stripped with the speed of lightning, and then scrubbed herself clean with black soap, which she repeatedly rubbed over a local sponge made from the bark of coconut shells. Osom vigorously worked her body like a carpenter focused on sawing away at a challenging log, using her plastic bowl to pour water over her body and rinse.

With her mind on school, she had the quickest bath she could recall having in a very long time as she watched earthworms crawling out from beneath the fence posts. Hurrying back to her room when she was done, she opened her window blades to the fullest for more light rather than use any electricity. Osom hurriedly got dressed, made her bed haphazardly, and marched into the small kitchen adjoining her bedroom.

She opened the severely blackened and deformed pot she had left sitting on the three-burner table stove the day before and sniffed its contents. Satisfied that there was no stale odour, she grabbed one of the two left-over cobs of boiled corn from the pot and kept shaking it to release some of the salty water as she scurried to her room. Then she grabbed her school bag, locked the doors, and began the twenty-five-minute walk to school. It was ten after nine.

A few steps away from their house, Vero—a neighbour with whom her mother often exchanged pleasantries—called out to her. "Ah, morning, Osom. Are you well?"

"Yes, I am, Auntie Vero," she responded quickly through a mouthful of corn. She knew that this was her neighbour's way of telling her that she was obviously even later for school than normal. She quickened her steps.

"Yum yum!" she mumbled, smacking her lips and scowling as she bit hungrily into the cob. In her hurry, she had forgotten that, ideally, she should have rinsed out the corn, as having left it in the pot overnight, it had absorbed much of salty water it had been prepared in, which had concentrated with the extended boil. She was not really enjoying the corn, but she was hungry, so she munched on anyway, wincing a little as she swallowed.

Osom's mind was in a frenzy as she tried to come up with a credible excuse she could give Ms. Claire for her lateness. The thought of Ms. Claire brought bad memories of her nightmare, and she almost choked as she mindlessly swallowed a mouthful of corn. Coughing hard, she dislodged everything in her mouth, then cleared her throat till she felt better.

With one final bite of corn, she tossed the cob into the bush by the sidewalk. "Okay, I've had enough," she told herself loudly, not wanting to choke again. As she continued on her way, she ran her tongue over her teeth and lips repeatedly, wiping her mouth with her hand to remove any remnants of her breakfast.

With that out of the way, Osom tripled her steps, jogging periodically, and soon saw the school building in the distance. In another five minutes, she'd be walking through the gate, but she still had no tangible excuse to offer Ms. Claire, who by now would have called the class register and marked her absent.

Nnem-oooo! Nnem-oooo! she cried silently, her heart pounding as it called for her mother.

"God, please help me," she prayed then. "What do I say?" Her face was a picture of worry and acute fear.

A few steps away from the school's entrance gate, Osom was still trying to find a lie to give as an excuse for her lateness, but just couldn't. Tired of racking her brain, she settled for the simple truth, hoping that "I overslept," accompanied by an apology, would suffice.

Whatever the excuse, Osom prepared herself for the long dressing down she would get from Ms. Claire, along with many probing questions, some of which she knew would insinuate a degeneration of her behaviour because her parents were away in Fonma. Osom didn't like the prospect of this allusion at all and hoped that Ms. Claire would remember that, even though she was home alone, she had been a well-behaved student so far. That way, rather than giving her the usual three strokes of the cane for lateness due to carelessness, maybe she'd only get a tongue-lashing.

"Jesus!" she muttered then, looking up at the sky. "Ms. Claire's tongue! I don't know which is worse, that spiky tongue of hers or the cane." Sighing, she looked directly overhead then. "To be honest, dear God, I think I prefer the cane, or I would if that were all I got. At least the cane is a swift punishment. But the scolding! Ms. Claire's words can sting like a scorpion. How did she learn to scold like that, eh, God?"

Osom finally brought her gaze down to the road and shook her head vigorously in frustrated disapproval of her class mistress's method of enforcing discipline.

On the school grounds now, she wasn't surprised by the silence that greeted her. The students were all in class, and lessons had begun. Osom began to run to her classroom, running her tongue over her lips once more to ensure there was no corn residue, at the corners of her mouth in particular. Then she wiped her lips with her left hand to be doubly sure.

As she got closer to her classroom, she found the door slightly ajar and began to say the Lord's Prayer, mixing in a Hail Mary in the hopes that this prayer mélange would be more efficacious in bringing about the result she desired. She made the sign of the cross several times the right way—and once the wrong way in her nervousness—and then stepped up to the door, took a deep breath, and lingered there, scared to push the door the rest of the way open.

Osom stood and waited by the door for almost a full minute, like someone expecting her chauffeur to open her car door. Steeling herself to finally do it, she had just begun to readjust her bag when the door flew open, and Ms. Claire stared down at her in complete amazement.

She'd come to the door to investigate what had looked like a shadow hovering around the door, and was shocked to find the student she had marked absent, no longer expecting her that day.

It was 9:25 a.m.

"Osom Semewe!" Ms. Claire exclaimed in surprise at the student who was standing at the door with her mouth hanging open.

"G-G-Good morning, m-miss," Osom stammered, even as she genuflected.

"Come in! Why are you standing there like a bouncer? Have you taken up a new profession as a security officer?" Osom shook her head in response and threw the class mistress a pleading look.

Stepping aside and waving her student into the room, the class mistress said, "You're very late today. What happened?"

Osom stood very still and tried to explain. "I'm so sorry, miss. The clock died this morning and did not ring like it does every day. So, I overslept. I walked as fast as I could and—"

"Just come in and settle down," Ms. Claire said impatiently, rolling her eyes. "And the clock did not *die*, Osom Semewe. It only stopped working." She was always unimpressed by inaccurate phrases like "the clock died." Osom could hear some of her classmates giggling.

Ms. Claire looked around sharply at her pupils then. "Shhh! What are you all laughing at?" she asked sternly. "Is someone hungry for the cane this morning?"

There was immediate silence, and she turned back to Osom then. Ms. Claire knew that the girl was doing her best to improve her English and maintain her "B" grade, but with her at form-five level now, she hadn't still expected to hear transliterations like "the clock died" from her. She wasn't sure whether to attribute her use of the phrase to nervousness, which had clearly overtaken her shaking student completely while standing at the door, or to a lingering lack of proficiency in the English language.

Osom walked into the classroom and stood by the teacher's desk, her posture hunched like a lamb drenched in the rain. She was certain what would come next and waited as still as possible for the very worst to happen: the fetching of the cane and the strokes across her palms as punishment. Instead, Ms. Claire took a sweeping look at her from head to toe, blinked slowly, shook her head, and then giving out a sigh that seemed to label this as a hopeless case, she instructed Osom once again to just go to her seat and settle down.

Osom's eyes widened in surprise, but she quickly turned around and marched to her desk, but not before rummaging through her bag, taking out her homework, and quickly giving it to Ms. Claire, who took it with a wry smile and placed it on top of the pile of submissions already gathered there.

Ms. Claire waited for about a minute to allow Osom to settle down, and her body language to signal her readiness, before continuing with the English lesson like no interruption had occurred, leaving Osom sober and confused.

She tried to concentrate and managed to be attentive about half the time, while far away in her own thoughts the other half. *Why is Ms. Claire postponing doomsday? I would have preferred to be whipped now, once and for all, and put it behind me. But, God, now I'll have to wait, the whole day maybe, for whenever Ms. Claire is ready to make me pay for my lateness."*

While postulating on the worst, she missed the teacher's instruction to the class to turn to a specific page in their textbooks. When Osom suddenly saw the commotion all around as her classmates flipped their pages, she quickly craned her neck to look at the one her colleague seated to her left had turned to, and she flipped to that page, sighing heavily in relief.

At the end of the lesson, Ms. Claire picked up the pile of homework and her teaching accessories, walked up to Osom, and quietly said, "Osom Semewe, see me in my office during the long break. Okay?"

"Yes, miss," Osom answered, looking up at the teacher, who quickly turned away and headed for the door.

When Ms. Claire walked out of the classroom, leaving the door wide open, Osom's eyes could not help but watch her feet and listen to the clack of Ms. Claire's heels hitting the floor of the corridor until the sound and sight faded in the distance.

In a turmoil of mixed emotions, Osom buried her head in her arms and rested at her desk, despairing as her mind tried to fully remember the previous night's dream. She again saw Ms. Claire laughing hysterically, with that axe raised overhead, and she began to cry. This postponement of her punishment was almost as tortuous as being in that dark cave.

It was another two hours and forty-five minutes before the long break and Osom's meeting with Ms. Claire. When the big bell sounded at ten-thirty for the short, fifteen-minute break, Osom rushed to see her childhood friend, Kenene, in the next class.

One look at Osom told Kenene that something was very wrong with her dear friend. "Hey, Osom, what happened? I looked for you this morning at the general assembly, and when I did not see you, I got a bit worried." Kenene said this hurriedly, peering into her friend's eyes.

Osom grabbed her hand and pulled her away from listening ears, walking with her to the field and then describing her ordeal from last night.

"Eeeh!" Kenene screeched, placing a hand over her mouth. She was dumbstruck by Osom's dream, but even more so by Ms. Claire's very uncharacteristic reaction to her friend's lateness. It all felt so eerie. She thought Ms. Claire was bad news—a sadist simply wanting to add fanfare to her extraction of the proverbial pound of Osom's flesh.

"Oh dear! I don't like the sound of this, Osom. I really don't. Why is that woman behaving like a witch?" She paused and stared pensively into space briefly before continuing. "But what can you do? When you meet her, try to beg her to forgive you right away, but you must prepare yourself mentally too because you and I both know how strict Ms. Claire is, and that her 'no' is as firm as an Iroko tree."

Both girls were silent for a while. Then Kenene sought to soothe Osom's frayed nerves. "Listen my friend, by God's grace, all this will be over in September when we graduate."

"I tell you, Kenene, I can't wait to get out of here! You have no idea! And in my next life, I pray never to cross paths with Ms. Claire. Though should I ever see her, I'll change my direction faster than the wind! I ask this in Jesus' name."

"Amen!" they chorused.

The bell rang, and the two friends walked back to their various classes. Before finally parting ways on the landing, which would lead them in different directions, Osom said, "I'll come to see you after I've seen Ms. Claire. For sure."

"Okay. Take care till later," Kenene replied regretfully and bade her friend goodbye.

At exactly 12:32 p.m., Osom was standing at Ms. Claire's office door. With a deep steadying breath, she raised her hand and knocked three times.

"Come in, come in!" called an impatient voice from inside the office.

Osom slowly opened the door, poked her head in to see if the invitation to come in would be repeated, and then walked in with a bit of a shiver. Unsurprisingly, Ms. Claire kept her head down, busily writing and flipping through assignment sheets. Osom had been to this office several times in the past and had received many tongue-lashing from the class mistress right here. So, she was very familiar with the layout of the bookshelves, the pictures and maps on the wall, and the various statues adorning Ms. Claire's table—unique pieces from Africa, Asia, and North America. There was no doubt that Ms. Claire was a "globetrotter" and an avid collector of bits and pieces from all over the world.

Osom stood in front of Ms. Claire's table, though some distance away, and folded her hands behind her back. "Good afternoon, miss," she said, genuflecting a little.

"Good afternoon, Osom. Please sit down." The class mistress pointed at one of the two visitor's chairs in front of her. Pleasantly surprised that the teacher had addressed her only by her first name for once, Osom sat down timidly.

Ms. Claire bit the bottom of her red Bic pen and swivelled her chair a little to the left, and then a little to the right, as though she were pondering where to start. Then she stopped swivelling, put the pen down on the pile of assignments, leaned forward, and clasped her hands in front of her on the table.

"How are you?" she asked then, with no emotion on her face.

"Fine, miss," Osom quickly answered, twiddling her fingers in her lap.

"You told me your parents went to Fonma. When are you expecting them back?"

"Yes, miss. They'll be back next Monday." Osom wasn't sure why her class mistress was asking about her parents as a prelude to punishment. *God! Why can't she just get on with the flogging? I'm tired of this torturous wait,* she thought to herself.

"Osom Semewe," Ms. Claire began, interrupting the girl's thoughts, "I know you think the worst of me ... that I'm a monster because I'm firm about discipline."

Osom's eyes widened. *Ah ha! I knew she was a witch! She even knows what I'm thinking and that I saw her in my dream! She knows!* Osom's mind was in overdrive, and she looked down, staring at her lap.

Ms. Claire could see her pupil's distress, so she continued in a much softer tone, one that sounded almost like a plea. "You're a bright student, Osom Semewe, and I know you'll excel in your academic work. I just want you to be a lot more organized. It's ironic, but I don't *know* if your parents' presence is in any way responsible for your often-shoddy ways. I must say that I've actually noticed that you've been a bit tidier and more focused this past week since they've been gone."

Osom looked up but found she couldn't meet her eyes. So, she fixed a remorseful gaze on the space just above the teacher's head.

"I'm sure they want to see you grow up to be a very responsible and successful woman though," Ms. Claire said then. "All parents want that for their children. I want it for my *own* children. So, believe me, that's my strong desire for you and *all* my students. When I'm strict, or whip you for doing something wrong, it is because I care about you. I really do care about all my students! You know you're not the only one I sometimes have cause to strongly caution."

Silence. Osom's eyes were fixed now on a single spot on the table, still expecting the worst to follow this sermon and too scared to look up. Something in Ms. Claire's words and voice had struck a chord though, making her think of her mother. The allusion to her parents had a sobering effect on her. If only Ms. Claire knew how unhappy and demotivating her home had become. She slowly looked up from the table and directly at the class mistress for the first time then, though she still could not bring herself to speak.

"Do you understand me?" Ms. Claire asked after a moment. "Do you understand that you must be better organized if you are to graduate in September? Do you understand how your success or failure will also be a reflection on your teachers—me included?" The teacher said this firmly, and then looked straight at her student and fell silent, awaiting an answer.

"Yes, miss. Please, miss, I'm very sorry I arrived late. I finished my homework very late, and the clock—"

Ms. Claire raised her hand to stop her. "It's okay. I understand about the clock dying, or whatever, and I don't blame you for that." The teacher paused suddenly then, as though an idea had just sprung into her head. Then she asked, "Do you know what you'd like to be in the future?"

Osom kept her gaze on the table as her mind went through a series of common professions. She had never really given her future much thought and became lost in the question. "Emm … no. But… But I think I'll become a famous drummer, and maybe a keyboardist too." She didn't know how or where this idea had come from. Even as she uttered the words, they sounded strange even to herself, and she wondered if she had gone crazy. Nonetheless, there was something liberating about this professional goal she'd just blurted out, and it made her happy. She just didn't know why.

Ms. Claire was taken aback, jerking backwards and frowning, wondering if she had heard Osom correctly. With raised brows, she asked, "Really? Have you ever told your parents that this is what you'd like to do in the future?"

"No." She shrugged. "They've never asked me really." Osom still didn't lift her gaze from the table. She still wasn't sure why her teacher had yet to fetch the cane.

While her pupil was thinking about the cane, Ms. Claire's baffled thoughts were elsewhere. The class mistress really didn't think that Osom had ever discussed this desired profession with her parents, but she could only guess what Mr and Mrs Semewe's reaction would be.

There were no local institutions offering majors in such musical instruments. Making a success of a career as a drummer or keyboardist would be extremely difficult. Osom would need to win a foreign scholarship, or else her parents would have to become wealthy enough to pay for such study overseas, and Ms. Claire was sad that, without parental guidance, her student was setting herself up for a huge disappointment.

She wondered if Osom had been watching too many international shows on TV and was being misled by the realities of other more-developed countries, which contrasted sharply with theirs. However, not forgetting her supporting role as a teacher, irrespective of the chosen career path, she relaxed back in her chair. Something about Osom's dream profession was bringing a smile to her face.

In Osom, Ms. Claire saw a fast-changing world from the one she'd grown up in, staring her in the face, or at least, staring down at her desk. Still not completely sold on the drummer and keyboardist idea, given the challenges of achieving such a dream, she took solace in the fact that Osom was still very young at only fifteen. The class mistress figured that many of her students either had no idea about what they wanted to do or become in the future or were at least indecisive. She believed, and hoped, that Osom might soon change her mind when other options presented themselves.

Ms. Claire sighed, leaned forward, and decided to give Osom a piece of advice nonetheless. "Listen, if becoming a drummer or a keyboardist is what you'd really like to pursue in the future, I'll advise that you find time to discuss it with your parents and not wait for them to ask you because they may have some other ideas or plans for you that are likely the extreme opposite of what you've just told me. It's also important that they're prepared to support you. Do you understand?"

Osom finally lifted her face up, looked at her class mistress, and nodded. "Yes, miss."

She found the idea of having a conversation about her future with her parents very strange; it actually scared her. Do parents really have such conversations with their children? Osom wondered and pouted as her peculiar choice of dream profession gradually unravelled. Defiantly, she thought, *Ha! Papa would look at me like he was seeing a ghost, and Mama will wonder if I've had too much palm wine.* Osom sucked in her cheeks to suppress a smile. She realized that, if there was one way to rebel against her parents and get them to notice and reflect deeply on how effected she was by their increasing estrangement, telling them she wanted to be a drummer was definitely it. They would at least be thinking about her then, wondering what in the world she was thinking and why.

Ms. Claire watched her student process this silently for a while; then she took a long breath. "Okay," she said finally, tapping the table with both hands. Then she pushed her chair back, stood up, and walked towards the bookshelf to her right, where she normally leaned the cane.

Osom turned slightly to spy on her from the corner of her eyes, certain the hour had finally come. Giving the conversation they had just had, and Ms. Claire's reassuring voice, Osom believed that she was unlikely to get more than two strokes of the cane and was relieved—in fact, she felt gratitude. As the teacher searched her bookshelf, Osom looked away to avoid Ms. Claire catching her eye and instead focused on her hands, gently pulling and playing with her fingers.

Ms. Claire returned to her chair with a box wrapped in brown paper, sat down, and held it out to her with a warm smile. "Here. This is for you."

Osom thought this was another dream. Shocked and a little suspicious, her hands felt frozen and wouldn't move as she looked back and forth between the teacher and the box. "Go on, here," Ms. Claire urged, thrusting her hand forward with the gift.

Osom kept her gaze on her teacher as she took the gift with shaky hands, holding it out as though she expected it to explode at any moment.

The class mistress could see her nervousness and felt the need to reassure her. "It's a gift from me ... and I hope you'll find it useful."

"A g-gift for me? Thank you, miss. Thank you." Osom bowed twice. Her shock made her legs shake, and she found herself tongue-tied as she examined the item in her hands from all angles, confused by this unexpected turn of events. She'd come here sure she was going to be punished for being late, but instead, here she sat, unpunished, and the icing on the cake was that she'd just received a gift from the most renowned disciplinarian in the school. Reflexively, she held the wrapped box tightly in both hands and clutched it to her chest as she stared at the teacher in disbelief, still at a loss for words.

"It's my pleasure," Ms. Claire said. "If there's any way I can be of assistance to you, at any time, please don't be scared to come to me. Do you understand, Osom Semewe?"

"Yes, miss. Yes, miss. Thank you, thank you, miss." Osom bowed repeatedly still clutching the gift to her heart.

Ms Claire rose from her chair then, prompting Osom to quickly stand up too, then leaned forward a bit, pointing her forefinger at the girl's nose and speaking very sternly. "Now, behave yourself, Osom Semewe, and pay attention to your studies. No more lateness. Do you hear me?"

"Yes, miss."

"Next time you're very late for school as you were today or submit a dingy or crappy assignment, I won't be lenient at all." She wagged her pointed forefinger in Osom's face. "Do I make myself clear enough now?"

Osom nodded vigorously, bowing repeatedly in gratitude. "Yes, miss. I'm sorry for today. Thank you very much, miss. Thank you."

Ms. Claire stood upright and breathed out audibly. "You're welcome. Now go have some lunch before the bell rings." She waved her student away. "And shut the door after you."

Outside the door and clutching her gift firmly, Osom turned and sent one last look of gratitude to the teacher she now found incredible.

Ms. Claire kept a straight face as she nodded in acknowledgement of her student, waited for the door to swing closed behind her, and then sat down, her thoughts immediately drifting to Osom as a drummer or keyboardist. She soon found herself clapping quietly as she started to laugh. *Children these days!* she mused and continued to laugh, tears of amusement welling in her eyes. *I am so old!*

Outside Ms. Claire's office, Osom began to run, skipping for joy intermittently on her way to Kenene's class. She could hardly contain herself. Kenene spotted her friend holding a brown package from the class window and ran out to meet her. They met on the field where they usually sat during the short break.

"You wouldn't believe it!" Osom said hurriedly, panting and pulling her friend down to sit on the grass. They both settled into lotus positions, and still out of breath, Osom held her chest so that her heart might stop racing as her friend watched her eagerly, waiting for her news, which was obviously good if the delighted look on Osom's face was any indication.

"No flogging, no nagging, no dressing down!" Osom spurted out in summary, taking deep breaths to try and calm herself before starting from the beginning, telling her friend all about her meeting with the class mistress.

When Kenene heard about the profession her friend had told Ms. Claire she'd like to pursue, she laughed so loud and so long that she had to hold her stomach. Osom now found it hilarious too and joined her friend in laughter.

"Hun? You mischievous thing! Drummer and keyboardist? Not even a poet? Where did that come from? Or did you just want to shock Ms. Claire so badly she'd forget what had brought you to her office and just chase you out of there?"

"I don't know, Kenene. Bang! The idea just came to my head. But interestingly, Ms. Claire sounded supportive and advised me to discuss it with my parents. That was another surprise for me today."

"Hun? Tell your parents what? That you want to be a drummer and/or keyboardist?" Kenene opened her eyes wide as she pushed her head forward. "I don't need to tell you that you'll be toast, do I?" she asked her friend rhetorically, blinking hard at her.

Osom wore a playful look as she pouted her lips and moved them from left to right. Convinced that Osom had hallucinated her crazy moment in Ms. Claire's office, Kenene dismissed the impulse to prod her friend further and relaxed a bit. "Well, your poor parents have their work cut out for them, I assure you. But first, they must buy you talking drums from Baba Pututu to practice with. As for keyboard, you had better book the church's organ and start learning from there. But do me a favour and please remember that you never had this conversation with me. I don't want your parents to think that I'm a bad influence."

Osom laughed heartily at Kenene's sarcasm and then continued while her friend was still laughing. "Anyway, here. This is the present she gave me!" She held up the brown-paper package.

Kenene had already been listening to a story that sounded incredibly unreal and almost screamed now as she looked at the gift. "Huh? Ms. Claire gave you a present? Tell me you're lying! She really gave you a present? Will wonders never cease?" She clapped and then held her chin.

Osom was more excited than she could adequately show her friend. "Yes, yes! Well … at least I think so. Look! This is a gift, isn't it? Or am I dreaming?" She shoved it towards Kenene's face.

They looked at each other, over the package, with their mouths agape.

"Wait! Wait, Osom! Let me get this again… You mean Ms. Claire did not tongue-lash you at all, even though she chose not to physically whip you?"

"No! She didn't. Can you believe it?" She paused briefly and then added, "Although, before I left, she did warn me not to be late anymore or submit work that's dingy or … em … some other word that sounded like 'happy' … hmm… I can't remember the exact word she used. You know Ms. Claire's a walking *Oxford Dictionary*. But I assume she meant untidy work. She usually does."

"That's all? Really? Please someone tell me: Are we missing something?

Has Christmas come early?" Kenene looked around as though there were others nearby who might provide such answers.

Osom pinched her own thigh to remind herself that she was really there. "I don't know, Kenene, but you tell me... Is this really happening, or have I gone mad?"

"Well, not completely, just on the nonsense drum and keyboard talk. But tell me..." She nodded at the gift then, leaning forward with wide-eyed curiosity. "What's in it?"

"I don't know. She didn't tell me. Go on, Kenene. Open it!" Osom pressed it into her friend's hand.

"Oh no," she said, placing it on the ground between them. "It's *your* gift. *You* must open it. So, go on and open it already!"

They looked at each other. Neither of them eager to actually unwrap it.

"Go on," Kenene said, then added teasingly, "Are you afraid?" They both began to laugh. Then Osom nodded.

"Well, wouldn't you be if you were in my shoes, Kenene?

Taking a deep breath, Osom began to unwrap the gift then, the two friends shooting nervous but excited grins at each other periodically as she tore one end open and then the other. When it was almost unwrapped, Kenene shouted suddenly.

"Wait! Wait! ... Let me just move away from you in case a spitting snake pops out of that box!" She giggled and sat a little further away from her.

"Bad friend," Osom said flatly. "With a friend like you, what do I need an enemy for? If it's a snake, then it's yours to bring home for dinner ... with all pleasure." The two friends laughed joyfully, thoroughly enjoying themselves now.

Osom shook her head. She couldn't stop imagining what she'd do without Kenene's friendship. It was at times like this that she found their acquaintance utterly invaluable. They complemented each other. Osom's best subjects seemed to be Kenene's worst and vice-versa, and so helping each other out was easy. They both loved the game of field hockey, and were excellent at it, relishing the rush of adrenalin they'd get as they shouted and prodded each other with shouts of *"Go! Go!! Go!!!"* at critical points of any game where they were playing on the same team, though that happened only very rarely.

Osom was a defender, while Kenene was a centre-forward, usually playing against each other. Osom always described the goal posts as her castle to defend against marauding pirates like Kenene, and Kenene in turn teased that *her* job was to break into that castle like a jet bomber and take defenders like Osom and the goalkeeper hostage for a huge ransom.

Eyeing her friend, now sitting at a "safe" distance, Osom tugged very gently on the last piece of glued paper, teasing Kenene as she drew out the suspense: "Going ... going ... open!"

Osom yanked the paper free then, revealing a small, plain-white box, with no photo or description of what it might contain. As Kenene watched on, Osom quickly opened it and withdrew a small, beautiful, brass table clock with dragon scales on its surface and gold-plated dragon legs on which it stood. The dragon's two-toned spiked tail of burned brass and gold curled backwards and up to the clock's crown to form the handle with which it could be carried.

"Wow!" the two girls exclaimed almost simultaneously, and Osom covered her mouth in awe.

"It's so beautiful!" Kenene said, moving forward and stretching out her hand. "Can I hold—"

"Not on your life!" Osom said, yanking it out of reach before her friend could even finish her request. "It's going to change to a spitting snake!" She held the clock behind her back, grinning playfully.

"Oh! Please, please, please!" Kenene said, begging like a child.

"Hmmm... I don't know. Next time I get a strange gift like this, will you sit closer?"

"Oh, yes! Yes, of course I will!" Kenene blurted, clasping her hands before her as she pleaded, smiling.

"Liar!" Osom poked out her tongue teasingly, eyed her friend, and then with exaggerated caution, she brought the clock back around and gave it to Kenene.

"God!" she exclaimed as she studied it up close. "It's really sooooooooo beautiful! It's even working already too! And look!" Kenene squeaked excitedly and scooched over so close to Osom that the sides of their heads touched. "When you turn it this way or that, the dragon opens or shuts its mouth and eyes!" She held the clock out and tilted it left and then right for

Osom to appreciate the dragon's changing expressions.

"My God!" Osom whispered in utter amazement. "I've never seen or been given anything this beautiful in my life before."

"Neither have I," Kenene raised her shoulders in agreement. After admiring the clock for a little while longer, she gently handed it back to Osom and felt a pang of envy as she did so, still dumbstruck by such a unique work of art. She admitted again that she had never seen anything quite like it before, then shook her head.

"Hmmm… Osom, I'm jealous-o. Maybe I should make my English notebook scruffy and come late to school tomorrow to get a gift too."

"Great idea, Kenene. In fact, why don't you enlist me to tutor you in scruffiness, and then try coming to school five hours late from tomorrow on. You'll get Ms. Claire's normal beautiful gift: a full mouth of insults and much, much more."

The girls laughed. Osom peered into the box then. "Hey, look! There's a manual to guide me in operating it."

"Very nice, my friend. Very, very nice…" Kenene paused as an idea popped into her head. "Hey, Osom, your nightmare! Do you think it was *meant* to be the *opposite* of reality?"

Osom grew pensive. "Maybe. I don't know." A moment later, she shrugged. "Maybe Ms. Claire's axe was a metaphor for her help, and the strangeness of the dream a symbol of today's shocking outcome… Who knows?"

As she carefully placed the clock back in its box, Osom repeated to her friend Ms. Claire's advice, promising to do her best not to upset the class mistress anymore with tardiness, scruffiness, or dinginess.

The big bell sounded then, and the girls jumped up, dusted themselves down, and started to walk back to their classes.

"I'm going to go thank her again as soon as school is over today," Osom said.

"Yes, good idea. You must do that."

As they climbed up the stairs with a crowd of other students, Osom bent towards her friend, grabbed her hand, and whispered playfully, "Tell me about the future. Should I become a crystal-ball gazer and dream interpreter rather than a drummer? I overheard that the neighbourhood sage who practices fortune-telling seems to be a specialist in telling everyone the same thing, just in different ways, and they say that a visit to his hut costs a lot of money—and I mean, *a lot*, Kenene."

Kenene chuckled, eyeing her friend, who was becoming impossible, and hissed before asking, "Is the sage very rich then?"

Osom struggled to suppress a laugh. "I hear he's the poorest sage in town."

There was no suppressing after that. The two friends laughed so loudly then that some students looked over at them, wondering what was going on. Just as they arrived on the landing, from which they would head off to their respective classes, Kenene turned to her friend, still grinning playfully. "I think I'll help your father drive you to a psychiatrist myself. Until then though, you better concentrate in class. Bye." With that, she hopped away, not even hearing Osom quiet assurance that she would try.

When the bell was rung at two-thirty to signal the end of the day, Osom quickly packed her bag and marched down to Ms. Claire's office. On her way, she made a mental note of how best to thank her and practiced it many times over to ensure that she chose the right words, with proper grammar, and was very disappointed to see a notice on the class mistress's door: "Closed for the day."

Osom sighed and turned away, promising herself that when she saw her in the morning as usual, she would thank her profusely. She was unsure whether to try and catch up with Kenene or just go straight home. She decided that she'd wait and see her friend in the morning as well, then checked her bag again to ensure she had taken everything she needed and began her long trek back home.

No sooner had she entered her bedroom than Osom took out her present from her bag, removed the clock from its box, and set it strategically on the table at eye level with her bed, so that she could look at it in infinite admiration. She read the manual, and after a bit of trial and error, she learnt how to set the alarm and turn it off, and was ecstatic to learn that the alarm had four different rings. She played with the four options for a while, dancing to each tune as she sat on her bed before finally deciding on the one she liked the most.

Osom had never received any gift this valuable and practical for her immediate needs, and being her first, the clock was exceptionally special to her. That it was also from Ms. Claire was something she simply had to get used to. Her negative perception of Ms. Claire hadn't disappeared completely. She was still somewhat apprehensive of her class mistress, even though this clock gift had helped to shift her former position a remarkable amount. Last night's nightmare had played with her emotions, flicking her mind on and off and making it difficult for her to relax in the face of the warmth Ms. Claire had shown her today.

As she looked at the pretty clock, she became increasingly fascinated by the dragon's eyes, which opened and shut when she turned the clock up or down, and looked sideways when she turned the clock to the left or right. Osom sincerely hoped that her class mistress would do such good deeds more often, instead of her normal harshness. Still, she didn't know what else she could expect of Ms. Claire if she herself didn't show consistency in discipline.

Each time she left the bedroom for a few minutes, she found herself hurrying back to look at the clock. Her eyes stayed fixated on it as she changed out of her school uniform and settled down. She changed its position on the table many times to find the most appealing to her eyes.

Osom was quickly becoming obsessed by the brass and gold-plated dragon clock. The dragon's eyes made her feel like she had another friend in the world besides Kenene, but this friend lived with her, right in the intimacy of her home, where in recent times friendship—or even companionship—had become a rare and expensive commodity.

That evening, Osom cooked herself rice and fish stew for supper. She was feeling very happy and looked forward to eating in her room, instead of in the dining room, so that she could keep looking at the clock. She whistled as she stirred the stew and danced to an imaginary song. She sang as she scooped some stew on top of the rice in a ceramic bowl, sniffed the enticing aroma in its the steam, swirled it around twice, and then headed for her room, striding like a model on a catwalk.

As Osom settled down to her meal, she found herself speaking to herself aloud between bites: "You were not whipped for being late, Osom... Unbelievable! ... You even got a present ... despite being very late... Can you even believe what happened to us today?"

As she ate and pondered, her eyes never left the clock, and she spoke to it now, instead of herself. "Dinner tastes so much better tonight... I wish you could eat with me, my new friend."

That night, Osom tidied up her cutlery, hurriedly wiped down her table, and settled down to do her homework as usual. It was a very humid day, and feeling sweaty and sticky all over, she took a quick bath before settling down to study. She managed to finish her homework on time, and feeling sleepy, decided to go to bed much earlier than normal, quite tired after the nightmare that had kept her from getting much sleep the night before.

Finishing with her bedtime prayers, she yawned, and stood up. "What a miraculous day it's been!" she said loudly to herself.

Then taking one more look at the clock, playing with it for a little while to watch the dragon's eyes open, shut, and study her, a contented Osom set the alarm for six a.m. Her eyes grew heavy as she sat on the edge of her bed and kept looking at the clock, so she finally put the lamp and some matches next to the head of her bed, and slipped under the covers, thinking about Ms. Claire and what a lovely teacher she was after all.

As she remembered her kind words, she couldn't understand how such a good-natured woman was being so effectively hidden beneath the mask of a strict disciplinarian. Osom wondered if other students would ever be as privileged as she had been this day to see this other side of the class mistress who was more feared than admired in the school. Still propped up and staring at her new treasure, Osom began to nod off. Each time her head fell to the side, startling her and making her eyes flip open, it was as though a bell had rung to warn her not to fall asleep.

It was almost ten o'clock when she gave up the fight. She couldn't stay awake anymore. Stretching out with a loud, drawn-out yawn, she blew the lamp out, and in no time was fast asleep.

The big clock on the wall softly chimed twice, politely letting the world know that it was two a.m., but Osom could not be stirred from deep slumber. Not by the chimes, and not by the small commotion that was going on in her room. Osom slept right through it like one who'd had too much wine. It wasn't until the commotion escalated to a loud crash that Osom was startled awake, sitting up abruptly in fright and listening hard.

Silence.

She frowned, wondering if a burglar had entered the house and straining her eyes as she looked around the darkness of her room. As far as she could tell, there was so one else there, but she quickly leaned over, felt for the lamp, and lit it, adjusting its flame to its lowest setting. Then holding the lamp up, she flung her legs down from the bed as its soft, orange light filled the room, and then sat there on its edge, with her eyes and ears focused keenly on the door, waiting for another sound.

After about two minutes in pin-drop silence, Osom shook her head, thinking that she must have just been dreaming. She suddenly remembered her new friend, the dragon clock, and decided to take comfort in looking at it. Turning up the lamp's regulator to slightly increase its glow, she turned towards it.

Osom's heart stopped. She could not believe her eyes. "I must be dreaming again," she whispered, rubbing her eyes and looking closely at her table, and then set the lamp down. Her pretty dragon clock lay smashed on the floor by the table's legs, surrounded by splinters of glass.

Osom was transfixed, her left hand covering her mouth as she whispered through it in despair, "This is another nightmare. This has to be another nightmare. Wake up, Osom!"

She stared at the dragon's covered eyes through the broken opening on the clock, and then reached out. Her hand shook as she carefully picked up the clock, and then the lamp, which she held high above her head so she could see every corner of the room, trying to figure out what was happening.

Just as she was about to give up, a large rat jumped out of her school bag and ran past her under the table, making her jump up in fright, setting the lamp to swinging in her hand. She hurriedly placed the lamp down on the table as clarity began to creep into her mind. With quivering hands, Osom clutched the back of the smashed clock to her chest, a deep sense of sorrow falling over her. She closed her eyes to take it all in.

"Please, God," she said in a quiet, broken voice, "tell me this is a dream... Please tell me this is a dream..."

She turned the clock in her hands and stared at as though hoping for a restoration miracle that would never happen.

"Oh God, why?" she lamented. "What have I done to deserve this?" Raw pain cut deep through her chest and entire body, but she couldn't cry. "I haven't even given Ms. Claire a proper thank you yet... I planned to but ... but now it's broken. Why? Why? Why?" Her head began to throb from the growing pressure of pent-up emotions.

Osom placed the clock on the table, pulled out a chair, and sat down, holding her head in her hands. Every now and then, she looked up at the dragon and felt the same sense of utter shock and disbelief, shuddering in disgust and anger at the image of that filthy rodent running amok in her room while she'd slept.

"What was that rat looking for on this table or in my school bag anyway? What?" Feeling the urge to investigate, she stood up, used her slipper to brush the glass splinters together into a small pile that would be easy to pack, and then lifted the lamp and began to inspect the table more closely.

"Oh my god!" she almost screamed then. "These stupid rats!!"

She could see tiny drops of dried-up fish stew on the table. She had wiped it down after supper last night before doing her homework, though not thoroughly enough it seemed, and the smell of fish had been too much for any rat to resist. Angry with herself, Osom smacked herself in the head as punishment, then gave out a long, loud hiss, placed her hands on her waist, and scowled in dismay as she looked around.

She was struck by another sudden realization then, and her eyes widened in fear. She snatched her school bag up from the arm of the chair and peered into it, then slumped down to the floor, almost fainting at what she saw. Her schoolbooks were torn up, her personal notes as well as her textbooks, and parts of the school bag itself had been bitten open in three places. She sat there on the floor, in utter denial, for a long time, her heart pumping heavily. Then she finally summoned up the courage and strength to get up. Turning her bag upside down over the table, she shook it vigorously so that all of its content would fall out.

"*OH NO!!*" she screeched, clutching her mouth as she watched pieces of her notebooks and textbooks flutter down to the tabletop like drunken moths. Osom went numb as tiny bits and pieces of paper flew everywhere in the slight breeze that was creeping in through the window slats. Her homework notebook had been the most viciously attacked.

Osom lifted the tattered remains of her bag up to her nose and sniffed it. *Yep,* she thought bitterly. *Fish stew.* She must have dripped a bit on it as she'd carried her supper into the room, and the rodents had traced the smell to her bag and started chewing away at the bag itself and everything inside. Tears streaked down her face past her wide open mouth as she began to sob, collapsing onto her chair, resting her head on her arms, and weeping desperately. Her pain was indescribable.

As the tears fell in torrents and her nose ran, she couldn't stop thinking that this was the worst catastrophe to have ever befallen her. She had not only lost her school books and her homework assignment, which had symbolized her quest for success and the ongoing determination to improve herself, but the clock as well, a special friend she had just been gifted and which she treasured for its promising potential to be her faithful companion in a home where she'd felt so lonely for so long. Osom wept with a bitterness that felt almost suicidal.

"What am I going to do? What am I going to do?" she sobbed. She couldn't believe that a simple meal of rice and fish stew had brought her whole world crashing down in the twinkle of an eye like a house being swallowed up by a huge crater in an earthquake, along with everything she cared about the most.

That train of thought brought her attention to her parents then, in faraway Fonma, and she froze, wondering what to do about her textbooks and feeling like running away and losing herself in some unknown land. Life at home was hard enough already with her father's cost-saving measures everywhere. She couldn't even imagine telling him that she needed new textbooks.

"No way! He'll roast me alive for eating in my room! I'd much rather just go on with whatever's left of these books, and failing, than ask Papa." Osom shook her head aggressively, as though to dismiss an evil thought. "If only I could ask Mama," she whispered wistfully. But Osom knew she couldn't do that either. Her mother was already supporting the family with the meagre income from her retail work. Asking her to buy new textbooks was akin to pushing her mother to beg, steal, or borrow. Her mind went to Kenene then, as it often did when she needed help, but she just couldn't figure out how her one true friend could be of any assistance to her when she had her own studies to worry about.

Thirty minutes later, seething now, Osom grabbed the lamp and stomped off to the kitchen to fetch a broom and a pestle. Then she marched back to her room like a member of the first battalion, set the lamp on the table, and like a sleuth, stealthily walked around, searching the corners of her room for any rat, the pestle raised in one hand and the broom in the other, ready to strike.

After a couple of minutes with no success, she sat on the chair by the table with the pestle and broom on her lap. "I'm waiting for you, rats! Come out! I dare you to run anywhere in this room! I'll smash your head to a paste, you stupid, destructive, little thieves!"

Livid, she stood up again and started pacing her scarcely furnished room, opening the wardrobe and the drawers and pulling out clothes and accessories with the broom, searching for the furry source of her wrath. Then she walked around the room, working her way through everything with the broom and pestle, carefully pushing things around, poking cardboard boxes and raffia bags with the pestle, and slowly turning things out of bags and cardboard boxes ... waiting for a rat to jump out. But there was nothing.

Beyond frustrated, she sat back on the chair, looking almost deranged, dropping the broom on the floor but keeping the pestle in her hand. After a long wait, remembering that her mother had once told her that rats were smarter and quicker than human beings, she breathed out heavily and put the pestle down. She was exhausted.

Osom looked down in misery at the shreds of notes and textbooks that littered the table and floor of her room. Each and every piece, large and small, looked to her like a fragment of her life, helplessly needing to be put back together and become whole again, free of anxiety and fear.

She got up from the table, taking the broken clock with her, and sat down on her bed, placing the pestle beside her, refusing to let go of the only weapon she believed could help her exact vengeance on the rats. Osom then began gingerly removing the remaining loose pieces of glass from the clock, and then shook it upside down to ensure that any pieces she had missed fell out. Looking at the dragon's closed eyes, she felt like her entire life had played out before her in the span of the twenty-four hours between her horrible nightmare and this terrible moment.

The thought of how her parents would react if they knew brought tears to her eyes. Even though she often wished for a more loving relationship with her parents, she *was* deeply grateful for the sacrifices they were making to see her through school, rather than sending her away like her siblings for a better life elsewhere. Her School Certificate exams were in about five months' time, and her greatest fear was not getting the required grades and letting her parents down. Almost debilitated by sadness now, she lay down, clutching the clock, and cried inconsolably for the rest of the night.

It was six-thirty a.m., but Osom had not moved a muscle and had no intention of doing so. The clock was standing next to her pillow, being held in place by her hands, when the dragon's eyes flipped open suddenly, surprising her and bringing a small glimmer of light to her heart. Those eyes seemed to be telling her that it was all going to be fine. Trying to believe that, Osom continued lying there, gazing sadly into the dragon's eyes.

At 8:15, there was a loud knock on the door and an equally loud call: "Osom? Osom? It's Auntie Vero! Are you well? You're very late for school today!"

"Good morning, Auntie! It's a bad period, and I can't go to school today, but I've taken some painkillers. Thank you."

Osom could not bear to be seen with her red, puffy eyes or face and having to explain what had happened and its likely effect on her newly thawing but still frosty relationship with Ms. Claire. Osom knew that neighbours—even genuinely caring ones—sometimes had a way of getting overly involved in other people's affairs, and she didn't want the entire neighbourhood to hear her story, overreact, and start to police her every move or emotion.

"Okay! Drink lots of hot water, tie a pillow on your stomach, and lie face-down. I'll come see you later, you hear?"

"Thank you, Auntie Vero," she called back, glad she wasn't insisting on coming inside to see her in person. "I'll do that."

At about nine-thirty, she began to feel sleepy again. Placing the clock on the table where she could directly look at it, she laid back down and slept soundly for three hours. At a quarter to one, she got out of bed and had a bath. Not very long after, she was back in her room and dressed when Vero knocked again, having brought Osom a bowl of hot, spicy-pepper soup made with dry fish, local herbs, and spices. The locals believed that unprocessed traditional spices were medicinal for period pain because they effectively warmed up the pelvis and acted like a balm to any pain there.

At the sound of her voice, Osom quickly grabbed her pillow and clutched it firmly below her stomach before opening the door.

"Good afternoon, auntie," she greeted in a low tone, feigning pain by wincing a little.

"How are you? But ... you've been crying! The pain must be terrible." Vero looked at Osom compassionately, and seeing the young girl's puffy eyes, her maternal instincts made her want to do more. "Don't cry. Here, look. I cooked you some spicy-pepper soup for your period pain. I do the same for my daughters, and they swear by it."

Vero held out the covered metal bowl of soup, holding it by its handles with thick, cloth napkins. Osom sniffed and put on a tired face, for more compassion, as she flung her pillow out into the living room and carefully took the bowl from her neighbour.

"It's got strong local nut spices in it, and it's piping hot, so be careful not to burn your tongue," Vero advised.

"Oh, Auntie, but what hassle I've caused you with this! Thank you so much," Osom said in an even lower tone, sniffing again, maintaining her phoney pained expression, and looked down at the bowl, feeling a pang of guilt for lying and making her neighbour go through the trouble of making a special delicacy for her.

"Ah, it's nothing at all. Look, my dear..." Vero reached out and touched her lightly on the arm. "Have some now while it's hot, sit up for at least an hour, and then have some again in the evening, but don't take those painkillers unless the pain continues tomorrow. Okay?"

"Okayy... Thank you, Auntie." Osom tilted her neck slightly to her left side, dragging out her "okay" like a sick child in need of a cuddle.

"Ah, don't worry, it's no problem at all. You'll feel better soon, I promise you. I'll come check on you again in the evening, and if you need anything else, just let me know. Do you hear?"

"Okay, I will. Thank you, Auntie." Osom genuflected twice, starting to feel hungry as the aroma of the soup wafted up past its cover. She couldn't wait for her kind visitor to leave, and as soon as she did, Osom locked the door and hurried to the kitchen to set her medicinal soup down on the stove. She lifted the bowl's lid to take a sniff, and her hunger struck her like a bomb. In fact, she realized that she was starving. She rushed to the three-shelf cupboard by the stove, took out a soup bowl and tablespoon, and quickly spooned in a good portion of the hot soup.

From another shelf, she took a quarter loaf of locally made bread, broke off a large chunk, and sat on the floor by the kitchen's door. Making a quick sign of the cross, she began to eat, dipping every morsel of bread into the soup and licking remnants from her fingers. She was amazed by how incredibly good Auntie Vero's pepper soup tasted, and in a short while, she had devoured the bread and the entire bowl of delicious broth, licking it clean. Osom had always thought that her mother was the best cook around and could win any cooking competition on any given day, but Auntie Vero's pepper soup, she had to admit, was in that same league.

"Ewo! It just can't get better than this," she told herself, shaking her head and licking her fingers, one after the other, but this positive outlook lasted only a minute or two before a gloomy feeling came upon her. Still seated by the kitchen's door with the empty soup bowl, the unfinished business in her bedroom flashed across her mind.

With an off mixture of satisfaction and distress, she stood up, washed the bowl and spoon, wiped them dry, and then returned them to the cupboard before heading back to her room. Once there, she sighed, still unsure where to start in an attempt to tidy things up, and just stood in her doorway for a while with her hands on her waist, staring at the mess.

Finally, sighing once more, she went back to the kitchen to fetch the plastic dustpan and returned, dropping it next to the broom. Then she retrieved her English textbook from the table, sat on her bed, and took time to closely examine the extent of its damage, flipping slowly through its pages one at a time. Then she did the same with her math textbook. Her assignment sheets had taken the worst of it though and were in a disastrous state. Lifting up a stack of tattered papers with just the very ends of her fingers, as though they were soiled rags, she tossed them to the floor in frustration, hissing and cursing. "God will kill you, rats!"

At 3:20, there were three loud knocks on the door, which irritated Osom, believing she was in for another intrusion by another neighbour. She was not in the mood for a visit, especially an uninvited one, and when she called out an answer, her tone did little to hide this fact.

"Yes? Who's there, ha?"

"It's Kenene."

Osom's mood changed in an instant, and delighted, she ran to the door to let her bosom friend come in. As deeply as she'd been wallowing in misery, she hadn't given much thought to her friend since disaster had fallen, but she now realized that she desperately needed to share her predicament with the only confidant she had. She badly needed Kenene's always inspiring words and threw the door wide open to welcome her friend.

"What's wrong, Osom?" Kenene asked before she could even say hello. "You didn't come to school. Are you sick? Is it your period?"

Kenene expression was very worried as she walked into the living room. She could see that her friend had been crying. She fixed her eyes sternly on her as she waited for an answer or explanation.

Osom shook her head, locked the door, and then took Kenene's hand and quickly pulled her to the bedroom, all without uttering a word. Not having been warned, when they reached Osom's bedroom, Kenene was shocked and confused by what she saw and found herself at a loss for words. It looked like a bomb had exploded.

Then she saw the clock, and her eyeballs almost popped from their sockets as she rushed in, screaming, "What?!"

Looking at Osom, she lifted the broken clock, examined its front and back, and looked at her friend again, waiting for an explanation as she placed it back on the table. Osom was just standing there like a statue though, and so Kenene started rummaging through the shreds of paper, lifting each textbook in turn, in utter confusion and disbelief.

"I don't understand," Kenene said. "Please, tell me what in God's name happened here?! How did this happen? The beautiful dragon clock you only got yesterday is broken! Who did this and why?"

Osom threw her hands up in the air, breathed in and out heavily for a moment, and then sat on the bed in despair. Kenene sat next to her, listening intently as Osom finally began to tell her story, interjecting only once to exclaim, "Oh my god! Rats?!"

Once the story was complete, Osom shrugged tiredly. "So, Kenene, that's my one-day life story, and I wish it wasn't true." She peered into her friend's eyes then. "What do I do? How do I solve this? I'm just as afraid of my parents as I am of Ms. Claire, even though my opinion of her has changed a little now. Tell me, Kenene... What am I to tell Ms. Claire? That instead of using the dining room, I was stupid enough to eat rice-and-fish stew in my room, on the same table where I do my homework, and didn't have the common sense to clean the table properly with soap and water? Tell me, Kenene... Wouldn't that just confirm to her how scruffy I really am?"

Osom paused and shook her head before continuing. "I haven't even thanked her properly for the clock, and now..." Tears streaked down her face again.

Kenene could perfectly understand her friend's predicament. She knew about her challenging home situation, which was why she had only visited Osom twice in the more than two years since they'd become close friends. Last year, during her second visit, Kenene had walked into a tense situation, finding her friend's parents bickering and too engrossed in their quarrel to even acknowledge the greeting from their daughter's friend.

When the argument had become heated, Osom had taken her by the hand, and together, they'd walked outside to a mango tree two streets away. In the comfort of its shade, they'd sat and chatted until Kenene left to return home. Kenene had never visited Osom's home again until today.

Osom only rarely visited her friend too, but Kenene understood that because the Semewes didn't have the convenience of domestic help, like her own family did, Osom's help was needed around her house much more than hers ever was. Each time her friend told her about a sour new domestic situation, Kenene felt like her own simple, humble life was actually luxurious. She had never seen or heard her parents argue bitterly, and imagining them doing so was hard enough. Imagining them not even being on speaking terms for hours or even days at a time, as Osom had told her was often the case at home ... well, that was unthinkable.

Whenever Kenene grumbled or complained about some inconsequential issue she was having at home, she'd remember Osom's home circumstances and feel like the proverbial man who cried because he had no shoes until he met someone without feet.

Kenene put her hands on her friend's shoulder now and tried to console her. "It's okay, Osom. Don't be too hard on yourself. Who *really* would have thought to clean the table with soap and water just because they ate rice and stew on it? I would have made the same mistake." She sighed. "I feel very pained that your beautiful, new clock is broken though."

Kenene paused and took a quick sorrowful glance at the clock. "But don't worry; we'll find a way to make things right." She gently shook Osom's shoulder then as a thought came to her. Sitting up straight suddenly, she spread her hands wide apart, and with an upbeat tone, said, "Hey! We can share my textbooks! We don't have the same lessons at the same time anyway, so you can come get whatever textbook you need when you need it and then return it afterwards."

Sharing Kenene's textbooks this way had not crossed Osom's mind, and the suggestion gave her some degree of comfort at least.

"Oh, my friend, thank you so much. I hadn't thought of that!"

"No problem. You can also use them for your assignments too if I don't need them. The only challenge will be what you'll do on those occasions when we both have English and math assignments on the same day." Osom nodded pensively, but Kenene quickly added, "But don't worry about that for now. We'll find a solution in school."

Aside from checking to ensure that her friend was alright, Kenene had also come to bring her some news, though she wasn't sure how to begin. Too much had already happened. Of all the reasons Osom might have had for missing school today, she never could have imagined what had truly happened.

The two friends stayed quiet for a while before Kenene stood up and walked over to the table. Looking around at the mess again, and getting angrier with every moment that passed, she suddenly blurted out a curse and started ranting: "Bloody rats!!! Terrible creatures!!! What does one do with such destructive animals?!" She turned to Osom then. "You must tell your parents to get a cat! Or rat poison! Rat glue works too, but these days, it looks like the rats are outsmarting the glue. We used to use it at home, but my parents now use rat poison. Oh God, I really hate rat poison, though, because the rats always die quietly in some invisible place after eating the poison-laced food, and you never know there's even a dead rat there until it starts to decay and smell."

Kenene frowned and pushed her upper lip upwards to touch her nose in a show of disgust. "Then the work of finding the dead rat or rats starts, and often, we have to move furniture and things around. I always empathise with our house helper when she has to search for hidden dead rats, but you should hear her jubilation when she finds one. You'd think she was praise-worshipping in church." Osom gave her a weak smile and nodded, wondering how to broach the subject of such traps with her parents.

"For me," Kenene continued, "the only real cure for rats in the house is a cat. One meow, and all the rats disappear. No poison, no glue, no trap, no smell, just another animal getting nicely fat, feeding on destructive rodents."

Osom nodded in agreement. "Yes, you're right. I think cats are the best remedy." Not wanting to get into a discussion about the challenges with telling her parents this, she rose from the bed and joined her friend by the table, lifted her torn English textbook, and refocused the conversation on the English teacher.

"But Ms. Claire is going to kill me this time. How do I explain this to her? Especially after her understanding and generosity yesterday? How can I, Kenene? She has always admonished me about being tidy and organized, and now this?" She pointed at the table. "This completely justifies everything she's always said about me ... and her anger as well." Osom's voice broke with emotion, her fear palpable now.

Not wanting her to break down again, Kenene moved closer, and gently said, "It's okay, Osom. It'll be okay. Please, don't start crying again. Look at your eyes. You look like you've been in the ring with a boxing champion."

She rubbed her friend's shoulder gently. "You've already cried your heart out, so how will more tears solve the problem?"

Kenene felt a bit mean being so direct, but she knew that indulging Osom's teary trend wouldn't get them anywhere. "I know how things are with your parents, so let's focus on the specific sharing challenge we identified earlier. Right now, that's the most important thing to think about."

To make it clear that she wanted her friend to move on from the problem and focus on the solution instead, she picked up the broom. "Look, let's clear this mess and give your room some semblance of order and sanity. Seeing it like this will just continue to make you mad, and it's driving me crazy as well."

With a sigh of resignation, hearing the wisdom in her friend's words, Osom joined her, and together, they picked things up, swept, and tidied the room.

"Look at this, Kenene." Osom had her fabric school bag over her shoulder and turned around so that her friend could see the holes that rats had chewed on every side.

"Jesus!" Kenene exclaimed. "They actually had your bag for dinner too!"

Osom laughed and pulled the bag off. "Yes, those rats must have been malnourished."

Kenene laughed with her friend, happy that she was finally beginning to see the humour in this painful incident.

Having completed the cleaning and tidying, Osom sat back on the bed, and Kenene pulled over the chair by the table and sat down facing her. There was silence for a short moment, and then Kenene spoke up.

"Osom, in addition to coming over to ensure that you were alright, I brought some news too. Ms. Claire didn't come to school today either. She's in the hospital after getting in a car accident yesterday."

Osom felt a sudden swing of emotions. "Oh my God! Are you serious?" she screamed, covering her mouth with her hand.

Kenene nodded. "No one knows for sure, but rumour has it that she's in a very bad way ... that she broke a leg, her neck, and has a big gash on her head. She can't speak, and has a fuzzy memory apparently, but she is able to recognize people."

"No! No, please tell me you're lying. Our class mistress, Ms. Claire? What hospital has she been admitted to? Can we go see her?" Osom's heart was pounding fast, and she could hardly contain her shock and worry.

"I hear she's in Take Care Private Hospital, where they have the expertise to manage her sorts of multiple injuries. I don't know if they'll let us see her at this stage, but we could try."

"Can we go now?" Osom asked, standing up before her friend could even answer and quickly adding, "We must go before it's too late. I must to see her and thank her for the clock! *I must!* Just give me a few minutes to change my blouse."

Kenene was pleasantly surprised by how Osom's emotions had immediately swung from self-centred and self-pitying to selflessness, with a swift call for action. She understood how deeply the news about Ms. Claire affected her friend and was happy to help her find some solace in an expression of gratitude to the class mistress before it was too late. She patiently waited for Osom to change her top.

In ten minutes, the two friends set out, hailing a tricycle, and were soon on their way to the hospital. As they started walking onto the grounds of the healthcare centre, Osom stopped suddenly.

"Kenene, since she can't speak, and we're not sure if she can even hear, why don't I write a thank-you message on a sheet of paper and show it to her, assuming they even allow us to see her."

"That's an excellent idea," Kenene said, clicking her right fingers in agreement, and then immediately proceeded to tear out a sheet of paper from her notebook, grabbed a pen, and handed both to Osom. She then turned and slouched so that her friend could use her back as a table.

Flattening the sheet out on her back, Osom started composing her message, boldly, using all capital letters:

"SORRY. THANK YOU, MISS, FOR THE CLOCK. MAY GOD BLESS YOU AND MAKE YOU WELL."

As it turned out, Osom and Kenene had arrived at the hospital just fifteen minutes before the end of visiting hours and had to beg their way into Ms. Claire's room after initially being refused at reception. Osom had begun to cry, refusing to leave, and Kenene joined in, though her tears were largely pretend. The receptionist had called a senior nurse when she couldn't handle the two friends anymore.

When the older woman arrived, Osom rushed towards her, sobbing as though she'd lost a close relative, and explained why she so desperately needed to see Ms. Claire, adding that she also had an urgent message to deliver to the class mistress.

Seeing how emotional and persistent Osom and her friend were, the nurse couldn't help but sympathize and agreed to let them see Ms. Claire, though for no more than five minutes. She then accompanied them to Ms. Claire's room, cautioning as they walked down the hall that the teacher had been strongly sedated and might struggle to recognize them.

Osom and Kenene were shocked by the state Ms. Claire was in. Her head was bandaged, her neck was in an uncomfortable-looking brace, and her left leg was in a POP cast, suspended slightly above the bed.

Looking at her, Osom was overwhelmed. Standing there, she suddenly realized that, idiomatically, she had carried a basket filled with her own problems to the market square only to find that her basket was the lightest. Against the vastness of the teacher's current difficulties, her damaged textbooks and broken dragon clock seemed like minor annoyances.

As the class mistress's neck was firmly restrained to keep it stabilized, the nurse told the girls to say their well wishes from the foot of the bed only. They nodded, moving into position and looking up at Ms. Claire. Her eyes were closed, and at first, they thought that she was sleeping. But when the nurse touched Ms. Claire lightly on the hand, she partially opened her eyes.

"Can she hear us?" Kenene asked the nurse.

"Yes, though faintly. Still tests to be done, but she seems to be straining a bit to hear."

As though in response to the nurse, Ms. Claire blinked twice at the girls. Her eyes were a little bloodshot, and didn't open all the way, but they did seem happy to see the two friends standing there. Kenene was certain the class mistress recognized Osom and seemed particularly happy to see her, as she was one of her students whose academic and personal development was very important to her and sometimes gave her cause for concern. The two girls stood there quietly, not sure what to do.

Osom believed there was something else in Ms. Claire's eyes that she hadn't seen there before, even in her office the day before: a genuine plea for her to keep working hard at her studies for her own sake. She remembered the day she'd first been asked to switch places with Nadia in the front row, because the class mistress had found her large eyes disconcerting, and suddenly realised that, whatever her motives might have been for that comment, and the switch, it hadn't been dislike.

Relieved by this new awareness, and realising that their time would soon be up, Osom smiled and raised her sheet of paper up in front of her so that Ms. Claire could read the message effortlessly and left it there for about a minute before lowering it again.

Meeting the class mistress's eyes then, she was pleased when Ms. Claire gave her a weak smile, blinking twice again, before drowsiness narrowed her eyes into a squint. Satisfied now that her message had been read and received, Osom clasped her hands together in gratitude and prayer and bowed to the teacher.

Kenene mimicked the gesture, and then the nurse moved to grab the curtain around Ms. Claire's bed, preparing to pull it closed. "We must leave the patient to rest now," she informed the girls with a professional air.

"Thank you, nurse," Osom said. "Can we come again sometime?"

"Yes, of course you can. I'm sure she was happy to see both of you today and to read your message. Her eyes said a lot."

Osom and Kenene began the long walk back to the street to flag a tricycle to take them home, with Osom clapping and skipping with joy.

"I'm so happy we were allowed to see her! That nursing sister is very kind. God bless her."

"Yes, she is. I was afraid at first she'd support her colleague's refusal, but Osom ... I think she just couldn't say no when she saw your tears."

"Yes, I'm sure, but your emotional display helped a lot too." Osom looked at Kenene in acknowledgement of her invaluable friendship and placed her hand on her own chest before continuing. "My heart feels at peace now. I think Ms. Claire was happy to see us and read the message. Did you notice how she blinked and tried to smile? Her eyes said it all."

"I did notice, yes. My mum always says that, like silence, eyes speak louder than words."

"True, Kenene, and they also say that the eyes are the mirror to the soul, and it is, isn't it? Even the nurse seemed to have noticed the message in Ms. Claire's eyes."

Kenene laughed and shook her head. "You know, something just crossed my mind. When my mum is mad at me, and she doesn't say a word, her eyes become a horse whip. Those looks send me straight to hell, feeling like a shrinking drop of water on a hot pan."

"Ha! I know exactly what you mean. I've been there too with my parents many times, as I'm sure you can imagine." Osom chuckled, patted her friend on the arm, and nodded.

In the tricycle, the two friends began to laugh and exchange anecdotes. Osom was feeling so much better and knew she was ready to face school again. For the first time since her meal of bread and pepper soup, she thought of Auntie Vero and her generosity. She also remembered that she still had some soup left. She relished the idea of finishing the rest and telling Auntie Vero that it had indeed helped cure her period pain when she returned her bowl later that night.

When they got close to the intersection where Osom had to get off, she and her friend said their goodbyes and hugged each other. Kenene pulled back from the embrace, wagging her forefinger playfully at her friend's face, admonishing and advising her at the same time:

"No more tears, Osom. You hear me? We'll find a way to patch up the clock. We'll even find someone to replace the broken glass. It may not be as good as new, but it will be okay."

"Kenene!" Osom almost screamed. "*That's a great idea!* In fact, I'll be over the moon even if we can just get the dragon's eye movements working properly again."

"I'm sure the repairer could find a way."

"Hey, Kenene, one more thing: Ms. Claire."

"Yes, what about her?"

"You know how I've always likened her to a wicked witch?"

"Well, who hasn't? Her ways can be very mean sometimes. We both know that."

"Yes. But seeing her lying in that hospital bed … she didn't look like a witch at all. I felt really guilty for having thought her so wicked and—"

"Hey, don't start blaming yourself now. Do you hear?"

"Okay. Okay. I'll try not to. I do feel better now though, so more tears. I promise."

The tricycle pulled up at Osom's requested stop, but before getting out, Osom looked at her friend. "Kenene, you know that my parents abandoned me a very long time ago. You're all I have. So … thank you for finding me worthy of your friendship. Good night."

Kenene was both touched and saddened by her friend's words and sought to reassure her. "Your parents love you, Osom. They've just forgotten how to show it. Remember you told me that things were different when you were much younger? Anyway, please don't worry. I'll never abandon you, my friend. I'll see you tomorrow in school. Goodnight."

Kenene waved enthusiastically as the tricycle sped away.

Ms. Claire was replaced in class by Ms. Ekita, whose laissez-faire style of instruction was significantly different from their former class mistress's. Osom and Kenene described the contrast between them as "coconut and cassava." Osom shared Kenene's textbooks as they'd agreed and also got creative about finding used ones she could use to minimize any inconvenience for Kenene.

She announced her need to her class, and Kenene did the same in hers, and only two days later, Imelda, a classmate she had never spoken to, brought Osom her cousin's used English textbook.

Osom was stunned and grateful. In a class of about forty students, she hadn't even known Imelda's name until the quiet student had brought her the textbook. Imelda explained that her cousin had scribbled a lot with pencil and pen on many of the pages, and when Osom asked if it would be okay for her to clean it up, she happily gave her permission. Pleased, Osom had painstakingly erased as many of the pencil scribblings as she could. And then the very next day, Kenene was given a used math textbook that was still in very good condition by her classmate, whose friend had graduated two years earlier.

With the issue of the textbooks sorted, Osom reprioritized her school-work. The clock's interior mechanism still worked, and so she used its alarm daily. Osom had to get used to not being driven by her teacher, as Ms. Ekita was so liberal, and worked hard to become more self-disciplined.

She hoped that someday Ms. Claire would return to teach, even if with a lighter workload, but she changed schools instead and began to teach in a secondary school out of town, much closer to her parents' residence so that they could act as caregivers as she recuperated. Osom never saw her anymore and missed her. Each time she looked at the dragon clock though, Osom smiled, remembering her former strict (but kind) English teacher, who had drawn such ire from her on that very first day when she'd accused her of having scary eyes and asked her to switch seats.

It was Monday, and the Semewes were due back from Fonma, so Osom ensured that nothing was amiss in the house before leaving for school. When she returned home in the afternoon, she heard her mother's loud singing in the kitchen from the front door and knew instantly that her parents had had a good time in Fonma ... and that something remarkable was making her mother particularly excited.

Ayere's version of Louis Armstrong's "What A wonderful World" made Osom smile, as she had changed the lyrics. "I see trees of green" had become "I see fish and meat," and "I see them bloom" was now "plenty, plenty food."

Listening to her mother belt out this adjusted classic, Osom's instincts told her that her mother, had just made up her own version of the famous lyrics in celebration of whatever it was that was making her so jubilant. True indeed, when she arrived in the kitchen to greet her mother, it looked like a restaurant buffet. Her parents had brought back enough takeaways to last a week, all of it contained in food warmers and cellophane bags.

"Good afternoon, Mama."

Ayere stopped singing. "Ah ha! Osom, you're back? Look. Food! We won't need to cook for a long time. In fact, I've decided that I'm taking a cooking sabbatical for two weeks. We must manage this food. Just look at what we have here!" Ayere waved her hand delightedly and began to open warmers, bowls, and pots so that Osom could appreciate the quantity and variety of food in the kitchen.

"It's really a lot of food, Mama. There must have been quite the excess at that wedding."

"Excess? Ha! That's an understatement! It was a river of food. Go ask your father. That couple's families are stupendously rich and showed it off. I can't even count how many cows, goats, and chickens they slaughtered for the three-day extravaganza. Go ask your father," Ayere said again, clapping in wonder. With a click of her tongue, she continued. "I ate and danced until my stomach warned me to stop or risk revolt."

Osom smiled. She hadn't seen her mother this happy and excited in a long time. "Wow! Are you serious, Mama? You and Papa must have had a blast in Fonma. I'm glad. So tell me, how are we going to preserve all these foods? There's only so much the fridge can take."

"Ha! Preserve? We must preserve them-o. I will force as much as possible into the fridge. Those over there," she said, pointing to two medium-sized bowls on the burner, "I'm taking to Vero in a moment. I'll also give Sister May and her neighbour some food. Thinking about it, we may actually need to store some food in Sister May's fridge."

Osom perked up at the mention of Vero, and she took the opportunity to tell her mother about the kindness she had showed her with the pepper soup. Ayere expressed her gratitude to their neighbour and promised to thank Vero when she saw her.

Seeing how much work needed to be done, Osom knew that she should give her mother a hand with the partitioning and storage process. "Let me go change, and then I'll come help you, Mama."

She hurriedly left the kitchen and went to her bedroom. As she was getting changed, she could hear her mother's vernacular remix of yet another classical song: John Lennon's *Imagine*. Osom smiled and shook her head as she heard her mother bellow loudly and out of tune:

"Imagine all the people, eating rice and meat, uh-uh-uh-uh-uh. Do not sayyyy I'm a dreamer -ah-ah; I have more than what I want. I hope more marriage will come, come, and all of us will eat as one."

It had been five weeks since Ayere and Tingatu had returned home from the wedding, and a relative peace had settled in the Semewes household. It was a cool Thursday in early June, and Ayere had just taken delivery of a new batch of second-hand clothes. Just as she usually did, she gave a few of the neighbours, who were regular patrons of her business, a heads up on her new stock, as well as the privilege of coming to her store to shop for themselves and their children before the general public. Sister May, who lived four buildings away at the back of the Semewes residence, was always the first among Ayere's primary shoppers to get this information.

It was early in the evening, and Osom had locked herself in her room to concentrate on her homework, so her mother decided to make a quick dash to Sister May's house to inform her about the arrival of her new stock.

"Osom!" Ayere called.

"Yes, Mama?" Osom's concentration was broken, and she abruptly stood up and opened her door. She saw her mother heading towards her bedroom but stop when she saw Osom standing there.

"Start frying some plantain for dinner. I need to go to May's and will be back soon," Ayere said as she tucked her blouse into her skirt.

"Alright, Mama. Should I make some sauce too?"

"No. We'll use some of the leftover stew in the fridge."

Osom breathed out in relief. Frying plantain only would be less work, and she could finish quickly and return to her schoolwork. She shut her bedroom's door and immediately went into the kitchen.

Ayere told her husband that she wouldn't be long, and tying her head with a scarf, she left Tingatu in the living room, lying on the couch and cooling himself with a raffia hand fan.

As Ayere approached May's door, which was wide open, she heard loud voices in animated conversation. Seeing her neighbour standing just outside, May stopped and excitedly welcomed her in with fervent wave, inviting her to sit and join the chat.

In the living room was a tall, burly woman that May introduced as Madam Santana. Spread out on May's coffee table were choice pieces of gold and silver jewellery. There were necklaces, earrings, bracelets, and rings; some gold or silver and others a mixture of the two.

"Santana, this is my good neighbour Mrs. Ayere Semewe, who lives some houses in front of me," May told her guest and then turned to her neighbour. "Ayere, as you can see, Madam Santana sells jewellery. I've known Santana forever. She's the one from whom I bought all those beautiful jewellery pieces you sometimes see me wear and compliment me on."

Santana raised an eyebrow like she had just learnt a well-kept secret, and as Ayere was sitting down, she turned to her with a look of pleased surprise and said, "Semewe? Are you Tingatu Semewe the trucker's wife?"

"Yes, I am. How are you? You know my husband, Tingatu?" Ayere was also surprised.

"Of course! I know Tingatu very well. He is one of my better customers. He buys jewellery from me. I sold him the unique set of earrings and necklace he bought you last year for your birthday, and the set of twin bracelets he bought you for Christmas."

Ayere's eyes widened, and she found herself leaning forward somewhat as Madam Santana continued. "You're one lucky woman. Those jewellery sets he bought you were a real bargain."

Santana turned to address May then, with pride in her voice. "May, my friend, you should see these gold pieces I'm talking about. Solid English gold—I swear on my last breath—not mixed or diluted. You know me and the quality of what I sell. I don't peddle cheap or nasty stuff."

The seated Santana danced in her chair as though to drive her point home as she carried on boasting about the pristine and high-society quality of her jewellery, oblivious to the inappropriate nature of some of the information she was sharing.

May sat further back in her chair, and smiling coyly, teased her friend with a touch of seriousness, believing at the same time that Ayere should feel elated by what she was hearing. "I see, Santo... So, you now bring me leftovers after the entire town has had the chance to choose the very best pieces."

"Of course not! You *know* I always prioritize you, May! It's just that Ayere's husband wanted something very special for his wife on those occasions, and being a woman, I know what it means to us to be shown such gestures of love and appreciation by our husbands." Madam Santana smiled and winked at May, as though she needed a co-conspirator in some grand plan to advertise her trade.

"Well, I certainly can't contest that, Santo," May said. "Besides, I still have some of the most unique jewellery in town. Even my neighbour here can confirm that. Isn't that true, Ayere?" May turned to Ayere with her brows raised high in question, but Ayere didn't notice. She was just sitting there like a statue with her heart pounding, stunned by all Madam Santana had said, and what she'd learned from her.

Snapping out of her thoughts just in time to notice that May needed her confirmation, Ayere replied offhandedly, "Oh, yes, yes. I agree with you, May."

Santana was excited to show off, so she continued on, unaware of how uncomfortable Ayere had become. "Still ... even though I wouldn't minimize anything I sell, I must say that the last sets Tingatu bought from me are truly one-in-town designs, May, and their prices reflect as much." She leaned forward, looking from May on her left to the Ayere on her right, and then whispered, "Now, this is privileged information, so please don't tell anyone. But just to let you know how special those sets of jewellery are, since it's Tingatu, I sold the earrings and necklace set for four thousand Shinpas, and the bracelets at three thousand Shinpas."

Ayere almost choked at the prices she had just heard.

May gasped, "Ewo!"

Santana turned to face Ayere, addressing her directly now. "I tell you, your husband got an extremely good deal." Santana relaxed back in her chair, clicked her tongue, and gave Ayere an envious look then, concluding with her arms folded across her chest, "You better protect those precious pieces you have because they're rare, and in a few years, their value will have skyrocketed."

Ayere was dumbfounded. Surely whichever Tingatu this Santana was referring to wasn't (and couldn't be) her own husband. *Impossible!* her mind screamed, trying to rationalise Santana's words. There were many Tingatus, and although Santana had gotten her husband's surname and profession right, and from all indications, seemed to know him well, Ayere believed that there simply must be some sort of mix up.

She was confused, but she didn't want to fish for more information from Santana, or for clarity either, lest she uncover what her ears and heart weren't prepared to have revealed. So, she opted for the best solution:

pretence. She and Tingatu were sometimes masters of faking emotions, but as she sat there and listened to Santana, her acting prowess seemed to be failing her just when she needed it most.

Her facial expressions kept swinging from shock to mild surprise, then to stoic neutrality, and finally, to a toothy smile. Ayere just wasn't sure what face to put on as her heart and head collided, and more than just embarrassed now, she was beginning to get angry and knew that she needed to control herself. She decided to act.

She opened her mouth, but before she could speak, May quickly began to tease her. "Aha, my friend, I'm jealous-o. Wish I had a loving husband like Tingatu to spoil me with expensive jewellery." May adjusted herself on her chair, leaned to one side, and wagging her hands playfully at Ayere, advised her humorously, "You better hold that husband of yours tight. Very tight." She put her two hands in comically tight fists in front of herself, and then released them before continuing. "Good men like Tingatu are hard to find these days."

Ayere smiled demurely, like a teenage girl on her first date, and replied in an almost childlike voice, tilting her head to one side. "Oh, May, I really feel blessed. Tingatu sure likes to spoil me silly when he can afford it. What can I say?"

Even before she had uttered the last word, Ayere was reminding herself that she had come to May's house for a reason completely separate from the ongoing conversation about jewellery. In times past, she would have loved to sit there for much longer, gossiping and admiring the beautiful pieces of jewellery glistening before her, even though neither she nor her husband could afford any one of them.

This evening, however, had been tainted by Madam Santana's revelation, and Ayere was desperate to get home. She smiled, clapped lightly, and then got up. "Okay, please forgive me, but I have to run. I told my husband I wouldn't be long. Thank you, Sister May. Lest I forget what brought me here, I came to tell you that I have new stock, so you can stop by before I put it out on the shelves."

She then turned to Madam Santana and sweetly said, "Madam Santana, I'm happy we met. Those pieces of jewellery my husband bought from you are truly the most beautiful pieces I have. Sorry that I can't stay longer to admire these lovely pieces in more detail. My husband will be pleasantly surprised to know that we met after all, even though I promise you, he wouldn't be happy to learn I know how much he spent on those gifts. In any case, I must go home now to make supper. Hopefully, we'll meet again some other time."

"Oh, please, please, please, pretend that you don't know the costs, Mrs Semewe. Tingatu would be very angry with me if he knew I had told you the amounts, and I don't want to lose him as a customer." Madam Santana clasped her hands in prayer and pleaded with her, a worried look on her face.

Ayere smiled, and waving her off, said, "Don't worry. I promise not to reveal all you've told me about the prices. Bye for now."

May rose and walked her neighbour to the door.

Ayere stormed into living room and met her husband, who was in the exact same position he'd been in before she'd left the house twenty-five minutes earlier: lying on the couch and fanning himself.

Stopping directly in front of him, she was finally able to stop pretending to be calm. "Tingatu Semewe!" she shouted. "So! You have a second wife or registered concubine, for whom you've been buying the world's most expensive jewellery, while your legitimate wife is struggling, doing her best to contribute to the upkeep of our house and ensure that our daughter gets the best education!" Her volume was growing with each word she said. "Tell me, Tingatu, you liar! You faithless, disloyal man! Tell me!"

Tingatu sat up and rubbed his eyes like he had just woken from a long slumber, even though he had been wide awake. "Hey, hey, hey… What's this madness?" he asked, looking genuinely confused. "What are you talking about?"

Ayere was boiling with anger, pushing her head forward and spitting furious words at him. "You heard me! Tell me how you've been catering to that second wife I've been unaware of until just now and buying her expensive jewellery from Madam Santana! While *we're* counting the pennies while buried in debt!"

"Look! Watch yourself, woman. Who is Madam Santana?"

"Liar!" Ayere shouted. "Don't play games with me! You don't know

Santana the jewellery retailer? Or do you call her Santo! You didn't expect that I'd find out, did you? Well, I just met her at Sister May's house, and she knows *you* very well! When she learned I was your wife, she assumed that the pieces of jewellery you bought for your wife's birthday, and for Christmas, were actually for me! Your wife!"

Ayere did a 360-degree turn, raised her hands up to the ceiling, brought them down to her waist, and then stood there akimbo, barking out her anger and pain until her voice went coarse.

"Tingatu Semewe, have you *ever* given me a birthday or Christmas present? Eh? Even once in the twenty-five years we've been married?! But your mistress? Well, being so much more important to you than me and Osom, your mistress has been receiving *lavish* gifts from you! While I'm left *borrowing* jewellery to wear from Sister May each time there's a special event to attend!" She was so angry she was shaking. "You've not only been unfaithful to me, but—"

"Stop!" Tingatu said sharply, raising his hand to reinforce the demand as he interrupted her furious shouting with a raised voice of his own. "What nonsense are you talking about, Ayere?! What mistress?! You're accusing me of being unfaithful to you?!"

"Tell me, Tingatu, what else should I accuse you of when you're having an extramarital affair! What else can I call you? Tell me! I'm all ears, Tingatu, you lying cheat of a man who *calls* himself husband!"

"Don't you dare insult me like that, Ayere! I'm warning you... Don't make me lose my temper!"

"Then stop lying to me like I'm an idiot, Tingatu!"

Tingatu was breathing heavily now as though he were being stripped of both his masculinity and control all at once. "I know Santana! Yes! I admit that! So what? Is it a crime to—"

Ayere clapped in his face, not letting him finish. "Oh, so, now you *admit* you know Santana?! Now we're getting somewhere, you liar!"

Ayere started wagging her index finger in his face, but he slapped her hand away. "Woman!" he yelled. "Stop this now! Stop or I will slap your soapy mouth! So what if I bought jewellery from Santana! What is wrong with me buying jewellery to resell for profit?! How else do you think I've been able to maintain my truck, eh?! Tell me! How?!"

"My god, Tingatu!! You're *still* lying!! You're lying through your teeth! When did you have seven thousand Shinpas to buy that jewellery at all, even if you *had* planned to resell it, which I don't believe for a moment! Where did that money come from when we owe the Cooperative, we owe your employer, *and* we owe your friend?! Tell me, foxy Tingatu! Where did you get that money from when we've only just skimped and scratched to finish paying Osom's school fees for the year, and her school cert exams, with no certainty that we'll even be able to pay for her next level of education when the time comes?!"

"Stop shouting and listen to me, Ayere!" Tingatu barked in turn, trying to interrupt his wife, but she wouldn't allow it, starting to scream even more loudly at him then and drowning out whatever else he'd been planning to say.

"No, *you* listen! When did you become a trader in women's accessories?! Why did you not tell me about *that* plan?! You told me all about wanting to branch out into selling building materials! I even have a shop of my own! So, among the two of us, who do you think is in a better position to sell jewellery?! And when—"

"Ayere! Just listen!" Tingatu shouted at the top of his lungs as he leapt to his feet, breathing down into his wife's face as she peered straight into his eyes, daring him to go on even as she wouldn't let him finish, waving him off like a fly.

"Don't 'Ayere, just listen' me! I married a shameless liar, and this is what I get after toiling through the last twenty-five years by your side!" Ayere was close to tears as she fell briefly silent, took a single step back, and then shook her head. "You know what? Since you have a second wife out there, you clearly don't need me. "We're done!"

With this definitive statement, Ayere stormed off into their bedroom, slamming the door shut so hard that it shook the building.

Osom had heard the shouting match and turned down the heat on the frying pan to enable her to go find out what was going on. Standing by the dining room's door, she watched her parents almost come to blows as they barked into each other's faces and gestured angrily with their hands. When things were great between them, Tingatu and Ayere were like teenagers in love, but they both had bad tempers. Ayere was just as quick to anger as she was to play or laugh, and whenever her parents were arguing, Osom did well to keep out of the fray.

Because of their tempers, Osom couldn't intervene, afraid she would either make things worse or become their punching bag. She had heard her mother's accusations against her father and felt betrayed as well. Now, with her mother locked in their bedroom, Osom looked at her father, who was carefully avoiding making eye contact with her as he put on his rubber flipflops, grabbed his truck keys, then walked out, slamming the door behind his just as her mother as done, so loudly that it rattled Osom's teeth and startled her.

She returned to the kitchen to finish frying the plantains and warming the stew. She couldn't help but wonder at how quickly a seemingly peaceful afternoon had changed so much. She had occasionally witnessed her parents bickering, and even have some very angry exchanges, but with her mother's accusations, this evening's quarrel seemed much worse than any of the previous ones. She hoped that her parents would cool off in a few days, as they usually did, and resolve their differences.

As she served herself some plantain with leftover stew for a sauce and sat by the kitchen door eating, Osom was afraid that something might have broken beyond repair this time and would never be the same again. This was the last situation she would ever want to be in as she prepared for her final exams.

When Osom finished her dinner, she walked to her parents' bedroom door and knocked three times. "Mama?" There was no answer. "Mama?" She leaned a bit closer and could hear her mother crying, talking to herself, walking about, and making a lot of noise, opening and shutting drawers and pulling things out. Osom knocked again, and not waiting for a response, said, "Mama, the plantain is ready. Should I serve you some dinner?"

When Ayere still didn't respond, Osom returned to her bedroom and tried to carry on with her schoolwork, listening at the same time for her mother to re-emerge.

At 8:45 p.m., Osom suddenly heard her parents' bedroom door open. She rushed out to the living room and found her mother there with a large overnight bag slung over her shoulder and pulling a medium-size trolley suitcase behind it.

Osom's heart began to race. "Mama, where are you going?"

Ayere didn't reply. She just sniffed and wiped her eyes with her hand.

Osom looked at her mother's puffy eyes and tried to take the trolley suitcase from her. "Mama, where are you going?"

"Leave it, leave it. I must go." Ayere tried to push her daughter's hand away from the handle as she carried on pulling the suitcase towards the front door.

"Mama, please, don't go! Please! It's late. Please, don't go!"

"Don't be offended, my daughter, but I can't live with your father anymore, and since he has a second wife anyway, he'll need to let her move in here. Right now, I feel like a laughingstock. If I stay, one of us will do something we'll regret later."

Osom walked out of the living room and into the street with her mother, clutching her arm, begging her not to leave. "Mama, please! I beg you in God's name, don't go! Please don't leave me!" Tears trickled down Osom's face.

All Ayere could do was cry, hearing her daughter's pleas, but she refused to change her mind. They stood by the roadside waiting for a tricycle or a taxicab, and when Osom sighted a car with a yellow taxi sign on its roof, her heart broke. "What about me, Mama? What about me?"

Ayere flagged the taxi down as it got closer, then turned to her daughter. "I'll be visiting you in school. Keep working hard. Do you hear me?"

Osom was silent.

A few moments later, she watched her mother load her bag and suitcase into the taxi's trunk and then climb into the back passenger seat. Before she could shut the door, Osom stepped closer. "Mama, you're letting the sun go down on me... Why?"

Ayere sniffed, wiped her eyes, and then with no good answer to give, she shut the door. The taxi drove off then, leaving Osom standing there, watching until she could no longer see the yellow taxi sign on its car's roof. Then she slowly walked back to the eerie-quiet of her home.

Her father had still not returned, and she decided to peep into her parents' bedroom. She was shocked by the dastardly nature of the mess she saw there. It looked like a tornedo had lingered in the bedroom, bringing down and destroying everything in its path. It seemed Ayere had almost literally turned the room upside down while she packed. The deliberate damage that had been done to things was glaring.

Some of her father's clothes and shoes had been ripped up. Files and papers were strewn everywhere. A black bottle of ink was broken, its content spilling onto some of her father's clothes on the floor. Osom remembered the night her dragon clock had broken and the state of her own bedroom when Kenene had come visiting. Yet, as she stood in the doorway of her parents' bedroom, she believed that comparing what stared her in the face at that moment to the state of her room months ago wouldn't be fair. Dealing with the mess in her room had been child's play in comparison.

She didn't know where her father would even place his foot on his return, and she definitely didn't want to see his face when he discovered what his wife had done. As Osom couldn't just tidy things up either, she pulled the bedroom's door partially closed and returned to her room.

Osom left the lights on though and kept listening for the slightest indication that her father had returned. Not sure what to make of her father's departure either, and whether her parents had both decided she was too irrelevant in their lives to even care about her wellbeing, Osom looked at her broken dragon clock with a sad smile and set the alarm.

Kenene and the clock were the only two friends she could count on in the whole world, and tonight, their friendship—the dragon clock's in particular—meant everything to her. Scared, she laid in her bed, wondering what to do if she ended up wilfully orphaned, not by death but by the sheer rejection of her parents, who should have inherently loved and cared for her but apparently did not. With the recent commotion in the house, she found concentrating on her schoolwork impossible, so she finally decided she'd wake up early the next day, go to her favourite spot by the valley, and do some revision before heading to school.

Osom didn't know when she had dozed off, but she suddenly woke up the next morning to the sound of her alarm. Her father immediately crossed her mind, and she jumped out of bed and ran to the living room, planning to peep through the window to see if his truck was there. On the way, she noticed that her parents' bedroom door was closed, but she could hear noises coming from inside. For confirmation, she tiptoed to the window and took a peek outside, feeling some relief on seeing her father's truck parked in its usual spot.

Osom remembered the state her mother had left their bedroom last night and imagined the shock and anger her father must have felt upon returning to the mayhem. She also knew that he had a lot to do, cleaning and tidying up the mess, and she felt sorry for him. Not wanting to interrupt or annoy him even more with an early morning greeting, she tiptoed back to her room to prepare for school.

A short time later, and without a word to her father, Osom left for school. For most of her classes, she struggled to stay awake and alert. Her English, math, biology, and Health Science teachers each called her up to stand in front of the class with her textbook when they noticed her nodding off intermittently in their classes. During their lunch break, Osom confided in Kenene about the latest goings on in her family as they sat in the field to eat.

"Oh no! Osom, you must come live with us. I'll tell my parents, and they won't mind at all." Kenene tugged on her hand.

Osom looked afraid, her heartbeat speeding up. "I don't know. It's not that I wouldn't love to come live with you, even just for peace, especially as our final exams are only a few months away, but I think me going away would only make things even worse between my parents."

"Make things worse? How?" Kenene was surprised and a little upset by her friend's show of empathy to her parents. "Tell me, my friend, your mama and papa... Do they really care about you? Your mama just walked out on you, at night, and who knows? Your papa could be thinking of doing the same. Suppose when you get home this afternoon, your papa is gone too, either hoping to spite your mama or preferring to go live with the other woman! Then what will you do, eh? Tell me what will you do then? Live all by yourself?"

Osom was quiet as her friend's words struck home, but she quickly decided on a compromise. "I tell you what, Kenene, if I get home, and Papa has left the house and doesn't return tonight, I'll pack up and come live with you. I promise."

Kenene sighed heavily in resignation and shrugged. "Well, okay. Just don't live by yourself. That's all I'm saying to you."

Osom smiled and nodded.

When Osom returned home from school, her father was not at home, but he returned around seven, going into his bedroom briefly before emerging and going into the kitchen. Osom heard his noises in the kitchen and knew he was probably making himself dinner. She stayed in her bedroom, debating whether to come out and greet her father or simply remain in the privacy of her room.

Tingatu didn't bother to check on his daughter. He had dinner, washed the dishes, and then returned to his bedroom. At nine p.m., he switched off the lights, and from the gap under her bedroom door, Osom watched the light from his lamp as he carried it about, doing one thing or another.

For five days after Ayere left, Osom and her father didn't speak, because even when they both knew the other was home, they didn't see each other. When Osom left for school, Tingatu was in his room, seemingly asleep. By the time she was back from school, he was out of the house, returning between seven-thirty and eight, having dinner, and then cocooning himself in his bedroom for the rest of the night. Osom and her father lived like two strangers sharing a flat, only meeting in communal facilities by chance.

On the sixth day, just before nine p.m., Osom heard three loud knocks on the front door, but though she wondered who it could be, she didn't bother to go check. Aside from May, their back neighbour who had twice stopped by at night, her parents never really had any visitors this late.

In a few minutes, she heard voices, but May's was not among them. They belonged to her father and another man. At first, she wasn't particularly interested, but when she heard an argument begin, she gently opened her door and left it ajar so she could better hear their conversation. Soon, who the visitor was and the purpose of his visit became crystal clear.

"It's been six months now, Tingatu, and you promised to pay me back in three! I need that money for my business. Two months ago, you begged me to give you till last month, and last month, you begged me to give you till the beginning of this month! Well, this month will end in two days' time, Tingatu, and now you're asking me to give you another month? I'm sorry, but I can't anymore. I am totally, completely broke. So, pay me whatever you have now, and next month, I'll come for the balance."

Her father kept pleading for more time, but the visitor wasn't backing down. Osom was afraid. She didn't know how this conversation would end, so she quietly stood up, opened her bedroom door wider, and quietly tiptoed over to the living room's door to watch and hear more, though she kept herself largely hidden behind it. From the last fight with her mother, she'd already known her father was badly in debt, to his friends, employer, and the cooperative, but the possible repercussions of that were only now dawning on her as she eavesdropped on the argument that was happening in their living room. Was this just the beginning of her father's debtors knocking on their door for payment? Osom panicked as she thought about how this was bound to unfold, and sooner rather than later.

Craning her neck forward to see past the door, Osom's heart broke when she saw her father kneeling in front of the stranger, with his hands clasped, begging and bowing as though to kiss the man's feet and then raising his head again.

"I know, my friend, I know, and I'm begging you!" Tingatu bowed repeatedly, pleading with him. "Business has been very bad, as you know, and I'm trying to find alternative ways to earn money. I don't have *any* down payment to make right now. Please, *please,* I beg you in God's name to give me just one more month. On the graves of my ancestors, I promise you that I'll pay you every cent then."

Even though her father had ignored her for many days, refusing to even recognize her existence, Osom felt shame, pity, and sorrow as she watched her father on his knees like a beggar. She didn't know which made her feel worse, witnessing her father in the most humiliating grovel she could have imagined, or having watched her mother's taxi drive off into the darkness, leaving her behind.

"Well," the stranger said finally, "then give me your truck until you pay up then. Otherwise I suspect that by the time I come back here next month, you'll have disappeared, and I don't want to have to go to the police. You know where you'll end up if you're arrested."

Alarmed, Osom covered her mouth with her hands. She knew that asking her father to trade his truck for his debt, even temporarily, was as good as bankrupting him and sending him over the cliff. She shook at the mention of involving the police, which would be even worse than bankruptcy, knowing how entangled her father would likely become in the tentacles of police involvement. Tingatu bowed his head until it was touching the visitor's ankle and carried on begging for more time, crying as well this time, now that his truck was on the line.

Any anger or indifference she might have felt in her heart for her father, broke free in that moment, dissolving as love and compassion rose to the surface, and she began to weep as well.

"Please, Tingatu," the stranger said. "It's getting too late for me, and I don't want to prolong this visit any longer. So, just give me the keys to your truck, and then when you have my money, you can come pick it up." With that, the visitor pushed Tingatu away from his feet and stepped back.

Osom couldn't take this anymore, running out of her hiding place and kneeling down by her father at the visitor's feet. "Please, sir! Please, for my sake, give my papa a little more time! Please?" Sobbing, Osom clasped her hands beneath her chin. "Please, imagine I'm *your* daughter. Please. My mama has left us, and my papa hasn't even finished paying my school fees, sir. Please." Tingatu pulled his daughter close and added his voice to hers as they knelt and pleaded with the man together.

The visitor looked at his friend and daughter, crying at his feet, and despite his anger, frustration, and resentment, he finally relented. He hissed, standing akimbo and gazing up at the ceiling for a while. Hating every bit of the decision he knew he was about to make, he looked back down and nodded briskly.

"Okay, for your daughter's sake, Tingatu. I'll give you another two months' grace because of her and only her. But listen attentively and mark my words." He raised his voice and gave a chilling warning then: "I won't ask you twice the next time I come for my money. That's all I have to say, so

I hope you've heard me loud and clear."

With that said, the visitor pulled the front door open angrily and stormed out into the night, leaving the door wide open behind him.

Osom quickly disengaged from her father's hug, and careful not to look at him, ran back into her bedroom and shut the door. Her father's hug had felt strange, and she believed it was phony, to say the least. She despised him for having acted like he cared about her before that stranger and wanted to keep her distance from him.

Tingatu watched his daughter flee the living room like lightning and felt ashamed. She had just saved him from being thrown into the stinking pit of desperation, though he didn't deserve it, and guilt, helplessness, despair, and self-loathing descended on him like a torrential rain. Tingatu crouched like a fetus, held his head in his hands, and cried in the realization that he had lost the most precious gift he truly had in the world: his daughter. Exhausted, he sat down on a couch, threw his head back, and disappeared into a sea of introspection.

Every material thing suddenly paled in comparison to the importance of his daughter's wellbeing. Tingatu didn't know when or how he'd begun to drift apart from Osom, but at that moment—the lowest of his life— nothing else mattered anymore, not even his truck, without which he'd once thought his world would end. He didn't expect Osom to like him anymore. Neglecting her as he had done was inconceivable. All he wanted now was for her to find a small place in her heart to forgive him for his selfishness and dereliction of his responsibility as a father. His biggest challenge would be figuring out how to approach his daughter and what to say.

At eleven that night, with heavy feet, Tingatu walked around the house like a zombie, switching off the lights, and then finally approached the metre box, standing in front of it with a look of hatred as though it were the source of all his problems. He pounded his fist three times on the wall beside the box before pressing the "off" button.

By early the next day, Tingatu had a plan and went in search of Ayere as soon as Osom left for school. When he didn't find her at the homes of one of her good friends or a distant relative, he had an inkling where she would most likely be. So, he drove for two hours to Ayere's elderly aunt's house on the outskirts of town, and indeed, she was there.

Ayere was shocked to see her husband standing at the door when she answered it. As though he were a smelly piece of trash someone had left on the doorstep, she looked at him with her mouth twisted in distaste and asked defiantly, "Yes? What do you want? Have you come to give me an invitation to your second wedding?"

Ignoring her sarcasm, Tingatu told his wife that he needed her to return home as a matter of utmost necessity. At first, Ayere refused, suspicious of his motives, and mocked him. "Ha! Will wonders never cease? Me? Return home?" Ayere clapped, laughing cynically, and then turned away, crossing her arms over her chest. A moment later, turning back just enough to look at him over her left shoulder, she asked, "What about your second wife? Has she thrown you out then?" Ayere looked her husband tauntingly in the eye. "Or is she lost?"

Tingatu brushed aside his wife's scoffing remarks and just explained why he was there. "Listen, I didn't come here to argue or fight. I need to go away for some time and don't want Osom living by herself. Or is that what you'd prefer?"

Ayere gave her husband a denigrating look, up and down, from the corner of her eyes, then hissed at his face, left him standing at the door, and disappeared into the house. Tingatu stood there for a moment and then began pacing around. He could hear his wife speaking with her aunt and hoped she didn't suddenly change her mind. In twenty minutes, Ayere came out with her bags.

"How's Auntie?" Tingatu asked, reminding himself that he was in the house of someone he regarded as family and needed to show respect and courtesy even if the elderly woman couldn't or wouldn't see him.

"She's sleeping," Ayere replied nonchalantly, waving him out impatiently so that she could step outside and lock the door. Getting his wife's message, Tingatu turned around and headed for his vehicle.

In a few minutes, Ayere was seated next to her husband in his truck, on their way back home. Neither of them spoke the entire journey. Ayere kept her body shifted so far away from her husband, one would have thought he had chicken pox, pressing herself so close to the door that she could easily have fallen out were the door to suddenly open. When they reached their destination, Tingatu had hardly put his truck in park when Ayere jumped out, grabbed her bags from the back seat, banged its doors shut, and marched off, quickly letting herself into the house.

Tingatu thought about Osom. He was determined to pay off all his debt in no more than a year and a half and start the process of building a relationship with his daughter. He hadn't always been faithful to his wife through the years of their marriage, and had indeed been cheating on Ayere more recently with a twenty-three-year-old lady called Nmanne, whom he'd met during one of his trucking trips a year and a half earlier. Nmanne was not a pretty woman—not anywhere as beautiful as Ayere—but Tingatu had been smitten by her constant smile, finding it disarming, heartwarming, and welcoming at a time when his soul had yearned for comfort.

Initially, he'd meant to just use Nmanne as a one-time-affair to drown his sorrow after a bitter quarrel with Ayere, but gradually, his relationship with her had blossomed, and he'd begun to spend extra non-trucking days with her and buy her exotic gifts, including the pieces of jewellery Madam Santana had referred to. Tingatu's extramarital affairs were a secret blot on both his marriage and character, and it was inevitable that he brought home his feelings of guilt and anger whenever those affairs broke down. He'd become increasingly estranged from Osom and developed anger-management issues and a proactive lying habit to quell any potential suspicion from Ayere.

In denial, and unable to deal with the fundamental issues in his marriage, Tingatu had believed that the surface solution of unfaithfulness was actually helping to keep his marriage to Ayere alive and kicking. Nmanne had just ended her relationship with Tingatu a month before his trip to Fonma with his wife, after a heated argument in which she'd realized that he wouldn't leave his wife for her, accusing him of breaking his promise and fidelity.

"What? I'm unfaithful to *you*, Nmanne? What then will my *wife* accuse me of?" he'd shouted as they argued.

"You're habitually disloyal, a green snake in the green grass, and a liar," Nmanne had shot back.

What Ayere didn't know, until she'd met Santana, was that her husband was often in emotional turmoil and borrowing more money than they needed in order to feed his bottomless pit of transient lustful desires.

Without saying more than "I'm going to work" to his wife, but happy his daughter wouldn't need to live alone, Tingatu packed up as soon as they arrived and left the home he shared with his wife and daughter.

As Osom approached her home on her way back from school, she noticed that her father's truck wasn't there but made nothing of it as this was nothing unusual. She simply assumed that he had gone out like he often did. When she tried to let herself into the living room via the front door, she was surprised, however, that the door wasn't locked. Osom's heart skipped a beat. She wondered if her father had changed his mind and handed his truck over to last night's visitor after all, in lieu of the money he owed.

Frowning, she walked into the house and went straight to her bedroom. Kenene had shared with her some examples of previous exam questions that her parents had bought from a bookstore to help with her preparation, and as Osom had studied the questions with her friend, she'd quickly realized that she needed to double down with her review and approach to answering some questions. She quickly changed out of her school uniform and went out into the kitchen to get some water. She was relieved that she wouldn't have to cook anything new today, as there were still plenty of leftovers from last night. As she was drinking, she heard footsteps walking towards the kitchen.

"Are you back?"

When Osom heard her mother's voice, when she'd been expecting her father, she jumped and spilled water on herself.

"Mama? Yes, I'm back," Osom answered, looking at her mother in wide-eyed confusion and surprise.

Ayere didn't say another word but rather brushed past her daughter and began to busy herself, opening pots and bowls. She suddenly felt a little short around her daughter, and for the first time, it struck her just how tall Osom had grown at only fifteen.

Osom followed her mother's every movement with her eyes, expecting some modicum of explanation, but when none came, she quickly put her cup away and scurried back to her room.

At seven p.m., Ayere knocked lightly on her daughter's bedroom door. "Come and eat," she said softly. "I've served your food, and it's on the dining table."

Osom opened her eyes and stammered, "Th-Thank you, Mama."

"And just in case you're wondering about your father, he claimed that he was going to find work," Ayere quickly informed her daughter to put her mind at ease.

Having been served food, rather than being the one doing the serving, was another shock to Osom. She couldn't remember her mother ever serving her dinner before, and as for coming to invite her to eat as though she were a queen? That was unheard of. She began to shiver as fear overcame shock. *What's going on in this house?* she asked herself rhetorically. Osom felt like she was caught up in a chess game between her parents, with her emotions as the chess board.

Osom was delighted and relieved at the same time to see that her mother had served food only for her. She would have dreaded having to sit next to her mother at the meal, self-conscious, stealing side glances at her, and eating in silence because there would have been nothing to say. She knew her meal would not have sat properly in her stomach were she not eating alone. So, with her mother busy in her bedroom, Osom said the grace with more gratitude in her heart for aloneness than for the food in front of her, and then ate with pleasure like a princess.

* * *

It had been over two months since Ayere had heard from Tingatu—since the day he had brought her home and left again without an explanation, returning her to her old routine with her daughter. Although she'd doubled her efforts to make her shop more profitable, spending more time there—uncertain whether or not her husband had finally left her for the other woman—she also now spent far more time taking care of Osom and the house.

She wasn't the only one working hard though. Tingatu had been working his fingers to the bones. He'd found work stacking shelves, cleaning, and running errands at a building-materials warehouse during the day, starting at six a.m. and emptying fecal waste in the evenings for another company. At ten p.m., he would then return to the warehouse to work as an untrained security night guard till five a.m.

He worked eighteen hours a day, getting only three hours of sleep, and little by little, he began to pay off his debts. As he consistently distributed his earnings among his creditors, he also built trust with them, and they extended his deadlines.

In September, Osom began her exams and was impressed by how well she believed she had done so far in the math, physics, and literature exams when she compared notes with Kenene afterwards. In the second week, however, she found the chemistry exam more challenging than she had envisioned and beat herself up for making silly mistakes on some answers she should have gotten right. She came home that day grumbling and with a long face, and her mother couldn't help but notice, questioning her about it that evening as they made dinner together in the kitchen.

"Osom, what is the matter? You have worn a face as long as an iroko tree ever since you came back from school."

Osom was picking spinach in the sink, frowning and pouting like she wanted to spit out a curse. After a moment, she clicked her tongue and then answered, "I think I'll fail the chemistry exam I did today. Stupid, *stupid* mistakes I made," she hissed.

"Eh? You've started your final exams? When?" Ayere stopped what she was doing and looked at her daughter as though she had just been informed that the sun had crash-landed in a nearby field.

"Last week," Osom grumbled almost inaudibly.

"Last week? This same last week that just passed?" Ayere moved forward and closer to her daughter, craning her neck to peer into her eyes for confirmation. She sounded like a fool and she knew it, realizing that she had inadvertently been careless and irresponsible.

Osom nodded.

"Why didn't you tell me you've started your exams?" Ayere asked, her hands on her hips.

Osom said nothing and continued to pick the spinach leaves from the stalk.

"I'm asking you, Osom, why didn't you tell me, eh? I've been back in this house now with you for more than two months."

Osom ignored her mother, but in her mind, she replied, *"As though you would have cared. What would you have done, anyway, even if I had told you? Write the exams for me?"*

Ayere decided not to press the subject further. She returned to her corner of the kitchen to carry on with what she was doing but did so half-mindedly. Her conscience whipped her as the words *"you've really not been a mother"* chorused in her head and haunted her soul.

Coming unbidden in her mind then were the words her elderly aunt had said to her when she'd arrived at her home, described the fight with Tingatu, and told her she had come to stay:

"Ayere! Ayere! Unbridled anger will destroy you! When you're generous and happy, you're like a massive waterfall, cascading from a mountain, but when you're angry, you're like red-hot lava, erupting from a volcano. When are you going to learn to be somewhere between those two extremes, eh? If you don't wish to fight for your marriage with Tingatu, I get it. But from all you've just told me, that is exactly with whom you have left your teenage daughter, without knowing for certain he will even remain to look after her. Are you truly sure that it's your husband who does not wish to continue your marriage? It seems to me that you are the one who ran from it, leaving your daughter behind, though nothing was chasing you."

After a long conversation, her aunt had advised her to take a couple of days to calm down and cool off at her place, and then return to her marital home. But Ayere wouldn't hear of it. She adamantly said she was done with Tingatu and would figure things out with respect to Osom.

Osom received only five credits of the seven subjects she'd chosen, failing chemistry with an F and scraping through Health Science with a P. She wasn't sure if she had done enough to gain entrance to the National Independence College (NIC), an elite school where Kenene (whose lowest score was a B-) would be going to do her A Levels. Admission to the NIC was very competitive. Places were limited, and upper middle-class parents whose children had grades like Osom's fought hard to help their children get in.

Osom needed to wait, hope, and pray. With her family in such disarray, she knew that she couldn't afford to lose Kenene—her best friend and the only person who truly felt like family to her—simply because of distance.

As though her daughter had received straight A's, Ayere sang and danced around the house with delight upon seeing Osom's report card. Later that evening, Ayere sat her daughter down in the living room after doing the foxtrot, the samba, and some hip-hop in the dining room, and out of the blue, asked, "How are you, my daughter?"

Osom had watched her mother indulge in elaborate jubilation over a very average report card and couldn't help but wonder how Kenene's parents would be reacting to their daughter's brilliant one.

Sighing tiredly, she picked up the discarded report card from the table, waved it at her mother, and quietly asked, "Mama, why is *this* the best you and Papa expect from me?"

Ayere was taken aback by the question. "Why wouldn't it be? You don't think that is an excellent report?"

"Kenene my friend has three A's, three B-pluses, one B-minus, and a guaranteed place for A Levels. Whereas I'll have to wait—"

"Listen to me," Ayere said quickly, leaning forward and interrupting her daughter. "Never compare yourself with your friend. You and Kenene are not the same. You're endowed differently, and so, your destinies are different. Do you understand me?" Ayere moved even closer forward to reduce the gap between her and Osom and peered into her eyes.

Osom was disappointed and angry and could no longer hide her emotions. "You're right, Mama. Kenene and I are not the same at all. She's got peace at home; her family is not dysfunctional like mine. She has parents who care about her, talk with her, teach her, and encourage her to excel in every way possible. I have done *this* well *because* of Kenene, Mama, and I can't begin to imagine how I would have fared in the world without her. Have you ever even asked me how I am out of a *genuine* interest to know? Do you know if I've started getting my period? Do you know what I've been going through in school, how I've endured bullying but been too scared to tell you or Papa because it would hurt even worse when neither of you cared? Have you noticed how tight my school uniform had become, Mama?

"So, you're right," she continued. "My friend and I *are* 'differently endowed.' But I've reaped the benefits of that difference. I've been tapping into Kenene's destiny for over two years now while you and Papa showed me nothing but indifference, just like you have done with my siblings."

This last accusation struck Ayere like a brick and almost knocked her out. "Osom!"

With a hiss, Osom got up abruptly, and stomped out of the living room, leaving her mother seated there alone and in a daze with her daughter's words tearing at her soul.

The minutes passed slowly as she sat there, looking off into space, piling one on top of each other and deepening the shadow of guilt and regret that hung over her, and as they did, it became increasingly clear to her that she had much to atone and apologize for. She just didn't know where to begin. "My god..." She covered her mouth with her hands suddenly as a frightening prospect crossed her mind. "Suppose Osom had gotten pregnant out of ignorance. I haven't told her *anything* about her body, the limits beyond which boys must not go with her, and precautions to be taken..."

In this horrified moment of clarity, she suddenly thought, *How irresponsible I've been!*

Ayere recalled her own teen years then. Her mother—called "Mama Praise" by most who knew her—had never noticed when Ayere began to get her period and never taught her anything about sex at all. Those topics had been taboo in her family, with Mama Praise leaving it for Ayere's school to educate her on such matters. Such lessons at school had been woefully inadequate to prepare anyone for everyday social life.

Ayere had discovered details about the biological makeup of women and men only by accident or from friends. She'd always imagined that her mother hadn't known any better and so couldn't be blamed for replicating the upbringing she'd received from her own mother, Ayere's grandmother, any more than she herself could be blamed for—

She hissed then, chiding herself for trying to justify her own lapse in this way. *Times have changed, Ayere. Why are you still living in Grandma's era when you're an educated woman with so many opportunities for enlightenment all around you? Why is Kenene's mother so obviously current and modern and able to bond with her daughter so closely that she can discuss things with her that you're unable to with Osom? Stop fishing for excuses, Ayere! You've had your priorities wrong all along. You can see that now, can't you? You've been selfish and done a very poor job at being a mother. Now get up and go speak to your daughter before you lose her forever.*

Ayere obeyed the voice in her head and stood up to go have a heart-to-heart talk with her daughter. After just a few steps though, she changed her mind. *I can't just go to Osom and say, "I'm sorry. Forgive me." No. Sorry isn't enough, and she wouldn't believe me anyway. I have to ask for her forgiveness in some other way...*

With a heavy heart, Ayere went into her bedroom and shut the door, imprisoning herself there for the remainder of the evening and not sleeping a wink all night.

Like all her emotions, which were far too often extreme, Ayere's guilt over Osom's neglect was overwhelming. So starting the very next day, she began to overcompensate, becoming excessively friendly and a little obsessed with trying to please her daughter. She would ask Osom how she was doing twice a day, serve her meals, share petty gossip about people Osom neither knew nor cared about, and forced small talk upon her.

Osom could see all the efforts her mother was making to get close to her, but she was unimpressed. It was both too much and too late. But she was happy to humour her mother, nonetheless, allowing her to reduce her own guilty suffering by finally giving Osom the attention and friendship she'd so fervently craved for so long.

Ayere was doing more to atone for the past outside the house as well. Every day for an entire week, she took Osom's final report—placed securely in her bag like an ID—and went to the NIC, requesting to see the principal or vice-principal.

As she left the house each morning, and continuing until she reached the school grounds, her mind replayed the same thoughts over and over like a mantra: *They must admit Osom to this school. They have to! I'm not taking no for an answer. The other students gaining admission here don't have two heads, so they must admit Osom also!*

After finally meeting with the school's principal, who told her they had reached their A-Level capacity, and that she would need to wait and see if additional places would open up, Ayere took a trip to the school three times a week, for the next three weeks, not caring if her presence became a nuisance.

When Osom's school announced that a send-forth workshop and party was to be held for the graduating class on the same day she would turn sixteen, Osom delightedly shared the news with her mother, who went into a frenzy of activity, swearing to dress Osom in the very best even if it cost her the last cent she had. So, withdrawing her savings, she took her daughter shopping for a dress, matching shoes, earrings, and a handbag, escorting Osom around the shops and boutiques for three straight days, looking for the perfect outfit for her daughter.

"Mama, it's just a secondary-school send-forth party, not a Hollywood red-carpet event," Osom laughed as Ayere rejected one outfit after the other, saying they were too dull or "not grand enough."

"For you, it isn't a red carpet, but for me? This is a once-in-a-lifetime, red and white carpet event, and I don't want other students looking more glamorous than you. So, let's find the dress!"

Although Ayere had begun to bond with her daughter, she remained regretful that she had negligently missed some very important phases in Osom's development and could never regain those lost times. Ayere's deepest fear was that her daughter did not trust her, seeing it in Osom's body language and expression—particularly in her eyes.

As part of the school's send-forth party programme, Ms. Ekita had asked Osom if she would read one of her poems, and she was thrilled to further develop one of the early poems she'd roughly scribbled while lying on her back in the field, near the valley, when she should have been in school.

Two days before the send-forth, Osom developed cold feet and almost pulled out of reading it. She didn't think she could face the crowd, but Kenene wouldn't let her chicken out, encouraging her to showcase a talent that was rare in their school. Playing the role of the audience so that her friend could practice, she got Osom to stand in front of her and not just read the poem but dramatize it ... over and over. Then for five days, Osom got to rehearse her poem with one of the teachers accompanying her on the piano.

When the day of the send-forth event arrived, Osom and her mother sat with Kenene and her parents in the same row. And when it was time for Osom's poem to be read, and she was called up, Kenene jumped from her seat and began to cheer and applaud as her friend walked up to the stage and all the students joined in.

Once Osom was ready, the pianist led things off with an introductory melody, and Osom began to recite her poem:

> "It's in the darkest, vilest nights the brightest day comes.
> In the heaviest rains, the loveliest, drowning flowers bloom.
> In ruins and floods find the hidden someone, one forlorn hope.
> It's in the dungeon of the new, over old, let strip slippery teary thorns.
> In presence, the tattered, loneliest heart tenderly crawls home."

At the end of the first stanza, she closed her eyes and imagined herself back in the field by the valley as the pianist led her into the second stanza. Then Osom opened her eyes and saw her father standing at the hall's back door. She hadn't seen or heard from him in about four months and had never imagined he would miraculously show up. How he'd even come to know about the send-forth was unclear to her. Shivering, she forgot the beginning of the second stanza, but the pianist, believing that she had developed a delayed stage fright, simply continued to repeat the intro, hoping Osom would join in at the right place.

Tingatu saw apprehension in his daughter's eyes and knew that she had spotted him, and that it was his presence that had left her tongue-tied. Looking at her, and seeing her looking back, he pantomimed applause and nodded at her encouragingly.

Osom shut her eyes again, remembering her dragon clock, and then smiled as the second stanza came flooding back.

"It's in the eyes, truth loses might, flight, or hide.
In the nothingness of pain find that beautiful world so wide,
Always there, here, waiting like the sleepy sun to rise.
Knowing, nature births one last dancing act of a good, bad song.
Like the lid of a boiling pot, lift ... set free this scorching steam
of sorrow.
Let it rise, oh rise, mingle into emptiness, our hearts heal
come tomorrow."

Only Kenene and the pianist knew that Osom had experienced a momentary lapse of memory, with the audience generally thinking that her silent pause had simply been part of the act, added for greater effect.

As Osom finished and was bowing to the resounding applause of the audience, she saw her father leave, and quickly stepped off the stage and ran out the door to find him. Seeing her quick exit, Kenene and Ayere assumed that she was pressed from nerves and anxiety and simply in need of the toilet.

Osom saw her father walking briskly to his truck and started running faster, catching up with him just before he reached his vehicle.

"Papa!" Osom called out to her father's back, panting a little.

Tingatu turned to face his daughter, took a deep breath, and finally told her what he had been meaning to for a very long time, unsure if the day would ever come for him to unburden his heart.

"Osom," he said, and then hurried on as though afraid his words could be stolen from his mind before he was able to finish, "I've been a despicable father to you. I know, and I'm really sorry for all I've done to you. I've also really hurt your mother, and I won't blame her if she doesn't want to be married to me anymore. I'm not asking you to like me, Osom. I don't deserve that feeling from you. But I know you've finished your final exams and are looking forward to doing your A Levels, and I just want you to know that I am very proud of you, whether your final results were good or not.

"Aside from the huge debts I owe, most of which I brought on myself with my own weakness and stupidity, I know that I have a lot of work to do on myself to become a better human being, a better husband to your mother, and a better father to you. I'm going to change, Osom. That I promise you. Please forgive me, will you? And give me a little time to work on myself? That's all I ask."

"So, you're not coming back to the house?" Osom asked, a little disappointed, for even though her parents had neglected her, she still wanted to live in a home with them both.

"No, not yet. I'm sorry, but I can't come back and just carry on being that old version of myself that I want to change. That I *need* to change. I'm not ready. I still have too much to do."

Osom nodded slowly but had no other response to give him. So, she just stood there and watched her father get into his truck and drive off without even waving to her. Instead, he just gave her a single nod, the meaning of which she couldn't decipher.

Feeling sad, Osom returned to the hall and retook her seat between her mother and Kenene.

"Wow!" Ayere exclaimed, struggling to keep her voice low so as not to disturb anyone. "I didn't know you write poems! That was *so* impressive! Well done, my daughter!" Ayere patted Osom's thigh, then took her hands and squeezed them, love and pride welling up in her heart. But there was pain there too, having realized once again just how little she knew about her own daughter.

Shutting out that thought, she refocussed on her daughter's achievement, babbling away. "Were you pressed? I don't blame you. Standing up there in front of this multitude of people to dramatize a poem? My god, my legs would have been jelly! I wouldn't even be able to open my mouth. I can't stand in front of even five people and give a presentation without stammering through it. This is a wonderful gift you have Osom, but you definitely didn't get it from me."

Having been waiting to get a congratulatory word in, Kenene quickly interjected, "Yes, my friend, that was amazing! I'm *so* proud of you!"

Osom smiled shyly, offering a feeble thanks, but her father was still weighing heavily on her mind. It was neither the time nor place to mention him though, so she didn't correct her mother's assumption that she had gone to use the toilet.

261

When they got back home, the time felt right, so Osom immediately told her mother about her father's attendance and her meeting with him.

"Eh? Tingatu?" Ayere seemed shocked and unhappy. "Your father was there? Who invited him?"

"I don't know, Mama. He must have visited the school and found out."

"I see. And did he apologise for failing you and hurting me? Did he say he'd change?"

"Yes, that was exactly what he said." Osom described the meeting fully then, sharing everything with her mother that her father had shared with her.

Ayere breathed out so loudly it was as though she'd been holding her breath the entire time her daughter had been speaking. Then after a moment, she gently asked, "And *can* you try to find it in your heart to forgive him?"

Osom was surprised by this question, having expected her mother to fly off the handle with countless accusations against her father, and in so doing, strengthening her grudge against him.

Osom shook her head and shrugged uncertainly. "I want to, Mama, but his refusal to just return home has left me wondering."

Ayere placed a comforting hand on her daughter's shoulder. "Osom, as you get older, you'll come to discover how truly complex we human beings are. Like me, your father is not perfect. Like me, he has his demons ... but he's not a monster. And neither am I. You are my daughter, Osom, but I don't even know you. In these past months, it feels like I'm giving birth to you anew, just beginning the process of breastfeeding, weaning, and fulfilling my role as a mother to help you grow."

Looking down with regret and shame clear in her expression, she continued. "Your father and I equally neglected you, Osom, and like him, I cannot tell you how deeply sorry I am. But I *must* tell you that *none* of what's happening is your fault and you must never entertain the slightest thought that it is. Your father and I both just need our individual space ... and some time."

Osom nodded, hoping that the space her mother was referred to wouldn't become permanent. She had always admired and envied Kenene's family, and even though she knew that hers could never be remotely like her friend's, she still wanted the façade of it all. She wanted to believe that, somewhere in the murky waters of living together and learning from their mistakes, her parents might just be able to really build a stronger, sustainable, and more trusting relationship.

Clearing her throat delicately, Ayere brought her hand down to signal the end of the topic. "Now, let's settle down and agree on what we'll have for dinner. That packet of finger foods and Fanta they served us at your send-forth has done nothing for my hunger. I need real food."

Osom smiled. "Me too, Mama. I'm hungry."

At three p.m. on the second of December, Osom was in her room, sorting her old clothes, when she heard her mother call out urgently as though the house was ablaze:

"Osom! Osom!! Osom!!! Come! Quick, quick!"

Panicking, the girl dropped the blouse she was looking over and ran out to the living room to find her mother waving a sheet of paper over her head and twirling around like she had lost her mind. "Here!" she shouted, seeing her daughter's arrival and waving the paper towards her, grinning madly.

"NIC has admitted you! I pushed, and pressed, and pushed!" she said giddily, pantomiming a tug of war. "I wouldn't give up, Osom!" She pasted the letter against her daughter's chest and then carried on dancing. "They have admitted you!"

Osom screamed excitedly as what her mother was saying finally sank in, and did a quick sprint in place, almost delirious with excitement. Then with her hands shaking, she read the admission letter for herself, did another quick stationary run, and then bolted back to her room. Quickly changing her clothes, she scurried back to the living room and found her mother lost in her own world, still dancing, jumping, and twitching to her own version of Lionel Richie's "All Night Long."

"Mama, I'll be back shortly. I'm going to Kenene's house to tell her the good news," Osom blurted as she ran out of the house, leaving the front door ajar. When she was only two houses away though, she stopped suddenly and ran back. Standing by the open front door and smiling at her mother, who was still shaking her bum to her own weird remix, she shouted, "I love you, Mama," and then turned and raced off.

Ayere smiled lovingly after Osom as she watched her sprint away, feeling the truth in her daughter's words at last and hoping to never again lose that feeling. Then the song and dance began anew.

Notes

Endnotes

1 Nunu: fresh milk from the cow
2 Mumu: fool/ignoramus
3 Nne: Mum